Maggie Hope was born and raised in County Durham. She worked as a nurse for many years, before giving up her career to raise her family.

A Wartime Nurse

Maggie Hope

EBURY
PRESS

3 5 7 9 10 8 6 4

First published as *A Time to Heal* in 1997 by Piatkus Books

This edition published in 2011 by Ebury Press, an imprint of
Ebury Publishing, a Random House Group Company

Copyright © 1997 by Una Horne writing as Maggie Hope

The Random House Group Limited Reg. No. 954009

Addresses for companies within the Random House Group can be found at:
www.randomhouse.co.uk

A CIP catalogue record for this book is available from the British Library

ISBN 9780091952969

To buy books by your favourite authors and register for offers visit
www.randomhouse.co.uk

Penguin Random House is committed to a sustainable future for
our business, our readers and our planet. This book is made from
Forest Stewardship Council® certified paper.

MIX
Paper from
responsible sources
FSC® C018179
www.fsc.org

Printed and bound in Great Britain by Clays Ltd, Elcograf S.p.A.

Acknowledgements

The early part of this book is based on the old hospital at Bishop Auckland. It was a workhouse hospital, which became a general hospital serving the people of south west Durham. During the Second World War, part of the hospital was used for the treatment of prisoners of war.

I was a student nurse there in the fifties and often heard stories of what happened in the war days from older nurses.

The characters and happenings in this book are entirely the products of my imagination and if there is any resemblance to real people it is accidental.

I am immensely grateful to the doctors and retired nurses who helped me with background details and apologise that there were too many to mention by name.

To the staff of Bishop Auckland General Hospital,
past and present

Part One
1936

Chapter One

'Don't go, Joss – please don't go. I don't want you to.'

Joss Wearmouth gazed solemnly at his sister, his eyes hopeless. 'I know, I don't want to go neither.'

They were sitting on a grassy bank speckled with wild strawberries and the tiny red fruit sparkled in the sun. A small, much-battered wicker basket which Theda had had as a child lay beside them, half-filled with strawberries. But now she had forgotten about the fruit altogether, for Joss had come down the garden path and out on to the bank beside the old waggon way and told her that he was 'surplus to requirements' at the pit.

'Well, don't go, you don't have to. You'll find a job here if you look hard enough, surely you will. There's the Railway Waggon Works at Shildon and there's Bishop . . . now there's bound to be something at Bishop Auckland.'

Earnestly she looked up at him, her Joss, the one who always looked after her and never talked down to her the way the elder brothers of other girls did.

Joss picked a blade of grass and rubbed it between his fingers, staring into the distance over the old waggon way and grassed-over mound which was an old pit heap really. Over to the ruined buildings of Old Pit, their harshness softened by distance and sunlight.

'You know we talked it all out yesterday, Theda. There is no other work,' he said at last. 'I'll get no dole, not when I'm living at home – not when Da's working anyroad. We should be thanking God his name didn't come out of the hat again like it did at Wheatley Hill. At least he's working.'

'Yes, but—'

'It's no good, Theda. There's you and Frank and Chuck and Clara to feed. You're only fourteen, but you know how it is. No, I'm sixteen, big enough to fend for meself. I said I'd go in the army and that's what I'm going to do.'

'I could leave school, I'm nearly fifteen,' she said. 'I can, I don't have to go till I'm sixteen just because it's the Grammar School. Everybody else leaves school when they're fourteen.'

Joss got to his feet and she scrambled up after him, looking into his face, her own so woebegone that he grinned and put an arm around her shoulders. 'What, and waste that scholarship we're all so proud of?'

'You could have had a scholarship, Joss. If you had, you'd have had a posh job in an office by now,' Theda countered. But she knew that Joss couldn't have taken up a scholarship, not when it fell in the year the family had had to move to Winton Colliery. He was the eldest and when he was old enough to go down the pit his money was needed, that was how it always worked. And, anyway, Joss had wanted to go down the pit; that was what men did.

'Aw, howay,' he said now. 'I'll help you fill that doll's basket and we'll take it in to Mam and then go swimming in the reservoir. How's that sound?'

'I don't know about the reservoir,' said Theda doubtfully, thinking about the amount of frogspawn there had been in the reservoir at Old Pit that spring. Not to mention what else might be lurking in the weeds that grew out ever further into the water from the bank!. 'Can we not go down the wood and paddle in the Gaunless?'

Joss laughed. 'Howay then.'

In the end, Frank and Chuck and little Clara trailed behind them down to the wood and the place where the bed of the Gaunless river was paved with large stones that didn't hurt their feet when they paddled, and just along from the paving a deeper pool where Joss could swim. They had pop bottles of water and slices of bread and fish paste and some wild strawberries for after.

'Keep an eye on the young ones, our Joss, and you an' all, Theda,' Mam had said. 'I don't know whether you should take them anyroad . . .' But there were howls of protest and in the end they all went. Mam watched them go from the gate of the back yard and Theda could see that her eyes and nose were red as though she had been crying.

'Are you sad, Mam?' Theda had asked. 'I wish Joss wasn't going, don't you? It's not fair, you know – I bet the gaffer cheated when he drew Joss's name out of the hat.'

'No, pet, Tucker Cornish wouldn't do that,' said Mam. 'No, I'm not sad, the army'll be the making of Joss. I'm just getting a summer cold, I think.'

Mam needn't have worried about the little 'uns. They never went near the deep pool, not even Frank. He was more interested in roaming through the wood than paddling in the stream anyway. So he wasn't there when Joss suddenly disappeared under the water. Theda, her woollen knitted costume hanging from her skinny body, was treading water when it happened. She blinked and rubbed her eyes with one hand – where had he gone? Panic rose in her.

'Joss? Joss?' she cried and dived under, for a streak of red was bubbling through the water at the spot where he had been diving. Taking a deep breath, she ducked under again. The water was brown and peaty but still clear enough for her to see that the top half of Joss's body was sticking out of a hole in the bed of the stream, his eyes wide open as he tried to move a rock that had rolled over, restricting the opening.

'Frank! Frank!' she screamed the moment her head was clear of the water, but there was no sign of Frank, only Chuck and Clara standing on the stones and staring at her.

'Stay there!' she shouted and swam to where she judged Joss to be before ducking under the water again. She heaved at the stone, adding her small strength to that of her brother, and for an eternity of perhaps two seconds she thought she couldn't do it. And then it moved and Joss shot up through the water and he was there, above her, and they swam the two or three strokes it took to reach the bank.

They hung on to the edge, gasping, until Joss summoned up enough strength to push Theda up on to the grass and then Frank was there, holding out a hand to his brother.

'What happened?' he asked, as they rubbed themselves down with the towels Mam had put in the carrier bag along with their picnic. Theda went behind a bush and changed into her cotton dress while Joss told the tale, for she couldn't bear to relive the horror of it. Then she bound up the graze on his leg with his hankie.

'Theda saved my life,' declared Joss, watching her.

'Well, I would have done,' said Frank, sulkily, mad that he had missed the excitement. And after a while they settled down and ate the sandwiches and drank the water out of the pop bottles and trooped away home for tea.

'Don't tell Mam or Da,' Joss warned the little ones, but of course Clara couldn't contain herself and the story came tumbling out as soon as she got in the door.

'No more swimming in the beck,' declared Mam. But Joss wasn't likely to; he was going away, wasn't he? thought Theda.

That night, lying in the bed she shared with Clara, Theda had a serious talk with God. She always talked to God rather than prayed as it was uncomfortable kneeling on the bare floorboards by the bed. She was sure God didn't mind her being comfortable when she spoke to Him. She told Him how lonely it would be without Joss and asked why they had been brought to Winton Colliery when there wasn't enough work to keep them all? And she asked a special favour: could He please look after

Joss for her when she was no longer able to keep an eye on him?

It was 1938 by the time the pit started working full blast again. Matt Wearmouth, Theda's father, came off the three-day week he had been working along with his mates and began working five and a half days and suddenly there was enough money in the house to feed the gas meter even on a Thursday night. The younger ones missed sitting in the firelight telling stories but Theda was glad because it meant she had more time to study for her School Certificate.

She had cried the day she had had to leave school to take up a job behind the counter at the Co-op store because she was doing well, and if only she had had another six months she could have done it. But Frank had left school and had been working on the screens at the pit for only a few weeks when he was laid off and times were desperate.

Theda had given up talking to God. There was Joss, thousands of miles away, in India of all places, with the army. And she hated her job at the Co-op; it was boring.

'I'm going to be a nurse, Mam,' she declared on the day she got the information on how to apply from Newcastle Hospital. 'If I have to have my School Cert, I'll work for it at night.'

'Aye, well, pet,' said Mam. 'If determination means anything, you'll make it.'

A year later, Theda had the certificate in her hand and sent it off to Newcastle along with her completed

application form and a reference from the manager of the
Co-op, given a bit reluctantly, for Mr Hodges thought she
didn't apply herself sufficiently to her work. She was
grateful that he gave it in the end, for she knew there was
some truth in what he thought, but how can you apply
yourself to tidying shelves and waiting while a customer
decides between a tin of peas or a tin of beans? There was
another reference from Miss Dart, the French mistress
from school who had helped her out by giving her extra
coaching.

'I wouldn't spend all my free time with my head buried
in books,' said Clara as she sat on the bed the day Theda
packed her cardboard suitcase. Clara was fifteen and
already a machinist in one of the new factories the other
side of Bishop Auckland. Safely out of sight of her
mother, she was trying the new lipstick she had bought
out of the five shillings Mam gave her back from her pay.
It was a bright cherry red and contrasted well with her
dark eyes and black hair. She pouted her lips and blew
herself a kiss in her compact mirror, well pleased with
the result.

'What do you think of that, our Theda?' she asked.

'A bit bright.' She looked up from her consultation of
the list that the hospital had sent her: two nightgowns,
three pairs of knickers, three vests, three pairs of black
stockings (lisle, no artificial silk), and two pairs of flat-
heeled black shoes. She had had to save up for weeks to
collect them, together with the list of textbooks.

Clara pulled a face. 'At least I won't look a frump like
you will in that lot. Anyroad, like I said, I think you're

mad to go in for nursing. Emptying bedpans all day long, that's what you'll be doing. Or cleaning up other people's snotty noses. But don't take any notice of me, I'm just your little sister. You think I know nothing.' Clara jumped off the bed. 'I'm away now, going into Bishop to the pictures.'

'Better not let Mam see you with all that muck on your face,' advised Theda. 'You know she said you hadn't to wear make-up until you were older.'

Clara grinned and pulled her red beret over one eye, just like Marlene Dietrich. 'I won't,' she said, and winked. Theda heard her tripping down the stairs and going straight out of the back door, calling goodbye to the family in general as she went.

'Wait – Clara!' her mother cried after her, but she was gone, escaping down the street to the bus stop.

Theda hadn't given much thought to what would happen when she began working as a probationer nurse. But though the work was hard – she fell into her bed at night exhausted and slept straight through until six o'clock, and every afternoon when she had a split day and two hours off she slept on her bed for the whole time – she liked it. The girls she was with were friendly and the patients were ordinary people, some of them from the mining villages around and some whose fathers and brothers were among the men laid off work at the shipyards along the Tyne.

What she hadn't bargained for was how homesick she would be. Though she was only thirty miles away, she couldn't get home every time she had a day off as she didn't have the fare.

You're eighteen years old now, she told herself. Don't be a baby. How do you think Joss felt, going all those miles away?

Gradually, her body adjusted to the hard, physical work and she learned to stay awake when she had to after night duty to attend a lecture. And by the time she finished her first year and was studying for her first exams, she was coming up to twenty-one and there was a war on.

Of course, she'd known it might happen. She had been worried at the time of Munich, just like everyone else, and had felt a great sense of relief when Mr Chamberlain came home waving his piece of paper. But the war had crept up on her unawares, somehow. She had been sitting in her room with her books, as she so often was, for she had preliminary examinations coming up, when she heard the excited voices outside and went into the corridor to find out what was wrong. The door of the common room was open and some of the girls were clustered around the wireless in there.

'. . . no such undertaking has been received.' It was Mr Chamberlain's voice coming over the air.

'It's started then,' Nurse Lewis, one of the nurses in her year, said. 'I have a brother in the Air Force, I hope he's all right. I suppose the men in your family will be all right, being down the pits? A reserved occupation, isn't it?'

'My brother's in the army,' said Theda defensively and turned away. But for her the war was something that was happening in the background; apart from the normal stab of fear for her country, which she imagined everyone felt, she wasn't worried for her family. Though Joss was a soldier he was far away, out of harm's way, in the Far East and the war could be over before he came home. The hospital had been an enclosed world to her this last year or so; the patients came from the outside, it was true, but it was the world on the wards and in the nurses' quarters that had been Theda's reality.

Then she went home one day to find that Frank had been called up.

'But, Da,' she protested, 'Why? He was working again, wasn't he?'

'Aye. But if you'd been taking more notice of what was going on you'd have known he was in the territorials, had been for a few months. So he got his papers straight away.'

'He's just a bairn!' her mother had burst out and Theda had felt exactly the same way. It didn't seem right.

Then there was Joss. There were no letters coming through from India but she discovered that some of his friends had landed from a troopship somewhere in the south of England. It was all very hush-hush and there was no information of more of his unit coming.

'It'll be because of the U-boats. They don't want to let them buggers know where our troopships are,' Matt had said, nodding his head sagely, and fear gripped her heart once again at the thought of a torpedo hitting a ship with Joss on board and him floating in the water trying to swim to safety. It reminded her of the day he'd got stuck in the pothole in the bed of the Gaunless, and she went off on her own down the garden to the strawberry beds and had a good cry. Then she wiped her eyes and went back to Newcastle as she was on duty that night.

Sometimes she went out with the other nurses to the Brighton ballroom or the Majestic cinema; it occupied her mind and the town was full of soldiers and sailors who liked to dance. Sometimes she even met a boy and had a date but nothing ever came of it. No one ever quite measured up to Joss. She was gaining a reputation for being quiet and studious and not much interested in boys. She was studying when Nurse Lewis knocked on her door one evening.

'Come in,' called Theda, looking up from her work. Nurse Lewis popped her head round the door.

'Mind, you're a dark horse,' she said. 'Here, I thought you didn't have a boyfriend, weren't even interested?'

'I haven't,' said Theda.

'Then who's this smashing fella waiting downstairs in the lobby? Tall, dark and handsome, with a gorgeous tan. A corporal, an' all.'

Theda hadn't time to answer, she was pushing past Nurse Lewis and flying down the stairs, and there was Joss, home safe, and a great weight lifted from her shoulders. She flung her arms around him and he swung her off her feet and laughed exuberantly. It was the same old Joss, only older and with his skin tanned to mahogany and his body filled out to that of a man.

'Steady on there, our Theda,' he said. 'I didn't come all this way just to be knocked over by a slip of a lass like you.'

They had a lovely time, dancing at the Oxford Galleries in the town, and she discovered that Joss was a great dancer, swooping around the floor with dash and verve. But, of course, he had to go back to his unit.

'I have to catch the 11.10 train to King's Cross,' he said, and showed her his docket. 'I only had forty-eight hours' leave. But when Mam said she thought it was your afternoon off, I had to pop up and see you, hadn't I?'

'I'm so glad you did,' said Theda, and behind her eyes the tears threatened. 'I can't come to the station with you, I have to be back at the hospital.'

'Aye, well, I'll be back. I can't tell you where we're going but if I see our Frank, I'll tell him you were asking after him.'

Chapter Two

Joss didn't see Frank, thought Theda sadly as she sat in the bus bringing her home to Bishop Auckland, the certificate confirming that she was now a State Registered Nurse safely in her shoulder bag. It took an hour and a half to travel from Newcastle to Bishop and that didn't include the fifteen minutes from the town to Winton Colliery.

There was something sad about leaving the nurses' home, having packed her bags and removed all her personal stuff from her room so that it became once again the impersonal little box with a bed and a wardrobe and dressing table that it had been when she moved in more than three years ago. On the bus she had plenty of time to reflect on the past and found herself doing just that.

Joss had come home from Dunkirk but Frank had not; Theda had gone back to Winton to be with her family for two days, which was all the time she was allowed.

'There is a war on, Nurse,' Matron had said, implying that Theda's was not the only family to be bereaved at this time. Theda felt like swearing at her. Of course she knew there was a bloody war on. Hadn't it just been brought home to her in the worst way it possibly could have been?

Now she moved restlessly in her seat on the bus, crossing her legs and folding her arms as she stared out of the window at the shops of Chester-le-Street where they had just come to a halt to pick up more passengers. The memory of that interview still made her angry though today she had more idea of what Matron had to contend with, running a hospital in wartime.

Joss was in North Africa now, fighting under Montgomery.

'The young ones didn't stand much chance,' he had said when he came home from Dunkirk. Too green altogether. We tried to help them but—' He had fallen silent and Theda thought, But *you* weren't much older than Frank. But she was well aware it was the scant experience he had had in the army as a boy soldier and then in the Far East that had helped him. So, after all, it had been a good thing Joss went to India.

The bus was pulling into Durham, turning off the great North Road at Neville's Cross and going down the bank into the city, under the railway viaduct and into the bus station. The cathedral towered overhead on the promontory on the other side of the Wear and Theda stared at it as she always did. It looked so grand; how could ordinary people have built it all those centuries ago? She didn't notice when a soldier slipped into the seat beside her until she felt the rough serge of his uniform against her leg.

'Sorry,' she said, 'Was I taking up more than my share of the seat?'

'It's OK.'

She looked at him. He wore the badge of the Airborne Regiment on his red beret and beneath that had a cheerful smiling face with twinkling blue eyes.

'I'm only going to Spennymoor. I won't be a nuisance too long,' he said. 'Well, I'm going home to Shildon really. I'll change to the Eden bus at Spennymoor.'

'Really?' said Theda. He was altogether too chatty; she wasn't the sort of girl to be picked up like that, on a bus. She looked away and out of the window as they pulled out of the bus station. But when she happened to glance back, the soldier was looking at her openly.

'You don't mind me looking at you, do you? After where I've been it's so nice to look at a pretty girl.'

'Well—'

'Oh, come on, I'm not trying to pick you up. We can be friendly just for the time we're on the bus, can't we? If you like I'll introduce myself – my name's Alan Price. I live at Shildon. Or I did before the whole world went crazy.'

He was so friendly and easy to talk to that before she knew it, Theda was telling him she was a nurse and newly qualified, going to work at the hospital at Bishop Auckland. And suddenly they were in Spennymoor and he was getting off the bus and waving to her through the window, giving a mock salute. The bus set off again and she was smiling, lifted out of herself by his open admiration and friendliness.

*

'Aw, come on, Theda. Come to the dance with me. You're such a stick in the mud! I can just see you in ten years' time – an old maid you'll be if you don't shift yourself and start taking an interest in lads.'

'You think anybody must be on the shelf if they reach twenty without getting engaged at least! Besides, if your friend Violet Mitchell hadn't been on night shift, you wouldn't have cared whether I went or not.'

Theda had a few days before she started at the hospital at Bishop Auckland and was enjoying just lounging about the house; doing nothing much was a novelty she appreciated.

'Well, are you coming then?' demanded Clara, and Theda sighed.

'Oh, all right, I'll come,' she gave in. The dance was at the church hall in Eldon; it wasn't as if it was a long way to go. And if she hated it, she could slip out and come back on her own. Clara was sure to find someone to walk home with.

Of course, she thought as she stood on her own, feeling conspicuous, her sister had been claimed by an eager partner as soon as she walked in the door but Theda herself was relatively unknown to the local boys, having lived in Newcastle for the last few years.

The band – well, really it was Mrs Phipps who played the church organ on Sundays banging away at the piano, and her white-haired husband twanging the double bass – was a bit of a comedown after the five-piece band at the Brighton or the full orchestra at the Oxford Galleries, she thought, smiling slightly.

Mrs Phipps played the veleta and the palais glide, and when they began a rather slow and sedate foxtrot, someone tapped Theda's shoulder and she jumped in surprise.

'Now then, it's the beautiful nurse, isn't it?' The soldier from the bus was standing there, handsome in his uniform, his red beret tucked into his shoulder epaulette. 'You dancing?'

Theda grinned. 'You asking?'

'I'm asking.'

'I'm dancing.'

She went along with the formula and followed him on to the dance floor, feeling lightheaded and relaxed. And when he took her in his arms and they began to dance, she liked the feel of it, the ease with which she could follow him in the slow foxtrot.

'I'm Alan, remember?' he said. 'Do you live around here? And if you do, why haven't I noticed you before?'

'I was away training as a nurse, I told you,' said Theda. 'Now I'm going to work at Bishop Auckland.'

'Lucky for me,' said Alan, and when the music ended kept his arm around her waist and drew her to where the trestle table was set up in the corner of the hall. He bought her a coffee and afterwards they sat drinking the watery brew and talked and talked.

'Just think, I might never have met you if I hadn't been walking down the street in Nuneaton and wondering what to do with my forty-eight-hour pass,' Alan commented after he had walked her to the back gate of her house in West Row at the end of the dance and kissed her softly on the lips. He held both her hands in his, not wanting to say goodnight, not yet.

'Nuneaton?' asked Theda, bemused.

'That's right. I was wondering where to go. Forty-eight hours wasn't long enough to catch a train home and go back again, and anyway I hadn't a docket. But there in front of me was a furniture van, *Rutherford's Removals, Close House, Shildon*. I wasn't lucky enough that he was going straight home, but he gave me a lift to Durham and there you were on the bus with an empty seat beside you. It must have been meant. I knew I would see you again, and here we are. I recognised you the minute I came into the hall.'

Alan struck a pose in the manner of Charles Boyer. 'It is our destiny, don't try to fight it.'

Theda laughed, even though half the boys she knew made the same quote at every opportunity. Oh, he was funny and attractive and it was so exciting to think that he was attracted to her too. She looked up at his face, though all she could see in the darkness was the shape of his head outlined by the starlit sky. Then she sobered as he drew her to him and bent his head to hers.

'Eeh, our Theda, what are you doing standing there with a lad? Does your mam know you canoodle with soldiers?'

Theda jumped back hurriedly as Clara's voice came out of nowhere. She felt a twinge of guilt; she had forgotten all about her sister and Clara had probably been waiting to walk home with her. But she need not have worried; Clara was with their brother Chuck and Norma Musgrave.

They did not linger but went on into the house, chatting and laughing.

'I have to go in now,' Theda said in the moment of silence after the door closed.

'Can I see you tomorrow?'

'No, I'm sorry. I have to be on duty in the afternoon and evening.' It was her new job as a Staff Nurse. Her first – oh, everything was happening at once.

'I'll see you in the morning then. Oh, come on, Theda, what do you say? Ten o'clock? I'll be going back on the last train tomorrow night and the Lord knows when I'll be back.'

As Theda hesitated, the back door opened and her mother looked out, letting a tiny beam of light into the yard.

'Theda? Is that you? Howay in now.' She closed the door at once because of the blackout regulations but the disapproval in her voice was evident.

'I have to go,' Theda whispered to Alan, and then, 'All right then. I'll meet you at the bottom of Eldon bank. Ten o'clock.' And she fled indoors and up the stairs without looking back to face the amused glances of her brother and sister and the disapproving one of her mother. Once in bed she lay and hugged this strange and exciting feeling to her. She was going to see him tomorrow . . . by, it was grand! He was a lovely man.

They walked along Old Eldon to the crossroads and waited hand in hand while the cows crossed the road and then they hid behind a barn and kissed. The farmer opened his mouth to tell them to move on and not forget to close the gate behind them, but there was something about them and instead he whistled up his dog and went on his way to inspect the green shoots in the pasture land which had had to be turned over to grain. The couple were young and judging by the lad's uniform had enough to put up with without his bothering them.

They had to go back to Winton, of course; there was Theda's new job to prepare for. Alan waited for her at the end of the row and went with her to the town on the bus.

'Don't come any further,' she said as they were passing the station. 'You go back to Shildon now.' She felt so bereft, the fact that she was starting her new job hardly entered her mind.

I'll write,' said Alan. 'And you know that song "Don't Sit Under the Apple Tree?" Soppy, I know, but I mean it.'

'I won't,' said Theda, and hurried off to the hospital gates. When she looked back, he had gone.

The layout of the hospital at Bishop Auckland might be different from that at Newcastle, but the work, the discipline and the comradeship were the same, Theda found. And as ever there was a chronic shortage of trained staff so she was kept busy the whole time she was on the ward, at first on a ward for officers, separate from the old workhouse section. Going back to her room in the nurses' home, tired and ready for her bed, she had little time to worry about her men at the front, Alan now beside Joss.

'You are always in my mind,' she wrote nevertheless in her twice-weekly letters to Alan. She sat one night, just before lights out, and thought about him, her writing case open on her lap in bed, the fountain pen he had sent her for her birthday in her hand. She looked at it, a blue marbled bakelite case with a gold nib. Somehow in the time since he went away they had grown closer. Every morning her heart beat a little faster as she went to check her pigeon hole to see if there was a letter from him, and when there was she would thrust it under the bib of her apron and save it for her break.

She would take it up to her room, foregoing her cup of tea and half a teacake, and devour the letter instead. She would kiss it in the place where his fingers had been, and smile at herself for being a lovesick idiot. Then the intensity of her worry for him would hit her with full force and she would close her eyes and will him to stay alive.

You only knew the man for a couple of days, she told her reflection in the dressing-table mirror as she sat in bed and thought what to write in reply. For she couldn't let him know just how terrified she was that she was going to lose him, have him snatched away by the war. The bloody war . . . who invented war, anyroad?

There was a small supply of the new wonder drug, Penicillin, solely for the use of the British officers on the ward. Understandable really, it was in such short supply and the officers were needed to win the war and save them all from the Nazis. But if anything happened to Alan, if he was wounded (God forbid!), would there be any of the wonder drug to save him? Oh, she hoped so. She hoped some doctor would use it to save her Alan.

*

He had been away for almost two years, apart from one Christmas when he came home on a fortnight's leave. Theda had been transferred to the Children's Ward and felt she had really found her niche – she loved working with the children. She had a week's holiday though, and when Alan climbed down from the train on Darlington station she was there to meet him. There was what looked like a whole regiment of red-bereted men, looking fit and sun-tanned and smiling hugely as they grabbed hold of their wives or girlfriends, but she knew Alan straight away, even though she had seen so little of him before he went away.

He dropped his kitbag and swung her off her feet and the first thing they did was buy an engagement ring at the jeweller's on the High Row: a gold ring with three small diamonds set in platinum, slightly on the cross, as was fashionable.

'I love you,' said Alan as he slipped it on to her finger. 'I want to marry you when the war is over.'

'Are you sure? Are you really sure?' asked Theda, looking up at him. She herself had been sure, had been filled with a wild elation when he stepped off the train and she had seen him again, for she had feared he would be not at all as she remembered him, had worried he would be different from his letters somehow. But he was the Alan she remembered and Theda knew now that she loved him.

'I'm sure,' he said and put his arms around her, there in the shop, and the shop girl had tittered and the jeweller had coughed drily and sent her into the back on some pretext or other.

They went into Binn's tea room and had spam fritters and chips and jam roly-poly and custard, and Theda was proud when all heads turned to look at the handsome, brave paratrooper sergeant and his girl.

Afterwards they went back to the station and took the local train, which wound its way through Aycliffe and Heighington and stopped at Shildon. They sat with their hands clasped all the way and anyone looking in their compartment for a seat changed their mind and left the young couple alone, standing in the corridor if they had to.

At Shildon, they got down from the train in the old station. 'The first passenger station in the world,' said Alan proudly. They walked their different ways then, he to tell his mother and father he was engaged to be married and Theda taking the Eden bus to Winton Colliery and then going in at the back door of the house in West Row to display her ring.

'Nobody asked me,' growled Matt.

'I'm sorry, Da. Alan only has two weeks, and we wanted to get used to the idea before he has to go back. And it was so handy, being in Darlington; we could look at all the jewellers.'

'Oh, Da, don't be old-fashioned!' cried Clara. 'I think it's grand, Theda. Congratulations, I wish you all the best, I do an' all.' And she flung her arms around Theda and hugged her, and after a moment so did her mother and father.

'You're not getting married yet though, are you?' asked Mam. 'Not for the duration, anyway.'

'Oh, Mam, we haven't even discussed it yet. But I

promise we won't go off and do anything daft like getting a special licence and going to the Register Office. No, we'll have a proper chapel wedding when the time comes.'

Theda suddenly thought that she didn't really know what Alan's thoughts were on the wedding; he could have completely opposite ideas. But he wouldn't, she told herself. She felt she knew him so well now. Sometimes you learned more about a person through what they wrote than what they said, she told herself.

'We haven't even met the fella,' commented Chuck when he came in.

'No,' said Mam, 'but Mrs Andrews down the row knows the family and she says the Prices are good, decent folk and his father's a foreman at the Railway Waggon Works. Alan has a good job, too, to come back to after the war, like.'

Theda gazed at her in amazement.

'Well,' said Matt, 'you didn't think we wouldn't make enquiries about a lad you were going out with, did you?' But of course, Theda hadn't even thought about it.

Alan came down from Shildon for tea to meet the family and they seemed perfectly happy with him, at least Mam kept persuading him to have some more tea, or another piece of her eggless sponge cake, and he had a great conversation with Matt and Chuck about the progress of the war. Afterwards, he and Theda sat in the front room on their own, a privilege allowed to a newly engaged couple.

'We could go away for a few days – why not?' said Alan, lifting his head from her neck where he had been nuzzling her soft skin. He looked as bemused with love as she felt, thought Theda, hot and bothered and shivery and melting, all at the same time. But she thought he must be joking and just smiled and kissed him again.

'No, I mean it, why can't we? We could go to . . . oh, Windemere, or Blackpool, or even just up the dales for a few days. Why not?'

Theda sat up straight. 'Alan, you know my parents would never allow us to – not to go away together. Let's just be happy as we are. We'll probably be married this time next year. The war won't last so long now, will it?'

He got to his feet and walked over to the window and his going left a coolness where he had been, close beside her. 'But why not? We're engaged now, why can't we go away together? You're all I've thought about for months and months. Have you no feeling for me?'

'Yes, of course I have, Alan, I want to just as much as you do. But we can't.'

'You could say you had to go back to the hospital—'

'Alan!'

He turned back and gazed at her, his expression pleading with her. 'Theda?'

'I can't. I won't lie either, Alan.'

He bit his lip, seemed about to say something else but in the end didn't, simply strode to the door leading to the kitchen.

'Alan. You're not going like that?'

He paused, hand on the door, and after a moment

turned back to her and smiled tightly. 'No, I'm not going. Sorry, pet, it was just – oh, I don't know. I want you so much.'

He sat down beside her again and took her hand and kissed her lightly on the forehead but something had gone out of his lovemaking. Their passion had dwindled. And after a minute or two he rose to his feet again.

'I have to go now. I promised I'd have a drink with Dad before he goes on the night shift.'

'Yes.' Theda felt miserable out of all proportion; nothing had happened after all. It was in the nature of lads for their passion to get the better of them and hadn't she always been taught that it was up to the girl to keep them in check? But no one had told her that the passions in herself would rise to such a pitch. What an ignorant girl she was! Almost twenty-three and she didn't know a thing about men or life or anything. She almost said she would try, she would do anything, she even said, 'Don't look like that, Alan.'

He smiled down at her. 'I really have to go, sweetheart. You look so worried. Don't you look worried; I love you, pet. It doesn't matter – I was being selfish. Come on, now, walk with me to the bus stop.'

'I'll see you tomorrow?'

'No one could keep me away; not Hitler himself.'

He kissed her goodnight at the bus stop and said something about her coming to meet his mother and father on Sunday. 'They want to meet you, of course they do. You'll like them, Theda, and they'll like you. Then we can have the rest of the week to ourselves, can't we?'

Yes, she thought, as the bus pulled away and she waved to him until it was out of sight, ignoring the giggling young pitlads on the corner who were pretending to make sheep's eyes at each other and sighing and making loud kissing noises while looking shyly at her to see her reaction. They could have the rest of the time on their own, but wasn't that asking for trouble?

'She looks bewitched, Matt,' said her mother as Theda came in the door, refused a last cup of tea and went straight upstairs to bed. 'By, I hope nothing happens to the lad, dear God, I do. He's the first one our Theda has shown the least bit of interest in, and I don't know what she'll do if anything happens to him. I reckon it must be a dangerous thing, this jumping out of aeroplanes an' all.'

'Why, woman, will you hold your tongue?' Matt answered, impatient as ever. 'He seems a sensible fella to me. And anyroad, there's not a thing in the world we can do about it so he'll just have to take his chance along with all the other poor sods.'

Chapter Three

Theda wore her new utility costume to go to tea with Mr and Mrs Price. It was a pearly-grey colour and she had a smoky-blue chiffon scarf to soften the rather military lines of the shoulders and lapels. There was one small pleat in the back of the skirt but the shortage of cloth being what it was, the overall effect was pencil slim and close-fitting. It suited Theda to perfection. She was glad she had stuck out and saved her clothing coupons to buy it and the neat grey court shoes that went with it.

Her hair was dark and shining, curling down on to her shoulders at the back and pinned up in a roll at the front. Clara had done it for her when Theda said she didn't have a hat to suit.

'You can't go up there looking like you're still stuck in 1939,' her sister had said. Clara lent her her own gloves, ones she had painstakingly cut out of an old gaberdine she had bought on the market and hemstitched round in surprisingly neat stitching. 'Just the right shade of grey to go with that suit,' she said. 'Now, are you going to let me pluck your eyebrows? And you're not just going to put on a smear of that Pond's vanishing cream, are you? What you need is a bit of colour. I have just the right shade of lipstick and how about some green eyeshadow?'

'I'm fine, thanks, Clara,' Theda interjected. 'I like my own paler lipstick and I really don't want my eyebrows plucked, I'm too much of a coward. You don't want me to go up to Shildon to see my future mother-in-law with tears in my eyes, do you?'

'Well, I wash my hands of you but you can't say I didn't try.' Clara began packing up her make-up huffily.

'Come on, don't be miffed,' said Theda. 'I'm really grateful for all your help, you know that.'

'Well, I have to say, you're not the best model to work on.'

But Clara was mollified. 'Hurry up now, here's Alan come for you already.' He was coming down the yard and Theda's heart gave a small skip and flutter when she saw him and Clara laughed when she noticed.

'Mind, you are in love,' she said. 'I never thought to see the day.' Theda pulled a face at her.

Alan rolled his eyes and whistled when he saw her. Walking up Shildon bank with him, their shoulders touching and their hands entwined, Theda felt she was in a dream, she was so happy. As they came to the entrance to the Black Road, part of the Stockton and Darlington Railway before Shildon tunnel was built, he drew her on to it.

'Where are you going?' she protested weakly, but followed him willingly.

'Oh, come on, it will be quieter up here. And it still leads to Shildon, doesn't it?'

There wasn't a soul on either path but Theda allowed herself to be drawn on up the old line, still clearly defined and black from the small coal and slag that went into its construction more than a century before. On either side the grass grew high and one or two goats were tethered out to graze. They looked up, thoughtfully chewing as Theda and Alan strolled past, the young ones bleating and running close to their mothers in mock alarm. Up above, a lark sang and they stood close together and squinted up into the blue to try to see it. It was Alan who spotted it first.

'There it is, look!' he cried, and Theda bent her head back eagerly to see and he slid his arms around her and kissed her full on the lips so that they toppled over into the long grass, the lark forgotten. His hand was on her breast and her instant response shocked her so that her eyes flew open and she scrambled to her feet.

'Alan, come on, your mother's expecting us,' she said. 'I don't want to be late the first time I come to tea, do I?' She smiled, trying to be cool and in charge of the situation. He lay back in the grass and put his hands behind his head, supporting it while he looked up at her soberly.

'Theda,' he said, and his voice was low and throaty, 'don't you want me?'

I do! I do! she cried silently but turned away from him, twisting Clara's gloves round and round in her fingers. After a minute or two he got to his feet and brushed bits of grass from his khaki trousers. He came over to her and took her hand.

'Howay, pet,' he said softly. 'Like you said, you don't want to be late for tea, do you? I know for a fact Mam got hold of some currants yesterday and she's made a cake 'specially for you. Just to prove to you that she's a hard act to follow, you understand. Oh, yes, her little boy is used to the best of food. The best of everything, in fact.'

Theda smiled weakly and after a moment they walked on up the bank to where the old line came close to the modern, tarmacked road.

Alan's parents lived in one of a neat line of semi-detached houses with small gardens to front and rear. Pansies grew in rows by the path from the gate and beside them rows of lettuce and spring onions. Salad for tea, guessed Theda as she waited by the door for Alan to open it.

Mr Price was an older version of his son, still slim and straight-shouldered under his Fair Isle pullover, but his mother was a surprise: small and dumpy and bubbling over with the desire to please her guest.

'He's our only son, you know,' she confided to Theda as she brought in the teapot under its knitted strawberry cover. 'Eeh, I thought he was never going to settle down with a lass. I'm that pleased for you both, I am.'

It was obvious that Alan was their only child. The piano in the corner had three pictures of him on the top and on the wall was an enlargement of him in his uniform, one eyebrow lifted in a quizzical grin which made Theda's heart melt all over again.

'Come on, lass, tuck in,' Mr Price invited when the tea was served, and Theda didn't like to say she wasn't hungry because she had not long eaten her Sunday dinner. But the meat had been suspiciously like whale meat and she had only had a small piece so she did justice to the corned beef and onion pie, and praised the currant cake, and even ate some stewed plums and custard.

They sat on into the evening, the Prices talking about their son and his exploits over the years and Theda drinking in every word while Alan kept trying to shut his mother up.

'All in all, a success, don't you think?' he asked as they took their leave at last, Theda promising she 'wouldn't be a stranger' when Alan was away. The thought made her feel cold but she thrust it to the back of her mind; she wasn't going to let it spoil the week – oh, no, she was not. And when she went to bed his kisses were still warm on her lips, her body still felt the imprint of his hands and the length of his body pressing against hers in their last embrace. And still four more days to look forward to.

Days which got harder and harder, she admitted to herself on the last of them. The weather didn't help. Though it hadn't been all that good a summer, the week of Alan's leave had excelled itself. The sun shone from dawn to dusk and the cool wind that had plagued the north-east all year suddenly disappeared.

They walked down the wood on the way to the Bishop's Park with a picnic basket, and Theda told Alan of the time they'd had a picnic in the wood and Joss had got himself caught in a pothole under the water and the

34

panic everyone had been in and how she could laugh at it now, though not then, oh no.

That was the nice thing about Alan, she thought. They could talk just as easily as she and Joss had talked, about anything. She'd told him all about her elder brother, of course, and how he was in Italy now.

'What's he like?' asked Alan.

'Like you, really,' she answered, and now she thought about it, it was true.

'I always wanted a brother,' said Alan.

'Well, after the war you can share mine,' Theda promised.

They sat on the grass by the bank of the Gaunless which had left the wood and now meandered through the park on its way to join the Wear. There was no one about; it was market day in the town and the streets were thronged with shoppers queueing for bargains while the children were in school.

Inevitably they kissed and inevitably it got out of hand while the picnic basket lay forgotten. It was like a drug, thought Theda, once you'd started it was so hard to stop. Alan loosed the top button of her blouse and put his hand inside and she weakened at the feel of his hand against her breast, the sudden thrusting of her nipple taking her by surprise.

'Please, Alan,' she whispered.

'Please yes or please no?'

'Alan, don't spoil it now, let's wait until we're married. When you come home, Alan, after the war.'

'Suppose . . . Suppose I don't come home,' he said,

holding her close against his shoulder, her head cupped in the hollow of his neck. His mouth was very close to hers as he bent over her and his hand lay still on her breast and she was filled with a terrible fear.

'Oh, no, don't say that, please don't say that,' she whispered. The day seemed to have darkened as though by an eclipse.

She could not see her own reflection in his eyes. If he had gone on then she would not have had the strength to stop him. He was going to war, for God's sake, how could she deny him? What sort of heartless fool was she? 'I'll do anything, Alan, I love you,' she said. 'But don't say that.'

Abruptly, he let go of her so that she fell against the grassy bank. He jumped to his feet and pulled her up after him. 'No, pet, no, you were right. I don't want you to do anything you're not ready for. There's plenty of time, we have our lives together. Nothing's going to happen to me, I'm too fly for Adolf, just you wait and see. Come on, love, let's go home.'

He lit a cigarette and stared at the stream while she adjusted her clothing and pulled a comb through her hair. He whistled tunelessly and when she came to join him, took hold of her hand and strode off up the bank to the path. She wondered if he realised he was whistling a song about angels and whether they would watch out for him. Probably not, she decided.

Theda walked up the yard to the back door, feeling dispirited. It was Friday, her day off, and almost a month since Alan had gone back to wherever he was going.

'I wouldn't tell you love, even if I could,' he'd said to her. But she knew that wherever it was it must involve parachuting out of planes and most likely over enemy territory. She was at the pictures with Clara and the news came on. She could hear the plummy voice of the announcer: 'This is Gaumont British News,' and there were pictures of paratroopers saluting cheerily before stepping out of a plane and floating down to earth. Except that one of the parachutes didn't open and the camera followed him down and got closer and closer, and when it was close enough she imagined it was Alan.

Sometimes, the parachutes all opened and she was ecstatically happy as they floated down but when they reached the earth they were surrounded by German soldiers with bayonets on their rifles and they were prodding at the paratroopers . . .

Theda shook her head to clear it and opened the door and walked into the kitchen. Her mother had a visitor, a man. Oh, God. Theda stood, just inside the door, staring as he got to his feet. It was Mr Price. Even as she saw the buff envelope in his hand she was telling herself that there were other reasons why he had come visiting; he could have had the day off and been out walking and just happened to be passing, he could be there for many a reason. Why should she jump to the worst conclusion?

Mr Price had risen to his feet and she gazed at him, begging him not to say the words. And Bea Wearmouth moved to her daughter's side and took hold of her arm and drew her in towards the fire.

'Theda, pet,' she began.

Chapter Four

'Oh, I wonder, how I wonder,
When the pit starts work on Monday,
Will the galloway pull the tub for me?'

Charles Wearmouth, resplendent in his Sunday suit, utility
though it was, combed back his Brylcreemed hair before
the press mirror as he sang. Bea frowned at his reflection
in the glass.

'Hush, lad,' she whispered. 'Can you not show a bit
more sense? You know Alan was always singing that
tune.' She nodded towards Theda who was sitting in her
dad's rocking chair, one elbow propped on its wooden
arm. She was staring into the fire as in a dream, her
thoughts far away.

'Aw, Mam, he always sang the proper words, you
know he did,' Chuck said, raising his eyebrows in pained
innocence. It sometimes seemed to him that he spent his
life tip-toeing round people's feelings. Why shouldn't he
feel happy that it was his day off and he was going to meet

his sweetheart? But still, Theda was his sister and remorse struck him.

'It's the tune, Chuck,' his mother began, but Theda interrupted her. She had not been so lost in thought after all.

'Never mind, Mam, I hear it often enough on the wireless anyway.'

By, thought Bea as she regarded her elder daughter, a large family was supposed to be a consolation in your old age. But these days, the more children you had, the more worry and heartache you had to go with them. She noted the shadows under the girl's dark eyes, and how pale she was. Were they working her too hard in that hospital? After all, she could hardly have got over poor Alan being killed, and so soon after he had been home on embarkation leave. Bea glanced at the girl's hand, noting she was no longer wearing his engagement ring.

Theda put the hand up to her stiff white collar and loosened the stud as though it had suddenly become too tight. She was still in her nurse's dress though she had removed her apron and white cap, revealing the way her hair was pinned up off her neck. Some dark tendrils had escaped the pins and curled over her nape and around her temples. Bea sighed. The poor lass seemed so vulnerable somehow. She cast around for something to engage the girl's attention; Bea didn't believe in morbid thoughts.

'Why don't you and Clara go out for a walk before chapel, pet?' she suggested. 'You look really peaky. The fresh air will do you good after being cooped up in that hospital all week.'

'Oh, I would but I promised to go over to Violet's house

today.' Clara was just coming down the stairs and heard her mother's suggestion. Her dark, curly hair, so like Theda's and indeed all the Wearmouth family's, was strained into rolls on top of her head in imitation of Lana Turner.

Bea tightened her lips in annoyance. Did Clara think of no one but herself?

'It's all right, Clara,' said Theda, who was well aware of her sister's plans for the day and certainly didn't want to spoil them. All she wanted was for her mother to stop treating her like a convalescent.

Clara grinned in relief and held out a black eyebrow pencil to her sister. 'Will you draw me in some seams?'

'Righto.'

Theda took the pencil from her sister's hand, which was stained as much as her legs from the 'liquid stockings' she had been painting on. 'Stand on a chair then,' she said, and carefully drew straight lines from the top of her sister's wedge-heeled shoes to the middle of her thighs, lifting her skirt to reach the last bit.

Behind her, Chuck finished combing his hair at last and stuck the comb in the top pocket of his jacket, ready for the frequent touching up he felt his hairstyle would need during his walk with Norma Musgrove, the overman's daughter. They had been walking out for a year now and still he dithered about getting married.

'Ta-ra,' he called as he strode out of the kitchen and down the yard. Bea watched him go up the row before looking back at the girls.

'Why don't you go with Clara, pet?' she asked Theda. 'I'm sure Violet won't mind. You can all come back for your tea; I'll open that tin of salmon I've got saved from last month's ration.'

Theda was hard put to it not to burst out laughing when she saw her sister's dismay. Clara and her friend had dates with a couple of soldiers, or were they Canadian airmen? She remembered Violet and Clara had been talking about the Canadians stationed at Middleton St George. They were going into Bishop Auckland to the pictures at the King's Hall. There must be more to it than usual too, Theda reckoned, for the airmen to come into Bishop Auckland; Middleton St George was nearer Darlington.

'No, Mam, I don't want to. I've made plans of my own for this afternoon,' she said quickly, and Clara's face cleared.

'Oh and what might they be?' asked Bea.

'I'm . . . I'm going to change and then I thought I would go over to see Alan's mum and dad. They've been asking me to go to see them and I said I might today.'

The idea of going to see Mr and Mrs Price had but that moment jumped into her head and she surprised herself by putting it into words for she dreaded having to go. But when she thought about it, it was true: Alan's parents had invited her and she had to go sometime. Might as well get it over with.

'Mind, I don't want you going upsetting yourself again,' warned Bea, looking grave.

'No, Mam, I won't. I'm all right now. And, after all, I'm not the only one to lose her fiance in this war, am I?'

Bea nodded. 'Though, please God, not many more now, eh? Surely it can't go on forever.'

*

It was almost six o'clock when Theda came out of the Prices' house in Shildon. The Eden bus wasn't due for nearly half an hour but she had made the excuse that she felt like walking the two miles home for she'd felt that if she didn't get out then she would go mad.

'The fresh air will do me good,' she had said to Mrs Price. She was too late for chapel but that didn't worry her much; chapel didn't mean a lot to her since Alan had been killed at Arnhem. Killed at Arnhem . . . Dear God, just hearing the words in her head sent such distress coursing through her; she wondered clinically if she could go mad.

She set off down the road, desperately seeking something else to think about other than those awful words. The wind lifted her hair off her forehead where it had escaped from her headscarf, cold and damp on her flushed skin.

It had been an ordeal sitting in the front room of Alan's home, surrounded by photographs of him and listening to his mother talking about him. She had forced herself to respond, to add her own reminiscences to those of Mrs Price. The older woman needed to talk about her lost son. Poor soul, he had been her only child.

Theda had steeled herself to sip the too-weak tea from one of the best china cups and eaten a piece of eggless sponge cake filled with home-made plum jam, though it had taken an effort of will to swallow it. And the feeling of desolation she had been keeping at bay ever since Mr Price had called to show her the telegram from the Ministry of War with the bald statement that Alan had been killed in action rose in her and threatened to engulf her altogether.

Walking down the bank from Shildon, the fresh air made her feel somewhat better. At least she had got the visit over. As she walked, she found the tune that her brother had been singing so light-heartedly earlier in the day running through her mind, but this time it was Alan's voice she seemed to hear singing it:

'Oh, I wonder, how I wonder,
If the angels way up yonder,
Will the angels play their harps for me?'

Oh, yes, she told herself as she rounded the corner into the pit rows of Winton Colliery. Oh, yes, Alan, they will indeed. And for her own brother, Frank, only eighteen when he was killed on Dunkirk beach.

Frank had been one of the young ones who had been in the territorials and so had gone with his marras, his mates, who had all been out of work practically since leaving school, until the year before the war when the country found a need for coal and the pit winding wheels started rolling again. Of course, that was before the government stopped the miners going to war.

'The young lads didn't stand a chance on those French beaches, strafed by the Luftwaffe,' Joss had said. She remembered it now and her mind filled with bitterness. But these days, even with the war nearing its end, she was bitter about everything. It kept her from thinking about . . . Her mind shied away, back to Joss.

Joss had returned with the troopship coming from Bombay, just like in that other song, he had gone through the North African campaign and on to the Italian one with the Durham Light Infantry, and had survived, thank the Lord. Did the German wives and mothers and sweethearts thank God? she wondered.

Theda controlled her rambling thoughts as she approached home. She stopped just before she got to their gate and blew her nose and took out the powder compact, which had been Alan's present on her last birthday, to powder her nose. Best not to let Mam see she had been upset again. Pinning a bright smile on her face, she walked up the yard to the back door.

'Was it all right, pet?' asked her mother anxiously as she went in.

'Yes. Don't worry, Mam, it was fine.'

Bea lifted the iron kettle, weighing it in her hand to see if it held plenty of water before setting it on the fire.

'Well, I'm glad you went to see them then, Theda,' she commented. 'It was only right. Mrs Price is a decent woman and Alan was her only lad. Now, I'll open that tin of salmon and if you butter the bread we'll have sandwiches for supper. Go and call your dad, will you? By the time he gets downstairs it will be ready.'

Obediently, Theda called up the stairs and after a moment Matt Wearmouth answered: 'I'm coming, I'm coming, there's no need to wake the whole row,' just as he always did.

She heard him cough as he got out of bed and the nurse in her paused, listening. Was it worse than it had been last year? Perhaps not. But she had little doubt that he was beginning to suffer quite badly from what he called 'the miner's lung'. Still, if he was no worse . . . Satisfied, she returned to the table and began to spread margarine thinly on the bread. The butter ration was too precious to eat with anything as tasty as salmon. Butter was best eaten on its own on new bread, when it could be savoured properly.

The tune that Alan had liked to sing was still running through her head, refusing to go away. The miners had taken it up, devising their own words to suit the melody.

'Will the galloway pull the tubs for me?' She found herself humming softly and the words brought to mind the time before the war when Joss had been fined five pounds for kicking a pit pony, a galloway that had refused to pull the tub and so threatened to put his whole weeks' wages in jeopardy. She'd been a young girl at the time, studying in her spare time so that she could pass the entrance examination to Newcastle General Hospital. She remembered the row there had been at home, though.

'How could you do it, lad, a poor dumb beast?' her mother had cried. 'And five pounds lad, it's a mint o' money.'

But Theda had known why he did it and so did his mother really. For weeks Joss had come home from the pit full of frustration because Bessie the galloway had found herself a nice narrow part of the tunnel and wedged herself there, refusing to move. Oh, she was a wily pony all right. She would turn her head and look at him, Joss would say, and he swore that in the gleam of his head lamp her eyes would be triumphant. In other circumstances it would have been funny but when it meant the difference between a living wage and a pittance, oh, yes, she understood. The seam of coal was poor enough as it was. It wasn't long after that that Joss's name had come out of the hat when the mine had to cut down expenses. The gaffer had decided that that was the best and fairest way to choose and Joss had lost his job and had to leave Winton. For some reason, thinking of that reminded her of wild strawberries . . . what a butterfly mind she had, she chided herself.

Theda cut the sandwiches in two and arranged them on a plate and got out the blackberry pie her mother had made with the last of the season's berries. She would have to be getting back to the hospital as soon as tea was over. There was flu among the nurses and she had to work extra hours.

On the bus going into town Theda was lucky enough to find a seat by the window and sat dreamily looking out of the window at the darkness. She thought about Alan, lying somewhere in the Dutch countryside, but for the first time her thoughts were not really melancholy. She had met him first on a bus and then at the dance at the church hall in Eldon. Oh, he was handsome in his soldier's uniform with the sergeant's stripes, his red beret tucked into his shoulder epaulette . . .

The bus had reached her stop. She struggled to the front and got out, pulling her uniform hat firmly down on her hair for the wind was strong now. At least, she thought, she had been to see Mr and Mrs Price. Alan would have been pleased with her about that.

Poor Alan. Oh, not because of how he had died – though bad enough, it happened to thousands in this hell of a war.

No, poor Alan for being landed with a girlfriend as stupid as Theda Wearmouth! Why hadn't she said yes that time, the last time he had been on leave? She should have gone away with him, anywhere so long as they could have been together, snatched a few days and nights on their own, gone to bed together. How could she have denied him?

But the pain of that thought was too much for her altogether so she set off up the path that led to the road outside the hospital, trying to concentrate her mind on the ward and the work that lay in front of her.

The Children's Ward was quiet, the patients already bedded down for the night, the lights dimmed. Sister was in her office finishing off the report and her junior nurse was walking softly round the beds and cots, giving sips of orange juice out of feeder cups to the one or two children still awake, fetching a bedpan for one little girl who was whimpering with the need to go and fear of asking.

'Nothing much to report tonight, Staff Nurse,' said Sister. 'By, the nights are cutting in, aren't they? I suppose before we know where we are it'll be winter.' She yawned and sat back in her chair; Sister was never in a hurry to get off these nights unless her husband happened to be on leave from his unit, something which wasn't happening very often these days to any of the soldiers, Theda knew.

She went into the cloakroom and took off her coat and outdoor hat and pinned on her apron and cap. She looked at herself in the tiny mirror and rubbed at her cheeks, trying to bring some colour to them. You're not the only one to lose your man, she told her reflection fiercely. But it didn't help. She was the only one to lose *Alan*.

Chapter Five

'What do you mean, you don't want to work with the prisoners, Staff Nurse? You'll go where you are directed, like everyone else. Don't you know there's a war on?' Matron stared sternly over her half-glasses at Theda.

'But, Matron, I don't understand why I'm being transferred? Surely I'm needed where I am, on Block Five? When we're short-staffed as it is—'

'Are you presuming to tell me my job, Staff Nurse?'

'No, no Matron. I'm sorry.'

Theda lowered her eyes and gazed at the floor, the habit of obedience to orders reasserting itself. It had been too long ingrained in her to do anything else. But at the same time a wild emotion was surging within her, churning her stomach, and the emotion was close to hatred.

'Flaming prisoners-of-war!' Chuck had said when it was first proposed that the wounded POWs should be nursed in the hutted wards of the emergency hospital, which had started out as a workhouse hospital. 'There's likely to be Nazis and worse in among them. Right in

48

the middle of the town, an' all! It's bad enough having the Italians giving our lasses the glad eye, but Germans! Well, I ask you. Someone should complain to the council.'

But the council had had little to say in the matter; it was a Government directive. And besides, the huts had been added to the hospital for the care of war casualties, and wounded were wounded whether they were allies or enemies. Theda had pointed the facts out to Chuck but he had simply snorted his disapproval. She dragged her wandering thoughts back to the present.

'You will start on Monday, Staff Nurse,' Matron was saying.

Theda lifted her head and answered meekly, 'Yes, Matron.'

Well, at least she had almost a week to accustom herself to the idea, she thought numbly as she left the office and walked over to Block Five.

A week to say goodbye to the children in this side ward, the ones with the sadly misshapen spines who had never known life outside the hospital. A week to say goodbye to all the other child patients, especially the long-stay ones she had time to grow fond of.

You're being stupid, she told herself savagely as she hung up her cloak in the tiny cloakroom and pinned on her all-enveloping cap. In all the years she had been nursing it had always been hard when she'd had to move to another ward, first in Newcastle General Hospital and then, these last two years, here at home. But this time it was different, this time she had to go to the hutted wards, separated from the old workhouse hospital by barbed wire and with sentries at the gates. This time she would be nursing Germans. One of them could actually be the one who had shot Frank on the beach at Dunkirk . . .

'You look as though you lost a shilling and found a penny?'

Theda looked up as the Senior Assistant Nurse on the ward spoke to her. Nurse Jenkins was English. She had married a miner in the Welsh valleys but he was killed in a pit disaster and she had returned to her native Durham where, when the war broke out, she became a nurse.

'Morning, Nurse,' said Theda for anything less formal was frowned upon as likely to cause a breach of discipline. But she smiled at the plump, good-natured woman, so loved by the children and yet immensely practical and a great asset on any ward. 'I've been transferred,' she added, and couldn't keep the dismay out of her voice.

'Oh, dear, I'm sorry to hear that, Staff. Are they sending you to Durham? My friend went there. Mind you, she likes the place all right.'

'No, not another hospital. I mean, I'm to go over to the other side. Hut K.'

Nurse Jenkins looked relieved. 'Oh, well, that's no so bad, is it?'

Theda was saved the necessity of a reply for just then she heard Sister coming in through the main door. It must be two minutes to eight and if they were not ready and waiting in Sister's office by the time she had removed her cloak and straightened her cap, ready to receive the night report on the patients, there would be trouble.

*

'Hello, Millie. That's a lovely doll you've got there, may I have a look at it?' Theda asked the child in the cot nearest the door of the disabled children's room. She held out her hand and Millie proudly gave her the doll. 'It's nice, isn't it, Nurse Elliot?'

Nurse Elliot, the young Assistant Nurse who was helping Theda change the beds, nodded her agreement.

'My mother sent it to me,' Millie said proudly.

'What's her name?' asked Theda, thinking how much better it would have been if Millie's mother had actually brought the doll herself, but she never came near the hospital. Still, at least she kept in touch.

'I was waiting till you came. I'm going to call her after you, Staff Nurse. What's you name?'

Theda laughed. 'I don't think you want to do that. My name's Theda – and no one's ever called Theda! Why don't you name her Clara? My sister's name is Clara. She's named after Clara Bow, the film star. Theda is after Theda Bara, another film star of long ago.'

'I've never heard of them,' said Millie doubtfully. Though she had not seen a film in her life, she was an avid reader of *Film Fun* and the *Silver Screen,* magazines which Theda brought in for the children every week. Millie could even read the captions on the pictures, unlike Jean and Mary, the other two girls in the room.

'Why don't you call her Lana after Lana Turner?' suggested Nurse Elliot.

'No, I will call her Theda after Staff Nurse,' said Millie. 'But not after that Theda Barry, mind.'

'Well, thank you, it's a great compliment,' said

Theda. 'Now let's get you sitting up in bed. Nurse Jenkins is coming round with the cod liver oil and orange juice, isn't that nice?'

The children beamed. They weren't so fond of the cod liver oil but they loved the concentrated orange juice which came to them courtesy of America. Theda left them sipping the juice contentedly and went to make sure the main ward was tidied up properly for Matron's round.

Every cot and bed wheel had to be turned to the correct angle, and every counterpane smoothed with just the right amount of sheet turned down over it, every pillow plumped up and the opening of the pillow case facing away from the door. Trouble was, the children tended to rumple the bedclothes as soon as they were straightened. And better so, Nurse Jenkins had remarked to Theda, for if the bed remained tidy it usually meant the child was too ill to wriggle about.

Matron came in on the stroke of ten and walked round the ward with Sister, pausing at each bed as they talked about its small occupant and each child gazed at her with round solemn eyes, impressed by such an important personage. As she was leaving, she stopped where Theda was laying the trolley in readiness for the dressing round.

'Oh, Staff Nurse Wearmouth,' she said. 'I want you to take your dinner hour early if Sister will spare you. You can go over to Ward K and have a word with Sister Smith. Best go early, she's off duty this afternoon.' Taking Theda's agreement for granted, she swept off the ward and into Sister's office, the deep triangle of her cap fluttering behind her.

'You can go as soon as Mr Kent has finished his ward round,' Sister said to Theda before she followed in Matron's footsteps. They would be closeted in there for half an hour, thought Theda rebelliously as she stared at the closed door, no doubt having a good gossip. And when was she supposed to eat the Woolton pie which was always on the dinner menu on Mondays? She dipped the large forceps she was holding into the boiler and fished out an enamel kidney dish, banging it on the trolley and filling it with sterile pads of gauze. She laid out the instruments and the sharp-pointed scissors she would need to take out David's stitches if Mr Kent gave the go-ahead. Finally she covered the lot with a sterile dressing towel from the autoclaved drum.

It was no good kicking up a fuss, it would only upset her more than anyone else. Besides, she had to keep cheerful for the sake of the children. They soon picked up any bad atmosphere in the ward. But nevertheless she felt pretty rebellious as she set off on a round of the ward.

Not long after Matron left, the opening of the ward doors heralded the approach of Mr Kent and his junior doctor.

'Bring me the case notes from my desk, will you, Staff?' Sister asked over her shoulder as she went forward to meet the surgeon who strode into the ward, his house-man trailing behind him. But there was someone else with them. Theda stood to the side as they passed and saw he was a soldier, an officer in fact, a major. A doctor friend of Mr Kent's home on leave, perhaps? she conjectured as she went to get the notes and bring them back to Sister. He walked with a limp, he could be on sick leave.

'This is Major Collins, Sister. Major, Sister Allison,' Mr Kent was saying. 'Oh, and Staff Nurse Wearmouth. Major Collins is joining us on the other side mainly, though he will be available for the civilian side if necessary.'

He was very tall, the major, Theda noted as she acknowledged the introduction. He looked down at her with level grey eyes from a deeply tanned face which nevertheless had an underlying pallor and grooves of pain etched between the eyebrows. But his gaze lasted for only an instant for Mr Kent was striding up the ward to his first patient, six-year-old David who had had his appendix removed the week before.

'Thank you, Staff,' Sister said quietly, dismissing her. 'Go and check that the side wards are fit to be seen, will you?'

At a quarter to twelve, Theda crossed the grounds to the hutted section of the hospital. The day was overcast and a bitter cold wind blew over the tarmac as she walked so that she wrapped her cloak more tightly around her slim body, thankful for its warmth. The sentry at the gate let her in when she showed her pass and she walked down the ramp to Hut K and opened the door. A long corridor stretched before her and she paused, trying to remember the layout of the huts. The door on the left must be the patients' toilets, on the right the bathrooms, and further along the kitchen. The last door on the left had to be Sister's office.

She walked towards it, her rubber-soled shoes silent on the highly polished composite floor. She knocked and went in as Sister Smith called 'Enter'.

'Oh, Staff, thanks for coming.'

As though I had any choice in the matter, Theda thought, but she smiled. 'Hello, Sister. Matron told me you wanted to see me.'

'Yes. Sit down, Staff. It might be a good idea to have a look round before you start next week. I don't think you've worked on the huts before?'

'No, just the civilian side. Children mostly.'

'And you don't want to move,' said Sister, observing Theda shrewdly.

'Like everyone else, I go where I'm told,' she answered, and Sister Smith nodded.

'For the duration, anyway.'

Theda had to suppress a smile. The expression had become common over the war years. Shops had notices stuck to their shutters, *Closed for the duration*, council services had been cut *For the duration*. It had almost become synonymous with *When the Boat Comes In*. Only that morning she had heard one of the children announce he was saving his sweet ration for the duration.

'No, Jackie,' she had protested. 'What do you think the duration means?'

'Everybody knows that,' he had declared stoutly. 'It means the big party we'll have when we beat the Jerries.'

He had been so nearly right that Theda hadn't contradicted him.

'You can eat your sweets now, Jackie,' she had said instead. 'There'll be plenty after the war.'

Sister rose to her feet and motioned Theda to the

window set in the wall of her office, overlooking the ward. Theda went to look over her shoulder.

The ward was long with no side wards, forty narrow beds lined up to either side. There were round black stoves at each end and some of the ambulant patients were seated round them on hard wooden chairs. In the centre of the ward was a table and other patients were sitting there, playing a card game. The beds nearest the door had men lying in them, some reading and some just lying looking at the ceiling. Theda gazed at them curiously.

Some of the ambulant patients wore their field grey uniforms, all with the yellow or orange-coloured patch sewn on the back of the jacket denoting their prisoner status. She stared at the men nearest her.

They were mostly young, though there was a sprinkling of middle-aged men there too. Many were wearing plaster casts on various limbs and two were in bed with legs strung up on systems of weights and pulleys. Fractured femurs, she supposed. Her gaze focussed on one boy – he *was* only a boy, looked to be no more than eighteen – who had his left arm in a cast and his leg in traction. His head moved restlessly on the pillow and his blond hair was dark with sweat despite the coolness of the day. Running a temperature, she thought to herself.

'You see, not one with horns or a tail,' commented Sister Smith, glancing sideways at her, and Theda flushed.

'No, of course not,' she murmured.

Sister laughed. 'I'm sorry, but if you could have seen your face when you came in here!' she said. 'Do you want to do a round of the ward? Have you time before you go back?'

Theda consulted her wristwatch which was attached by the strap and a safety pin to the pocket of her dress. It was already twelve-thirty.

'I haven't had anything to eat yet and I have to be back on the ward by a quarter to one, Sister.'

'Oh, well, no matter. Come back sometime, Staff. How about Friday? I'm on duty all day.'

Theda agreed to return on Friday and tied on her cloak ready for the walk to the dining-room. As she opened the door, she was startled to come face to face with a German officer and jumped back hurriedly. But he too stepped back and gestured courteously for her to pass him, clicking his heels together as he did so in a gesture entirely foreign to her. She mumbled something incomprehensible and walked past him, taking with her an impression of light-blue eyes and dark hair, and an odour of carbolic soap and something else that was indefinable.

'Oh, Major Koestler, do come in,' she heard Sister say before the door closed behind him. 'I wanted you to look at—'

Whoever it was Sister wanted the German to examine, Theda didn't wait to discover. She hurried to the dining room where she took a plate of luke-warm Woolton pie and mashed potatoes and sat down to eat before finding that her appetite had left her.

For some reason she hadn't thought there would be a German doctor ministering to the prisoners. But, after all, it was only logical when she thought about it. If a doctor were taken prisoner, then of course he would be useful to his own countrymen. If nothing else, he could speak their language. But was she expected to take orders from a *German*? Her very soul rebelled against the idea. The first chance she got, she decided, she would see Matron and find out what the position was.

Abandoning her meatless dinner Theda went back to Block Five, breathing a sigh of relief as she heard children's voices from the ward. This was where she ought to be, she loved working with children.

There had been an emergency admission, an eleven-year-old boy who had been playing with his friends among the abandoned pit buildings at Black Boy colliery and fallen fifteen feet from the rusty wire rope of what had been the aerial flight, the overhead transport system which, when the pit was working, had carried tubs of coal. The boy was unconscious with a possible fractured skull and broken arm.

Theda's afternoon and evening were fully occupied, attending the houseman as he examined the boy and carrying out his instructions. The patient was laid flat and a temporary splint put on his arm until he should be judged well enough to go to the X-ray Department, which had been provided by the government along with an operating theatre in the hutted section of the hospital.

Nurse Jenkins helped Theda to tie a pillow carefully over the bedhead, just in case the boy should thrash about and catch his head on the iron bars, and then it was a case of watching and waiting and keeping the rest of the children quiet. And, of course, trying to allay the fears of the boy's parents who hovered in the corridor as they were not allowed in the ward just yet. Sister was having her two hours off-duty so it was up to Theda to usher then into the office and talk to them.

'I've told the lads till I'm sick not to play on the old aerial flight!' the father said the moment the door was closed. 'It's not safe, it's not been safe for years, I don't know why it wasn't cleared away years ago. All that scrap iron and they leave it. No, they'd rather take down folk's perfectly good railings to get iron for their factories. Eeh, I don't know how their minds work, I don't. If they have any minds, that is.'

He stood in the middle of the room, a man of medium height but with heavy powerful shoulders as most miners had. He spoke nervously, angrily, almost as though he didn't know how to stop once he'd started.

'Mr Patterson,' said Theda before he could go on, and he closed his mouth and put an awkward arm around his wife who was gazing anxiously at Theda, her lips working spasmodically.

'He's going to be all right, isn't he, Nurse?'

'We'll known soon enough, Mr Patterson,' she answered. 'Mr Kent, our consultant, will be here shortly to have a look at him.'

'I know you, you're Bea Wearmouth's lass, aren't you?' Mrs Patterson spoke for the first time. 'I heard she had one a nurse.'

'That's right, Mrs Patterson,' said Theda. 'Now, would you like a cup of tea while you're waiting?'

'By, I'm glad it's you – we can talk to you. But never you mind bothering with tea for us, you've got plenty to do without that, I fancy. Eeh, I'm that glad you'll be looking after the bairn, I feel better in my mind now. I'm not much good talking to doctors and nurses and such.'

'Sit down, do, Mrs Patterson,' Theda said gently. 'And you too, Mr Patterson. You look pretty tired yourself. Have you been on fore shift?'

'Aye, that's right. I hadn't been long in, just had my bath when the lad came running in to tell me Peter had had an accident. A good job I had an' all. I didn't have to come here in me black, like.'

'It wouldn't have mattered. Well, I'll get Nurse to bring you some tea anyway. The doctor won't be long and maybe there'll be some good news about Peter. Then you can go to your bed; you look as though you could do with it.'

'I couldn't sleep anyroad.'

The miner shook his head but sat down alongside his wife, and, bending forward, took his cap out of his pocket and began twisting it round and round in his hands. There was nothing more to say so when the tea tray arrived, Theda excused herself and withdrew, murmuring something about checking on Peter.

He was just the same. The young auxiliary nurse she had set to watch him for any signs of change stood up as she approached the bed. Theda felt his pulse; it was thready but could have been worse.

'Let me know if there's any change at all,' she said to the auxiliary. 'Mr Kent shouldn't be long anyway.'

The girl nodded and sat down again, staring fixedly at Peter's white face as though she was frightened she would miss something. Ah, well, better that than someone who let her attention wander with thoughts of her boyfriend or the like.

Chapter Six

It was half-past nine and a wet, cold night with the raindrops mixed with hail when Theda descended from the bus at the end of the rows in Winton Colliery.

'Got your flashlight, Nurse?' asked the conductor solicitously before he closed the door after her. 'You want nothing wandering about on a night like this without one.'

'Yes, I have it here, thanks, Tom. Goodnight then, see you tomorrow.'

The blue-shaded headlights of the bus gave a ghastly glow to the houses as it went around the corner on its way back to town, and then the blackness was absolute until Theda switched on her flashlight. Pointing it to the ground, more from habit than the fear of an enemy plane overhead spotting the light, she set off. It had been a long time since a German plane had been seen over this part of County Durham, she mused as she increased her pace to a fast walk towards West Row. In fact, the last one had been during the Battle of Britain and that was in daylight. It had dropped a bomb on the old pithead at Black Boy, missing the pithead further down which was in full production. The children had spent hours searching around for bits of shrapnel despite dire warnings from the authorities about the danger. There was not a child in the street that didn't have a piece of shrapnel hidden away.

They didn't see danger, that was the trouble. Which was why Peter Patterson was lying in a hospital bed right now. She sighed. At least he had pulled out of his coma to open his eyes and see his mother and father hovering anxiously at the bottom of the bed.

'Are you going to play war with me, Dad?' his first words had been.

'We'll see about that,' Mr Patterson had answered. 'How do you feel now, lad?'

'Sore.'

'Aye, well, it likely serves you right.'

Theda had ushered the parents away once the immediate danger was past; they were not allowed on the children's ward unless the child was dangerously ill. The powers that be had decided it upset the children too much.

West Row was very dark and the back street quite deserted, every window closely curtained with the black-out material obtainable from the Co-op store. The band of blue paper that shaded half the beam of her flashlight reduced visibility further but Theda walked confidently to the gate of her home and turned up the brick-paved yard to the back door. The scene that greeted her as she stepped into the kitchen was all the brighter for the gloom outside.

'Now then, how's my best girl?'

Dad was sitting in his rocker, dressed in his pit clothes

for he was on fore shift and Mam sat opposite him with a smile on her face bright enough to break any blackout regulations. But it was the soldier standing before the black-leaded range with his hands on his hips and a wide grin on his face who had spoken. Theda flew across the room and flung her arms around him.

'Joss! I didn't know you were back in England, let alone coming home on leave. Why didn't you let us know?' She leaned back in his arms and gazed up at him in delight before giving him an extra hug for good measure.

'I didn't know myself, that's why,' answered her brother, laughing down at her. His eyes were strikingly dark, as were all the Wearmouth eyes. But in his case his face was dark too, tanned deeply by his years in India where he had served as a young soldier after being laid off at the pit. The tan remained, thanks to his time in North Africa and, later, Italy.

'I'm just making supper, Theda,' Bea interjected. 'It's a shame we used the salmon yesterday. If I'd known – well, never mind, I still had the corned beef and I've made a hash and dumplings. There's plenty for an extra one.' She lifted the lid of the pan, which was sitting half in the fire and half on the bar, and an appetising smell wafted through the kitchen.

'Well,' said Joss, 'I thought I'd had enough bully beef in the army to last a lifetime. And here I am, coming home to it!' He winked at his father.

'Oh,' said Bea, distressed. 'It's all I have, lad. I've made herby dumplings though, I had a bit of suet from the butcher today. Your dad and Chuck get eightpenny-worth of extra meat each for working down the pit but I have to take it in corned beef.'

Joss put an arm around her and laughed. 'Only joking, Mam, I love your corned beef hash. It bears no resemblance to what we get in the army anyway. Fetch it on, I'm starving.' He thought of something and fished in the pocket of his battledress to pull out a paper. 'You can get more meat tomorrow, I've brought my emergency ration card. Just forty-eight hours' worth but better than nothing.'

Theda watched happily as the family gathered round the kitchen table. By, she thought, it's grand to have him home. It was almost two years since they had last seen him but now he was here it seemed as though they had seen him yesterday.

After supper, Theda and Clara reluctantly decided it was time they went to bed.

'I have to be up at five to catch the bus,' said Clara. 'Violet and me are on day shift this week.'

'Well, mind you take your flashlight this time,' Theda said drily, and they all laughed but Joss.

'What's this then?' he asked, looking from Theda to Clara.

'Aw, take no notice, Joss, they're just getting at me,' said Clara crossly.

'Clara missed a shift last week,' her mother explained. 'She was late getting up and by the time she was ready the others had gone and she had to walk to the bus on her own. And then she forgot her flashlight. She decided to take a shortcut across the gardens and ended up getting lost in the dark.'

Clara frowned fiercely at the amused expressions around her. 'It wasn't funny,' she observed. 'I thought I'd never find my way. I'd been walking round in circles and somebody's goat frightened me to death. *And* I tripped over its dratted chain and fell into the muck and messed up my trousers.'

'No, pet, I can see it wouldn't be funny,' said Joss solemnly, and then spoilt it by bursting out laughing.

Clara tossed her head in the air. 'I'm off to bed. Mind, don't make so much noise neither. Think on – my work is just as important as yours, and hard an' all in that munitions factory.'

'Yes, Clara. Goodnight, pet.'

Joss managed to keep his face straight while his young sister made a dignified exit, and then he pulled down the corners of his mouth and gazed round at the others wickedly.

'Aye, well,' said Matt as he laced up his boots. 'She's right there. Mind you, sometimes she comes home with more of that yellow powder on her than I have coal dust. It cannot be good for her. By, it smells like fire-damp gas! But the pay's good, I'll give you that. She fetches in more than I do.'

In fact, Clara earned more than any of them, Chuck included, and he was on top wages at the pit, hewing, thought Theda as she too said her goodnights and followed Clara up the stairs. It was a bone of contention with the miners that though they worked an extra day during the war they earned little more than they had done before, unlike other workers. But at last there were some signs of its being put right, the government currently negotiating with the union.

Next morning, when Theda went down to the kitchen, there was a brown paper bag on the table and a note from Joss with her name on it.

'I thought you could take these for the bairns on the ward,' was written in his careless scrawl.

Theda picked up the bag and opened it. Inside were six oranges and four bananas. The bananas were slightly over ripe but not spoiled and Theda gazed at them in delight. It was four years since she had last seen a banana and she lifted one to her nose, breathing in the almost forgotten aroma. Smiling, she slipped it back into the bag. She had to get on if she wanted breakfast before she went to work.

The kettle was still warm and she placed it on the gas ring by the side of the range and lit the gas before spreading margarine on a slice of bread she had cut from the loaf and covering it with a smear of jam. There was a small amount of dried egg left in the packet but she would leave it for someone else, and she had eaten her four ounces of bacon on her day off. But the milkman had come early so at least there was real milk for the tea.

'Gosh!' said Nurse Elliot, peering over Theda's shoulder at the exotic fruit she was cutting up and spreading on bread and butter to make it go further. She placed a piece on each of the children's tea plates along with a section of orange, careful that there was an equal share on each. 'Don't bananas look funny, Staff Nurse? I'd forgotten what they were like. Do you know, I used to love banana custard before the war.'

'We didn't see many bananas before the war,' commented Theda. 'Not even in the local Co-op store. There wasn't much call for them in a mining village with most of the miners out of work.'

Nurse Elliot, a Red Cross nurse, looked at her blankly. She was not from a mining village, her father was a bank manager in the town.

'Come on,' said Theda, 'let's get them on the trolley and pass them out. I want to see the children's faces when they taste the banana.'

The reactions of the children were all she could have hoped for. Only Peter Patterson was not well enough yet for solid food but Theda was thankful that he was at least taking an interest in his surroundings now. He had been to X-ray but no skull fracture had been discerned, though he had been badly concussed. His arm, now plastered and supported in a sling, lay heavily on top of the bedclothes.

'And lucky for you, young man, that you weren't killed,' Sister had said sternly. 'Or at least suffered a fractured spine. Why, you could have been paralysed for life.'

'What's a factured spine, Nurse?' the boy had whispered to Theda after Sister had returned to her office.

'Fractured spine,' Theda had replied. 'And it means a broken back.'

Peter had blanched. He knew well enough what that was and he lay quite still for the rest of the day. Mr Gates, a man who lived at the other end of his street, had a broken back from the pit and had to be wheeled about in a long carriage as though he were a baby.

David, the boy recovering from an appendicectomy, gazed dubiously at his bread and banana. 'I'm not sure I like it, Nurse,' he said.

'Go on, have a bite,' urged Theda, and he took a tiny morsel in his mouth. His face cleared and he grinned.

'By, it's lovely, isn't it?'

All in all, the fruit, especially the bananas, were an enormous success, Theda reported to Joss that evening.

'Where did you get them? I didn't know they grew bananas in Italy, Joss,' she said.

He tapped his nose and looked mysterious. 'Now then, careless talk costs lives.'

'Oh, aye, and where is the German spy who might be listening in here?' asked Chuck, sitting in his black having just come in from the pit as he had worked overtime on his back shift. Chuck was training to be a deputy overman and had ambitions to raise himself to manager at least in time to take over from Tucker Cornish when he retired. Norma, his girl, fuelled his ambitions. She fancied rising above the pit rows and becoming mistress of the manager's house on the outskirts of the village.

Next morning Joss travelled into Bishop Auckland with Theda, his forty-eight-hour leave over, gone in a flash. Now he had to catch a train to somewhere in the south of England to join up with his regiment and then they would be off again, to somewhere on the continent.

They walked up the path from the bus stop together, Joss with his kitbag on his shoulder and Theda in her nurse's uniform. They paused on the station bridge where she had to turn left for the hospital and Joss had to cross the road for the station.

'Mind you look after yourself, our Joss,' she admonished. 'Don't walk under a tank, especially not a German one.'

Joss grinned. 'Nay, lass, you know me. I keep my head down all right, I'm not one for trouble.' He gave her a quick peck on the cheek and then changed his mind and hugged her tight so that the passers by turned to look at the handsome soldier and his girl saying their goodbyes and Theda thumped him on the chest.

'Behave yourself, our Joss,' she said, and his grin grew wider. He stepped back and waved cheerily before striding the road, whistling merrily: 'I'm Going to Get Lit Up When the Lights Go On in London'.

Theda gazed after him until he had rounded the corner into the station before she continued on her way to the hospital. Oh, well, she thought, Joss had survived Tobruk and the landings in Sicily – maybe he did bear a charmed life. In any case, it was no good worrying about it. With a bit of luck the war would be over soon.

The following Sunday, Theda had to report to Sister Smith on Hut K. A man in hospital blue came out of the toilets as she entered the ward.

'*Morgen*, Nurse,' he said, bowing his head in what she knew was a courteous gesture though it seemed very foreign to her.

'Good morning,' she answered, nevertheless. There were two more ambulant patients in the kitchen, she saw, murmuring in what she presumed was German as they washed up the breakfast pots. Of course, she thought, they would have their own men working as orderlies. Well, it would save the nurses a lot of cleaning work, she didn't object to that. She took off her hat and coat in the tiny cloakroom and put on her apron and white cap. Taking a deep breath, she walked down the corridor to Sister's office and knocked on the door.

Afterwards, when the day was over and she was free to leave Hut K, Theda was startled to realise she had almost forgotten her patients were anything other than British. Which was strange, she mused as she walked down the ramp between the wards to the dining-room, for there had been plenty of reminders, what with the difficulties with the language and the exuberant behaviour of the few Italians, whose favourite game appeared to be to flirt with the junior nurses, calling out outrageous remarks to make them blush. She was pleased that most of them were convalescent; they would soon be on their way back to the main camp at Weardale.

The young boy she had noticed on her first visit to the ward was still poorly. He was first on her long list when she set out round the ward with her dressing trolley, accompanied by a Red Cross nurse, a pretty nineteen-year-old with rosy cheeks and green eyes. Nurse Cullen, she introduced herself as, and pushed a lock of bright auburn hair back under her cap before Matron came round and saw it dangling on her collar.

'I haven't seen you before,' said Theda as they turned down the sheet from the boy's arm and shoulder.

'No, I only came last month,' Nurse Cullen admitted, and Theda's spirits sank.

'Can you take off the bandage while I scrub up?' she said, and backed out of the screens. As she took up the scrubbing brush at the sink at the end of the ward, she thought, well, she would see what sort of a nurse the girl was going to make soon enough. By the end of this dressing round in fact.

Surprisingly good, she had to admit later. Nurse Cullen had gentle hands, safe and sure, causing the minimum of discomfort to the patients as she worked and seeming to know just what Theda wanted her to do.

The young soldier, Johann his name was, according to the chart on the end of the bed, was cause for concern. He had an inflamed wound on his shoulder which Theda guessed was probably causing his pyrexia and as she cleaned it with Eusol and packed it with sterile gauze she could feel that his skin was hot and febrile and hear him muttering constantly and incomprehensibly.

The dressing round was hardly over and Theda was washing her hands when the main doors opened and into the ward came Major Collins, favouring his left leg a little, Theda noticed, even as her heart sank as she saw the German doctor at his side. Sister was on her break, she remembered, still had ten minutes to go. The doctors were early.

Major Collins halted at the door of the office and looked up the ward directly at Theda. She finished drying her hands and went to meet him.

'Morning, Doctor. Sister isn't back from her break,' she said, acknowledging Major Koestler with a brief nod.

'No matter, Staff, I have something I want to do in the office. Will you take the round with Major Koestler this morning?'

No! was Theda's instinctive reaction. For a moment she thought she had shouted it out loud but it resounded only in her mind. She tried to control her expression, not let it show on her face, but something must have done.

'You will do the round with Major Koestler,' said the Englishman, and this time it was an order.

'Yes, sir,' said Theda.

Chapter Seven

Theda walked across to Block Five during her dinner break. She had the latest copy of *Film Fun* for the children in the side ward and wasn't feeling very hungry anyway, the last hour on the ward having taken away her appetite. In any case, she felt like a chat with Laura Jenkins if the ward wasn't too busy.

Major Collins had made her feel like a naughty child, she thought rebelliously. Surely it was natural to feel some resentment toward the German doctor? After almost five years of war, and Alan and everything? Oh, he had said nothing, he hadn't needed to: it was his tone of voice when he spoke to her; it was the steely look in his eyes when he looked at her.

'Perhaps you would find it easier if you called me Doctor?' Major Koestler had suggested, looking at her keenly. Obviously he was well aware of the tension in the atmosphere and what had caused it.

'If you insist, Major Koestler,' she had said stiffly, and he instantly turned his attention to the patients, saying no more to her than was absolutely necessary for them to get round the ward. But the constraint she felt soon eased as her professionalism took over.

The Italians, usually so vociferous, especially when there were pretty nurses about, fell silent as he approached their end though Major Koestler did not examine them, most of them being medical rather than surgical cases anyway, Theda realised. They had been prisoners since the North African campaign and their main camp was further up the dale.

'Good morning,' he said to them. They stared back, their normally merry faces impassive, but he didn't appear to notice anything, merely going smoothly to a middle-aged German who was sitting by the stove, one arm in a sling.

'Don't get up,' he said in German, or at least that was what Theda surmised he said for the elderly soldier half-rose from his seat and then subsided again.

Afterwards, when the round with Major Koestler was over and she had gone back into the office with him to leave the case notes, the English doctor had looked at her impersonally, almost as if he had trouble recollecting who she was. Sister was back and he was deep in an animated discussion with her over Johann Meier.

'Oh, Helmar,' he greeted the German, and barely glanced at Theda. 'We were just discussing the shoulder wound, Meier. I think we should withdraw the Sulphapyridine and try—'

Theda heard no more as she left the office, closing the door behind her. She carried on with the work of the ward automatically, dishing up mince and cabbage and potatoes for Nurse Harris, a new auxiliary nurse, and Nurse Cullen to give out to the patients who, practically to a man, looked in horror at the grey meat and watery vegetables. Yet all the plates were cleared when they came back to the kitchen, she noticed. Food was food after all in this year of war, 1944.

Laura Jenkins was coming off duty when Theda got to Block Five and waited while Theda delivered her comic book and had a few words with the children. Then they walked together to the dining-room.

Over plates of mince and vegetables, exactly the same as those eaten by the prisoners earlier, Theda gave an account of her morning. Laura ate steadily saying nothing, until she put down her knife and fork and went to the counter to bring back two plates of rhubarb and custard.

'Well,' she said as she sat down again and picked up her spoon, 'at least you have got over the first time. It will get easier, I'm sure.' She pulled a face at the taste of the rhubarb, sweetened with saccharine and tasting like it, but carried on eating stolidly.

'I'm all churned up though,' said Theda, who was pushing her spoon round and round in the custard and eating little. 'And I don't see why I should feel in the wrong. Surely anyone would feel the same as I do in the circumstances?'

'Aye, I can see you're right upset,' agreed Laura. 'What I reckon is, you're just going to have to get used to working there. What can't be cured must be endured, as my old man used to say.' She put down her spoon and gazed across the table at her friend. 'Oh, look, I know how you feel, believe me I do. You're still raw from losing Alan, I know that.'

Theda stopped playing with her food and began eating stolidly, the stab of pain at the mention of Alan's name fading slowly, robbing her of her appetite. But after all, she had to work the rest of the day and needed the energy. Laura was right of course, she knew it, and moaning about it wasn't going to help. At least it was her day off tomorrow. She could go back to Winton Colliery tonight and forget about the hospital for a while.

It was a dark and bitterly cold morning when Theda awoke in the bedroom she shared with Clara when she slept at home. She snuggled down under the bedclothes, leaving only the tip of her nose in the icy air. She heard voices downstairs as her sister came in from the factory, her mother's greeting and Clara's reply. Her father would still be at work, he didn't usually get home from his night shift until almost midday, and Chuck was at the pit too.

She could help her mother with the housework today, she thought. Clara would be in bed and they would have the house to themselves for most of the day. But not yet. It was so lovely to be able to stay in bed a little longer, snug under the blankets.

Theda must have dozed off for the next thing she heard made her sit up, careless of the cold, and look across at the other bed. Clara was already there, she could see her from under the pile of blankets which was heaving slightly and hear what sounded very like sobs coming from underneath.

'Clara?'

The sounds stopped and the blankets became still but Clara did not answer. Grabbing her woollen dressing gown from where it lay at the bottom of her bed, Theda hurriedly pulled it on and went over to her sister. There was nothing to be seen but the top of her head.

'Are you all right?' she asked softly, and Clara turned on her side, still keeping her face hidden.

'Just the sniffles, let me sleep,' she replied. 'I have to go to work tonight, remember.'

Theda stepped back. Maybe it was just a cold, though that wasn't what it had sounded like to her. Still, if Clara didn't want to talk . . . oh, maybe she did just need a good day's sleep.

'Has Clara got a cold, Mam?' she asked later as she speared a slice of bread on the end of the toasting fork and held it to the bars of the fire.

'A cold? No. At least, she seemed perfectly all right when she came in this morning,' Bea answered. 'Why? Does she look poorly to you?'

'No, it's nothing, I just thought – no, it wasn't anything,' said Theda. She took the toast off the fork and went to the table. There was some dripping Bea had made from beef fat that she had managed to get from the butcher and Theda spread some on the toast and bit into it before the dripping melted altogether. Sighing happily, she sat in her father's chair before the fire and stretched her legs out along the steel fender towards the blaze, feeling the heat seep into her bones. The day was very dark and the main light in the room came from the fire, gas was too dear to light during the day. Bea could not get used to the idea that they were all working and bringing in money now, she was still careful with the gas.

Toast and dripping eaten in the half-light – how it reminded Theda of family suppers before the war when they would sit around the range and Da would tell them stories because it was too dark to read. Thursdays mostly, the night before payday when there was no penny left to feed the gas meter.

It was a black moonless night when Theda walked up the yard and to the end of the row to catch the bus back to the hospital. She had an extra few hours to work because of the number of nurses off sick.

It had started to rain and wind was stirring the few remaining leaves in the gutter so that they eddied and swirled around her legs, making her shudder. She pressed the switch on her flashlight, creating a small pool of light around her feet as she turned the corner and set off across the small piece of waste ground to the road to Winton village. The buses to Winton Colliery stopped early and so she had an extra half-mile to walk to catch another.

As she walked, Theda thought about Clara. Her sister had got up about six o'clock, looking puffy-eyed and pale, but then she often did when she had had insufficient sleep and no one else seemed to notice anything. Perhaps she had been wrong, it was all her imagination, Clara was just grumpy and tired from working night shift.

It had been a relaxing day, in spite of her niggling

worry about Clara. Theda had ironed the clothes her mother had washed the day before, standing at the kitchen table ironing her father's shirts on an old blanket while Bea sat by the fire, leaning forward to the light as she sewed on buttons and darned and mended frayed patches. They had listened to *Workers' Playtime* and laughed and chatted as they worked, Theda exchanging a cooling flat iron every now and then for a hot one from the bar, spitting and making it sizzle to make sure it was just the right temperature.

Bea told her of the new scare story in the rows. Her neighbour, Mrs Coulson, had her daughter-in-law Renee staying there, a cockney girl who had married one of the Coulson boys in 1939 when he went to London in search of work. When her husband had gone into the army and the bombing started, the girl had fled up to the safety of her mother-in-law's house with her young baby and stayed there, for her parents' house in London had been bombed and she had nowhere to go back to. She swore she had heard a bloodcurdling scream and been followed in the dark one night as she took the short cut from the bus stop, and only escaped because she had run for her life.

'But then,' Bea had commented, 'I suppose she's always been used to living in a town. There's likely a lot of things frighten her here. It was likely that fox that's been about, I've heard it myself.'

There was news from Germany too. Betty Young's husband, Billy, who had been missing, presumed killed, had turned up in a prisoner-of-war camp.

'An' I only hope he is getting as good treatment as those ones in your hospital,' Bea had said as she finished sewing on a button and bit through the thread. 'There now, I'm about finished. We'll have a cup of char, will we?'

Theda smiled as she walked on down the road. Her mother picking up expressions from the wireless. But the smile disappeared as she heard the bus in the distance. Goodness, she was going to miss it! She began to run and dropped her flashlight which promptly went out. Theda stumbled over the kerb in the blackness. Oh, where was it? She was torn between running for the bus and finding her flashlight – she would need it and they weren't so easy to replace – when she heard a man's footsteps. And suddenly she was nervous, remembering Renee Coulson's tale; she began to run towards where she could see the outline of the first houses in Winton village and was just in time to see the lights of the bus as it rounded the corner and set off on its return journey to town.

She bumped into the fence at the side of the path, catching her shoulder painfully, and moved out into the middle of the road, beginning to run headlong for the village as the footsteps grew louder. She had reached the houses, which were all dark and blacked out, and thought she would knock on a door anyway – surely the inhabitants would be inside on a night like this? – when she felt a hand on her arm and was pulled roughly back on to the path. She had opened her mouth to scream when he spoke.

'Staff Nurse Wearmouth, isn't it? What are you doing out here at this time of night?'

Theda pulled herself away and closed her mouth before a scream escaped. 'Major!' she cried, her voice sharp with shock. 'What do you think you're doing, grabbing me like that? You frightened me half to death.'

Major Collins laughed. 'I was only trying to help. You seemed in danger of falling on the road. Due back at the hospital, are you?'

Theda took time to catch her breath before replying. Across the road the front door of the Pit Laddie public house opened and a beam of light spilled across the road. As she gazed up at him she saw he was smiling, looking almost human. Why couldn't he be like that in the hospital?

'Close that door!' roared someone from inside the pub. 'Do you want me to be summonsed for showing a light?'

'Sorry,' replied the man who had come out, and hastily closed the door, cutting off the light. Now the major was just a dark shape beside Theda again.

'Yes, I suppose I'll have to walk now,' she replied.

'I can give you a lift, if you like? I was going back in any case. My car's just around the corner.'

Theda hesitated, tempted. If she walked back she would be late and Home Sister could be snotty about the rules. On the other hand, if she were seen getting out of Major Collins's car, there could be more trouble. But she couldn't really spend yet another night at home, the ward would be short-staffed. She would just have to swallow her resentment of him.

'What's the matter, don't you want to accept a lift from me?'

'Oh, it's not that,' she said. 'Just, you must know what Home Sisters can be like. If she sees me getting out of your car at this time of night, she'll think I've lost my virtue or something.' As soon as she said the old-fashioned phrase, Theda felt embarrassed. He would think her a fool.

'I'll drop you off on the corner,' he offered, and she realised he understood what she meant. Of course he would, he was used to hospital rules.

'I would be glad of a lift,' she admitted, and walked with him round the corner to a Hillman car and waited for him to open the door for her. Rain was falling heavily now and she was glad to get inside. The major soon had the car on the road and headed towards the town, blue shaded head-lamps lighting the road poorly and glinting eerily on puddles in the gutters. There was very little traffic; all was dark and silent except when they passed a pit head with the wheel whirring above and the twinkle of rights as the cage came to the surface and spilled out its load of miners with their lamps.

Theda glanced sideways at her companion. All she could see was the outline of his face, darker than the night outside the car, and a faint flash as he sensed her eyes on him and looked down at her.

'By the way,' he said, 'what were you doing in Winton?'

'I live there. At least, my family lives there. It was my afternoon off and I was visiting them.'

'Oh? Then you will know my uncle, Mr Cornish? He's the manager at Winton Colliery.'

'Yes. Well, of course I know him. Everyone in a pit village knows the gaffer. But my father and brothers are just ordinary miners.' Theda bit her lip, she hadn't mean to sound as though she had an inferiority complex about it.

He glanced at her again. 'Does that matter? After all, I understand Uncle Tucker started as an ordinary miner. Worked his way up from the bottom, so it's said.'

Theda sighed. 'Sorry. Of course it doesn't matter, not nowadays, I was being silly. I'm tired and have to work four hours tonight *and* I'm on days tomorrow.'

'Almost there.'

The car was entering the town now and he turned into the road that ran along the side of the hutted wards, though nothing could be seen of them even in daylight for they were surrounded by a high wall surmounted by rows of barbed wire. He stopped the car before he got to the corner, about a hundred yards from the nurses' home and the entrance to the hospital.

Theda gathered up her flashlight and gas mask from her lap and turned to him. 'Thank you for the lift, Major,' she said. 'I would have been late if I'd had to walk.'

'Not at all, it was no trouble,' he replied, almost as formally as she. 'Best hurry in now, before Home Sister catches you.' Theda got out of the car and hurried off down the road, looking back only the once as she turned for the gate of the home. The car was still there, headlights dimmed, but as she went up the path to the door she heard the engine rev up to go on.

It was nice to think that he had watched over her until she was safely inside, she mused as she went up to her room and took off her wet coat. Not that there was anything to fear on the streets of Bishop Auckland, but still . . . it was nice. It reminded her of the way Alan . . . Good Lord! What on earth was she thinking? She certainly didn't think of Major Collins in that way. Why, it was only three months since Alan was posted missing at Arnhem. The familiar ache started up as she thought of her dead fiance.

Theda did her stint on the ward. It was quiet, only the occasional snore from the sleeping men, and some muttering when the porter came in to replenish the stoves and the clattering noise of the coke going in woke them. She busied herself refilling dressing drums for the autoclave.

Dear Alan, she thought miserably, how I loved you. The misery she had felt when she learned of his death returned full force and was still with her when she slid between the icy sheets of her narrow bed in the nurses' home. She cried into her pillow for a moment or two before looking for a handkerchief in the drawer of her bedside cabinet and blowing her nose.

That's enough, she told herself sternly. There's work to be done tomorrow. Settling herself down once more, her body gradually warmed up and, against her expectations, she fell asleep.

Chapter Eight

The week before the Christmas of 1944 was a comparatively happy time at the hospital. There was a new mood of expectancy; everyone thought the war would be over soon, or at least the British did.

'Won't be long now,' said Tom, the guard on the gate to the POW section, as Theda showed her pass. 'Hitler's in for it now. Our lads will be in Berlin before the spring, you'll see.'

'I hope so,' she replied. 'I think we've all had enough of this war.'

Even the prisoners were different, she thought as she walked down the ramp and into the ward. There was a much lighter atmosphere altogether as some of the men made wooden toys for the children's ward and the singers among them, having formed a choir, were practising singing carols at the far end of the ward.

One lot of prisoners from another ward, who were fit enough to be allowed out to work the regulation three hours on surrounding farms, had brought back bunches of holly and tree ivy and shared it out so that all the huts had greenery decorating the windows. Some was sent over to the civilian side too. Nurses were forever dodging bunches of mistletoe hung by enterprising Italians.

'I'll be glad when they all go back to the camp,' commented Nurse Harris. 'They shouldn't have been on this ward anyway – it's surgical.'

Nurse Harris was becoming quite knowledgeable about hospital ways. At the moment she was busy laying yet another dressing trolley with freshly sterilised instruments from the stainless steel boiler and flashed a cheerful smile at Theda as she said it.

'You're in a good mood this morning,' commented Theda as she reached across the bench for the drum of dressings and swabs, freshly autoclaved overnight by the theatre porter. She smiled to herself. Nurse Harris spoke with such an air of knowing it all, considering the scant time she had been working in the hospital. The Italians were in the ward because the medical wards were overflowing with chest infections this winter. They were all convalescent and considered non-infectious.

'My boyfriend has seven days' leave over Christmas,' explained Nurse Harris. 'I had a letter this morning. Sister says I can have Christmas Eve and a half day on Boxing Day.'

'Oh, that's grand,' Theda said warmly, and was genuinely pleased for her colleague despite a stab of envy and aching regret that it wasn't Alan coming home. In case the other nurse had noticed anything, she turned away as she removed her cuffs and rolled up her sleeves before she scrubbed up.

Nurse Harris's sweetheart was a Durham Light Infantryman but since the Italian campaign when he had caught a lump of shrapnel in his shoulder he had been reduced from A1 fitness category to C3. Consequently he was confined to home duties though stationed far from his home somewhere in the south. Theda knew him slightly; he had worked at Shildon Railway Shops, the same place as Alan before the war.

'How are you today, Johann?'

The young boy stared up at her and refrained from answering. One of those, she thought. Brought up in the Hitler Youth no doubt. She hadn't been on the prisoner side very long but had soon learned to recognise them. The best thing to do was ignore their attitude; most of them softened after a while.

'Your temperature is nice and steady now,' she remarked as she returned from washing her hands and begun to clean the wound in his shoulder which Nurse Harris had already uncovered. The dressing she removed was almost clean, Theda saw, the wound nearly healed. There would be a nasty scar but at least he would be able to use his arm as normal. He lay passively, accepting her ministrations, but keeping his head turned away.

'It won't be long before you can leave us and go up to the camp among your friends,' Theda said. 'Now you have the plasters off your leg and arm.'

She knew he could understand English but he didn't answer her.

'Waste of time talking to him, Staff.'

They finished the dressing and made him comfortable in bed, cradling him in their arms and lifting him up against the pillows. He was a tall boy but thin, only just beginning to put on a little weight as his appetite returned. He would have been easy to lift were it not for the fact that he tensed as they held him, his face turned away in disdain.

'You will soon be going up to the main camp up the dale,' Theda persevered. 'This afternoon we will get you out of bed, we must have you walking again.' She smiled at him. He was so like her own brother Frank had been, patriotic as only the young can be. He was just a boy after all.

'I will get away,' he said, surprising them both as they were in the middle of removing the screens from around the bed. It was the first time he had spoken to either of them.

'Don't be silly!' snapped Nurse Harris, her patience exhausted. 'Where do you think you will go?'

'I will get away,' he repeated. 'You will see, I will escape. It is my duty.'

His voice had risen and he raised himself from his pillows, his face flushed as he glared at them. 'It is the duty of us all, everyone who is prisoner. Some have forgotten—'

'Private!'

A sergeant had risen from his seat by the stove and was stamping down the ward as fast as his game leg would let him. He raised his walking stick as he reached the bottom of the bed and drew himself up.

'You will be civil to the nurses, Private, you hear me?'

Johann's flush deepened. He subsided on to his pillows, muttering something Theda took to be a yes. Obedience to authority was too well ingrained in him for it to be anything else.

'What is happening?'

She turned and saw that Major Koestler had come into the ward and was standing just behind her. He looked very inch the arrogant Prussian officer, she saw, completely different somehow.

'It is nothing, Doctor—' she began, but the sergeant was speaking in rapid German and Major Koestler was asking questions and completely ignoring the nurses.

'Come on, Harris,' she said. 'We have plenty to do without joining in their squabbles.' They moved on to the next man to be dressed and pulled the screens around the bed.

'Let them sort out their own,' said Nurse Harris. 'What do we care what a silly kid thinks? Mind, you'd expect him to be grateful at least for what we've done for him. I bet one of our lads wouldn't have got the same treatment in Germany.'

Theda didn't answer. The man in the bed was looking from one to the other of them, straining to understand what they were saying. He caught the gist of it for he nodded his head vigorously.

'Oh, yes, good treatment in Germany,' he said.

Theda smiled at him. 'I'm sure there is, Hans.'

'Well, come on then, let's have a look at your leg. We haven't got all day, even if you have.'

The corner of the ward where Johann lay was quiet now, the boy seemingly asleep and the sergeant back by the stove where he was whittling a small horse from a piece of wood. Theda watched his hands, swift and sure as they formed the head, the mane flying back as though in motion, the legs at the gallop. All the time he chatted easily to a friend or whistled under his breath, turning the wood in his hands, bringing it alive. He felt her gaze upon him and looked up.

'I clean up after,' he said, indicating the chips of wood on the red-tiled surround of the stove. He was a man in his forties – 'Poppi' the other prisoners called him – old enough to be the father of most of them, though not so old as some of the recent prisoners. Regular army, she supposed.

'That's all right,' she replied. 'Just so long as Matron doesn't see the mess.'

'She will not.'

She returned his conspiratorial smile. It was hard to keep her distance from men like the sergeant, enemies though they were. Every day there was a further chipping away of the reserve between them.

The sergeant could have been her father, carving a wooden dolly for her when she was younger out of the discarded end of a pit prop, sitting by the fire and letting the bits drop on to the tin hearth plate, being told off for the mess when her mother saw it. Mam would bustle about with a brush and small shovel, sweeping up the chips and throwing them on the fire so that they flared up with blue and orange flames, just as these did when the sergeant threw them in the stove.

The dressing round ended and Joan Harris went for her break. There was no sign of Major Koestler who must have left the ward. Theda couldn't get used to calling him 'Doctor' as he had asked, for he was a surgeon. If he had been English she would have called him 'Mr Koestler'. In any case, he was still in the army and he *was* a major.

Theda went to help Nurse Cullen who was going round the bedfast patients treating their pressure points with methylated spirits and dusting powder to keep away bedsores. The red-haired young nurse was flushed and angry, her eyes beginning to look suspiciously damp as a group of Italians clustered around the stove at the top of the ward, began calling to her, goading each other on.

'You can rub my back, Nurse, I get into bed now, eh?' one said, and made as though to get undressed. 'What's the matter, Nursie? You like to wait till tonight? *Romantica*, yes?'

His companions were laughing, whispering suggestions to him. He was a dark-eyed man in his twenties, thick moustache curling as luxuriant as his hair. He held out his arms in mock entreaty. *'Bella! Bella!'* he cried, turning up his eyes to the ceiling and smacking his lips.

Theda scowled heavily at him. 'Stop that this minute!' she snapped. 'You will show Nurse Cullen some respect or I will put you on report.'

The Italian pulled a face and turned away, muttering to his companions. She caught some of what he was saying, sure that it was derogatory and about her but ignoring him.

'Now then, Nurse, I'll give you a hand to finish. There's plenty to do yet before dinnertime.' Theda spoke briskly as she seized hold of the trolley and moved it on down the ward, giving Nurse Cullen a chance to recover herself.

'Something will have to be done about those Italians,' she said later as she sat in Sister's office having a cup of coffee with her while Sister went over the bed list. They act as though they are in a . . . a . . .' She paused, searching for the expression she wanted.

'A brothel, Staff?' Sister Smith grinned at her. 'I suppose their own hospitals are staffed by nuns,' she said. *'That* must cramp their style! In any case, they're going back to the main camp tomorrow, Major Collins tells me.'

They must be expecting a new influx of wounded prisoners, thought Theda, but even though she and Sister were alone in the office she did not say it aloud. One never knew who was listening, as the poster on the wall, *Careless talk costs lives*, implied. Someone on the ward could be a spy, could be giving the enemy warning of a big attack, someone could have a wireless set hidden in a crutch . . . Theda smiled to herself. She was letting her imagination run away with her.

The thought reminded her of her brother Chuck, a frustrated soldier if ever there was one. He had drilled with the Home Guard every Sunday morning since he was old enough. He scanned the *Northern Echo* every day for news of battle, exulting when the allies were victorious, discussing developments with his marras from the pit and anyone else who would listen. When the Americans were halted in their advance he considered it a national character defect. If it happened to the British, it was the fault of the generals of course.

Dear Chuck, she thought, he worshipped Joss, listened eagerly to everything he said about the war, would have changed places with him like a shot. As Joss would change places with him, no doubt, she thought with a wry smile. Or maybe he wouldn't. Now he was out of the pit he probably wouldn't want to go back.

'You're not day-dreaming, are you Staff? No, of course not. Just thinking about your work, weren't you?'

Sister Smith's voice cut into her wandering thoughts. Theda sat up and put down her coffee cup.

'Sorry, Sister. What were you saying?'

'You must be ready for your day off,' said the ward sister. 'Well, come on, I'll check the drugs with you and you can do the medicine round before Ken Collins gets here. I want to get off in good time today – looks like we'll be busy enough next week.'

Chapter Nine

Kenneth Collins was in his office running over the lists of wounded prisoners he had to fit into the available beds somehow. He stretched out his right leg under the desk. It always ached but this damp December weather intensified the pain, making it more and more difficult for him to control his limp or even keep his thoughts on his work.

Icy rain rattled the window of his office, and he sat back, sighing. It must be hell on earth out there on the German border, he thought. Why wasn't he there, doing what he could for the wounded? There would be plenty, he was well aware of that; the Germans wouldn't give up easily but would fight every inch of the Allied advance to Berlin. Which was pig-headed of them and most of them knew it, the officers in particular. It would be so much better for them if the Western allies got there first, rather than the Russians.

Ken sat back in his chair and gazed out of the window at the rain. He considered taking extra medication for the pain in his leg but decided against it; he couldn't afford to dull his reactions, he had a theatre list in the afternoon. He got painfully to his feet and went to the cupboard in the corner. A couple of Anadin he could take. Pouring himself a cup of lukewarm coffee from the almost-cold pot, he swallowed it with the aspirin, pulling a face at the taste of the bitter liquid.

At least it was Thursday tomorrow, his day off. Tonight he would go out to Winton village to visit Uncle Tucker. Tomorrow he would take some of his precious petrol ration and go over to Marsden, see the family, his mother and his gran.

Suiting action to deed, he picked up the telephone and got through to the operator.

'Shildon 29, please.'

After a short delay he heard Uncle Tucker's voice. He had rung directly to the mine office for, since the death of Aunt Betty the year before, there was unlikely to be anyone at the house. Tucker had picked up the phone, probably to stop its irritating ring, but was still talking to someone in the office.

'Number 9 seam on Busty, I want—'

Whatever he wanted was indecipherable to Ken as Tucker must have turned away from the mouthpiece. Ken waited, letting his thoughts drift idly again. He remembered the last time he had been out at Winton Colliery, a few weeks ago now. A dark, miserable November night, and he had given the staff nurse from Hut K a lift back in to the hospital. A pretty girl, if you liked dark eyes and hair. Very dark her eyes had been that night, in the gleam from his flashlight. And very big and frightened too. Who on earth did she think he was – the bogey man? The ghost of a tommy knocker? A dead entombed pitman?

'Hello? Manager's office. Cornish speaking.'

The voice of his uncle cut into his thoughts. Ken sat forward carelessly, jarring his leg against the side of the desk and wincing at the stab of agony that coursed through it.

'Uncle Tucker?' he forced himself to say.

'Ken? What is it? What's wrong?'

'Nothing . . . nothing's wrong. I just thought – I have the evening and tomorrow off, and wondered if I could invite myself to dinner? It's a while since I was out. If you haven't anything else on, that is?'

'Delighted, old lad, any time. Pot luck, of course, but I'm sure there's something in.'

'I can get some food points . . .'

'No, no need. Mrs Parkin will have something in. You know her, she'll rustle up something. It'll be grand to have a chin-wag, looking forward to it. See you about seven, then? Have to go now, Ken, things to do.'

Ken replaced the handset, his melancholy mood of the morning lifted. Uncle Tucker was right. It would be grand to have a good meal and a quiet talk in front of a roaring coal fire like the ones from his childhood instead of these infernal electric heaters or, worse, the smelly coke stoves in the huts.

He pulled the theatre list and pile of notes to him and opened the case notes of the first name on the list. There was the afternoon to get through first. The orthopaedic man was coming in from Darlington. There was a fractured tibia that had to be broken and reset for the man had lain for almost a week in the mud at the front. A man who must be fifty-years-old at least, though he swore he was only forty-five. Poor devil, he must have been in the last show. Defeat twice in a lifetime was too much for anyone.

Ken worked away steadily, reading the notes to remind himself of each patient on the list, then he went over the bed list which Matron had prepared for the whole of the section. When he had finished he rose and took it along the corridor to her office.

The sitting-room fire in the manager's house in Winton Colliery did indeed roar up the chimney as Ken had known it would. He sat in an armchair opposite his uncle and stretched his legs to the blaze, feeling relaxed and cosseted for a change. There had been fish for dinner, bought in fresh that morning from Shields and queued for by Mrs Parkin at Campbell's fish shop in the town. Bless the woman! And thank God fish wasn't rationed too.

'More whisky, Ken?'

Tucker Cornish held out the decanter and poured some into his nephew's glass and Ken added water from the jug on the occasional table by his side. Taking a sip, he smacked his lips in appreciation.

'How did you manage to get hold of it? Single malt, isn't it?'

'Glenmorangie. I bought it in 1939. This is the last bottle, I'm afraid. Still, with any luck the war will be over soon, and things will get back to normal.'

'I'm not so sure. Oh, not that the war will be over soon, at least the war with the Germans. I mean that things will get back to normal. I don't think we will be able to afford luxuries. The country has taken a battering. It's going to take an awful lot to get it back to normal. Wars don't come cheap either in men or money.'

Tucker stared into the fire, his face sombre. 'Now we have to win the peace. We can't let it happen again as it did after the last show; the miners and others thrown on the scrapheap. Something will have to be done, as the Prince of Wales said before the war. Not that he did anything, nor anyone else either. It took a war to do that.'

'I think Labour will get in. The soldiers coming home this time won't stand for what happened between the wars. There'll be a revolution else.'

The room grew quiet, both men staring into the fire as they contemplated what would happen after the fighting ended. Ken wondered if his uncle remembered the miners' strike of '26 and the long depression which had lasted for years after. He himself had been a small child at the time and living on a farm by the coast, but he could remember the unrest at Marsden Colliery. The poverty was all around him, the children stricken with rickets and other results of malnutrition.

He also remembered the murder of the mine agent in Winton and the trials of Tucker's natural father and half-brother. How Wesley Cornish, Tucker's father had been found guilty. Ken's mother was the daughter of Meg and Jonty Grizedale, her childhood sweetheart, Meg told him all about it when he moved to Bishop Auckland to work in the hospital. She feared he would hear it from local gossips. Jane was born after they moved away to Marsden. She had told him how Wesley had deserted her and her two boys, Jack and Tucker, and moved in with Sally Hawkins.

Now Tucker was the only Cornish left in Winton. Ken wondered why his uncle had not changed his name to Grizedale when his mother married Grandda Jonty, perhaps it would have been better.

'No, it can't happen again,' Tucker said, breaking into his thoughts. Ken watched his face in the firelight. Funny, he had not noticed before that he resembled Ken's own grandmother Meg. The same fair complexion, though Tucker's bore the blue-marked scars which were a legacy of working in the pits; the same steady, open gaze which was fixed on himself now.

'Well, lad, mebbe you should be away to your bed? You look properly done in.'

'Aye. But it's been good to talk, Uncle Tucker. Good to relax.'

Ken got to his feet and stretched his long body, yawning hugely. 'I'll say goodnight then.'

'Right, lad. Mrs Parkin will have put a bottle in the bed, you know which room by now.'

'Thanks. See you in the morning then.'

He left his uncle staring into the dying embers of the fire, a pensive expression on his face. It must be lonely for him now, Ken reflected, with Aunt Betty gone to her Maker and his cousins away in the army.

*

Ken drove up to Marsden next morning. It was still early for he had breakfasted with his uncle on a dried-egg omelette before he left for the mine office.

'Tell Mam I'll get up as soon as I can, mebbe this Sunday,' said Tucker. 'Depending if there's nothing in the pit needs my attention. I'm sorry I haven't got there sooner, but you know how it is.'

Indeed Ken did. His uncle had been working seven days most weeks since the war began, for with the men's week extended to six days the safety work had to be attended to on Sundays. And the equipment down below was getting desperately old and worn; make do and mend was the order of the day. The owners were reluctant to spend good money on new equipment when the nationalisation of the mines was a prospect looming large after the war.

'I'll tell her,' Ken promised.

Now, as he drove through Spennymoor and across to the Great North Road where he turned left for Durham City, he hummed softly to himself, looking forward to seeing his mother and grandmother again.

The opportunities for such visits had been few when he first came home from Italy, and no doubt they would be few and far between in the next few months, now that the allies were so close to Germany. He expected quite a list of POW casualties to filter through to Bishop Auckland. Then there were the ones on the medical side coming down from the camp up the dale; chest infections were rife among the new prisoners, the winter and the poor diet they had had in the last years of the war exerting the usual consequences.

Ken eased his foot on the throttle. Now he was on a good road his speed had been creeping up. There was little other traffic about but he was approaching New Elvet on the outskirts of Durham and being so early in the morning there was still a covering of frost on the road. He had to watch out for pedestrians.

School children were walking to school in twos and threes, muffled up against the cold, pixie hoods knitted from scraps of wool on their heads and mufflers round their necks, crisscrossed over their chests and tied behind their backs. On the ridge behind the houses stood the cathedral, standing guard over the little city. Ken spared it a quick glance, his spirits lifting as they always did at the sight.

Coming out on the other side of Durham, he took the Sunderland road. He had to go along the coast road through the town, skirting round the ruins where the bombs had fallen earlier in the war, smiling spontaneously as he caught his first glimpse of the sea.

That was it, that was what he had missed since he left Marsden: the sight of the North Sea. All this time in Africa and Italy, when he had often been so close to the sea, had not made up for this. It was different somehow, the smell of the North Sea, even the wind freezing his bones as it swept down from the Arctic.

What a fool he was! he thought. The smell was a mixture of fish and salt and sea coal, mingled with the down-blown smoke from the stacks in the pit yards of the coastal collieries. He grinned at his own sentimentality.

He was still smiling as he drove into the farmyard along the lane from the mining village and stopped the engine. As he climbed out of the car his younger brother Walt appeared in the doorway of the stable, grinning widely as he saw who it was sweeping into the yard, scattering the hens and making the drake honk and spread his wings in defence of his geese.

'You're back then,' was all the greeting Walt gave, in spite of his grin. 'Look at you now. Causing havoc already, you are.'

The pet porker that had been rooting about in the yard had panicked and fled, squealing, knocking the clothes prop from the line of washing which had been fluttering high above the yard and was now dangerously close to the muddy ground. Ken bent to pick up the prop and put it back in place before answering his brother's greeting.

'Ken! Why didn't you tell us you were coming? By, lad, it's grand to see you, it is that.'

'Hello, Grandma,' he said, bending again to kiss the white-haired old lady who had rushed out of the kitchen door. 'I thought I would surprise you all. Of course, if you don't want to see me, I can soon go.'

'Don't be daft, lad. Howay in and see your mam. Walt, tell your uncle we're having our elevenses early now Ken's here.'

Ken glanced back at his brother before following Meg, his grandmother, into the big old-fashioned kitchen. Walt's welcome had been genuine and warm enough; he never was one to show a lot of emotion. He was a born farmer, like most of the family on both sides. Their father had been killed in 1933 when his tractor rolled down a bank on top of him and their mother had sold up the small inland farm they had owned and brought her boys back to the farm, which her father, Jonty Grizedale, had bought when he first brought Meg and her two boys away from Winton Colliery.

In spite of his love of farming, Walt had been envious of his elder brother's scholarship to the Medical School of Durham University in Newcastle. And then, tied as he himself was to the farm when war broke out, he was envious of Ken's going into the army. Of course he might have enlisted himself, but couldn't leave his uncle the only man on the farm apart from Ben, a fifteen-year-old boy who intended to join the navy as soon as he was old enough.

So Ken had felt the need to tread softly in his dealings with Walt. The question was, had his brother matured enough by now to forget his envious feeling? Perhaps.

The kitchen was exactly the same as he remembered it. Still the same red-tiled range with shining steel hinges on the oven door, the terracotta tiles on the floor which Grandma had had laid just before the war. Only a new proddy mat before the fire – bright red in the middle and grey round the edges with what looked like strips from his and Walt's old school trousers – was different. The table was still scrubbed white and the old rocking chair still stood by the fire, the one Grandda Jonty had rocked slowly back and forward in when Ken was small.

'Fetch me my slippers, lad.' Ken could almost hear Grandda's voice from the past. And he and Walt would squabble over the slippers, in the end taking one each for the pleasure of being lifted up, one on each knee, and being allowed to bring out the old man's watch from his waistcoat pocket and hear it chime the time when Grandda pushed the button.

Today, though, it was his mother in the rocking chair, sitting forward and looking eagerly towards the door as he entered but evidently not strong enough to get to her feet. Ken was shocked to his core as he saw her. Even though she had been fine-boned and ethereal-looking ever since he could remember, she had never looked so frail as she did today.

'Mam, how are you?' he asked as he strode over to the chair and bent to kiss her. His professionalism stood him in great stead, his voice was steady even though he could not quite prevent his feelings from showing in his eyes.

'It's nothing, son, just a touch of the flu,' she assured him. 'You know what I'm like, soon knocked down.'

'Have you had Doctor Brown out? Mam, you know you have to be careful. Why didn't you let me know you were ill?'

'Don't fuss now, Ken. I told you, it's just a touch of the flu. Doctor Brown agrees with me, he's given me a bottle. I knew you were busy anyroad, else I would have written. I was going to today at least.'

'Touch of the flu!' Meg said sharply. 'By, our Jane, you know full well the doctor said you'd had congestion of the lungs. Who do you think you're fooling, like? Have you forgotten the lad's a doctor? Nay, man, he's a surgeon now, aren't you, Ken?'

Ken didn't reply. He picked up his mother's wrist and felt her pulse – not all that fast or erratic, he noted. And her skin was fairly cool. She must have got over the worst of it.

'I was telling her, Ken,' Meg went on, 'she should keep that Thermogene vest I made her on till the weather gets better at least. But she minds me not at all, thinks she knows better. Now tell her, lad, she'll have to look after herself – she's as weak as a kitten.'

'Why don't you get the kettle on, Grandma?' he asked mildly. 'I'm ready for a cuppa after that drive, and won't the men be in for theirs in a minute?'

Reminded of the job in hand, Meg picked up the heavy iron kettle and went into the scullery to fill it.

Jane smiled. 'If I was half as strong as your gran, I'd be doing fine,' she said, forgetting she had just been saying there was not much wrong with her. 'As it is, I feel just about ready for the knacker's yard.'

'Mam, don't you talk like that,' he replied, his face stern. 'You just feel weak from the flu. You'll be all right in a couple of weeks if you eat properly and keep warm.'

'I know. Sorry, Ken. I'm lucky really, living on a farm. At least we have more to eat than some poor beggars. But, by, it's good to see you! As good as a bottle of Parrish's Food. Does your leg still bother you, pet? I think about you working in that hospital, all hours an' all. I'm sure you could have been invalided out of the army long before now. Doctor Brown could do with an assistant, you know. Don't you think—'

'Mam, I'm a surgeon, not a general practitioner. I want to work in a hospital.'

Ken looked at his mother and smiled. This was practically a straight continuation of the conversation he had had with his mother the last time he had been here.

Walt and Uncle Jack came in, removing their boots at the door and walking into the kitchen in their thick woollen socks. Meg had fresh singing hinny scones and farm butter ready, a great luxury to Ken.

'Grand it is,' he said, licking his fingers after picking up the last crumb from his plate. 'The scones too.'

'I never could get away with margarine,' said Meg. 'I would just as soon do without anything on my bread. Luckily we usually have enough to do the house after sending in the quota. I can let you have half a pound, Ken, and some for Tucker an' all.' She gave him an anxious glance. 'How's he getting on? We don't see much of him, not since Betty died. He's not doing too much, is he? He forgets he's getting on now, time he let the younger men do their share.'

'He told me to tell you he would try to come on Sunday, Grandma. But he's fine. I spent the night there, Mrs Jenkins looks after him well.'

'Not like a wife, though,' she commented.

'I should hope not an' all,' said Uncle Jack, and laughed.

'Aye, well, you can laugh but I worry about the lad.'

The idea of Tucker with his grey hairs being classed as a lad made Ken smile. Grandma never changed. She was even known to call Walt 'the bairn' at times, big as he was.

'I'll be getting on with the fencing,' he said, pushing

back his chair. 'The sheep will be in the winter wheat if I don't fix the fence in the far field.' He hesitated before looking at Ken. 'I don't suppose—'

'I'll give you a hand,' Ken offered quickly, pleased at this overture from his younger brother. He found spare overalls in the scullery and an ancient pair of Wellington boots. Walt stood patiently as he pulled them on then strode away up the path to the gate to the pasture and on up Sugar Hill, to the expanse of ploughed land. At the top he turned and waited for Ken who was finding the going hard with thick clarts sticking to his boots.

'Eeh, sorry, I forgot about your leg,' he said when Ken finally caught up with him, breathing heavily.

'That's all right.'

They stood there, looking round. There was a good view on all sides, the land sweeping down to the sea to the east, the smoke stacks and winding wheels of the colliery right on the edge, seeming from here almost to be rising from the sea itself. Beyond, a couple of collier boats were steaming south. A trawler was coming in, making for Shields with gulls wheeling above it, their harsh cries carrying on the cold wind.

The hedge to the north, where the ploughed land stopped and a small windbreaker wood began, its trees bent all at the same angle by the prevailing wind, was neat and dense, well cared for.

'You the hedger, Walt?' asked Ken and nodded approvingly when his brother admitted it.

Ken turned towards the fence that bounded the farm. It looked in good condition to him and he said so.

'Aye? Well, wait till we get a bit closer,' Walt grinned. And, indeed, close up there were a few weak places which sheep would soon break through if they got the chance.

The brothers worked companionably for the next couple of hours, saying little apart from commenting on the job in hand. But that feeling of resentment which Ken had once felt coming from his brother was absent; they were back again to how they had been as young boys, sharing the work, though Ken sometimes had to look to Walt for what to do next.

It had been a grand day, he thought as he drove back to Bishop Auckland. The manual work had tired him but relaxed him too. And it had been good to be with the family again. Perhaps he would get a position at Sunderland Infirmary after the war, then he would be close enough to drop in more often. After the war, he thought, and sighed. For the duration at least he would be staying in Auckland. Well, it wasn't too bad. Funny that his grandmother and grandfather had set out from there all those years ago and now he was directed back. As his uncle had been drawn back, he thought.

Perhaps he would call at the manager's house on his way back. Uncle Tucker should be home. He had the butter to deliver in any case. As he drove along the road at the top of the rows of colliery houses, towards the lane that led to the manager's house, he found himself looking out for Staff Nurse Wearmouth. If she was there, perhaps he could give her a lift back to the hospital again.

There was a girl just turning into West Row. Ken

slowed for a moment and she turned her face towards him. But no, this was a younger girl, very like the staff nurse but white-faced and with a scarf tied carelessly round her head, dressed in slacks with a mackintosh over the top. Ken dropped a gear and accelerated on up the lane.

'Do you know the Wearmouth family, Uncle Tucker?' he asked after they had eaten their poached eggs on toast and apple dumpling and custard.

Tucker looked up in surprise. 'Why, of course I do, lad,' he said. 'Been here as long as I have. Good solid workers all of them. I was sorry when two of the lads went in the army, I could have done with them now. The youngest was killed at Dunkirk, I heard,' he paused for a moment and lit his pipe before sitting back in his chair. 'Why do you ask?'

Ken shrugged. 'Oh, nothing but idle curiosity, I suppose. The daughter is a staff nurse at the hospital. I gave her a lift back not long ago.'

'That would be Theda,' nodded Tucker. 'The youngest, Clara, works in the munitions factory over at Aycliffe.'

He said no more, but looked curiously at his nephew. Could it be that Ken was at last interested in a girl?

Chapter Ten

'I think they could at least let you have Christmas day off,' grumbled Bea as she watched Theda chop up dried prunes to make pretend currants for the Christmas cake.

'Mam,' she said patiently, 'if we all had the day off, who would look after the sick?'

'Let them look after themselves,' said Chuck from where he lay sprawled on the horsehair sofa in the corner of the kitchen. He was reading the *Daily Herald* but as usual never missed a chance to show his resentment of the German prisoners his sister was nursing.

It was half-past four in the afternoon and Chuck was on fore shift. He had come in from the pit a couple of hours before and was bathed and fed and lying in his stockinged feet and braces until it was time for his date with Norma Musgrave. They were going to the pictures in Eldon Lane; the Working Men's Club there had a picture house built over the club house. The entrance was only fourpence, so much cheaper than going into Bishop Auckland, and they were saving all they could for the future. Mostly Norma's idea, Theda suspected. Chuck had always been free with his money until he began going out with her. Norma was careful with money to put it mildly.

'Chuck, get up off that couch and go and pull me some Brussels sprouts,' his mother said sharply. 'Your da will be coming in before we know it and the dinner not ready.'

He pulled a face but went to do as he was bid.

'They could let some of you have Christmas Day off, anyroad,' Bea continued the conversation as she sifted dried egg and dried milk into the flour for the cake and added cinnamon and a pinch of bicarbonate of soda. Theda finished cutting up the prunes and began grating carrots before she replied.

'It's fairer if no one gets it off,' she explained, as she was sure she had explained every other Christmas since she had entered nursing. She raised her hand and brushed a lock of dark hair away from her forehead with the back of her arm.

'Hmm,' her mother snorted. She began beating margarine and white sugar together, for brown had been unobtainable in the Co-op where her ration books were lodged. Her strong arms were soon bringing the mixture to a light fluffy texture so she could add the other ingredients.

'I've got Boxing Day afternoon,' offered Theda, as a sort of consolation prize.

'Well, I'll just have to save some of the goodies for you, won't I?'

Though the blackout restrictions had been eased to a 'dim-out' recently, the kitchen curtains with their black lining had been drawn as soon as it became necessary to put a match to the gas mantle over the table. So they didn't see anyone coming up the yard until there was a knock at the door and Violet Mitchell came in, her arm around and supporting Clara. A white and trembling Clara, fighting to hold back the tears glistening in her eyes. Both Theda and her mother dropped what they were doing and started towards her.

'Whatever—' Bea began, but was interrupted by Violet.

'It's all right, Mrs Wearmouth,' she said. 'Clara wasn't feeling very well, that's all, so instead of working overtime I thought I'd bring her home.' She practically carried Clara into the kitchen and set her down on the sofa where she lay against the raised end and closed her eyes.

Theda went to her at once, feeling her rapid pulse, the clammy coldness of her skin. 'What happened?' she asked as Bea hovered, looking anxious.

'She was sick, that's all,' explained Violet. 'Then she fainted. I blame the powder. I'm telling you, the smell of that stuff is blooming awful. It's enough to make anyone throw up.'

It passed through Theda's mind that Clara had worked among the yellow gun powder for a year or two now but it had not made her sick before. Looking at her sister, she had her own suspicions and they were pretty dismaying.

Clara suddenly sat up and lifted her head. 'I'm fine now, really I am. Don't fuss. I couldn't fancy the dinner in the canteen, that's what it was. And then afterwards I was hungry.'

'I'll put the kettle on, pet,' said Bea. 'You can have a bite of something. You an' all, Violet. It was good of you to come home with her.' She shook her head at her youngest daughter. 'I don't know, you're nowt but a worry to me, you're not. You never do eat enough. You should be thankful for what you can get to eat these days, never mind not fancying anything.' She was working herself up, venting her alarm in sharp words now she felt there was nothing seriously wrong with Clara.

Theda intercepted a meaningful glance between the two younger girls. There was something going on here, she could see, and it probably meant trouble. But surely Clara hadn't – no, she was much too sensible a girl. But so many sensible girls had got caught in this war, what with soldiers only home for a day or two at a time before going back to France.

'Thanks, Mrs Wearmouth,' said Violet, backing towards the door. 'I think I'll be getting on home now, but thanks anyway for the offer.'

After she had gone, her quick footsteps echoing on the bricks of the yard, Clara sat up and unwound the pink scarf from her neck. Theda looked at it. The pink was discoloured in patches by an ugly sulphur-like yellow. Maybe that was the cause of Clara's sudden illness. But a glance at her sister's face, the tears glistening unshed and the dark shadows under her eyes, made her think otherwise.

Bea was spooning the cake mixture into a tin lined with the paper the margarine had come in. She was working quickly now so as to get the cake out of the way, prepare a snack for Clara and begin the dinner for the menfolk. As she stooped behind the heavy iron door of the oven, Theda's questioning eyes met her sister's.

Clara lifted her chin and looked back defiantly. 'I'm all right, our Theda,' she snapped.

Bea closed the oven door carefully and pulled the coals in the range back from the oven flue to lower the temperature. 'Course you are, pet. I'll make you a sandwich now, and you'll be as right as rain.'

Theda said nothing but at the first opportunity went upstairs and peeped into the top drawer of the chest in the room she shared with Clara. There was a full pile of clean rags which were used for sanitary purposes every month; she herself was not due for another five days but was well aware that Clara's courses usually preceded her own. And though she hadn't thought anything of it at the time, she remembered that the pile was undisturbed last month too when she went for them.

Sitting down on the bed, she drew a deep breath. It had to be that Canadian pilot or navigator or something, the one from Middleton St George airfield. Dear God, the stupid, stupid girl! After a moment she got to her feet and went downstairs. Bea was peeling potatoes on the table and looked reproachfully at her as she went into the kitchen.

'I know it's your day off, but I'm going to be well pushed to get the meal ready for six,' she said.

'Sorry, Mam. I'll do those, shall I?'

Theda took the knife from her mother who went out to the pantry for the soused herring she had cooked earlier in the day to go with the potatoes.

'Don't say anything, please.'

Theda had been avoiding Clara's eyes but the hoarse whisper made her turn and gaze at her.

'She'll have to be told. Goodness knows why she hasn't put two and two together already.'

'I know, but don't tell—'

'What are you two whispering about?'

Bea had come back into the room with the baking tin containing the soused herring and put it on top of the oven to warm. But she was speaking casually, Theda saw, as she didn't really think anything of it.

'Nothing, Mam, nothing really,' she said, and Clara cast her a grateful glance.

There was no opportunity for Theda to talk to Clara on their own until after the meal and even then it was just a few whispered words. Matt came in and they ate the soused herrings and potatoes practically in silence. Their father was white and tired under his layer of coal dust. He ate automatically, pushing the food into his mouth and chewing and swallowing, one forkful and then another. He had washed his hands before eating but the rest of him was still black. Theda found herself watching the red mark of a new scar on the back of one hand, contrasting starkly with the white skin, and as he raised his fork to his mouth, the black of his face.

'You should have had a dressing on that, Da,' she said, and he lifted his gaze briefly from his meal and looked at her, the white of his eyes gleaming like those of the singer Hutch whom she had seen once in a short filler film at the pictures.

'A touch of coal dust in the blood doesn't hurt,' he replied, and went on with his meal.

Afterwards she brought in the galvanised tin bath and placed it in front of the fire and ladled in hot water from the boiler by the side of the black-leaded range. Chuck went out to meet Norma and her mother stayed in the kitchen to wash Matt's back so she and Clara were the only ones to retire to the front room while he had his bath. But the dividing wall was thin. There was no chance of having a real heart to heart.

'You're right, I've fallen wrong. I don't know what to do,' Clara whispered frantically, the moment they were on their own. She moved as far away from the kitchen as possible and turned back to her sister. 'Tell me what to do, Theda.'

'Are you sure? I mean, have you seen a doctor?'

'A doctor? How could I see a doctor? How could I go to Dr Oliver? Anyroad, they say the doctors can't tell until you're at least four months gone, so what's the point of going? I have to do something now!'

'Missing a period doesn't always mean you're expecting,' said Theda. She was casting about in her own mind for anything that might prove they were wrong, and it was a false alarm. The eloquent look she got from her sister made her dismiss that possibility.

'Oh, Clara, what were you thinking of?' she whispered sharply, taking refuge in anger and in that moment looking remarkably like her mother. She jumped visibly when the door to the kitchen opened and Bea came in. Clara whirled round and stared fixedly at the picture of

Grandma and Grandda Mason which hung on the wall. She rumbled in the sleeve of her cardigan for her handkerchief and blew her nose, blinking rapidly. But her mother wasn't watching her, she was rooting in the drawer of the chiffonier for a clean towel. Finding one, she stood at the open door for a moment before going out.

'I hope you two lasses aren't quarrelling,' she said. 'I thought you'd grown out of that sort of thing?'

'I think I'm getting a cold,' mumbled Clara.

Bea sighed. 'Aye, well, I'll make you a hot drink and you can go to bed. I've got some blackcurrant jam left; I'll put a spoonful in a cup of hot water. That's the best thing to mend a cold.'

When she went out the sisters fell silent. All that could be heard was the splashing of their father as he knelt by the bath and sluiced the top half of his body with clean water from the boiler, and the ticking of the wall clock which hung beside the photos of their grandparents.

It was cold in the room. It had been Matt's turn to give half his allotment of coal this month to Mrs Hutchinson up the road, whose husband and two sons were in the forces. Theda shivered and walked over to Clara. She put her arms around her and hugged her.

'I have to go now, pet,' she said. 'Look, try to put it out of your mind for the minute. It's always possible you're just late, anyway. I'll try to get back tomorrow but if not I'll see you at the weekend. Howay now, pull yourself together. A good night's sleep will help. Drink Mam's blackcurrant and take the oven shelf to bed.'

Clara was shivering. Theda realised with a shock how

thin she was, she could feel the bones of her back through her cardigan.

'All clear,' called their mother. 'Howay in beside the fire, it's too cold to stay long in there.'

'Leave it for now,' Theda whispered to Clara. 'There's still a chance your period is just late. You've let yourself get right down on the bottom. Look how thin you are! Anyway, try not to worry too much. I'm sure the lad won't let you down.'

Though even as she said it she wondered: What did any of them know about these young lads from the other side of the world? If it *was* him. She was shocked at her own thought. How could she think her sister was promiscuous?

Theda put her arm around Clara. 'Bear up now,' she whispered. 'You don't want to worry Mam if it's only a false alarm.'

'No.' Clara shook her head.

'I'll have to be getting back, you know what Home Sister is like,' she said to Bea as the two girls went back into the kitchen. The room was filled with a rich aroma from the cake baking in the oven despite its make-shift ingredients.

'Aye, standing there with a stop watch in her hand,' said Bea. 'She forgets about the state of the buses these days.'

Theda laughed at the picture of Sister Brown standing at the door of the nurses' home with a stop watch in her hand. Her mother was inclined to exaggeration if it enhanced her point.

'Mam, she doesn't,' Theda protested.

'Aye, well, she might as well do,' her mother replied, unabashed.

As it happened, when Theda got to the bus stop there was a queue of twenty-odd people waiting, surprising at this time of night. They were standing quietly, huddled into their coats and blowing on their hands as they looked along the road for the sight of the blue-dimmed headlights – not grumbling though. After five years of war most people had learned there was little point in complaining. When at last the bus hove into view, the whole queue shuffled forward.

'Workers only,' called the conductor, a middle-aged chap with a limp and a strained, tired expression.

Theda gazed anxiously at the inside of the bus. It was packed with people, the seats all full and the aisle crammed with standing passengers. Some of the queue fell back and allowed the workers to go to the front, Theda amongst them. But one old man had reached the end of his tether.

'What the hell?' he whined. 'I have to get home tonight. What do you want me to do, camp out in this cold? What happened to the last bus anyroad?'

'Sorry, Dad,' said the conductor. 'It broke down and we had to bring this one out from the garage. So this *is* the last bus really. And there won't be another the night.'

Theda moved past the old man, feeling really guilty. She managed to climb aboard the bus, just, and had to push herself tight against the front window as the door was closed. After that, she stood on the steps, holding on to the rail as the vehicle lurched around the corner, springs squealing a protest as the weight of the passengers bore down on the axles.

She stared fixedly at the notice pasted on the window. Though the light in the bus was very dim and she could not read what it said, she knew it by heart: *Is your journey really necessary?* Well, she had to get back to the hospital all right but she could have stayed there in the first place. After all, she had seen her family once this week. That old man was probably on his way back from visiting his family, his daughter maybe. Oh, well, he would have to stay there tonight.

'What the—' There was a chorus of exclamations as the bus gave an extra sickening lurch and stayed leaning to one corner. If the passengers had not been packed so tightly they would have been thrown to the floor. As it was, they held each other up. Theda herself was thrown against the pole that held the handrail, catching her ribs a painful blow and taking the breath out of her. For a minute or two the world whirled around her.

'Get out a minute, lass, let me past,' the conductor was saying to her as she came to herself. He leaned over her and opened the door. Painfully she climbed down the steps. She must have banged her knee at the same time though she hadn't felt it. She stood outside on the pavement and felt for the spot, flinching as she found it. There'll be a right bruise tomorrow, she thought dumbly. Just when she was working the whole day too.

The driver and conductor were looking at the bus and she looked too. No wonder it was down. One wheel was missing. It must have come off as they turned the last corner.

'There it is, Jack, t'other side of t'road,' the conductor pointed out. 'Now what?' He sounded like a man past being surprised by anything that might happen.

'Best get everyone off, lad,' said the driver. 'We'll be going nowhere tonight.'

'Aye.'

Sighing, the conductor went to the door of the bus. 'All off now, please. Come on, hurry along. It's shank's pony from now on. All off, I said.'

They were about a mile from the town, Theda reckoned, maybe a mile and a quarter from the hospital. Ah, well. Taking out her flashlight, she set off. She couldn't afford to waste time hanging about, she would be late as it was. A long string of people followed her and there was some muttering and grumbling now. But then someone began to whistle 'There's a Long, Long Road a-Winding' and others took up the tune and set off in the face of the bitter wind which had sprung up, almost on cue.

'Bloody hell,' one man was saying to himself as he strode past her. 'I'm sick to blooming death of this flaming war.' As are we all, agreed Theda mentally.

By the time she reached the hospital she was about dead on her feet. She had taken the shortcut by the railway to get there, a mucky dark place at the best of times but thick with clarts in the winter. And of course she had almost fallen, slipping and jarring her injured leg as she put out a hand to stop herself and splashing mud up her arm and her stockings.

To cap it all, it began to rain, great sleety drops which stung her face and drenched her hair through her navy blue outdoor cap. What an afternoon off! Surely nothing else could happen? With the aid of her flashlight she picked out the gate to the hospital and thankfully walked through it, her whole leg throbbing by this time.

'Ah, Staff Nurse. Good evening.'

She rubbed her hand across her eyes and blinked to clear the rain from her lashes. Major Koestler was standing there with Ken Collins, both of them looking curiously at her.

'Staff Nurse Wearmouth,' came the voice of Sister Brown from somewhere on her right. 'Where have you been? You're late!'

Chapter Eleven

It was just as well that nurses wore black stockings, thought Theda as she painted gentian violet antiseptic on to the grazes on her leg. She was fresh out of a hot bath. Thank God for the bathrooms in the home, at least she wasn't confined to the old tin bath which they all had to use in West Row. Straightening up, she winced and put a hand to her ribs. There would be a bruise there tomorrow, she surmised.

Sighing, she sat down in front of the dressing table and towelled her hair dry as much as she was able. She was dead tired, would just have to go to bed with it damp. Laying a fresh dry towel on her pillow, she switched off the light and climbed into bed, snuggling up under the bedclothes.

The room was black dark, not a chink of light from the moon which, perversely, had come out after the rain. Slipping out of bed, Theda drew back the curtains at the high window before running back. There was a full moon and its light beamed in over her bed, strangely comforting.

Drowsily she watched the white disc with its ring of frost, feeling her body relax in the comfort.

How embarrassing it had been when she went through the door to find Ken Collins standing there with Major Koestler. She squirmed at the memory. And then to be dressed down by Sister Brown in front of them! What was the German doctor doing there, anyway? He was supposed to be locked up in the prisoner's area, wasn't he? After all he was a prisoner-of-war. She remembered the way he had looked down his nose at her, unsmiling, his pale eyes expressionless.

'Are you all right, Staff Nurse? Has something happened?'

It had been Ken who stepped forward, holding his hand out to her.

'You're late,' Sister Brown had repeated. 'For what reason, may I ask?'

'I . . . The bus broke down, I had to walk the last mile, I fell . . .' Theda found herself stammering like a first-year probationer. Pulling herself together, she turned to Ken. 'I'm all right, thank you. I just grazed my leg and got a bit of a shock.'

'Best go straight to bed. Don't forget you are on duty at half-past seven in the morning,' said Sister.

'I'd better look at your leg,' Ken began, but Theda was backing away.

'No, thank you, it's nothing. I can see to it myself.'

She fled. As she turned the bend in the staircase she saw the German say something and the three of them laughed and looked up at her. Now don't get paranoid, she told herself, they could be laughing at anything.

She lay on her side and looked up at the moon, deliberately trying to think of something else. Anything, a song. The first lines of 'In the Mood' ran through her head, and maddeningly ran through again and again. Poor Glenn Miller, missing over the channel, most likely dead. So near the end of the war too and he not even a combatant. 'String of Pearls' had replaced 'In Tthe Mood' now, its melody haunting. It had been Glenn's biggest hit, Clara was always singing snatches of it. Clara . . . Don't think about her, not tonight. Theda put sad thoughts out of her mind by concentrating on how cosy it was under the blankets and after a few moments her eyes closed and she fell deeply asleep.

She woke with a start. She had been dreaming about Clara when they were both small girls and out on the Sunday School trip to Seaton Carew. They were paddling in the sea. Theda had her dress tucked into her knickers and was bossily telling her little sister to do the same but Clara wouldn't and a wave came in and wet her up to her waist.

'Eeh! Mam will play war. Do something, Theda,' Clara had cried, and she had backed off up the beach and fallen down at the edge of the water, wetting herself even more. Theda put out a hand to pull her to her feet and just then there was a tremendous roaring and a motor boat came bearing down on them both and Clara screamed and Theda couldn't manage to drag her out of the way in time. All the time the boat drew closer she was filled with a blind panic . . . and then the dream ended abruptly.

Theda sat up in bed, shaking. The room was black dark again, the moon had gone behind the clouds and rain spattered on the window. There was a droning outside – an engine. Surely not a bomber now, not at the tail end of the war? No, of course not, it was a bomber all right but a British one. It was in trouble. The sound drew nearer and nearer, almost overhead. Good Lord, it *was* overhead and the engine was cutting out, spluttering and stopping, and then there was the sound of a crash . . .

A crash! Theda jumped out of bed and ran to the window. There was nothing to see, nothing at all. No, wait, there was a glow over by the football field. Hurriedly she pulled on her clothes. Surely someone was hurt, and extra staff would be needed. She paused as she was lacing up her shoes. There was the sound of the ambulance revving up and going out of the gates.

She was the first of the off-duty staff to get to Outpatients and Admissions but as she opened the door Major Collins caught up with her. Sister Brown, who was doubling as Night Sister, was talking into the telephone.

'Three, you say? Oh, well, that's not too bad. Oh, here's Major Collins now.' She handed over the phone to him.

'Am I needed, Sister?' Theda stepped forward.

Sister Brown turned to her. 'Yes, Staff Nurse. A Canadian plane has come down by Bracks Wood, on the grammar school field, thank goodness. Three hurt, we think. You can go up to Block Two and see that beds are prepared and everything ready. It's Nurse Atkinson on there, she's on her own.'

'Yes, Sister.'

Theda went out of the back door of the block and crossed over to the next one. Both the blocks had formed part of the old workhouse hospital and the upstairs ward of Block Two was used for British officers. Nurse Atkinson was an Assistant Nurse of some years' experience and they soon had the beds ready and stone hot water bottles put in them for the Canadians.

'I don't suppose we'll have them for long,' commented Nurse Atkinson as she switched on the steriliser to boil up the surgical instruments, just in case. 'We haven't had any Canadians before, I suppose they go to Darlington Memorial. No doubt these will be transferred as soon as they can be. I wonder what the plane was doing so far off course?'

'Only eleven miles,' Theda replied. 'The way the engine sounded, I'm surprised it got back at all.'

'What's going on?'

A querulous voice came from the row of beds and Nurse Atkinson hurried towards it. There was nothing else to be done in the ward now until the patients arrived so Theda went back to Outpatients.

Only one airman was there, laid on a stretcher with Ken Collins bending over him. Theda caught her breath as she recognised the smell of scorched cloth and burnt flesh, a smell she had encountered two or three times before – once when a child had crossed a smouldering pit heap and his leg had gone through the crust, and once when fire damp set coal dust alight down a mine and two miners had been burnt.

In all her nursing years she had never got used to that

127

smell and hesitated now before crossing over to the
stretcher, for she had to steel herself against what she
might see.

'Hold this, Staff,' said Ken. 'Come on, come closer,
do.'

'Yes, sir.'

The answer was automatic as she sprang to do as he
asked, hold the collar of the man's flying jacket away as
the doctor moved his head so that he could more closely
examine the burns on the neck. Theda looked down at
the airman. His eyes were closed, the lashes and
eyebrows singed, but thankfully his facial burns seemed
to be first degree. It was his neck and chest which
appeared to be the worst. He must have had his flying
jacket open. And his hands . . . how on earth had he
managed to pilot the plane home with his hands in that
state? Parts of them were already black. He must have
used them to beat out the flames.

'Right, Staff, see that theatre is notified, will you? I will
have to clean him up there. We won't try to take off any
of his clothes – not until he's under anaesthetic anyway.'

Ken was business-like as he covered the man's neck
with gauze soaked in saline. The pilot moaned and
moved his head and the moan became a cry of pain and
his eyes flew open, causing a tiny drop of blood to appear
in the corner where his lashes had fused together. But he
didn't seem to notice. His eyes had locked on Theda's
and they were the bluest eyes she had ever seen. Then the
lids drooped and closed again and she looked at his dog
tags before turning away to telephone theatre. Eugene

Ridley, date of birth January 1921, followed by his service number. He was the same age as Alan had been.

Ken was in the smaller treatment room and as Theda passed she saw Sister Brown was in there too, pulling the blanket over the head of another airman. She came out shaking her head.

'He hadn't a chance, shot in the abdomen,' she said sadly. 'The other one is dead too, poor lad, he didn't look more than nineteen.' She nodded to the stretcher which was just being taken out of the door by a porter. 'He's for theatre?'

'Yes, Sister, I've just notified them.'

'He's a lucky man. If you can call it lucky. Well, Staff Nurse, you may as well go back to bed, we can manage fine now. Thank you for your help.'

Wearily Theda went back to her room and threw off her clothes. Suddenly she felt deathly cold and tired to her core, every muscle aching, especially her ribs. It was half-past three in the morning; another two and a half hours and she would be called to begin her day duty. She was too tired to think, sure she was too tired to sleep, but within a minute or two she did. And her dreams were confused and incomprehensible and dominated by a pair of astonishing blue eyes.

The next morning there was an air of suppressed excitement on the ward amongst the younger prisoners. Those who were ambulant huddled together in groups, clustering round one of the stoves, casting glances at the nurses as they went about their duties.

'No doubt they are talking about the plane that came down,' commented Nurse Harris. 'They'll think of it as a triumph.' She was polishing the table in the middle of the ward as Theda got out the medicine glasses from the drawer at the side. 'Have you heard how that pilot is? You were there when they brought him in, weren't you?'

'I was. But I haven't heard anything this morning.' Theda lined up the glasses on the medicine trolley and took it back to the end of the ward to begin the round. Johann was off his sulphur tablets now; he was much better, his shoulder almost healed. After Christmas he would be allowed up on crutches. Now he smiled at her as she measured out his dose of iron tonic. But it was a cold smile, full of hatred.

Theda sighed. 'Come on now, drink it up. You should have it as soon as possible after breakfast.'

He took the medicine and tossed it down his throat before handing the glass back to her without a word of thanks. Then he lay back on his pillows and began to whistle. Badly, almost tunelessly, but nevertheless she could recognise '*Deutschland, Deutschland Uber Allës*'. Ignoring it, she went on to the next bed.

'You will see, we will push the Americans into the sea and you British will be finished.' He had been unable to contain himself, as she turned back to him she could see that. But the ambulant patients were surrounding him, talking to him rapidly in his own language.

The incident soon passed over and nothing else was said by any of the other patients. It was not until Theda went to the dining-room for her break that she found out what he had been so excited about.

'The Germans have mounted an assault in the forest of Ardennes. Took the Yanks by surprise an' all, or so I gather,' Nurse Jenkins said gloomily. 'Mebbe the war's not going to be over so soon after all.'

Chapter Twelve

'Merry Christmas, Staff Nurse,' said Tom, the guard on the gate. 'Merry Christmas, Sister.'

'Christmas 1944,' Sister Smith commented to Theda as they walked down the ramp to Hut K. 'Do you think it will be the last of the war?'

Theda pushed her pass into the pocket of her uniform dress and considered the question. 'It all depends,' she said, 'whether the Germans do still have enough reserves to break out.' Bleakly she thought of Joss. He must be somewhere over there and still fighting, even if it was the Americans who were taking the brunt of this push.

'If it had been against the British they wouldn't have got so far,' Chuck declared the last time she had seen him. 'The Yanks thought it would be just like the pictures.'

'Howay, Chuck, they're just soldiers doing their best like all of them. They came over here and joined in, didn't they? They could have stayed at home, you know,' Matt had argued.

'Aye. An' I feel sorry for them, poor lads, all that way

from home. Their mothers must be going through it, I can tell you.'

Bea had closed the oven door on the dish of panhagelty she was making for supper and hung the oven cloth on the brass rail under the mantelpiece. She had stood there for a moment or two, staring into the fire, and Theda knew she was thinking about Joss.

'They took their time about it though, didn't they? Late for everything, the Yanks.' Chuck had nodded his head sagely.

'You look as though you're in a brown study,' said Sister Smith now as Theda pushed the door open and they went in.

The ward was festive with greenery and paper chains the men had made – goodness knows where they had got the coloured paper from. Theda took off her cloak in the tiny cloakroom, pinned her cap on to her hair and tied a clean white apron crackling with starch over her dress. She stared at her image in the looking glass. Her face was pale and her mouth drooped.

Other years she had not minded doing twelve hours on Christmas Day, eight in the morning until eight at night. But other years her patients had been English, and the last couple of years she had been on Children's Ward. Oh, well. Pushing the corners of her mouth up with her forefingers, she grinned at herself and went out to start the day.

Dodging the bunches of mistletoe hung by the few Italians left on the ward, just in case one of them was lurking about, she went into Sister's office to hear the night report.

'After the dressings have been done, I want you to go with the choir,' said Sister. The report had been read, the night staff had departed. 'There are plenty of nurses on today for a change and no patient dangerously ill.'

'Oh, I thought the choir went over the other side last night?' said Theda. She was pleasantly surprised. She would see the children all excited about their presents, maybe even be there when Santa Claus came. 'Thanks, Sister, I'll enjoy that.'

In the ward the men were jovial, even Johann muttered something which Theda took to be Happy Christmas. And the men had assembled toys on the table in the middle, wooden dolls and tops and soldiers and cars. No guns – they had been stopped from carving guns or tanks. But there were circus clowns tumbling on ladders when a string was pulled, and jointed cows and sheep. Now they were all wrapped up in bright paper the prisoners had painted themselves, pink for girls and blue for boys.

They were waiting for the guards who were detailed to go with them, and of course Major Koestler who was the choir master. But at last they were through the doors and joining the group from the other wards. Major Koestler fell in beside Theda.

'Good morning, Staff Nurse,' he said. 'Happy Christmas to you.' He bent slightly, his head going down and up in a stiff little bow, his face solemn. 'I trust you had a good Christmas Eve with your family? I think you were with your family, for you were not with us, were you?'

Theda agreed that she was not. She hadn't been home either. She had spent the evening in her room, washing her hair and generally relaxing. But she didn't feel like going into details.

'We had a good time, you know. You should have been there,' said the major. 'We sang carols to the children and then we went to see the new mothers and their babies and sang for them too.'

'Lovely,' said Theda for want of anything else to say. She was glad when one of the sergeants fell back beside the Major and asked respectfully if he could speak to him. Koestler looked annoyed but slowed his pace a little and Theda drew ahead.

They were speaking in German, she heard the name 'Von Runstedt', but of course couldn't make head nor tail of it anyway. Von Runstedt, she mused as she followed the rest of the prisoners through the main door into the old part of the hospital, hadn't she heard that name mentioned. Oh, yes, the commander of the German troops in Belgium, that was it.

The choir stood in the middle of the children's ward and sang *'Stille Nacht, Heilige Nachf'*, and the children listened dutifully though their eyes were straying to the parcels that the singers had put round the tree when they entered the ward. They sang another, a beautiful lullaby but with the words still incomprehensible to the children, and then Laura Jenkins led her small charges, at least those fit enough to sing, in 'Away in a Manger'.

Millie and the other two disabled children, Jean and Mary, from the side ward, were pushed into the main ward in their cots, all ready for Father Christmas's visit. Millie's normally pale face was flushed with excitement and her eyes sparkled as Theda propped an extra pillow behind her to support her twisted spine.

'What do you want from Father Christmas?' asked Theda, and Millie shook her head.

'It doesn't matter, Staff, anything. But do you think he will remember me?' The smile slipped from her face and an anxious look came into her eyes. Poor Millie, thought Theda, she expected little and little was what she usually got.

'I'm sure he'll have something special for you,' she said, and at that moment looked up and caught one of the Germans, a young boy of no more than eighteen, smirking as he looked at Millie's twisted body, outlined under the sheet only too plainly as the blanket had slipped down. He said something in his own language to a group of prisoners and they all looked at her and there was some giggling.

Theda bent over the child and drew up the blanket to cover her. Her own face was flushed with anger as she looked at the child to see if she knew what was going on. But Millie hadn't noticed. She was gazing at the door, watching for Santa Claus. Theda moved closer to the group of prisoners and they looked at her, surprised.

'You're not making fun of disabled children, are you?' she demanded. The men looked at each other and there was a chorus of dissent. Theda felt sick, her face hot and her hands clenched and sweaty as she glared at them and they gazed blandly back, though one looked away, blushing.

'In Germany we would keep them separate. No one should have to look at them.' It was the one who had first drawn the others' attention to the deformed children. He sounded unabashed now.

'Oh? And there was I thinking, you being the master race, that all your children would be strong and healthy and you wouldn't have any to hide away so that ordinary people would not be disturbed.'

Theda was keeping her voice to little above a whisper, she could not be heard by anyone apart from this group and kept her back turned to the rest of the ward. But there must have been something about her which showed her anger for the next moment Major Koestler was beside her, speaking rapidly to the men before taking hold of her elbow and drawing her into the small passageway which led to the side wards.

'I hope the boys have not said something to upset you, Staff Nurse? They are young, sometimes a little exuberant.'

Theda looked up at him. He was standing very close to her and still holding her arm. What could she say? Nothing, not now. She couldn't say anything that would cause ill feeling, not on Christmas morning and certainly not on the Children's Ward. But, by heck, she would later. Oh, yes, indeed she would. She would tell those louts what she thought of them. The first time she had Ward K to herself, they would feel the edge of her tongue.

'Nurse?'

Theda swallowed hard. 'Nothing, it was nothing.'

'They made you angry?' Major Koestler persisted. He moved close to her, his strangely light eyes glinting in the gloom of the passage.

'It was—' Luckily at that moment there was a commotion at the door of the main ward. The children began to cheer and the two-year-old in the coat by the door to scream in fright as a man in a red suit and white beard with a sack on his back strode into the ward. In another moment she would have told him, he was so insistent. 'Leave go of my arm, please Major,' she said instead, and his hand dropped immediately.

Theda hurried down the ward to where Laura was picking up the screaming toddler and cuddling him and Santa Claus was wisely turning away to speak to some of the older children.

'I'll take him, if you like. You go and help him dish out the presents,' said Theda, and took the child to the rocking chair where she rocked him against her shoulder until his sobs began to ease. 'He's a nice man,' she whispered in his ear. 'A grand man, just like your daddy.'

'What was all that about? I mean with the German officer, what's his name, Koestler?' asked Laura Jenkins. 'Oh, never mind, you can tell me after when the pandemonium dies down a bit.' She went over to join Santa Claus.

It was Ken Collins playing Santa Claus, Theda realised, as she rocked back and forth, back and forth. She had thought Mr Kent was coming as he usually did the honours. Ken was good with the children, she noticed. They were eager to see what he had in his sack for them and when he had been round all the beds, he helped Major Koestler hand out the parcels that the prisoners had made.

But soon it was time to move on. There were the other wards to go to, and in any case the children had had enough excitement, they needed to be quiet again.

Theda helped push Millie and the other two back into their side ward, Millie lying quietly now, clutching a wooden clown in a befrilled outfit with enormous red spots all over it and painted blue eyes under huge, black, surprised eyebrows. And a knitted horse with improbable legs sticking out at the corners, no doubt knitted by a Hospital Friend. Theda said goodbye to them and hurried on after the choir, though somehow for her the magic had gone out of their singing. Taking her watch out of her pocket, she saw it was already eleven-thirty. Oh, good, she would have to go back to the ward soon to help serve dinners anyway.

She caught up with them on Block Two, upstairs in the ward which had been designated for British Officers at the beginning of the war. There weren't many of them in at the moment, just half a dozen, overspill from the military hospital at Catterick.

The choir was giving their rendering of '*Stille Nachf*' yet again and the officers were politely listening. But afterwards little was said and the choir shuffled out, a guard in front and one behind.

'Nurse!'

Theda turned her head and looked in the side ward from where the call had come. It was the Canadian – oh, what was his name now? She couldn't think. But there was no forgetting his distinctive blue eyes, looking out from a swathe of bandages. Bandages covered his hands and forearms too, up to his elbows.

'I'm not on this ward, but if you need something I can get it. Or shall I fetch one of the others?'

His voice sounded strange, muffled by the bandages, but so much like Clark Gable's voice in *Gone with the Wind* that she was half-convinced he must be putting it on, rather the way Chuck would imitate Charles Boyer or Douglas Fairbanks.

He moved his head slightly from side to side and then winced.

'Oh! I shouldn't have done that,' he exclaimed. 'I forget sometimes. It's you I want, Nurse. Come in, will you?'

'Well . . . I ought to be getting back.'

'Come on, the Krauts will manage without you for a few minutes, I'm sure. And if Sister kicks up a fuss refer her to me, Pilot Officer Eugene Ridley, ma'am. At your service. Or I would be if I could get out of this bed.'

Theda went into the side ward and stood by the bed. 'I'm Staff Nurse Wearmouth. Do you want me to get you a drink? Orange juice? Water?' She was looking at his lips, dried and cracked and only just visible through a split in the bandages.

'No, thank you. Staff Nurse, eh? Is that something special?'

'It just means I'm fully trained, nothing special at all,' she admitted.

'I remember you, that night I came in, standing over me like a beautiful angel. I thought I'd died and gone to Heaven. What did you say your name was?'

'Staff Nurse Wearmouth.'

'No, your first name. You do have a first name?'

'Theda.' She smiled as she said it, remembering the night he had come in – how she had dreaded looking at him and how relieved she had been when she saw he was not badly disfigured with burns after all. He could talk. Oh, yes, he could talk all right. His facial muscles and his mouth could not be damaged.

'Theda? Like the film star? You could be in films, you know that?'

'Hmm. Do all you Canadians talk like this? Where do you expect such flattery to get you?'

'I'm not Canadian, I'm an American. And it's not flattery, it's the truth. And I expect it to get me everywhere.' She could have sworn that underneath the bandages he was grinning, she could hear it in his voice. And she couldn't help laughing in return, almost as though he had made a great joke.

'I'll have to go now.'

'It's Christmas Day, Nurse – can't you take your lunch hour and stay and eat with me? Here I am, alone in a strange land, no one to care for me in my suffering. You can't be so hardhearted?'

Oh, yes, thought Theda, I could cheerfully stay if I wasn't on duty. His light-hearted banter was just what she needed to cheer her up, make her forget about last Christmas Day and how Alan had been at the gate of the nurses' home in the evening with a forty-eight-hour pass and they had gone to the Wear View Hotel and, instead of the hospital supper of bubble and squeak from the leftovers of Christmas dinner, had eaten steak.

A suspiciously fishy steak though the price had been scandalous and Alan had declared it was whale steak.

The sudden flash of memory sliced through her like a knife. Her smile disappeared, leaving her looking stricken. She stared at the American for a second before turning blindly for the door.

'What did I say? Hey, look, I'm sorry, come back . . .'

But his voice was fading away as Theda rushed for the stairs and ran down and out of the front door and across the tarmac to the hutted section. A few yards from the gate, she slowed to a walk. What a fool she was. The guard would think something was wrong. He was watching her approach curiously.

Stopping, she took out her handkerchief and blew her nose, composing herself before showing him her pass, which was mandatory even though he knew her well by this time.

'Something wrong, Staff?' he asked, his face showing his concern.

'No, just late,' she mumbled. 'I think I have a cold coming on too. Just my luck when I'm off tomorrow.' She hurried through the gate and set off down the ramp, leaving Tom gazing after her.

The American was just being sociable. He probably flirted with all the nurses, and was probably as bad as the Italians, she told herself. For goodness' sake, woman, pull yourself together.

'Staff?'

The voice came from right behind her. Turning, she saw Ken Collins, his Father Christmas suit changed for his usual major's uniform, a set of case notes under his arm.

'Oh, hello, sir. Merry Christmas.' Blast it all! The last thing she needed was a telling off from him. What had she done now? He was solemn-faced, completely different from the jovial Santa Claus of the Children's Ward.

'Merry Christmas,' he said, automatic in his response. 'You're going to the ward? Good. I wanted to have a word with you. Major Koestler seems to think there was some misunderstanding between you and the men in the choir this morning. Is that right?'

Theda's patience snapped. 'There was no misunderstanding, sir,' she said tightly.

Ken looked at her consideringly, then he nodded. 'Oh, well, the major must have been mistaken.'

'Yes.'

'Er . . . it's your day off tomorrow, isn't it? I wondered, would you like a lift back to Winton Colliery? I'm going anyway. Say ten o'clock at the main gate?'

Chapter Thirteen

I should have refused the lift, thought Theda, the bus to Winton runs every half-hour. But instead she had climbed into Major Collins's car which had been standing discreetly down the road from the main gates of the hospital.

'Good morning, Staff.'

'Good morning, Doctor.'

The greeting was stiff and formal as he pulled away into Newgate Street which was empty of people, the shops shuttered on this Boxing Day.

'*Was* there a misunderstanding between you and Major Koestler yesterday morning?'

Ken was manoeuvring the car around a greengrocer's cart pulled by a sturdy dales pony with feathery legs and large brown eyes which it turned disdainfully on the car as it passed. Theda watched it as he abruptly broke the silence.

'No,' she said, and stared out of the window. The car slowed down at the lights and then turned into South Church Road.

'It's not wise to get too close to one of the prisoners, and Major Koestler is a prisoner.'

Theda looked at him in astonishment. What was he talking about? 'I don't know where you get the idea that I am interested in him or any other German,' she said with some heat.

'As I came into the ward yesterday you looked to be quite close to him. He was holding your arm, in fact.'

'Did you offer me a lift so that you could lecture me about Major Koestler?'

Ken had the grace to look uncomfortable. 'No, of course not. I was just wondering, that's all.'

Theda considered telling him to mind his own business. She certainly wasn't going to tell him why she had been talking to the German doctor, though she was still angry about the other prisoners' attitude to the disabled girls. Let him think what he liked. Though how he could think there was any romantic involvement . . .

'Never mind, I'm sorry I brought it up,' said Ken. She glanced at him. He was staring straight ahead at the road but his ears and cheeks were pink.

'Yes, well, considering that only a week or two ago you were complaining that my attitude to him was unneces- sarily antagonistic . . .' she said. Luckily, by this time they were turning into the lane where the manager's house stood, slightly set back from the road behind a wooden gate. The gate had replaced the ornate cast iron one that had been taken down at the beginning of the war and still stood waiting, leaning against the hedge, to be taken away to be melted down to make armaments.

'You can let me off here. No need to take me down to West Row,' said Theda. 'It's not far to walk.'

'Sure? It's no trouble.' But he was slowing down already and she had her hand on the door handle. As she climbed out of the car she couldn't resist a parting shot.

'There's a war on, you know, the country can't afford to waste petrol on unnecessary journeys.' And as an afterthought, 'Thanks for the ride, anyway.'

Before he could say anything else she had the door closed and was striding away down the lane, the collar of her short, brown utility coat turned up against the bitter wind. A daft thing to do, she thought ruefully as icy shafts of sleet began needling her unprotected face and head and she began to run as soon as she was round the next bend. Arriving breathless and with her wet hair sticking to her scalp at the back door, she burst into the kitchen.

'By heck, our Theda,' commented Bea, 'where's your head scarf? Could you not have covered your head?'

'In my bag,' she admitted. 'I forgot all about it.'

Bea raised her eyes heavenwards before taking the kitchen towel from the rail under the mantelpiece and throwing it at her daughter. 'By, for somebody who's supposed to be clever, you can be as gormless as our Clara,' she said. 'Go on, dry your hair and we'll sit down and have a cup of tea. Your da's away to the pit, he's working today so he can have New Year's day off. Chuck an' all. And Clara's gone to Violet's, so we have the place to ourselves for once.'

Theda looked closely at her mother when she mentioned Clara but it was obvious that Bea still knew nothing about her pregnancy. Misgivings filled Theda as she went to the pantry to the tap and filled the kettle.

They drank the tea which tasted slightly funny because Bea had run out of cows' milk and was using goats', from the nanny kept by Mr Allen, one of the neighbours, at the bottom of his garden. But the slice of Christmas cake she had saved for Theda tasted surprisingly good despite the imitation currants.

'One of the doctors brought me down. He was going to his uncle's,' Theda volunteered.

'An' who might that be?'

'Major Collins. I must have mentioned him before. His uncle is Tucker Cornish.'

'The gaffer? I didn't know he had any relatives around here.'

The Wearmouths were relative newcomers to Winton Colliery in that they had moved there in the early-thirties. They had come from a mining village the other side of the county where Bea had known everyone and it still galled her that she didn't know everything about everyone else in these rows.

She listened to everything the rest of the women talked about when they were standing in the queue at the Co-op store or the fish shop. If she heard some intriguing snippet about anyone she would worry at it until she had the whole story. And, of course, she had soon found out that Tucker Cornish was related to the most notorious family who had ever inhabited Winton, Colliery or Village. But she had never managed to get all the facts.

'Eeh, they were a funny family, those Cornishes,' she

said now in the strong lilting accent of her native Wheatley Hill. 'I did hear that Sally and the lass an' all were no better than they should be, though I don't think Sally was Tucker's mother.' Bea shook her head, looking puzzled. 'Yet they have a lad a doctor, have they? A cousin mebbe, is he?'

'Mam, I said Tucker was his uncle.'

'Oh, aye.' Bea nodded but her eyes took on a faraway look and Theda knew she was wondering who would tell her about Tucker's nephew next time she was down the Co-op.

'Do you wish you could have stayed in Wheatley Hill, Mam?' Theda asked, not for the first time, and Bea looked exasperated.

'Why, what do you think, lass? I was brought up there, all me friends were there. But never mind, we've been fine here, haven't we?'

Theda nodded. For herself she liked Winton, liked being near the town too. Almost twelve years they had lived in Winton Colliery, she mused. Da had often told the tale of how his name was drawn out of the hat at Wheatley Hill when the Agent reckoned there were too many working there when demand for coal was so bad and going down. And Matt was one of the unlucky ones, even though he played the cornet in the colliery band and they had gone down to Crystal Palace in London and been placed in the brass band championships.

Theda remembered that, and the celluloid doll Da had brought home for her, and a pink teddy bear for Clara and a blue one for Chuck.

148

'You daft thing, Clara's too old for a teddy bear,' Bea had commented. But nevertheless Clara still had it, sitting on the chair by the side of the bed. The celluloid doll was long gone, Chuck having thrown it in the fire in a paddy. Theda still remembered the way it had flared up into strange green and violet flames.

Matt and Chuck came in from fore shift at one o'clock and the family sat down to cold belly pork and chicken saved from the Christmas dinner, and potato and turnip mashed together and fried in the iron frying pan on the fire. Christmas pudding had been impossible this year and there was no rice to be had either. So Bea had made a huge milk pudding with the goats' milk and barley and part of the sugar ration she had been saving for weeks and there was enough left over to warm up too.

Theda's thoughts were still running on those early days when they had come to Winton Colliery. When Chuck and Matt had had their baths and Chuck had gone out to meet his girl, she sat opposite her father by the fire. Bea was sitting back in the leatherette chair, newly bought when Matt got his rise at the pit, her apron over her head. She was having her two minutes, 'resting her eyes'.

'Tell me about how you came to Winton, Da?' said Theda.

'Eeh, lass,' he answered, leaning forward and poking a newspaper spill through the bars of the grate to light his pipe, 'I've told you many a time.'

'I know. But I've forgotten.'

Matt puffed at the pipe until he had it going to his satisfaction and then he sat back. 'You know me name came out of the hat.'

Theda nodded. 'I was just thinking about it this morning.'

'Aye. Well, there I was, four bairns still at school and no work. And we had to leave the house, it belonged to the colliery, you know, and if I didn't work there, well . . . Anyroad, I reckoned I would get a job if I looked hard enough. I walked round the county looking an' all. Five weeks it took but then I stayed one night with your grandma at Ferryhill and next morning I went to Chilton pit.'

Matt fell silent. His pipe had gone out and he lit another spill and puffed away.

'And you got taken on?' Chilton pit was eight miles away from Winton.

Matt grinned. 'Aye. Well, I had my cornet with me, I was taking part in a concert that night. And, praise the Lord, they were short of a cornet player for the band. Only trouble was, there were no colliery houses empty in Chilton. But the pit here belonged to the same company and there were houses here, so here we came.'

'But how did you get to work?'

'I got a bike on a five-pound club from the Co-op. It was grand that first fortnight. But then some flaming . . .'

'Matt!' The exclamation came from under Bea's pinny.

'Aye, well. It was enough to make a saint swear. Me bike was pinched from the pithead yard. I had the eight miles to walk back and forth till the club was paid and we could afford to get another. Aye, well. At least I got transferred here at the beginning of the war.'

Theda stared into the fire, thinking of the hard times before the war. The days when the food her mother could put on the table made today's rations seem like an abundance. Maybe things would change after the war, who knows? If the pits were nationalised Utopia might come.

Matt went to his bed and Bea had fallen into a proper sleep under her apron. Theda sat half-dozing herself, memories of Alan crowding in on her. There was no bitterness, just his face laughing down at her, a lock of his hair, free from Brylcreem, falling over his forehead.

They had been to a dance at Coundon and had a great time, jitterbugging to a band made up of piano and drums and the trumpet played by the cornetist from the colliery band, and it sounded funny somehow, not really like the records of Glenn Miller or Joe Loss which they heard over the wireless on the Forces network. But they had danced nevertheless, Alan swinging her off her feet and whirling her round so that she ended up a breathless heap in his arms. And afterwards they had walked the couple of miles home to Winton Colliery, one couple amongst many but spread out along the road so they were quite alone under the stars.

Alan had pulled her gently into the shade of a tree at the entrance to the bunny banks and they had kissed, softly at first but then with increasing urgency, and he had undone the buttons of her coat and slid his hands inside and ran his fingers up and down her back, and shivers of ecstasy had engulfed her. And he had cupped her breast with one hand and the nipple had thrust out against his palm and he moaned.

'Marry me, Theda,' he had said. 'Marry me . . .'

She sat up with a start, disorientated. She must have fallen asleep. The feeling of happiness and love fell away from her, leaving her bereft and cold. Picking up the poker, she pushed it through the bars of the grate and stirred the fire, then raked coal down from the shelf at the back on to the red and grey embers. The fire crackled and spit and sent showers of sparks up the chimney.

'Shale in the coal,' said Bea, sitting up straight and smoothing her apron down over her hips. 'The coal here isn't as good as the roundies we got at Wheatley Hill, not by a long chalk.'

'Are you expecting Clara back soon?' asked Theda. The nagging worry about her sister had returned, deepening the depression she felt as the dream of Alan faded. She would have to have a real talk to her.

'After tea, I expect. I don't know what gets into those girls' heads, I don't really. All our Clara cares about is being away with Violet. Chasing lads, I shouldn't wonder. I don't know. I reckon it's not good for them to earn so much money, that's the trouble. It can't be good for them.'

'I think I'll go for a walk before tea,' said Theda, a feeling of restlessness taking hold of her.

Bea looked out of the window at the darkening sky. 'Mind, it'll be cold enough out there. You'll want your top coat buttoned up, and don't forget to wrap your scarf round your head. Nurses can catch pneumonia an' all, you know.'

'It's stopped raining at least.'

'If you walk up by Old Winton you can take the

accumulators for the wireless – they've ran down. Tommy Handley's on tonight, I always get a good laugh from him.'

'It's Boxing Day, won't the place be closed?'

'No, he always opens up for a couple of hours in the afternoon.'

Theda placed the two accumulator batteries in the old basket kept for the purpose and set off up the back row for the shop. She turned round by the corner shop, closed and shuttered, the faded letters of 'Armstrong's' peeling away from the wood above the window and an equally faded notice stuck to the shutters, 'Closed for the duration'. She smiled as she remembered buying a penn'orth of black bullets there but now Tommy Armstrong was under the sod somewhere in France, had been since Dunkirk along with Frank. Now the only place to shop in the village was the Co-op and, of course, the bicycle shop where she was heading, with the shed behind where old Mr Jones mended wirelesses.

There was a strong smell of accumulator acid in the shed. Theda wrinkled her nose as she waited for Mr Jones to replace the batteries with newly charged ones.

'I hear Churchill's away to Athens for a conference,' he remarked. 'Must be nice to go off to the sun, eh? All right for some? Old bugger!'

Theda smiled to himself. There was a running battle going on between the Tories, and Churchill in particular, and the mining folk since the last war when he had ordered in the troops to South Wales. Evidently Mr Jones was one of those who wasn't going to let a little thing like

Churchill's being a great war leader alter his opinion of him. 'Attlee would have done as well, mebbe better,' was a comment he often made.

Looking at his gnarled hands, Theda noticed the acid burns on them, some just pink scars and others more recent, angry and red.

'You want to be more careful with your hands,' she told Mr Jones. 'Haven't you got some of those industrial gloves? Our Clara wears them when she's working with gunpowder; they save her hands a lot.'

Mr Jones gave her a scathing look. 'Aye, well, your Clara's a lass now, isn't she? A few burns aren't going to hurt me.'

Suitably told off, she paid over her eightpence and picked up the basket, carrying it carefully now. Acid from the accumulators could burn holes in clothes and she couldn't afford a new coat, not yet, though she had the coupons left.

Outside, the winter's afternoon was closing in, a cold, dark mist beginning to swallow up the houses only a few doors away. Theda tucked her headscarf inside her coat collar and burrowed her chin into the soft, woollen folds. Dark was approaching fast but at least she didn't have to use her flashlight. Now that the blackout was reduced to a dim-out there was a little light seeping through the curtains of the houses though the street lights had not been lit since 1939.

There was a car parked on the end of West Row. As she drew near she saw it was Major Collins's. Now what did he want? It wasn't time for her to go back to the hospital, it was far too early for her. She wanted to have a quiet word with Clara.

There was an unpleasant smell from the earth closet, which stood by the coalhouses at the end of the yards. Normally she didn't notice it, but now, with Ken here, she was embarrassingly conscious of it. I bet there's a water closet in the manager's house, she thought to herself. But why should she care what he thought? He knew well enough the conditions . . .

Her thoughts were cut off as, staring at the car and not looking where she was walking, she stumbled against the base of a blacked out street lamp and the basket jerked in her hand. Acid slopped out on to her feet and ran down inside her shoes, stinging and burning so that she cried out in agony.

Chapter Fourteen

Ken had spent the day with his uncle. Simon, Tucker's son, was on leave from the RAF and he and his wife Anne, who was six months pregnant, had come up for the Christmas holidays.

'Can't you come home, at least for one day?' Ken's mother had asked wistfully. But he was on call and had to stay near a telephone, close enough to the hospital to be able to get in if there were any emergencies. Mr Kent, the senior surgeon, lived in Darlington.

It had been a good day at Winton, though. Uncle Tucker seemed to have forgotten about the pit for a while. He was happy with his family around him, displaying a dry wit which kept the atmosphere bright and cheerful as they sat around the dining table.

'We're going over to Marsden to see Grandma Meg and the others tomorrow,' Simon said as they gathered round the fire in Tucker's comfortable sitting-room after the meal. 'Come with us, Dad. You too, Ken. Let's make it a proper family day.'

'Oh, yes, why not?' Anne enthused. She was a pretty girl, obviously madly in love with Simon. Her blonde hair was cut in the style of Veronica Lake, hanging loose over one eye, and she flung it back now in a gesture that was becoming habitual.

'Sorry, I can't get leave,' Ken answered. 'Give my love to them all, though.'

'No, I can't go either,' said Tucker. 'The pit will be going full blast by tomorrow.'

The afternoon was wearing on. It was cosy there before the fire, with Simon reminiscing about holidays spent on the farm at Marsden and Tucker and Ken putting in the occasional word. Thankfully, the telephone didn't ring to summon either of them to work. Anne and Simon sat close together on the leather couch, and Ken watched them indulgently.

Oh, how they reminded him of himself, not long ago it seemed, when he was waiting to go to North Africa with his mobile hospital unit and there had been Julie sitting just as close beside him on the couch in Grandma's front room.

Julie . . . he hadn't thought of her for ages, deliberately put her out of his mind. He had no choice, anyone in his position had to otherwise they would go mad. But now he felt the old aching longing for her. How she had clung to him when he got his orders!

'You come back, you hear?' she had said. 'No heroics now.'

'I'll come back,' he had promised, and kissed her and hugged her to him. It had been raining and her tears mingled with the raindrops as she held her face up to him.

He had come back, limping it was true but whole. It was Julie who had been taken, as she worked with a team of doctors and nurses and first-aid men down at the quayside in Newcastle during an air raid.

Ken moved restlessly in his chair, uncrossing his legs and crossing them again the opposite way. He was only one amongst many. Julie was one amongst many. But his memories were hard to bear, his contentment with the afternoon and the company gone. He got to his feet.

'I think I'd better go, I might be needed at the hospital,' he said.

Tucker looked at him in surprise. 'Oh, we'll be having tea in a minute or two. And I thought you were staying for supper? Mrs Parkin has gone off to see her daughter but I can soon fettle something. She said there would be cold rabbit pie and pickles.'

'Sounds tempting,' Ken admitted. 'But needs must . . . In any case, I gave a nurse a lift here this morning, I'd better see if she needs a lift back.'

'Theda Wearmouth, would that be? You mentioned her before and she's the only nurse I know lives in Winton Colliery,' Tucker answered.

'Yes. She lives in West Row.'

'A bright girl,' said his uncle. 'Good-looking, too.' He looked at Ken, his gaze thoughtful. 'A shame about her fiance.'

'Her fiance?'

'Missing at Arnhem.'

Ken nodded. Another victim of the war, he thought.

Simon and Anne walked with him to the door, their

158

arms entwined. It was as though they couldn't bear not to be touching.

'I hope we see you again soon,' said Anne. 'After the war, eh? It won't be long now.'

Not long now . . . Ken opened the car door and got in. 'Not long now' was the phrase on everyone's lips. He only hoped this German push in the Ardennes was soon crushed, otherwise it would delay the ending of the war yet again.

He was about to turn his car round when he thought again of Staff Nurse Wearmouth. He hadn't really promised to do it but he would go into Winton Colliery and pick her up. No doubt she would be glad of a lift. And he needed to be with someone so that he couldn't brood about Julie. What with hearing about yet another soldier killed at Arnhem and then seeing Simon and Anne together . . . He frowned, shying away from his dismal thoughts. Best think of something else. What had he said to upset the Staff Nurse so this morning? Nothing but the truth.

Parking his car at the end of West Row, he sat for a moment, feeling a bit of a fool for he wasn't sure which of the houses was occupied by the Wearmouths. Of course he could knock on the door of the end house and ask, that was the obvious thing to do. He was about to get out of the car and do just that when he heard a woman's footsteps coming down the back street. He would ask her.

But whoever was approaching was walking rapidly in spite of the blackout and suddenly there was a dull bump and something fell to the ground, and Ken jumped out of the car as whoever it was gave a startled scream of pain.

Taking his flashlight from the dashboard, he jumped out and shone it on the woman and saw it was Theda.

'What have you done?'

She fell silent and tried to stop hopping about. But she couldn't keep still, the pain was so sharp. Backing away, she limped to her gate.

'Wait! Let me help you,' said Ken, and putting his arm around her, supported her up the yard. Opening the back door without knocking, he helped her into the kitchen.

'What on earth is the matter?'

Bea started up from her chair by the range, looking alarmed.

'Nothing, it's nothing . . . just stumbled and spilled some acid from the accumulator batteries on my feet.'

Ken practically carried Theda over to the settee and sat her down, lifting her legs and swinging them round and up on to the cushion.

'By, our Theda, you want to be more careful! You know what that stuff's like—' Bea began, but stopped in mid-flow when Ken interrupted.

'Get me some water, will you, Mrs Wearmouth? The sooner we can wash the stuff away the better.'

Bea bustled away to the tap in the pantry, coming back with an enamel dish of water. Meanwhile Ken was easing off Theda's shoes and cutting away her lisle stockings.

'I can do it myself,' she protested. 'Really, it's not too bad. It was just the shock at first, I'm all right now.'

Ken was sluicing her feet and one leg with water and the pain eased as if by magic. The relief made Theda lie back against the hard horsehair of the couch end with a sigh.

'Yes, well of course you can,' he said, glancing up at her white face. 'But I'm here, aren't I? Does that feel better?'

'Oh, yes,' she said fervently.

'Now just lie still. It's not so bad but you've had a shock. Have you any bicarbonate of soda in the house? Clean white cloth? Bandages?'

'Yes, of course. Theda *is* a nurse.' Bea took the first-aid box out of the press and made up a solution on his instructions.

'Look now, it's not so bad,' said Ken. 'Mainly first degree, though some blistering. And if we exclude the air—'

He laid the makeshift dressing soaked in the solution across the reddened skin and bandaged it loosely. His hands were so gentle yet so capable, strong hands with the square nails of a surgeon. 'There now, you'll be back walking the wards in no time. It won't even leave a scar.'

'Tomorrow, I hope. It's Sister's day off, I'll have to go in. Anyway, it's not half so bad as I thought it was. It feels fine now.'

'Hmm. Now you're talking stupidly.'

Theda bridled. His tone was so cool, his blue eyes level and expressionless – quite different from when he had been attending to her feet. He seemed a different man.

'You said yourself the burns are nothing. I'm sure if I have a good night's rest and keep them covered, they'll be fine,' she said defensively.

'Eeh, our Theda, don't talk so soft!' her mother put in, and Theda blinked. She had almost forgotten Bea was there. 'Take no notice of her, Doctor. Of course she won't be coming in tomorrow. You can tell Matron, can't you?'

Theda sighed. Maybe she was being a bit of a fool, acting as though the hospital couldn't do without her. No one was indispensable. In any case, she felt tired to death. Shock, she supposed. And her feet, the left one in particular, felt like they were on fire again in spite of the dressing.

'Yes, of course.' Ken rose to his feet and smiled at Bea. 'Well, I'd better be going. I just came because I thought that Theda would like a lift. Lucky I did, really. I was able to see to her when she stumbled.'

I wouldn't have stumbled if you hadn't been there, thought Theda. She felt thoroughly out of sorts, angry at the world. 'If I don't go in, I'll have to have a doctor's note,' she said grumpily. 'It's the rule.'

'Oh, I'll explain to Matron,' Ken said easily. He stood looking down at her as he drew on his gloves, a faint smile on his lips – as though he were humouring a child, she thought.

'Won't you stay and have a cup of tea, Doctor? Or perhaps something stronger?'

Theda's heart sank. The only drink her mother had in the house was home-made ginger wine and half a bottle of cheap rum which she used to flavour the Christmas pudding. It was the only alcohol they ever had in the house, though they were not as strongly Methodist as some of the miners' families. But Ken was declining the invitation, thank goodness.

'No, thank you very much, Mrs Wearmouth. I must get back,' he answered, and headed for the door. Before he got there it opened and Clara came in, her hair done up in a turban formed from her head scarf and her cheeks red with cold. Just behind her were Chuck and his girlfriend Norma.

Clara stopped just inside the door with her brother and his girl crowding in behind her. 'Oh! For a minute there I thought I was in the wrong house.'

'This is Doctor Collins from the hospital, he just came to offer our Theda a lift in. He was visiting his uncle, Mr Cornish,' explained Bea. 'Doctor, my younger daughter, Clara. And my son Charles and his friend Norma.'

'How do you do? I'm sorry I have to go, I'm late as it is.'

The trio stood aside as Ken made his exit, rather hurriedly, Theda thought. He probably felt overwhelmed by the number of Wearmouths.

'Well, our Theda,' said Chuck, as he came into the kitchen and stood before the fire, warming his back. 'How long had this been going on?'

'Chuck! Behave yourself!' cried his mother. 'You know it's not five minutes since—' She stopped abruptly, horrified that she might say something that would bring all that unhappiness back to Theda. It didn't matter. The silence was uncomfortable. They all knew what the end of her sentence was going to be.

Not five minutes since Alan died, though Theda, and lay back on the cushion and closed her eyes for a moment.

'Aye, well, it's the first time a doctor has bothered to fetch her home, isn't it?' said the irrepressible Chuck.

'Just you take the brush and shovel and get out there and clear up the mess,' Bea said sharply. 'Theda fell and dropped the accumulators and burnt her feet. And now I won't be able to listen to Tommy Handley neither. I was looking forward to it an' all.'

She looked at Theda, suddenly realising what she had said. 'Eeh, pet, I didn't mean – well, it doesn't matter about the wireless, so long as you aren't burnt so badly.'

'No, I know what you meant, Mam,' she answered.

When Chuck came back he triumphantly bore a whole accumulator which looked none the worse for wear, the acid level seeming normal. The other was chipped and spoiled, its acid level well down, though even it might be salvageable, he pronounced.

'I'll take it in the morning,' he said. 'When I come in from fore shift.' He wired the accumulator into the wireless and switched it on while Bea made tea and toast with cheese and onion melted together in the oven. 'American cheese,' she said, her voice full of disgust. 'I don't know what the Ministry of Food is thinking of, saying the miners need extra protein, whatever that is, and then giving them four ounces of this hard rubbery stuff and telling them it's cheese. You could sole your shoes with it, you could. There's nowt else to do with it but melt it.'

The family ate it, however; four years of war following on the harder years of the depression had instilled in them the habit of never wasting food. Even Theda ate half a slice, though it lay like lead on her stomach after. It wasn't long before she went to bed, wincing a little as she put her feet to the floor and walked to the staircase.

'That's right, pet,' said Bea, 'you go up. You'll likely feel a lot better the morn.'

'I'll come up too, so I don't disturb you later on,' said Clara.

'Goodnight then.' Theda climbed the stairs slowly and carefully, undressed and thankfully got under the bedclothes. She lay on her side, so that the weight of the blankets did not press on her burns, or rather the one burn in particular which lay across her instep and was the only one to have blistered.

She had wanted to talk to Clara but didn't feel up to it now. All she wanted was sleep. Another day coming, she thought.

'Theda?' Clara had come into the room and was preparing for bed. She climbed in beside her sister. 'Theda?' she said again, though softly. Evidently she wanted to talk. But Theda lay with her back to her sister, her eyes tightly closed, and after a moment Clara too turned away and appeared to be sleeping.

The wireless was still on downstairs, Theda could hear her mother's chuckles as she listened to Tommy Handley on the Forces Network and Chuck laughing loud and clear. Her mother hushed him, reminding him the girls were trying to sleep.

Her mind wandered to Major Collins. He was a kind man, even though at times he seemed cold. Sometimes she felt an affinity with him, which was silly. She didn't know anything about him; she didn't even know if he had a girlfriend or ever had had one. But it had been nice, just for a second or two, to lean on him.

Chapter Fifteen

Next morning Theda woke feeling much better than she had expected to, just a faint throbbing from her foot. Clara had already gone to work, and Theda turned over in the big brass bed and stretched out luxuriously. Maybe she should go in, she thought, there was practically nothing wrong with her, and after all, Sister was off today. Swinging her legs out of bed, she pulled on a robe which Bea had crocheted for her last Christmas out of scraps of wool unravelled from old jumpers. Wincing only a little as she walked stiffly to the head of the stairs, she went down to the kitchen.

'By, lass, you won't take a bit of rest when you get the chance, will you?' demanded her mother. 'I was just about to bring you up a nice cup of tea and a slice of toast and dripping. How are your feet, anyroad?'

'Oh, practically back to normal,' said Theda. 'I might go in to work this afternoon, I feel a fraud.'

'Hmm. That bicarbonate of soda must have worked wonders then, I'm sure,' said Bea, sounding sceptical.

'Here, sit down and have your breakfast now I've made it for you. Then we'll have a look and see. Did you sleep all right?'

'Fine.'

Theda had lain awake until about one o'clock as it happened, and then, when she heard her father and Chuck going down to get ready for their shift, she had given in and followed them, taking a cup of tea from their pot and swallowing a couple of Anadins with it.

'Mind, you want to be a bit careful with them batteries, I thought you had more sense,' Matt had growled at her, but she could see he was concerned.

'Aye, you might have burned a hole in the pavement,' grinned Chuck.

Back in bed, warmed by the hot tea and a short sit by the fire, she had soon fallen asleep.

'Cold tea you want on that,' her mother pronounced as she inspected Theda's feet after she had removed the bandages. She firmly believed that her own remedies were quite as good as anything the medical profession came up with.

Tannic acid, thought Theda. This time she's probably right. Her right foot was a bit angry-looking but the redness had faded a little and was sore rather than painful. There were two blisters on her left instep, about the size of a sixpenny piece. All they needed was a sterile dressing. But it would please Bea to apply a dressing of cold tea.

'Go on then,' she said.

After dinner, fortified by another couple of Anadins,

Theda insisted on going in to work. It was one o'clock when she knocked on the door of Matron's office. She had gone in on the bus, so her foot wasn't aching too much.

'I thought you weren't coming in today? I've arranged for someone to take your place,' said Matron as Theda went in and stood before the desk. 'I understood from Major Collins that you had suffered burns to your feet?'

'Not too bad though, Matron,' said Theda. 'They were much better this morning.'

'Hmm.'

Matron was studying a list on her desk. Theda stood for a moment or two. She stared out of the window above Matron's head, feeling her left instep stinging a little. It must have rubbed against the dressing. Perhaps she had wasted her time coming in, she thought, feeling as grumpy as Matron looked.

'Well, they are short-handed upstairs on Block Two this afternoon – you can give a hand there. There's a short theatre list scheduled for three o'clock.'

'Yes, Matron. Thank you, Matron.' Theda turned to go, thinking that her superior had showed little interest in just how badly burned she had been. But as she reached the door Matron spoke again.

'I'll have a word with Major Collins. He'll find time to look at your foot, I'm sure.'

'Thank you, Matron.'

Block Two, the British officers' ward. Well, it made a change. Theda walked through to the next block and up the stairs to the ward. It wasn't long since she had been there with the German choir. Some of the men recognised her and as she came in they smiled and waved. At least the ones who were convalescing did; two in the main ward were screened off and she could hear Sister's voice from behind the screens.

'Lie still a moment, Captain—'

Theda put her head through the opening. 'Matron has sent me along to help, Sister.'

'Goodness, has she really? Things must be quiet in the rest of the hospital,' Sister said. She smiled briefly as she straightened from her position over the bed where she had been coating the Captain's abdomen with antiseptic. 'Still, we certainly can use you. Why don't you take over here so I can get on with something else? The Captain here, he's for an appendicectomy, and ditto the next bed. Both to prepare and administer the pre-op. I'm sure you can manage, can't you?'

The question was hypothetical. Of course she could manage. Theda scrubbed up and put on a gown and mask. A junior opened the screens for her and she went in, taking the forceps holding the sponge soaked in antiseptic from Sister's hand.

She worked carefully, covering the whole of the abdomen with the orange liquid and then placed a sterile dressing towel over the area. As she finished she glanced at the Captain's face. He looked white and ill, but managed a smile. 'I'll do anything to get out of parade duty,' he joked.

'Hmm. Well, I'll just get you your pre-med and then you can drop off to sleep. Before you know it you'll be back in bed with it all over. No doubt you'll get a spot of leave and then it'll all have been worth it.'

As she moved the screens she saw that the theatre porters had come in to take the first patient on the list to theatre. It was the American from the side ward. So he hadn't been transferred yet. He must be having his burns attended to under anaesthesia.

He was awake. As she watched he turned his head on the trolley and saw her. 'Just my luck!' he said. 'You come in to brighten up the ward and they take me away.'

Theda had to smile. 'Go on with you. I'll still be here when you get back.'

'That's what I'm afraid of – I'll come back asleep. Promise you'll be here when I wake up?'

'I'll be here.'

The porter took him off to theatre and Theda went to the sink to scrub up again and prepare the next patient. A nice man, she mused, and by the look of him he wasn't going to be badly scarred. There were his hands, of course . . . what agony it must have been in that burning plane! She thought of the pain in her own foot, a burn so trivial compared to what the American had suffered.

The afternoon wore on, the three patients on the list came back from theatre and had to be made comfortable and watched until they came fully round from the anaesthetic. The Captain who had had his grumbling appendix removed was nauseous and one of the two juniors on duty had to stay near so as to hold him up when he felt sick. And all the time, in the back of Theda's mind, she was expecting Ken Collins to come in to see her as

Matron had said. Not that it mattered to her if he didn't, of course.

'You can take your tea break now, Staff,' Sister said as she passed by and Theda glanced at the clock, surprised to see it was already five o'clock. 'Then you had better go back to your own ward, we will manage fine,' she added. 'Thank you for your help.'

Theda, just finishing the last Penicillin injection, picked up the kidney dish containing the empty syringe and took it down to the sink at the end of the ward. Penicillin, she thought as she washed the syringe in the sink and rinsed it under the tap before putting it in the steriliser. The new wonder drug. Maybe after the war there would be enough to use on the civilian population, not just the British Forces. Why, it could cut a swathe through infections of most kinds. Well, according to her old nursing tutor it would. Half the hospital beds would be empty.

Before leaving the ward, she looked into the room where the American had been sleeping peacefully since his return from theatre. After all, she had promised to be there if he woke. Eugene Ridley, she read as she looked at his chart on the end of the bed. Eugene Ridley. An outlandish name – she couldn't imagine anyone calling a baby Eugene. But Ridley was a local name. Idly she wondered if his ancestors had come from the area.

The line showing his temperature was down, almost normal, she noted. Putting down the chart, she moved to the side of the bed and looked at his face. She eased her left foot slightly, holding it off the floor. It was sore; she would change the dressing when she went off duty.

The American slept on, his mouth slightly open and showing white even teeth. His face was visible now; only a bandage around his forehead remained and one under his chin. The skin was a patchy red but healing already and his lashes were growing again, the roots must not have been destroyed. Fair they were, with a reddish tinge, though not as fair as some of the Germans'. There was a dimple in his chin. She smiled. It was just like her gran's.

'Hello, Angel.'

Theda jumped as his eyes flew open and he grinned, albeit a little lopsidedly as the new skin on one cheek refused to crease so easily.

'I knew it was you, even with my eyes closed,' he said softly. 'Thank you for staying.'

'I'm just on my way to tea,' she said, slightly flustered. 'Then I have to go back to my own ward.'

'Oh, come on, you can stay a few minutes, can't you? Have pity on a poor lonely man in a strange land, thousands of miles from home.'

He was used to charming girls, Theda thought, he must have used that line hundreds of times. It was not surprising, the way he looked and with that accent – most girls had only heard it on the films. The thought reminded her of Clara and her trouble. Oh, Lord, it was easy to understand how and why her sister had got into the mess she was in.

'Staff, I thought you were going to tea?' Sister's disapproving voice came from the doorway of the small side ward.

'I am, Sister.'

As she turned, Theda saw that Ken Collins was standing beside her, frowning.

'I thought you were having today off at least,' he said. 'I was surprised when Matron asked me to look at your foot.'

Theda began to explain but he cut her short. 'Come on then, let me see it now, I haven't got all day. Go into Sister's office and take off the dressing. I'll be along in a minute. I just want to check on the post-op cases here.' He stood to one side to allow her to pass.

In the office, she took off her shoe and stocking and unwound the bandage from her foot. One of the blisters had burst.

'Damn it all,' she said savagely to herself. She had felt it stinging. It must have been the friction as she walked about.

'Damn it indeed,' he said behind her, and she jumped. 'Don't you ever do anything you are told?'

He cleaned the foot gently with saline and painted on gentian violet before covering the burn again. In spite of herself his ministrations were soothing. Theda sat back in her chair and sighed with relief.

'That better?'

'Oh, yes, much, thank you.'

'It's not bad, it will be better in a day or two. Just an awkward place, that's all. Now I'd better be getting on, patients to see to. But do try to keep off it for today at least.'

'Yes, Doctor.'

Theda looked up at him; he was smiling now, friendly

again. He really was the most exasperating man, she thought. She couldn't always tell what he was thinking and that could be disconcerting.

'Well, I must go and check on your friend the pilot,' he said lightly, and she opened her mouth to say the American was not her friend but he had already gone.

When she was alone she pulled on her stocking and shoe and stood up. It felt fine. If she hurried she would just have time to eat the beans on toast that were invariably on the menu on Tuesdays then go back to Ward K.

By New Year's Eve, Theda's foot was almost back to normal. She felt quite light-hearted as she travelled the few miles home. It was her evening off. She had finished at six o'clock and hadn't to be back on duty until one o'clock tomorrow afternoon, for she had the morning free too.

There was no one in but her mother. Bea was on her hands and knees scrubbing the kitchen floor, 'getting the dirt out for New Year', as she called it.

'I'll be but a minute,' she said as she got to her feet and wrung out her floorcloth in the bucket. Her forehead was red and beaded with sweat. She pushed back wisps of damp hair with one hand.

'I could have done that, Mam. You should have waited,' said Theda, vexed to see the work had been such an effort for her mother.

'Aye, well, it's done now.'

Theda took the bucket from her mother and emptied it in the sink in the middle of the yard. Everything was sparkling clean: the seat and floor in the netty, the outside earth closet scrubbed, even the brick-paved yard had been swilled with soapy water, and the steps of both the back door and the back gate scoured with sandstone until they gleamed yellow in the light that came out of the back door as she opened it.

Bea made a cup of Camp coffee as the tea ration was running short and they sat down by the fire to drink it, Theda wrinkling her nose at the taste of the chicory. The fireside mat was still up. Chuck hadn't come in from the pit and would have to have his bath so Theda slipped off her shoes and rested her feet on the burnished fender. It was peaceful there, letting the heat of the fire soak into her, smelling the liver and onions Mam had cooking gently in the oven.

'What about this Major Collins, then?'

The question dropped into the silence, startling Theda for a minute. 'What about him?' she asked.

'Well, I mean, what's he up to, coming round here, do you think?'

'Mam, he's not up to anything. I told you, he was just visiting his uncle and gave me a lift. Common courtesy, that's all.'

Bea gave her an old-fashioned look. 'Aye, I know you told me. But it seems to me he was awful interested in you.'

Theda pulled a face at her. 'Now, Mam, don't you be going reading something into nothing. Anyway, I'm not interested in men any more. I'm going to go in for a grand career in nursing. I'll be Matron one day. Or maybe, when the war is over, I'll go off to Sunderland and take my Midwifery Certificate, even be a District Nurse. I don't intend staying a Staff Nurse all my life.'

'Aye, well, I know it's not long since . . .' Bea caught a glimpse of Theda's face closing up and thought again about what she had been about to say.

Up until that moment, Theda hadn't given any really serious thought to her future now Alan had died. But once she had put it into words, she realised she was ambitious, still as she had been when she first entered nursing. She would love to rise to the top, or at least as far as she could go in nursing. She stared into the fire, watching the coals redden and crumble, fancying she saw pictures in the ashes, just as she had when she was small. She could do it, she knew she could, and the war *was* almost over, surely it was? Though there was Japan . . .

Her thoughts were interrupted by the arrival of Chuck, black from the pit, and shortly afterwards Clara came in. Then everything was hustle and bustle as Bea called Matt from his bed and the meal was eaten and then Chuck had to have his bath. The talk was all about the New Year's Eve dance at the church hall.

'I never learned how to dance,' Bea said wistfully. 'Your grandda was strict chapel. For meself I couldn't see any harm in it, like.'

'Well, I'll be staying in with you, Mam,' said Theda.

'Get along with you,' her mother said sharply. 'You go along with your da. You want nowt staying in on a New Year's Eve – you'll be staying in all year if you do. You might as well enjoy yourself.'

'Aye, your mother's right,' Matt put in. 'You come with me, pet, you'll have a grand time. You an' all, Bea, I don't know why you can't come.' Matt was Master of Ceremonies at the dance which was organised by the Working Mens' Club to raise money for the children's summer picnic.

'Nay, Matt, I'll stay here and make sure we're ready for the new year.' Bea shook her head. 'It'll be nice to have the house to meself for an hour or two, I can listen to the wireless.'

In the sitting-room, while Chuck had his bath, Theda found herself alone with Clara as Bea had slipped out to see a friend. Clara was obviously waiting for the opportunity to speak to her and Theda's heart sank. Her sister had a brittle air about her, vivacious and smiling and bright-eyed, but she was obviously having trouble keeping still. She rushed over to the fire and turned to stare at Theda.

'Are you going to help me?'

Clara hissed out the question, her voice low but insistent. Her face was pale, but for two spots of colour high on her cheeks, and there were dark shadows under her eyes. Why her mother hadn't tumbled to the truth, Theda couldn't imagine. Except that she would never ever think it could happen to one of her girls . . .

'Well?'

'Clara, I don't know what I could do, really I don't.'

'Don't tell me that! You could if you wanted to, you a nurse. You must be able to get anything you want, if you would only try.'

177

'Clara, I've seen girls coming in to the hospital, bleeding, some of them dying, because they've done something to themselves, taken something. You know yourself there was Mrs Downs from Winton Village – she almost died after taking something. It's not worth it, Clara.' Theda felt like weeping for her sister.

'Whisht, Dad'll hear you! Keep your voice down, for God's sake!' Clara whispered fiercely. She walked over to the sideboard on the opposite side of the room and stared fixedly at the wooden manger scene Matt had whittled. The baby in the manger was a tiny celluloid doll, an improbable shade of pink, its golden hair painted on along with bright red lips and china blue eyes. Suddenly she lifted her hand and swept the whole thing off the sideboard so that the doll flew across the shiny linoleum which covered the floor and landed, feet sticking up, in the proddy mat by the fire.

'I swear I'll go to that old wife in Shildon. I've got the money, you know!'

Theda was down on her knees, picking up the tiny figures and scraps of straw which littered the floor. She glanced anxiously at the connecting door to the kitchen but Chuck was singing 'You Are My Sunshine' tunelessly as he washed and evidently neither of the men had heard anything, thank goodness. Her mind was working furiously, she had to get Clara to think sensibly.

'Don't do that,' she said, forcing herself to keep her voice down. 'I promise I'll see what I can do. But I wish you would just tell them—'

Seeing the desperate misery in Clara's eyes, she stood

up and dropped the figures on the sideboard and put her arms round Clara's thin shoulders. They were both of them shaking, Clara struggling to recover her self-control.

'I'll help you. I will, Clara. I promise. But what do you think Dean would say if he knew what you were planning on doing?'

How she was going to help she had no idea, and immediately after she mentioned Dean she was sorry. It wasn't a fair thing to do.

Clara moved away from her, turning her back. Theda's words had had a calming effect on her. Now she had the promise, Theda doubted she had even heard the mention of the Canadian, but she had.

'Dean's dead, you know,' she said, all the passion drained from her. 'I know it. Violet and me, we went to the camp and asked for him. Missing over Germany, they said. I know what that means. So it's just me who has to face it.'

Chuck began to whistle, his usual signal that he had finished his bath and was decent again. A few minutes later, the back door opened and they heard Bea's voice. The girls went through to empty the bath and finish tidying up the kitchen before their mother could do it all herself.

'You'll have a fine time with us tonight,' Clara was saying brightly as they went through the connecting door. 'I'll paint the seams on your legs for you if you like, and you can borrow my pink scarf I got for Christmas.'

'You want nothing with that flighty lot, our Theda,' advised Chuck. He was in his favourite position before the mirror in the press door, applying a generous coat of Brylcreem and combing his still damp hair into a quiff. 'The last time me and Norma met her and Violet at a dance, Norma didn't know where to put herself, she was that embarrassed at the wild way they were jitterbugging. Lord knows where they learned to jump in the air like that, showing all their legs and even their knickers.'

'They didn't, did they, Chuck?' asked Bea, scandalised.

Seeing his sister's furious face and realising he had said a bit too much, Chuck grinned sheepishly and backed down. 'No, Mam, no, I'm only having a bit of fun. Of course they didn't. Well, no more than that lass from that picture, you know, Betty Grable—'

'Chuck!'

'All right, all right, like I said, it was only a joke. Keep your shirt on.' He turned back to the mirror and carefully combed a stray hair back into place, winking at Theda in the glass.

Chapter Sixteen

The New Year's Eve dance was packed to overflowing. The Wearmouth family were there very early as Matt was one of the organisers, but they were far from being the first. All the seats around the floor were taken and Theda, who had hoped to be able to sit quietly in a corner, had to resign herself to standing with her sister and her friends in a group along the side of the hall. Ranged in a line opposite were the boys, hands in pockets, most of them young miners but with a sprinkling of khaki and Air Force blue among them. There was even a sailor standing there, his cap pushed to the back of his head, legs apart as he surveyed the girls.

The band was warming up, strange sounds coming from the stage at the end. The club had done them proud, she saw, hiring Phil Mason and his Swingers, a band well known in the area for their lively playing. Most of them played in the colliery brass band too, Phil being especially famous for his playing of 'The Last Post' at the Armistice Day parade. This didn't seem to affect their rendering of

'In the Mood'. They drew themselves into it heart and soul as they struck up the first quickstep.

Theda stood back behind Clara and her friends from the munitions factory; she felt set apart from them somehow. Most of her own friends were from the hospital and they were either working or at their own local dos. In any case, she was quite happy listening to the music and watching. In a minute she would go and give a hand in the supper room behind the stage – the Sunday School room it was really, but for tonight there were trestle tables set up with tea urns at one end.

She watched as Clara was claimed by a shiny-faced young miner from one of the rows, his fair hair slicked back from his pink forehead and smooth cheeks. He was trying hard to look more than his seventeen years, his 'spiv's' tie a flamboyant orange and red against his blue utility shirt. For a minute Theda thought her sister would refuse him but she had been well-schooled in the manners of the dance halls and hesitated only briefly before smiling graciously and accompanying him on to the floor.

Now Clara was a different girl from the one who had been pleading so passionately with her only a few hours before. She sparkled, dark luxuriant hair dressed high in a roll over her brow and at her temples, and at the back flowing loosely over her shoulders. Her cheeks were no longer pale, her elaborate make-up saw to that, and her eyebrows were darkened even further by eyebrow pencil. She wore a deep blue crepe-de-chine dress, which hugged her figure and ended just above the knees. Theda reckoned it must have wiped out her clothing coupons for the next six months. But then, perhaps she had bought it for her Canadian, Dean whatever his name was.

Theda herself was wearing a plain black utility skirt with a thin box pleat in front but had lightened it with a white embroidered blouse, and stuck a diamante brooch Alan had brought her just under the collar. She had had the blouse for years. That was the advantage of having to wear uniform for most of the time, your good clothes lasted longer.

Most of the girls were dancing now, and the floor was filling up. A sedate quickstep, this one; it was still early in the evening. They hadn't quite got into their stride as yet.

Theda edged her way along the side of the dance, aiming for the supper room, but before she got there she was stopped by the sailor.

'You dancing?'

Automatically the response came. 'You asking?'

'I'm asking.'

She grinned as he led her out on to the floor, threading his way through the bystanders until he came to a space. He was a good dancer, she realised, holding her firmly but not too closely, concentrating on the music. She relaxed, getting into the rhythm. They circled the hall, passing Clara who winked at her and then grimaced as her partner trod on her toes. On the stage, Matt was talking earnestly to the band leader but looked up as he saw Theda dancing and gave her a pleased smile.

'You live around here?' the sailor asked, and she waited while they executed an involved turn before replying.

'West Row. In Winton Colliery.'

'That right? Wha's your name then?'

'Theda. Where are you from?'

'Bishop.'

The conversation was cut short as the dance ended and the dancers split up, most of them going to their own side of the hall. He grinned at her and murmured thanks and then she was back in the crowd of girls.

'By, it's a wonder I have any feet left,' remarked Clara, bending down and rubbing her foot. 'Take my tip: if you see that one heading for you, hide in the lavatory. He'll soon make your foot bad again.'

Matt announced an old-time waltz and then threaded his way through the dancers to his daughters. 'Howay, then, Clara. I'll show you how dancing should be done,' he said.

The evening was getting underway properly; the hall, which had been cold at first, was warming up. Phil was leading the band in the 'Blue Danube' and some of the older people were joining the dancers and circling the floor.

'May I have this dance?'

The voice came from over her shoulder and Theda jumped. She had been watching her father and Clara and thinking over her conversation with her sister earlier on, her thoughts sombre.

'Oh! I'm surprised to see you here!'

Ken Collins raised his eyebrows. 'You are? But you know I often come out here, I stay with Uncle Tucker, remember?'

'Yes, but—'

She stopped speaking as he took her arm and led her on to the floor. She could hardly say that she thought this humble dance, put on by the Working Mens' Club, wouldn't be a place she would expect him to frequent. But that was the truth. Yet when she thought about it, Tucker Cornish always came to these things, even if he only put in a token appearance and left early.

'Yes, but what?' asked Ken as they began to dance. His limp was hardly noticeable but it was there and provided a reason.

'Well, I mean, with your bad leg—'

'Oh, it's not so bad. I don't need crutches anymore. Perhaps you've noticed I get around the wards under my own steam. Though I may ask you to sit down early if the dance goes on for long.'

They circled the floor in silence and she was very conscious of his arms around her, the smooth feel of his uniformed shoulder under her hand. She caught the eye of her father as he danced majestically round with Clara on his arm and looked away hurriedly, not wanting to see his speculative expression. The music came to an end and the dancers stood for a minute as the band changed their music for the second part.

'We could sit down, if you don't mind?' said Ken.

'Of course, if you wish,' she answered. She almost called him 'Doctor', she was feeling so awkward.

There were no available seats in the hall and the supper room was still closed. It was another hour before it would open. Ken glanced quickly around and then took her arm.

'All the seats are taken. Shall we go outside? It's a clear night, we can sit in the car and look at the stars.'

Oh, dear, Da wasn't going to like that. Even for the so-called fast girls this was a bit early to be going outside with a chap. Theda's doubt showed on her face.

'Look,' he said a trifle impatiently, 'I'm not about to seduce you. I simply want to sit down for a while, and I would like your company while I do. That's all there is to it.'

He did look a little strained, it showed in the tired lines around his face. Theda looked around quickly for her father but he was nowhere to be seen. Oh, well, he probably wouldn't notice anyway, he was so happy that the dance was obviously going to be a great success.

'Of course,' she said. 'I'll come.'

Outside it was indeed a lovely night, cold and crisp with a clear sky showing the stars and a broad frosty ring round the moon.

They sat in the car, Theda wondering weakly what she was doing there. The moonlight filtered dimly through the windows, showing only his profile. There was no light escaping from the hall except when the doors opened. And of course the streetlights, which before the war had been lit by gas from the pit, were dark and had been for more than four years.

A shaft of moonlight lit the top of the hedge close by and Theda shivered with the beauty of it.

'Cold?'

'No, it's just—'

But Ken was reaching into the back seat of the car for a rug. There was a sudden commotion as a jeep swept up to the doors of the hall, headlights full on in contravention of the dim-out, and out spilled four airmen, laughing and talking, obviously Canadian and full to the brim with high spirits. They swept into the hall, the doors swinging to sifter them, and shortly afterwards the band began to play boogie-woogie harshly and loudly and insistently.

'They have to let off steam,' said Theda, as if she was making excuses for them. 'It must be terrible for them to have to go out over Germany night after night, never knowing if they will make it back.'

'I didn't realise they came so far away from the base. Did you already know Pilot Officer Ridley before he was admitted to the hospital?'

'No, of course not, I would have said.'

'I just thought . . . you seemed so friendly, you and him?'

'He's a friendly sort of bloke.'

No doubt the Canadians had been invited by some of the girls from the munitions factory, thought Theda, but kept it to herself.

The noise became louder, they could hear the stamping of feet above the music. Ken turned to her and put his arm around her and she stiffened.

'You're cold,' he said. 'Do you want to go back in?'

'No, I'm fine,' she managed to answer, though she was amazed at her reaction to his nearness. A languor was creeping over her and she knew she should get out of the car now while there was still time, but somehow . . . Ken bent his head and kissed her on the lips, gently at first, then more insistently.

187

'You don't want to go back in there, do you?'

'I do.' Her voice was unconvincing.

'I want to talk to you. I think about you a lot,' he said into her hair. 'It's too noisy in there, and too cold here. You don't really want to dance, do you?'

'My family—'

'They're having a good time. Look, there's no one in at Uncle Tucker's, he's away. Why don't we go there? I can make you a cup of real coffee.'

'If you like.'

Theda's hesitation was practically non-existent. Of course she shouldn't go, but not even with Alan had she felt like this, carried along with no will of her own. All the old rules that had been dinned into her were forgotten. She couldn't believe she was agreeing to go with him into the empty house . . . what was she doing? She wondered what Laura Jenkins would say if she could see her now. 'A randy lot, these doctors, Theda, never give them an inch,' she heard her friend's voice in her head, but the warning was meaningless.

The feelings – Alan had awakened in her which had lain dormant these last few months – were pulsing through her. Poor Alan. If only she had given way to them. How could she have let some stuffy old rules that belonged in the age of Victoria stop her from making him happy before he went to his death?

She closed her eyes and Ken saw the emotions chasing across her face in the pale moonlight. She looked lost for a minute and he felt the urge to comfort her, to kiss away whatever made her look so tragic. And it was so long since he had held a girl in his arms and made love to her. Not since Julie died.

Julie seemed very far away now. She was gone forever, and nothing was going to bring her back. And just now he didn't know if he wanted to bring her back. This nurse, this girl, was taking over his senses. Life went on. It was trite but true. He kissed her lips and her eyes flew open, large and dark and searching.

He had been lying, even to himself, he thought. He did want to seduce her. He badly wanted to make love to her. And she lay in his arms, gazing up at him, and surely she wanted him too?

Ken started the car and manoeuvred it out from behind the jeep. In the background, Theda could hear the band playing 'If I Could Hold You in My Arms'. A slow waltz, dreamy. She could get out now, she could tell him to stop the car and he would. But she did not. The sound of the music followed them along the lane, diminishing as they turned into the drive of the manager's house.

Ken opened the door for her and she climbed out and stood in the porch, the frost making her shiver despite the rug around her shoulders. She had left her coat in the cloakroom, of course. And even now she thought what a complete fool she was being.

'Come on, into the sitting-room. It will be warm in there.' Ken put an arm around her and led her into the house and through a side door into a room where it was warm, beautifully warm.

'Wait here,' he said, leading her to a large leather

armchair with worn arms, which smelled of pipe tobacco. 'I'll only be a minute or two with the coffee.' She sat obediently, staring into the fire, until the chiming clock on the sideboard struck ten and she sat up, startled.

While he waited for the milk to boil on the range and spooned coffee into the pot, Ken was wondering at himself almost as much as she was. Not that he had brought her here – oh, no, he had wanted to do that, he was more attracted to her than he had been to anyone since Julie had died. But he had sworn he wouldn't get involved again, never again, not while this rotten war was on. And Theda was a nurse – he had to work with her. But surely there was no harm, not in having a cup of coffee with a woman? He was lonely, that was it, so lonely. And there was no harm. She had been engaged, her sweetheart was dead, and she must have some experience of men. Look at how Major Koestler looked at her, and that American flier too. They had been laughing together that day on the ward, even though Ridley had not long returned from having his burns dressed and must have been feeling a certain amount of pain. Ken shook his head.

He carried the tray back into the sitting-room, balancing it on one hand as he opened the door. Theda looked round quickly at him. She had risen from the armchair and was standing by the sideboard, looking at the pictures Uncle Tucker had there: Grandma Meg, his Aunt Betty with a baby on her knee, then the baby grown and in his Air Force uniform, standing with his feet apart grinning hugely at the camera.

'Oh, I'm sorry, I was just looking—' Theda said. 'I hope you don't think I was prying?'

'I don't think anything,' said Ken. 'Come and sit down and have your coffee.' She looked so slender in that black skirt and her hair was almost as dark and curled down on to her shoulders, shining in the light from the overhead lamp. As she held out her hand to take the cup and saucer from him he noticed how delicate the bones of her hands were, the nails cut short and unadorned by polish as a nurse's nails had to be.

'You wanted to talk to me?' she said, breaking the silence.

Had he said that? Well, he must have done. What on earth was it he had meant to say? He could hardly say he wanted to make love to her, could he?

'Yes.' He drew a chair up close to hers and took a sip of coffee. It was piping hot and strong, almost the last of the coffee he had brought back from the Middle East and given to his uncle because he knew he was fond of it.

'I just wanted to say – well, I thought we'd got off on the wrong foot when we first met at the hospital,' he said.

'Did we? How do you mean?' She thought of their first meeting, how he had looked at her when she had shown how she disliked working with the Germans and Italians. Her own resentment. Funny how she had got used to it, quite liked some of them, though not all. 'Oh, I know what you mean, you didn't like my attitude – oh!'

She stopped talking abruptly as the lights went out with an audible click, momentarily confused.

'Oh, hell!'

Ken got to his feet, shoving his coffee on to the side table and slopping it into the saucer as he did so. For a moment he was just a dark shadow in the faint light from the fire, then he picked up the poker and stirred the coals until they burst into flame.

'I'd better see if it's just a fuse blown or a power cut,' he said. But he stood there, not moving.

'Take my flashlight,' she suggested. Carefully she put down her cup and stood up to get it from the pocket of her coat before she remembered that she didn't have her coat.

'I'll have to go if it's a cut,' she said. 'The dance will be stopped and everyone will be going home.' She was very close to him; the buttons on his uniform twinkled and gleamed in the firelight and so did his eyes. He didn't answer, but put his arms around her and kissed her and she was lost. They forgot all about the lights.

After a moment they sank down on to the thick fur rug before the fire. The short hairs on the back of his neck were crisp under her fingers, his mouth on hers warm and demanding. And it was sweet and compelling and she was going to stop him, but not yet, not yet. Even when he took off his uniform jacket and unbuttoned his shirt and began to unbutton her blouse, she was still going to stop him. In a minute.

'Come to bed. We're alone in the house, no one will be in. Not tonight, not tomorrow,' he whispered, between nibbling her earlobe and kissing the nape of her neck.

Go to bed? Her eyes flew open. Of course she wasn't going to go to *bed* with him. She hadn't gone to bed with Alan and would be eternally sorry she hadn't, on the last leave before he went to Holland. And she wasn't engaged to Ken, she hardly knew him!

'I can't do that—'

He was stopping her mouth with his own; she could taste his tongue between her lips. His fingers were on her spine, moving, making her feel faint. When his hand touched her breast, she gasped. She hardly knew what she was doing except that it was urgent, compelling, there was no will left in her. He was taking off the rest of her clothes and she was helping him and suddenly they were both naked on the rug and she opened her eyes and saw the firelight playing on the bare skin of his chest and shoulders and she was gasping for fulfilment.

The pain came as a shock and she cried out but he was holding her against him and murmuring: 'It's all right, my love, all right, relax.' It was the climax which took her completely by surprise. Never had she expected it to be like this. She was exultant, filled with delight as he suddenly relaxed on top of her before rolling to one side, taking her with him and holding her close so that she could hear his heart pounding against her bare chest.

They lay like that, touching closely the whole length of their bodies, and the clock chimed again. Incredibly it was only a quarter after the hour. Her whole life had changed in a quarter of an hour. And then she felt him hardening against her thigh and he cupped her breast and brushed his thumb against the nipple and it took on a life of its own, hardening instantly.

'It will be easier this time,' he said. And it was.

Chapter Seventeen

The pit hooter did not blow to bring in the new year of 1945. If it had, perhaps it would have woken Theda up, but as it didn't, she slept on in Ken's arms on the rug before the fire in the manager's house. She did not stir until the telephone rang, shrilling out, loud and shocking, in the quiet room.

'Hell!' said Ken. He turned over on to his back and yawned hugely. It was very dark, only a dim light from the dying embers of the fire showing as he stumbled to his feet and felt his way to the door to the hall. Luckily there was a candle on the hall table with matches beside it for use in the now frequent power cuts and he groped around and found them and lit the candle before answering the telephone.

'Yes?'

Theda turned her head to watch him. She felt groggy and hardly knew where she was. She could see only the outline of him as he listened to whoever was speaking. He was naked and she looked curiously at him, the broad planes where the candlelight fell on him and the dark shadows. Of course she had seen naked men before, through necessity she had dressed their wounds and prepared them for theatre, given them bed baths. But this was different, Ken was different, she thought dreamily. A feeling of complete contentment lay like a blanket over everything else.

'I'll come right away, be there in half an hour. See theatre is prepared, will you?'

With a start Theda came out of her dream. Dear Lord, what was she doing here? She was supposed to be at home and bringing in the New Year by now. Da would be looking all over for her! Where were her clothes?

Ken came in carrying the candle. 'I have to go, there's an acute abdomen. Strangulated hernia, I think.' He began swiftly drawing on his clothes but found time to look at her as she struggled with her knickers, catching her foot in the waist elastic and almost falling over before she got them on straight. He grinned.

'I would stay and give you a hand, my love, but duty calls. Another time, maybe?'

Theda ignored him. She was fastening the buttons of her blouse, in her haste getting them all wrong and having to do them again. 'I don't know what I'm going to say. I promised I would be back for the new year, what time is it?'

'The clock says two o'clock,' Ken said. He was into his uniform and now sat down to fasten the laces of his shoes. He paused and gazed at her. 'Will you be in trouble?'

Theda thought of her mother, waiting at home for them all to come in for the New Year celebrations. She thought of her father and how angry he was going to be when she did turn up. 'That's the understatement of the year,' she admitted.

Ken finished tying his shoelaces and got to his feet. 'You're not sorry it happened?'

She looked up into his face, all shadowy in the candlelight, and for a moment they stood motionless, their haste forgotten. And then the light came on, bright and harsh and directly on them both. Tentatively she put out a hand to him.

'I'm not sorry,' she said. 'I'm glad. I'm very glad.'

Ken took hold of her and kissed her gently. 'That's good. I'm glad too.'

The magic was still there, she thought, ready to flare up into ecstasy at any time. The knowledge was there inside her, a lovely, comforting, exciting ball of feeling at her very core. She had forgotten about Da and what he was going to say. But Ken had understood.

'Come with me to the hospital. You can tell them I asked you to, that I needed you there.'

'No, I can't do that. There's no way of letting them know, and they'll worry until they hear from me. No, I'll just go home and face them.'

'Sure? Shall I give you a lift to West Row?' He was already pulling on his greatcoat and gloves, his mind on the emergency once more. She couldn't detain him.

'No, no, I can easily walk. There will still be people about, first-footing the New Year.'

'Well, if you don't mind . . .'

He was ready, waiting for her to go so that he could lock up the house. She hurried past him and out on to the driveway, the gravel bumpy under the thin soles of her dancing shoes. By the car he turned again to her and pecked her on the cheek.

''Bye, dear. I'll see you tomorrow, no doubt.' Getting into his car, he started the engine and drove off in the direction of Bishop Auckland.

He almost said 'Let's do it again, sometime', she thought miserably. That was all it meant to him, an interlude for sex. They hadn't even been to bed. Well, that was her fault, she told herself, as she started down the lane. It was very dark and she didn't have her coat and was shivering. He had forgotten she had left her coat in the church hall. He hadn't even noticed she wasn't wearing one.

She began to walk faster and faster, to keep herself warm, but when she turned into West Row, she hesitated, not wanting to go in. She could hear laughter and music coming from the house. There were some neighbours in likely. She was still hesitating at the gate when a crowd came out of next-door and she found herself seized by the sailor she had met earlier in the church hall and waltzed round the yard.

'Happy New Year. Please will you give me a kiss?'

There was a laughing, tipsy crowd of neighbours, evidently well on with their journey round the houses, letting in 1945 to each one, and they just about carried Theda into the house through the open back door. The kitchen and front room were packed with people, pitmen and soldiers and a handful of airmen with 'Canada' blazoned on their shoulders, and one of the Canadians had his arm around Clara – a laughing, sparkling Clara, bubbling over with what she had to tell her sister.

'Theda! Where've you been? We were looking for you.'

'I . . . I didn't stop for supper, I thought I would come home and then I got delayed . . .'

It sounded very lame in her own ears and she faltered to a halt as she looked across the room at her mother and father but they weren't even listening, they were watching Clara and the Canadian with stunned expressions on their faces. Clara, clutching the arm of her airman, pushed over to Theda.

'Theda, Theda, this is Dean. He escaped! What do you think of that? He was in a prisoner-of-war camp and he escaped, wasn't he brave?'

'How do you do?' said Dean gravely, and held out his free hand and pumped Theda's enthusiastically. 'I understand you will be my new sister-in-law?'

Theda gazed up at him, her mouth open. She felt dazed, unable to follow what they were saying. But there was no mistaking the happiness which spilled from them both.

'Dean just went up to Da in the dance, Theda, and asked him if he could marry me. Wasn't that sweet? And all his mates were cheering and they carried us round on their shoulders. Oh, Theda, it was great, why weren't you there?'

'I—'

But Clara wasn't listening, she was off to the other side of the kitchen, laughing and talking, and Chuck was thrusting a glass of ginger wine into Theda's hand and the lot of them were suddenly in a ring singing 'Auld Lang Syne' then the crowd were off out into the night, visiting the next house on their rounds and taking the Canadians and Clara and Violet with them.

There was a sudden hush in the kitchen and Matt and Bea sat down suddenly in their accustomed chairs and looked at each other.

'Well, that was a New Year to remember,' said Bea. 'I think I'll away to bed now, I don't think I can take any more surprises.'

'Yes, me too,' said Theda.

'Mind, I don't know where you got to, our Theda,' Matt began, but then he seemed to forget about it. 'You could have knocked me down with a feather when that lad came up to me and asked if he could marry our Clara. What could I say? If he's the one she wants, well . . .'

'I only wish he didn't live on the other side of the world,' said Bea, looking pensive. 'Manitoba, did he say?'

Matt patted her shoulder. 'That's what it sounded like to me. Aye, well, he seems a decent enough lad.'

Incredibly, they didn't seem worried about where Theda had been. 'I'll go up now,' she said, thinking it best to leave before they looked at her properly and noticed something was different about her for she was certain that it must show.

'Aye, you look tired, pet,' said Bea. But she spoke

absently, staring into the fire. 'I'm glad you had a good time. Join in the Armstrongs' party, did you? They always put on a good party.'

Theda nodded and turned for the stairs, hurrying up them before Bea could ask any more awkward questions. As she undressed for bed, Theda realised they never thought for an instant that she could have been doing anything they would consider wrong; they trusted her. And that was the reason she hadn't realised Clara was pregnant – it was something which just didn't happen to one of their girls. Fervently she hoped that Clara would be married and away before they found out.

Climbing into bed, she stretched her aching limbs, feeling aches and pains she hadn't known she had, wincing as she turned on her side and caught her breast against a lump in the mattress. How sore it was. She should feel guilty, she knew. But she did not, she was glad, just as she told him she was glad. He had said he was too, hadn't he? Maybe he did love her; he was just one of those men who didn't say it all the time. She would make him love her, she thought, she could do it.

Chapter Eighteen

Theda's thoughts were still muddled the following day when she began working on the ward. The patients were subdued, no doubt because they had heard the news that the German advance had been halted and the allies were once again surging towards the Rhine.

Many of the prisoners were being transferred back to the main camp up in Weardale and the staff were kept busy preparing for a new influx of patients. Theda managed to push her personal problems to the back of her mind as the day-to-day routine of the ward took over.

Even so, when the doors to the corridor swung open and she saw the doctors walking up to Sister's office and going in, her pulse beat rapidly and she bent her head over the pillowcase she was replacing as a wave of heat rose in her.

'I'm saving my clothing coupons until spring,' Nurse Cullen was saying as she went to the next empty bed and stripped off the sheets in one capable sweep and flung them in the dirty linen skip. 'I fancy a yellow silk dress with a heart-shaped neckline and a lovely full skirt for when my lad gets home. Do you think I'll get one on utility?' She giggled at the thought before turning to look at Theda, expecting her to share the joke. But Theda wasn't even listening – she was looking at the doctors as they came out of Sister's office.

It was the look on her face which made Nurse Cullen stop smiling and follow her gaze. There was Mr Kent and Major Collins and Sister Smith with an armful of the brown folders that contained the patients' notes. Well, nothing strange about that: it was Mr Kent's day for coming round. In any case, he was advising Major Collins on whether any more patients could be sent back to Weardale. She turned back to Staff Nurse.

'I'll take the slip back to the sluice and empty it,' she said. Sister hated there to be a mess in the ward when the consultant came round.

'Yes,' said Theda absently. She stuffed the pillowcase on top of the other linen. And then Ken was there, walking by the end of the bed with Mr Kent. Theda smiled at him.

'Morning, Staff Nurse,' boomed Mr Kent.

'Morning,' murmured Ken. And walked on by, his smile polite and impersonal, and Theda felt as though he had slapped her face which was silly, she knew. Did she expect him to take her in his arms in front of everyone? Liaisons between the staff were frowned upon.

'Staff, will you put the screens around Private Stern, please? Nurse Cullen seems to have disappeared.'

'What? Oh, yes, Sister.'

She hurried down to the end of the ward for the screens.

At least it gave her a minute to compose herself and when she came back with them her face was as impassive as Ken's.

The rest of the day was filled with work; new admissions always caused a flurry of activity for both doctors and nurses and through necessity Ken was on the ward quite a lot. Rather belatedly, Theda's training was coming to her rescue, however. She was able to immerse herself in her work and put their personal relationship out of her mind until at last it was time for her to go off duty.

Walking down the ramp to the gate, passing the entrance to the theatre, she was searching in her bag for her pass to show Tom when Ken stepped out of the doorway.

'Staff Nurse?'

Theda jumped. It was dark, only the tiny light at the door of the theatre lighting up the path, and as she turned to face him he was little more than a dark shadow before her.

'Yes, sir?'

'Theda,' he said quietly. 'Meet me by the footpath on the railway bridge?'

'I have to get back for supper. I'm staying in the nurses' home tonight,' she said. During the day she had decided that was the best thing to do; in the home she would be away from temptation, Night Sister saw to that. No matter what, she couldn't let it happen again. And even now, when he was so near and she could smell the soap he used and, faintly, the unique scent of his skin, she could feel herself melting. It took an effort of will not to sway towards him.

'Meet me,' he said. A group of nurses was coming down the ramp and he put his hand on her arm and drew her to one side as they passed. 'Good evening,' he said.

'Evening, Doctor,' they chorused, and Ken began to speak about the treatment he wanted for a patient on the ward and Theda thought, Well, they won't be fooled. They'll wonder why he didn't say it all on the ward.

'Meet me,' he said as the nurses' footsteps died away and they could be heard greeting Tom, one of them laughing at something he said.

'I can't, it's too public'

'Where then?'

She looked up the ramp. A group of nurses was just coming out of Hut C. 'Rossi's,' she said, naming a coffee shop in the town. 'I'll be having a cup of coffee in Rossi's.' It wouldn't hurt to meet him in Rossi's, there would be a few people in the cafe but there were enclosed booths, it was fairly private.

Ken nodded and went off up the ramp, whistling 'String of Pearls'. Theda walked on down without looking back and showed her pass to Tom at the gate and answered him as he said something or other, though what she said she hadn't an idea.

She bought a cup of coffee in the coffee shop and took it down to the far booth near the door at the back. She sat, stirring away at the muddy liquid, waiting for Ken to come, her nerves on edge. The feeling of euphoria which had enveloped her last night was fading; there was only the memory now overlaid with doubts.

When he did come she would tell him that it was over.

She wasn't like that really; he had caught her at a bad time because her boyfriend had been killed at Arnhem and she was still too upset about it to think straight.

She would tell him that she couldn't meet him again. It was hopeless when they worked at the same hospital; she couldn't afford for the hospital grapevine to get hold of any gossip about her which would harm her career. And besides, there was Mam and Da . . .

'Hello.'

She was jolted out of her thoughts as he slid into the seat opposite her. 'Hello,' she said.

'I'll take you home when you've finished your coffee.'

'No, no, I'm not going home. Thank you.'

He raised his eyebrows over his coffee cup and smiled and the skin crinkled round his grey eyes. 'Well, then, come for a drive.'

The front door opened and Theda popped her head round the wooden partition of the booth. 'It's Nurse Cullen and Nurse Elliot,' she whispered.

'Does it matter?' he asked, then as he saw her expression he realised that it did. 'Come on then, we'll go.'

They slipped out of the back door as the nurses were ordering cups of Bovril at the counter. 'Is there a cream cracker with it?' Nurse Cullen was asking as the door closed behind them.

The car was round the corner in Kingsway and in two minutes they were on their way. He cast her a sideways look as they sped down the road and his eyes were dancing with merriment.

'Exciting, isn't it?'

'Are you making fun of me?' Theda demanded.

'No, but I'm not sure I see the need for ducking about in doorways.' He took one hand from the wheel and put it over hers. 'It's no business of the hospital, you know – we're both free. I mean, we're not on hospital property now, are we?'

'No.'

She pulled her hand away and stared out of the window. She tried to remember all the arguments she had marshalled in her head but her thoughts were too confused. They were approaching Winton Village, turning up the lane that led to the manager's house, she suddenly noticed.

'Where are you going?'

'Well, I thought we needed somewhere to talk. Uncle Tucker will be back, I want him to meet you.'

'I'd rather not go in. Anyway, I know him, of course I do.'

Ken slowed the car to a snail's pace. 'He'll be pleased to meet you properly, though. And he's not the sort to pry into my affairs. We'll be able to talk privately after dinner, he'll be working in his study.'

'Still, I'd rather not.'

Ken stopped the car and turned to her. 'Where would you like to go then?'

'I have to be back at the hospital soon.'

'But you're not on duty until the morning.'

'No,' Theda conceded. 'But when I'm sleeping at the hospital I have to be in at a reasonable time. You know what Home Sisters are like: moral guardians of the nurses.'

'You can stay at home tonight then.' He started the car and accelerated down the lane. He turned the corner and sped up to Durham Road, and out into the country. He said no more until they were turning up a lane beside an inn about seven miles up the road. She should object to his high-handedness, she thought, but she did not.

'Come on, we have to talk somewhere and I for one am not sitting out in the cold.' He was holding the door of the car open for her. Biting her lip, Theda got out and allowed him to take her arm and lead her through a door labelled 'Snug'. It was a small room with only a hatch from the main bar where drinks were served. Ken rang the bell at the side of the hatch and stood drumming his fingers on the counter. Theda sat down in the corner and watched as a man came to the opening.

'Evening, sir.' An elderly man, he barely glanced at her as Ken asked for whisky. 'No whisky, sir. Beer only. Pint? Maybe a shandy for the lady?'

As Ken placed the glasses on the table and sat down beside her Theda heard a piano tinkling away out of tune in the bar next-door. But the barman must have closed a door between them for the sound was cut off suddenly and they were alone. She was very conscious of his nearness.

'I can't stop thinking about last night,' said Ken. 'What about you, do you want to go on?'

He was very direct. Theda gave him a startled glance then stared at her glass. The lemonade had put a thick white froth on the top of the beer. She lifted it to her lips for something to do and it put a white mark on her upper lip which she licked away quickly with the tip of her tongue.

'Well . . .' What was she going to say to him? Oh, yes. It was never going to happen again, she had been caught at a bad time last night, that was it. She was very aware of him beside her, and wished he would move away. He was clouding her senses. 'Yes,' she said.

Ken kissed her lightly on the forehead. 'Wait here,' he said, and walked out of the snug. Going to the lavatory no doubt, she thought, she would have to go herself soon. She looked around the tiny room, the wallpaper so brown from tobacco smoke that it was practically indistinguishable from the dark-painted woodwork. There was just one light-bulb, hanging from the ceiling in a fly-blown glass shade. It gave out very little light. Still, she didn't suppose they needed much light, the folk who came here.

The door opened. 'Come on,' said Ken, and held out his hand. She rose to her feet and took it. He led her outside and round the back of the inn and through another door and up a flight of stairs. She thought of asking him where they were going but didn't, simply followed him into a bedroom which was almost filled with a double bed and washstand with a blue and white jug and bowl set and a single chair by the bed.

'I must use the lavatory,' she said and could have bitten out her tongue.

'Down the hall. Second door on the right.'

'All right?' asked Ken as she slipped back into the room. He smiled. 'I told the landlord I was on leave and we only had one night together before I had to go back to France.'

A remnant of her former self was sceptical. 'I bet he believed you too.' He laughed and took her in his arms and she melted, feeling the hardness of him against her. Her will was gone. It was like a drug, she thought as they undressed and fell into bed, sinking into the feather mattress. There was nothing else to consider, nothing else mattered.

'Julie,' he murmured, sometime later in the night, and turned to her and ran his tongue around her nipple. She clung to him for she was newly awakened and hadn't heard what he said.

'Six o'clock, sir!'

Theda extricated an arm from under Ken and turned over on to her back to stretch luxuriously. He barely moved.

'Six o'clock, sir!' the landlord said again, opening the door slightly so that he could be heard.

'What? Oh, right, thank you,' said Ken.

'Will you be wanting any breakfast, sir? Only we haven't got a lot in, a bit of toast mebbe.'

'No, it's all right – we have to leave straight away,' Ken called back, and the landlord closed the door. His footsteps could be heard retreating along the passage and down the stairs.

'Good morning, pet,' said Ken, and dropped a kiss on Theda's nose. He jumped out of bed and poured cold water from the jug into the basin. 'You'd think there would be a proper bathroom in the place,' he muttered.

She watched him, his body lean and brown, no doubt from the hot sun in North Africa and then Italy. There was a vivid scar running down the length of his thigh, red for the most part with slight puckering at the end where there was a bluish cast. He picked up a thin towel from the rail on the end of the wash stand and dried himself.

'Come on, get a move on. We'll have to be away,' he said. She felt shy, didn't want to get out from under the protection of the bedclothes, which was silly she knew after the night they had spent in the bed. She could still feel his hands on her body . . .

'Come on,' he cried, and flung back the clothes so that she scrambled out of bed and began pulling on her underclothes, feeling herself blush all over. But he wasn't looking, he was buckling on his belt and then combing his hair back from his forehead. 'I'll pop down and pay the man,' he said, and she felt suddenly dirty.

'Ken, do you love me?' The words sounded loud in the room; she couldn't believe she had actually asked him.

'You're adorable,' he answered, and smiled at her as he opened the door. 'Must get on, a lot to do today.'

Theda stripped off her knickers and bra and poured fresh water in the bowl and washed herself all over, working fast, barely drying herself before pulling her clothes back on. She found her comb in her bag and pulled it through her hair and then stopped mid-stroke to stare at herself in the mirror. There were dark smudges under her eyes but otherwise she looked just the same, and marvelled that it should be so.

'Theda?'

His call came through the open window. He was standing beside the car, impatient to be off. Adorable, she thought. He hadn't said he loved her but he would. Oh yes, he would. Picking up her coat, she went out and down the stairs, passing the landlord at the bottom.

'Good morning, missus,' he said, and smiled knowingly. She nodded and fled.

In the car, Ken had the engine running and barely waited for her to climb in before setting off on the road back to Bishop Auckland. He glanced briefly at her.

'Are you free this weekend?'

'No, of course not,' she replied. 'Sister has Saturday afternoon and Sunday off, I have to be on the ward.' Was this all he wanted, stolen nights in out-of-the-way places to gratify his sexual urges?

'Pity. I wanted to take you over to the coast. You'd like it on the farm where I was brought up. My family still live there.'

Oh, why was she so suspicious of his motives? 'I'm free the weekend after,' she said.

'Good, I may be able to change my leave.'

The dawn was grey and mizzly, patches of mist obscured the bottom of Parkhead Bank. Ken had to concentrate on his driving until he swung the car round the bend into the market place.

'Let me out here,' said Theda.

'Sure?'

'The walk will do me good and I've plenty of time. Clear my head.'

He drove along beside the Barrington School and

stopped. There were very few people about, just a paper boy coming out of Armstrong's the stationers and an almost empty bus standing at the stop for Weardale. Ken looked quickly around and kissed her on the lips, lingering a moment. Theda looked up at him, perplexed. She didn't know what he was thinking half the time, that was the trouble.

'I'll let you know,' he said softly, and she got out of the car and watched as he drove to the corner and turned into Newgate Street. After a moment she began to walk after him, hugging her coat round her in the chill of the morning.

Chapter Nineteen

'I expected you'd be coming home last night,' Bea remarked as Theda came in. It was eight-thirty in the evening and the warmth from the kitchen rushed to greet her as she closed the back door behind her and hurried over to the fire. She stood for a minute or two, letting the heat seep into her.

'I was tired so I thought I wouldn't bother.'

It wasn't exactly a lie though naturally her mother thought she had stayed at the hospital. I'm a grown woman, she thought. We're almost through the first half of the twentieth century; what I do is my business.

'By, you look tired all right,' said Bea. 'Likely you haven't got over New Year. You're going to have to take better care of yourself, pet. Sit down, I've got cheese and onion in the oven. I'll just make you a couple of slices of toast and there's a tasty bite for you.' She opened the oven door and checked on the bubbling cheese, frowning. 'Though, mind you, it's that blooming American cheese your dad got in one of those iron rations parcels at the pit.

How the soldiers manage to fight on that sort of stuff, I'll never know.'

'I don't really want anything, Mam.'

'Oh, aye? What's the matter with you then? Sickening for something, are you?'

'No, I'm just tired.'

Theda took off her coat and hung it behind the door. Sitting down in Da's chair, she slipped off her shoes and propped her feet on the steel fender, spreading her toes to the blaze.

'Mind, you'll get chilblains. How many times do I have to tell you not to do that?' asked Bea, but she spoke mildly. She knelt before the fire with a slice of bread on a brass toasting fork.

'I'll make it anyway. You have to eat something, our Theda, you're getting dead skinny.' She was silent for a minute, watching the toast, turning it when she judged it brown enough. 'What do you think of our Clara's lad then?' she asked, abruptly.

'I don't know, he seems all right – a nice lad,' Theda replied.

'They want to get married right away, he's getting a special licence.' Bea looked thoughtfully at her. 'You don't suppose there's owt wrong, do you?'

'Oh, Mam.' Theda didn't know what to say but thankfully her mother interrupted her.

'No, no, of course not. Our Clara might be a scatter-brain but she's not wild, not like that lass next-door.'

The 'lass next-door', Renee Coulson, was a cockney, married to the soldier son of the house and not a bad girl at all once you got to know her. But Bea couldn't get over the fact that she often went to dances in the town with Clara and Violet and their mates, and her with a husband away fighting and a bairn to look after!

The toast was ready and Bea put it on a plate and poured the milky cheese and onion mixture over it. 'Howay and eat it while it's hot,' she advised. 'Then we can sit round the fire and have a nice listen to the play on the wireless.'

Surprisingly, Theda found herself enjoying the food once she started it. And it was nice to sit about the warm kitchen with no one to disturb them, for Matt and Clara were both on night shift and Chuck was out at his first-aid class down in the Working Mens' Club, something he had to do for his deputy overman's tickets.

The play was Noel Coward's *Blithe Spirit* and the two women were chuckling together over it when there was a thunderous banging on the back door.

'Mrs Wearmouth, Mrs Wearmouth – are you in?'

'Who the heck's that?' Bea asked Theda, getting up to switch off the wireless. 'They might have waited another ten minutes anyroad, just till we heard the end.'

Theda opened the door to find Mrs Patterson standing there, wringing her hands. 'Whatever is it?' she asked.

'By, lass, I'm glad to find you in,' said the little woman, stepping into the kitchen. 'It's my lad, Peter, that's what it is. He's come out of the bedroom window on to the roof of the pantry and fell to the yard. What he thought he was going, I cannot fathom. I tell you, his dad'll kill him when he gets in from the pit. Anyroad, he's all shook up and his arm looks funny an' all. And he's bleeding all over the place. Can you come, lass? You were the only one I could think of to ask.'

'Have you sent for the doctor?' Theda was pulling on her coat as she spoke.

'Aye, but he's out somewhere, the maid said. I don't know what to do!'

'Have you got a first-aid kit?'

'No, just a bottle of iodine and a bandage. I thought I'd better not—'

'Here, lass, take ours.'

Bea opened the door of the press and handed her the cardboard box with the kit Matt had bought cheap from the St John's Ambulance Brigade.

'Don't worry, our Theda will see to the lad,' she assured Mrs Patterson, a note of pride in her voice.

'Eeh, thanks, love. Thanks for coming.' The woman was practically running down the yard and along the end of the rows to her own house and Theda found herself running after her, her own tiredness forgotten.

Her former patient Peter was sitting in his pyjamas, his arm held out in front of him with blood welling from a deep cut in the wrist. His pyjamas were covered with blood and he had a towel on his lap saturated with it. At least it didn't seem to be arterial blood, thought Theda, though she was shocked at the amount the child had lost.

'What have you been doing now, Peter?' she asked as she took a dressing from her box and put it over the wound, applying as much pressure as she dared considering the strange angle of the arm.

216

'I was playing at getting out of the house in case there was an air raid,' Peter said, his voice small and squeaky and very young. 'Billy Potts said he could do it in three minutes flat and I wanted to beat him.'

Theda sighed. She'd have to have a word with Billy Potts or perhaps his mother. The main thing was to get him to a doctor as soon as possible, she thought. Seeing a copy of *Picture Post* lying on the table, she took it and bandaged it round the arm. It was thick enough to use as a temporary splint.

'Have you somebody can go down to the club?' she asked.

'I can go,' said Mrs Patterson, but the boy, who had been sitting pale-faced but dry-eyed, suddenly burst into tears.

'No, Mam, don't go off again – I want you to stay here,' he wailed, clutching his arm to his chest even as Theda tried to fit a sling round it.

'Sit with him,' she said. 'I'll go.'

'If you're sure?' the older woman replied. She put an arm round her boy and wiped his nose with a rag she took out of her apron pocket. 'Whisht now, pet,' she said. 'You'll need all your tears for when your dad comes in, mind.'

'I'm not going back to that hospital,' he sobbed.

'Aye, well, you should have thought of that a bit earlier, shouldn't you?' said his mother. 'By, you'll have me white-haired afore I'm forty, you will that.'

'I'll be as quick as I can,' said Theda.

She had her flashlight in her pocket so took the path

across the fields from the end of the rows. But when she got to the club the first-aid class was just about over.

'Dr Oliver was called out, lass,' advised the steward. 'Your Chuck's here though, will I get him to give you a hand?' But Chuck was already coming out. He soon grasped the situation.

'The baker's van's stood outside the store,' he said. 'I'll knock him up, he just lives up Winton Village. He'll take the bairn in to the hospital, I'm sure. I cannot think of anybody else with a car working round here.'

'There's a car stood outside the gaffer's house,' volunteered one of the men who had followed him out and were now standing round Theda curiously.

'Right then, that'll do. Get away back, our Theda. The lad might be needing you.'

He was very capable, thought Theda as she hurried back up the road. No wonder he was trying to better himself; the bosses would be crazy to refuse him.

Chuck strode away and up the lane and Theda went back up the fields to the colliery rows. Peter was lying down on the sofa now, his eyes closed with lashes fanned out on his pale cheeks. She explained what was happening to Mrs Patterson while she checked the dressing on the boy's arm.

'Eeh, I'll have to leave a note for my man coming in from work. His dinner's in the oven already, anyroad . . .' Mrs Patterson bustled about, finding a pencil and paper and putting on her hat and coat. 'I don't know what he's going to say,' she sighed once again.

Her mind busy with Peter, somehow Theda hadn't

given any thought to the fact that the car outside the manager's house would be Ken's. But suddenly there he was, bending over Peter, looking at his arm.

'Came out of the window, eh? Did you think you could fly?'

'No, of course not,' the boy said. 'I just fell, that's all.'

'Well, I'm afraid you'll have to go in to Lady Eden's cottage hospital. It'll have to be X-rayed.'

'It won't be for long, Peter,' Theda said. 'You'll be all right.' The boy nodded. He seemed to have got over his moment of panic.

'Are you coming in with us to the hospital,' Ken asked her. 'You did a good job, by the way.'

'No, I'll not come in. Mrs Patterson will go, though. I'm staying at home tonight.'

'I'll see you tomorrow,' he said. 'About next weekend—' Theda glanced anxiously at Mrs Patterson but she either hadn't heard or attached no significance to what Ken was saying. All the same if she had, Theda thought angrily as she closed the door. The key was on a string inside and she pulled it up through the letterbox and turned it in the lock before putting it back. He just didn't care about her reputation at all, she thought miserably. He should know what mining villages could be like for gossip. But Ken had settled the boy and his mother in the car and walked back up the yard to Theda.

'Don't look so anxious, love,' he said. 'Come with me on Saturday and I promise you everything will be all right.'

What does he mean? she asked herself as she walked

back to West Row. Was he going to ask her to marry him? Was that why he wanted her to meet his family? Or did he just mean the weekend would go well?

Anyroad, she told herself as she let herself back into the house, I'm not sure I want to be married. It's far too soon after Alan's being killed. And she wanted to take more qualifications, wanted to be a midwife, perhaps go on the district, be of some use to her own folk. She could look after herself, she didn't need Ken, of course she didn't.

'How's the lad, pet?'

Theda loosened her coat and took off her scarf and gloves before she answered her mother. She was cold and tired and dispirited. 1945 hadn't got off to a good start, she thought. Though it had been so wonderful on New Year's Eve. So . . . so . . .

'Theda? How's the bairn, I'm asking you?'

'Fine, Mam. Peter's fine. Well, not exactly; he has a fractured wrist, I think, and a nasty gash on his forearm. But he's gone to the hospital now. He'll probably spend the night at least on the ward.'

'I'm beginning to think that lad's accident-prone. By, he'll be one to watch. I wouldn't like the bringing up of him, I would not.' Bea shook her head. 'Go on, get to bed. I've put the oven shelf in so it'll be nice and warm.'

Chapter Twenty

It was like an early-spring day with the sunshine warming the inside of the car as Ken and Theda travelled over to Marsden. The wind outside was biting enough, but in the car it was a little cocoon of comfort with the worn leather seats fitting round them beautifully. Theda sat back in hers, enjoying the luxury of it.

'Not a bad old car, is it?' asked Ken.

She laughed. 'Any car is a good car for me after travelling on the buses, especially since the beginning of the war. Do you know what it's like on a utility bus, packed to the roof with people?'

'Yes, I do know, I've done it in my time. I'm lucky having the car, though, and being able to get the extra petrol because I'm a doctor, I admit is an advantage. But it is nice, isn't it? Am I supposed to be filled with guilt every time I use it for pleasure and not work?'

'No, of course not. I appreciate it anyway. And young Peter would have been in trouble if you hadn't had the car with you last week.'

'Hmm. Scamp that he is! He might have broken his neck. I thought he had learned his lesson after last time. Have you seen him since he came out?'

'Yes. He seems fine. I gather he comes in very handy as a casualty when the lads play war games. With his pot an' all.'

They were rolling down into the valley of the Browney, a small stream that ran into the Wear, and the countryside was laid out before them, hedges bare and dusty in the sunlight, fields brown and ploughed. Nothing was to be seen of the coming spring on the trees that clothed the riverbank and stretched away on the horizon but as they passed a small farm there was a gleam of early snowdrops along the front of a stone wall and the lime-washed farmhouse gleamed white.

Theda sighed. 'By, I love this road into Durham,' she said. 'I used to travel along it a lot when I was training in Newcastle.'

'I trained in Newcastle too,' said Ken. 'But after the war I would like to work in Sunderland. I'm a home bird really; it will be nice and handy for Marsden.'

It was the first time he had volunteered anything about his personal life, Theda reflected. She glanced at him. He looked relaxed and rested. Had he once been a dare-devil like Peter Patterson? She was filled with curiosity about him, wished she knew him better. She wanted to know everything about his childhood, about his ambitions. But at least he was taking her to meet his family.

'I would have thought there would be more scope for you at Newcastle,' she ventured. 'If you want to be a top surgeon, isn't it better to belong to a teaching hospital? It's not very far from Marsden after all.'

Ken frowned suddenly. 'No, I don't want to go back there.'

There was a silence in the car. Theda was left with the feeling that she had said something wrong, butted into something that was none of her business. But what?

'Why not?' she pressed him.

'I just don't, that's all.'

The sun went behind a cloud just then and the temperature in the car rapidly went down. She folded her arms across her chest and stared out of the window as they travelled through Durham and out on to the Sunderland road. A spatter of rain hit the windscreen and Ken switched on the wipers. She watched as the blade went from side to side with the water running down beneath, almost hypnotised by it. She shivered and rubbed her hands together.

'Cold?'

He reached into the back seat without taking his eyes from the road and handed her a rug which she wrapped round her knees. And the moment of coldness melted away as the rain stopped and he smiled down at her. 'Soon be there.'

The sun had come out again and the enclosed farmyard was quite warm as they stepped out of the car. Hens picked away between the cobbles and a black and white border collie barked furiously at them until it recognised Ken and wagged its tail.

'Hello, Sam.' Ken bent down and scratched the dog's ears as the back door opened and Walt stood there.

'It's you, is it?' he said. 'I might have known you would smell the tea.' He glanced curiously at Theda. 'Brought us a visitor, have you?'

'My brother Walter, Theda. Walter, Staff Nurse Theda Wearmouth.' It was the briefest of introductions as he ushered her into the low-beamed farmhouse kitchen. The family were sitting round about drinking their mid-morning cup of tea and Theda was suddenly conscious that her stomach was beginning to rumble in response to the smell of freshly baked scones and farm butter, something she hadn't smelled in a long time. She'd had no breakfast, she remembered – had been too keyed up to eat.

The room seemed full of people but she was used to that at home and after Ken's introductions soon sorted out grandmother and uncle and the frail-looking woman sitting by the fire as being Ken's mother. And she couldn't help noticing the way they all looked at each other significantly when she came in. It was Grandmother Meg who came forward with a welcoming smile and shook her hand and found her a seat before pouring her a cup of tea and putting a plate with a scone oozing butter into her hand.

'I'm pleased to meet you, pet. You come from Bishop, do you?'

'Winton Colliery.'

'Oh, yes. I don't remember any Wearmouths there, though?'

'Well, my family came from Wheatley Hill in the thirties. My father was out of work and got a job at Chilton. The only free house belonging to the owner was at Winton.'

Meg's face took on a sad faraway expression. 'Aye, I remember what it was like.'

'Grandma, stop quizzing the lass, let her have her tea.' Surprisingly, that was Walt. Theda looked at him. He was very like Ken except that his eyes were darker and his complexion ruddy as befitted a man who worked outdoors most of the time. He had a pleasant open expression and she warmed to him.

After the initial surprise, the family seemed to accept her presence quite naturally and she was able to sit back and enjoy her tea and scone as they asked how Tucker was and talked about the doings on the farm and the likelihood of the war ending soon. And then Jack and Walt were putting down their cups and going back out to work and Meg was clearing the table.

'I'll help,' Theda offered, and without any demur Meg agreed and took her out to the scullery, leaving Ken to talk with his mother.

Meg asked after the people she knew in Winton: asked if the Armstrongs still had the newspaper shops around the town, and mentioned how she liked the bands in the Bishop's Park on a Sunday afternoon. And Theda told her what was happening as far as she knew, which ones had got married, which families had lost their men in the war. They got on well, she thought, as though they had known each other for years. Meg reminded her of her own grandmother back in Wheatley Hill.

Afterwards Theda walked with Ken up the fields to the wood on the skyline to see the view: the land sloping away down to the sea, neat fields, well-tended by the look of them, and the tiny figures of Walt and his uncle carting hay to the sheep which gathered in a corner of the field, baa-ing and jumping over each other to get at the food.

'It's lovely, Ken,' Theda said. 'I don't know how you could bear to leave it.' It was, too; even the smoke stacks from the colliery by the sea looked a natural part of the scene, their smoke blending into the clouds.

'If we go now we'll just have time to walk along the cliff edge to the lighthouse – the rock formations are unique,' he said, and they ran down the path past the farmhouse and out on to the road. The pit yard and rows of miners' cottages were as grey and dreary as any other mining village but that was more than compensated for by the dramatic coastline with its steep cliffs and Marsden Rock standing against the breakers, connected to the land only by a natural bridge formation. Gulls wheeled about crying mournfully and in the distance a fleet of trawlers was making its way into the harbour at Shields.

Theda stood quietly watching and Ken put an arm around her shoulders. The primary school bell rang out and children began to march out of the nearby school yard in orderly rows which broke into yelling, racing gangs as they left authority behind.

'Time for tea and then we must be on our way back,' said Ken. He smiled down at her and kissed her lightly on the lips.

'"Oh, soldier, soldier, won't you marry me?"' girls' voices shrilled as they were surrounded by a pack of ten-year-olds, their faces alight with mischief. 'Is she your sweetheart, soldier? Go on, give her a proper kiss!'

Ken laughed and made as if to chase them and they scattered, shrieking with pretend alarm.

'It's been a lovely day. Thank you for bringing me,' Theda said. They walked back to the farm and ate the rabbit pie that Meg had made for high tea and then it was time to go.

'Come back whenever you like, Theda,' said Jane. Though she had sat quietly by the fire for most of the time Theda was there, she looked better than when they had first come; her cheeks had a tinge of pink and her eyes were bright as Ken bent down to kiss her cheek.

'Aye, you do that,' said Walt, who was busy putting on his boots yet again so as to go out and lock up the hens. 'At least you're friendlier than Julie.' A small silence greeted this remark and Theda glanced from one to the other. Ken was looking thunderous and it was Meg who jumped in, covering up, filling the moment with small talk.

'I've packed a dozen eggs for your mother, Theda, and a bit of butter. And don't forget to take Tucker his,' she admonished Ken.

They drove back as darkness was falling, made even thicker by the storm clouds that had gathered suddenly, spilling even more rain, which slanted across the windscreen, obscuring their vision. Ken was quiet, concentrating on his driving, and Theda was content to sit quietly too.

He dropped her on the end of West Row, making no suggestion that they go anywhere for the evening. And it was only as she watched him go away up the lane towards the manager's house that she remembered that he had said there was something they needed to discuss.

'Did you have a nice day, pet?' asked her mother as Theda put her parcels down on the kitchen table.

'Lovely.'

Bea looked at her curiously. Theda was disinclined to talk, she could tell, she knew that closed look she had on her face. No doubt she would hear all about it when her daughter was ready to tell her.

'I hope you thanked them properly for the eggs and butter,' was all she said now. 'By, it must be lovely to have a farm nowadays, eh?'

Clara came in like a whirlwind and bolted her food down, anxious to get washed and changed so that she could go and meet Dean in Darlington.

'I don't know, our Clara,' said Bea doubtfully, 'a young lass wandering all that way on her own . . . it means two buses an' all, and you're going to be pretty late.'

'Don't fuss, Mam,' was all Clara answered, and Theda covertly studied her. She was radiant with happiness for Dean had been grounded for the foreseeable future and their wedding plans were proceeding apace.

'You don't look very happy. What's up? I thought you had a date today?' Clara asked, but she wasn't really interested, too full of her own doings. Theda saw her mother frown fiercely and mouth, 'Alan!', and it was even more depressing that it had nothing to do with him; she hadn't even thought of him all day.

Theda soon made pressure of work an excuse for deciding to go back to the hospital that evening instead of the following morning. It was almost impossible to have any privacy in the tiny house in West Row and privacy was what she needed so she could think things out. She felt that events were running away with her, and that she had no control over them at all. The feelings she was developing for Ken were beginning to dictate all her actions and she still had enough common sense to know she couldn't allow that to go on.

Back in her narrow room in the nurses' home, she went early to bed and lay on her back, hands behind her head. Julie . . . she would give anything to know who Julie was, and what had happened to her. It was obvious by the way Ken had reacted that the girl had some sort of hold over him. In which case it was no good her going on fooling herself that she could make him love her. For that was what she had been doing, she realised that now. She loved him, that was the trouble.

And it wasn't only physical, though the attraction between them was so powerful. She wanted him, the very thought making her body ache for him. If he had suggested a place for them to go tonight she would have gone, though she had told herself all day she wouldn't. And she had been so critical of Clara! What a hypocrite she was! Turning over on to her side, Theda closed her eyes resolutely. She would get over this, oh, yes she would, she told herself for the thousandth time. She was her own woman, nobody else's.

'What do you think? There's a new registrar. We've got a civilian one now,' said Sister. It was the next morning and Theda and Sister Smith were taking the report from the night staff.

'A new registrar?' echoed Theda's voice, sounding stupid in her own ears.

'That's what I said.' Sister leaned back on the desk and folded her arms across her spotless apron. 'Major Collins has been recalled to Europe somewhere – I can't say where. It all happened in a tremendous rush. Our new man comes from Durham. Just until they get a military man from Catterick, I suppose.'

'But—' Theda began, and stopped. She bent her head over the report, feeling faint. Picking up the book, she pretended an intense interest in the fact that a new patient had arrived during the night, a suspected gastric ulcer: Wilhelm Foch, ex-submariner. No doubt his ulcer had been brought on by the dreadful diet the submariners had to put up with, according to the others they had nursed. Or the stress of being cooped up in a submarine . . .

''Bye, Sister. 'Bye, Staff.' The night nurse was going. Sister Smith was looking out the case notes ready for the rounds.

'I hate getting used to new doctors,' she said crossly. 'Don't you, Staff?'

'What? Oh, yes, Sister.' Had he left a letter for her? Of course he would have done. When she went on her break there would be one in her pigeon hole outside the main office. But why had he had to go so suddenly? Or had he known yesterday, was that what he had been going to tell her?

'It was very sudden, wasn't it, Sister?'

Sister Smith looked up from the notes and stared at Theda. 'What was?'

'Major Collins going,' she managed to get out.

'I don't know, I'm sure.' Sister shook her head impatiently. 'Oh, come on, get a move on, Staff. You'll have to get things organised or Mr Kent will be here to see the new man before we get the ward tidied up. And Major Koestler will be wanting to examine him.'

Somehow, Theda got through the morning, her training taking over so that she was able to put her mind to the jobs in hand. But when she had a few minutes to herself she hurried over to the cubby holes in Block One. There was no note from Ken. She couldn't believe it. She even put her hand in and touched the bare wood of the hole. Later, instead of going to the dining-room for lunch she went to her room and lay on the bed, staring at the ceiling.

The afternoon was little better. She told herself Ken must have let a message with someone but no one came up to her and gave her a note or a letter. Of course he could have posted a note to her . . . he probably had, she reckoned. There was nothing to do but wait for the postman to bring her word from him.

She couldn't go home that evening, had to work extra hours as the Staff Nurse on Block Two was again off work sick. Which was just as well, Theda told herself. She didn't think she could face the family without breaking down and howling her frustration at the world and the unfairness of it and the war and the way individuals were sent arbitrarily away at the whim of some nameless person, moving names around on a map. And without so much as twenty-four hours' notice.

It was only as she sat in the dining-room with a fork in her hand, pushing around the mashed potatoes and tinned beans covered in dark brown gravy and pretending to eat it whenever someone she knew came in, that a horrible suspicion rose in her mind. Perhaps he had known about it? Perhaps that was why he'd seemed so cold yesterday evening? He just didn't know how to tell her he was going away and didn't think that what they had together was worth carrying on.

Well, she thought, sometime during the night, to hell with him! She wasn't going to let a man like that get her down. So she had been a bloody fool, but she had learned something. It most definitely wouldn't happen again. Oh, no, it damn well would not. She didn't need a man and she definitely didn't need *that* man. Not her.

Deliberately she forced herself to think of her future. Tomorrow she would apply to go to Sunderland Infirmary to begin her midwifery training. The war was almost over, so she should be able to get a transfer. There was bound to be a baby boom when the soldiers came back and the Government would be well aware of that. They would need all the midwives they could train, not least because a lot of the older ones had stayed on past retirement age because of the war and would want to retire as soon as it was over.

Then, later on, she would train to go on the district; that was what she really wanted, had always been her ambition. That was the trouble with women, she told herself sternly. They were too easily distracted from their ambitions and lost sight of their goals in life. To hell with men, and especially doctors. Especially handsome doctors with cool grey eyes who took advantage of gullible nurses and then left them high and dry.

Theda turned on her side and wept. She wept for Alan and how she had betrayed his memory, and she wept for herself. Then she got out of bed and went to the bathroom and washed her face and neck in icy cold water, rubbing hard at the skin with a rough towel. Going back to bed, she burrowed under the clothes, shivering until the warmth from the blankets seeped through to her bones and then she felt calmer. It would be the last time she wept over a man, she thought.

'Bugger!' she said aloud into the silence but the word wasn't strong enough. She fell asleep as she was trying to think of a better one.

Chapter Twenty-One

'There's an urgent message for you, Ken,' said Tucker when he called in on the Saturday evening with his basket of eggs and butter from the farm. 'You are to ring the hospital, right away.'

Ken groaned. That was just what he needed: an emergency at the hospital. All he wanted to do was retire to his room and try to analyse his mixed-up feelings. The day hadn't gone at all as he had intended it to, at least the end of it hadn't. And it was his fault, he was well aware of that. Julie had been dead for two years now, and it really was past the time he should let her memory overshadow his life. And there was Theda now, his feelings for her were . . .

'Ken?'

'Yes, righto. I'll ring now, if I may?'

It took only a minute or two to get through to the porter on duty at the hospital.

'A telegram for you, sir, from the War Office,' the man informed him. 'It's marked urgent, sir. Shall I read it out? It's been here two hours.'

'Two hours? Then why didn't you try to contact me? I left word of where I was.'

'Yes, sir. But I thought you would be back tonight anyway, and it seemed a shame to spoil your leave.' Ken remembered the porter was an old soldier invalided out of the army only the year before. He probably had the fighting man's philosophy that if there was bad news that would wait until tomorrow, why let it spoil today? 'Shall I open it and read it out to you, sir?' he asked again helpfully.

'No, I'm coming in now.'

Ken's personal problems were forgotten when he got in to the hospital and opened the telegram. His orders were to proceed to Hull the following day, Sunday, and board a ship leaving at 8 p.m. for Le Havre, and from there onward to 'somewhere on the Rhine'. His precise destination would be communicated to him once he was on board.

Ken felt a surge of excitement. He had thought his part in the fighting had ended with his posting to look after prisoners-of-war and now he had a chance to go on to the end. He rubbed his hand over his injured leg. It was fit enough now – there was no reason why he shouldn't go back into service at a field hospital, tending his own countrymen.

'I'm going back to the front,' he informed the porter, a grin of anticipation lighting up his face so that the man was astonished. It was the last thing he himself would have been glad about. Still, it takes all sorts, the porter reflected. And that explains why the powers that be have brought in that new registrar, Doctor Strange, all of a sudden. A pity, because Major Collins was a good bloke.

'If that's what you want, sir, good luck to you,' he replied.

Ken went back to his rooms and packed his bags before making his way to the doctors' dining-room. It was deserted and he felt frustrated at having no one to talk to about his new orders. He ate his solitary dinner and retired to bed.

If he set out early enough he would be able to go back to Marsden and say goodbye to the family and take the train from there to Hull, then he could leave his car at the farm. He would write to Theda, he decided, as he wouldn't have time to call and see her in Winton and she wouldn't be back at the hospital until Monday. Still, she would understand. Anyone who had been through this war understood that orders were orders.

He wrote a note to put in her pigeon hole: 'Sorry, I have been ordered back overseas in a tremendous rush. I'll write to you. Love, Ken.' When he had a moment, perhaps on the boat, he would think things through before writing to her properly. But not now.

The following morning he was ready to be off by eight o'clock, the only difficulty being he had to wait until Dr Strange came at nine so as to hand over. Not that there was a lot to discuss, most of his patients were fairly straightforward, but courtesy demanded it. Well, he could say his farewells to Major Koestler and if he were very quick, he would have time to rush round the wards and do the same to the nursing staff.

It was all happening so quickly. He wondered why

there should have to be such a hurry as he started out for the prisoners' section. If only he had had time to talk to Theda. But he was worried about his mother, had to go over to the farm to reassure her he would be all right. It was very unlikely he would be going near the fighting. She was so frail now, that was another thing, he had hoped to have a talk with her doctor . . .

'Good morning, Major Collins.'

It was Major Koestler coming up behind him with a white-coated stranger who could only be the new registrar.

'It's lucky I've met you – I wanted to say goodbye. I have been ordered away,' said Ken, after acknowledging his replacement.

'I heard so,' Major Koestler said gravely. 'I am sorry to see you go. May I ask where it is you are going?'

'You may ask but I can't tell you,' Ken replied, smiling.

'No, of course not.' Major Koestler looked thoughtful. He stood aside as Ken had a few words with Dr Strange. They began to move towards the huts when Ken remembered the note for Theda.

'If you don't mind playing messenger boy for me, you could take this up to the staff pigeon holes and leave it in Staff Nurse Wearmouth's,' he said to the German. 'Dr Strange and I can go over the patients' notes and then I'll be away all the sooner. I've a long way to go.'

Dr Koestler nodded. 'Of course. Have a good journey.' He took the note and walked back to Block One. He was the only German on site who was allowed out of the prisoner-of-war enclosure and even he was supposed to have someone with him at all times. But the staff were used to seeing him about the place and no one questioned his lack of an escort.

Inside the swing doors of the main block, he walked past the notice board and pigeon holes and went into the lavatory, locking the door. Perhaps there was some clue as to Major Collins's destination in the note? One never knew what might be important. But there was nothing of importance in the note, which was disappointing. Tearing it up, he flushed it down the lavatory bowl. It had too obviously been tampered with for him to put it where it was meant to go.

As soon as she was off duty that Monday, Theda checked her box again, even though she knew it was too late. Ken was long gone, and he certainly couldn't have come back to leave a note for her. She was being irrational, she told herself, and had to forget about him. Going to her room, she got out her writing case and composed an application to Sunderland Royal Infirmary to be considered for the midwifery course. Then she changed into her everyday clothes and went out to catch the bus to Winton Colliery, posting the letter on the way.

It wouldn't be as easy as that, she was well aware, but at least she had taken the first step. If she was accepted it would be easier to go before the Board to ask for her release from the hospital.

She managed to find a seat on the bus, which was something to be thankful for. It was raining once again, streaking the dirty window as she stared dismally out at the blackness, relieved only by her own reflection and the dim glint on the raindrops running down the windowpane. The man sitting next to her got up and worked his way to the door and someone slipped into the vacant seat, but Theda didn't turn away from the window.

'You not speaking to me now, Theda Wearmouth?'

Theda looked round. It was Renee Coulson with Maurice, her toddler on her knee, his face pale and tired-looking and his thumb stuck firmly in his mouth as she stared at Theda with wide blue eyes. His mother grinned cheerfully at her.

'You were miles away there, all right. In love, are you? Come on, tell Auntie Renee all about it. I could do with a bit of amusement. It's bloody murder hanging about for buses in this weather – I wouldn't be surprised if Maury caught his death. Workers only, indeed! If this isn't bleeding work, hauling a kid about with you all the time, I don't know what is. I tell you, it's a break to get off to work after this. I'll have to rub his chest with Vick when I get him home or he'll keep me awake with his coughing all the bleeding night.'

Theda forced herself to smile. 'Sorry, I was thinking about—'

But Renee wasn't listening. She looked stricken for a moment. 'Gawd, my big mouth! I forgot about your Alan, dear. It's not so long since he went missing, is it? What a bleeding world, it is, isn't it?'

'That's all right,' Theda murmured, but Renee wasn't really listening. She was off on a monologue, the gist of which Theda couldn't catch so she just sat there, nodding or shaking her head according to what seemed most appropriate. She wondered what Renee would say if she knew the truth: that it was a new man occupying her thoughts, not Alan at all. She was a traitor to Alan's memory.

At the bus stop she helped Renee off the bus with her bags and Maurice. The child had gone to sleep and now he had been wakened as his mother pushed her way through to get off the bus and was tetchily crying and refusing to be put down to walk, clinging to Renee's shoulders with tiny iron fists.

'I'll carry the bags,' offered Theda, thus condemning herself to walking slowly by their side in the rain as Renee struggled up the bank to the colliery rows, hugging the boy to her and yet managing to talk all the time: about her mother-in-law, about her husband still overseas, about how she had nowhere to go now if she went back to London and no one to go to now her family were all gone. And wasn't it lovely that Clara was getting married on Saturday?

'Saturday?'

'That's right, didn't you know? You could have knocked me down with a feather when I heard. Isn't it lovely and romantic? Of course it isn't so nice that Clara will be going away. She's been a good friend to me—'

'Well, here we are, Renee. I'll give you a hand in with your bags. That young man looks like he'd be better off in bed.'

'Yes.' Renee broke off talking to look fondly at the blond head on her shoulder. 'I won't bother to bath him tonight; he can wait till tomorrow. Straight upstairs for him. His gran will wash him tomorrow while I'm at work.'

If she'd been asked to hazard a guess, Theda thought, she would have said the boy hadn't had a bath last night either as he smelled a bit stale. She followed Renee into the house and put the bags down on the kitchen table before saying goodnight and going back out to her own back door. She stood for a moment, hand on the sneck, composing herself. Then, fixing a smile on her face, she went in.

'What a rotten night it is,' she commented as she took off her sodden scarf and raincoat. 'What's for supper?'

'Eeh, I haven't had time to think about supper,' said Bea. She and Clara were sitting side by side on the settee, sewing at a length of material, which Theda recognised as parachute silk.

'See what Dean brought me, Theda,' cried Clara, her cheeks flushed and her eyes sparkling with excitement. 'He's got a special licence – we're going to be married on Saturday! We're making a wedding dress now.' She suddenly shrieked as she stabbed her finger with her needle, and thrust it in her mouth, sucking loudly.

'Aye,' Bea remarked drily. 'But it's me that's doing most of the sewing and Clara who's going to have a red-spotted dress if she's not careful.'

'Can you get Saturday afternoon off?' asked Clara anxiously. 'It's going to be in the chapel. We've asked the minister and he says it will be all right. Eeh, I hope you can come, our Theda.'

'We'll see,' she said, and picked up the kettle, taking it

into the pantry which held the only tap. 'How about having some of those eggs I brought yesterday?'

'Nay, lass. I did boiled eggs for your dad and Chuck, then I've had to use the rest of them for the wedding cake. Can you not smell it? It's just about ready to come out of the oven now. I got some real currants an' all. It's going to taste grand. There's a tin of beans, though. Why don't you have them?'

Theda sighed. 'No, I'm not hungry really. I'll just have a cup of tea.' She looked at the two heads bent over the sewing. They weren't really with her; she had never seen Clara being so industrious with a needle, she who hated to sew on a button. 'I think I'll just go up to bed, Mam,' she said.

'Righto, pet,' her mother answered absently. 'Have something at the hospital, did you? That's all right then. Did you have a bad day an' all? Tiring, I mean?'

'You could say that,' said Theda. 'Goodnight then.'

She trailed up to bed feeling very low indeed. She hadn't even wished her sister well, she realised as she crawled between the sheets. But Clara didn't appear to have noticed.

Chapter Twenty-Two

'I will expect you to work every weekend for the next few weeks, Staff Nurse,' said Matron. She stared disapprovingly at Theda over her glasses.

'Yes, Matron.'

'I don't deny that you will want to go to your sister's wedding, but after all you have had a lot of Saturdays free lately. More than your fair share. It's not fair to the rest of the staff.'

'No, Matron.'

'Well, go along then. No doubt you are needed back on the ward.'

'Yes, Matron.'

Having been dismissed, Theda walked back to Hut K, automatically checking her pigeon hole as she passed, feeling the familiar pang of disappointment when there was nothing in it. Fool that she was, she didn't know why she'd even looked. It was obvious she had just been a diversion for Ken for the brief time he was in Bishop Auckland. Julie was the girl he loved, whoever she was.

For herself, Theda was determined to put him out of her mind altogether.

The trouble was her mind vacillated all the time. She was determined not to think of him, not to let him affect her at all, and then a moment would come when she yearned to see him again, her body longing for the touch of his hands and the surge of feeling they could induce. What a weak-minded woman she was! Ruled by her senses. But, no, her feelings for Ken were more than that, surely. She shook her head as though that would clear it of such thoughts. There was work to do.

Dr Strange was in the ward with Major Koestler when she got there. Sister was off duty and only Nurse Elliot was with the doctors so Theda put on her cap and apron and went up to them.

'I'll take over, Nurse,' she said, and took the bundle of case notes from her colleague.

'*Morgen*, Staff Nurse.' Major Koestler beamed at her. 'How nice to see you. And looking so beautiful too.'

Dr Strange looked rather startled and gave them both a quick glance then coughed. 'Er – I would like to examine this patient, Staff,' he said.

As she arranged the screens around the bed, Theda frowned. She could do without any man showing he was interested in her, let alone a German. Wasn't the Major being a little too friendly? And in front of Dr Strange too. If he did it again she would have to choke him off and that would be a pain. Or perhaps she was reading too much into a friendly greeting? Goodness knows, German courtesy was different from English. But at least it wasn't as heavy-handed as the Italian way.

The ward round finished, and after a sojourn in Sister's office, the doctors went away. Theda took off her cuffs and rolled up her sleeves and worked alongside the other nurses, making beds, giving bedbaths to the patients who were confined to bed, doing the thousand and one mundane tasks that made up the ward routine.

At least she was free on Saturday, and could go to Clara's wedding. For a minute there when she had gone into Matron's office and asked for it, grovelled for it almost, she had thought she wasn't going to get it. Now all she had to do was find something to wear and buy a wedding present. She would forego her lunch and go into town and try to find something. If she concentrated on each little task as she was doing it, she got through the day quite well.

At five to two on Saturday afternoon, Theda went into the chapel with her mother, both of them only a little breathless after the mad rush to get the tables in the schoolroom set out with the spam sandwiches and ham and beetroot and fancy cakes they had had delivered from the Co-op bakery, and the three-tiered wedding cake, which Mrs Coulson had iced.

It was only a single wedding cake really, the top two were made of cleverly disguised cardboard and hired from the Coop, but you could only tell if you looked very closely. And there had been extra food points issued for the wedding, though nothing like enough to cover all the goodies, and Bea had had no compunction about flitting about begging things from family and friends.

'Mind, though I say it myself, it looks grand,' she announced after she'd insisted on popping in to the schoolroom to check it all over, even though the groom and his friends were already in the chapel and the car had gone to pick up Clara and her father.

Theda closed her eyes and tried to send up a prayer for Dean and Clara but somehow the Lord seemed particularly remote just then and she couldn't believe He actually heard her. Well, look at the mess the world was in – surely He had enough to think about?

She looked across the aisle to the bridegroom's side. It was a bit sparse but there were two rows of Air Force blue with bright shiny buttons gleaming almost as much as the brilliantined heads above, uncovered as they were in this hallowed place. All alike, she mused, all in a row like toy soldiers.

Then one turned and smiled at her and with a shock she realised it was the American she had nursed only a few weeks ago, one side of his face unnaturally smooth and shiny but not at all badly burned. She smiled back at him and he gave a tiny salute and then the minister was there and the organ was playing and the congregation was standing as Clara came down the aisle, looking amazingly beautiful in her creamy silk gown and her mother's wedding veil.

Amazing because only a couple of hours ago there had been hysterics in the front room of the house in West Row as one of the seams hastily sewn by the bride and her mother (most likely the bride) came apart and there had had to be some running repairs. Thank goodness the main seams had been sewn by machine before the last machine needle broke and put it out of action.

'We are gathered here today—' the minister began, and beside Theda, Bea shuffled up to allow room for Matt to come in to the pew after he had said 'I do' when asked who gave the bride away. The afternoon sun streamed through the plain side window of the chapel and lit up the couple standing so close together at the front, and for a moment Theda allowed her guard to drop and imagine what it might be like if it was herself standing there and a British Army officer's uniform the groom was wearing. A slightly shorter groom with a bit of a limp. A man with cool grey eyes, which would light up when he looked down at her and said the vows . . . The daydream was cut short as the congregation stood to sing Charles Wesley's hymn, 'Love Divine, All Loves Excelling'.

Afterwards there was the wedding tea in the Sunday Schoolroom with everyone bowing their heads as the minister said grace – and when they opened their eyes there was Joss.

'Tra la!' he cried, throwing his arms wide as though to embrace them all, and Bea jumped into them and he hugged her and swung her off her feet in the middle of the horse-shoe arrangement of tables and danced around with her which the minister didn't even seem to mind at all, even though no dancing was allowed on the chapel premises.

'How long do we have to put up with you this time?' asked Chuck.

'Now then, less of the impudence, young Charles,'

replied Joss, 'or I'll be having to put you on a charge. Anyroad, I have a whole week to mend your manners.' He turned to Theda, who had jumped up from her seat to crowd round him along with the rest of the Wearmouths. 'And how's my best girl?'

Love flooded through her as he smiled the well-remembered smile that crinkled up his eyes and tilted his head to one side. She glowed as she hugged him.

'Lucky man,' breathed the American, but no one heard him. Space was made at the top table for Joss and everyone ate what they wanted for a change. Even Renee's lad Maurice was allowed to eat two fairy cakes before he had any bread and butter. And it was real butter. No one in the street had eaten their butter ration that week; they had all saved it for the wedding.

They drank toasts to the bride and groom in blackberry cordial and ginger wine, though the Canadians brought out hip flasks of some sort of spirit. They were quickly persuaded to keep it until the evening celebration, however, and the minister pretended he had not seen it.

Everyone walked back to the house together, apart from the bridal couple who drove back in the airman's jeep, sitting so close together on the back seat they could have been Siamese twins. The walkers took the short cut through the fields, having to form a crocodile along the path that ran diagonally across what once was called the play field but now, when every spare piece of land was being used for growing crops, was just showing the green of young barley.

'No one would believe that not a drop of alcohol has

been drunk so far,' observed Eugene Ridley. Somehow, as the wedding party thinned into twos to go across the field, it was he who had ended up walking with Theda.

'That's true, an' all,' she said. The airmen were singing at the tops of their voices something quite indistinguishable, and the home crowd, led by Joss and Chuck, were doing their level best to drown them out.

'I wangled an invitation today. I wanted to see you again.'

'Did you, Pilot Officer Ridley? Why was that?' Theda's mood had lightened these last few hours as she'd tried to put her own problems behind her and enjoy her sister's wedding but now her spirits sank slightly.

'Call me Gene, everybody calls me that. I wanted to see if you were as attractive as I remembered you.' They were coming out of the field now and forming into groups and Violet and Renee and four Canadians were in a line across the road, dancing the palais glide to Violet's high-pitched rendering of the 'Lambeth Walk'.

Gene put an arm around her shoulders. 'Come and join in,' he said.

'Are you flirting with me?' asked Theda lightly, and laughed, trying to extricate herself without giving offence. 'No, come on, be a good boy. We want to get back before Clara and Dean go away, don't we?'

The newly-weds were going to stay in a hotel at Scotch Corner for two nights, before Clara had to go back to the munitions factory and Dean to his job on the base. And after that they would be separated until he managed to get them a place in Middleton St George.

'OK,' agreed Gene, but he looked sideways at her, his eyes questioning. He put a hand to his neck and pulled his scarf up around the worst of his scarring and Theda realised he thought she might be put off by it. So she smiled radiantly at him and he took hold of her hand and grinned back, reassured.

The house was heaving with people, the big kitchen overflowing into the yard and the front room into the garden. Matt and Chuck had borrowed a piano from the Hugheses up the row and manhandled it into the front room and someone was already playing boogie-woogie on it.

'Would you like a drink?' Theda asked Gene. The blackberry cordial was out, this time topped up by rum, which Chuck had brought in from the club. Gene looked doubtfully at it. 'A cup of coffee would be nice,' he said.

'Well, there's only Camp,' said Theda, wondering what he would make of the chicory-flavoured stuff, which was all Bea had been able to get at the Co-op. And he reached into his overcoat pocket and pulled out a packet wrapped in brown paper.

'I forgot. I brought this as my contribution,' he said.

They were all drinking coffee, flavoured rather peculiarly with goat's milk because Bea insisted on keeping the cow's milk for the tea, when Dean and Clara came downstairs ready to go and Bea started to cry.

'Don't mind me,' she sobbed, and flung her arms around Clara.

'Oh, Mam! You'll crease me dress. Behave! I'm not going to Canada for a while yet. I'll be back to plague you next week.' And Bea laughed and everyone gathered for the big send-off in the jeep, which was tied up with ribbon and had strings of old pit boots and tin cans tied on the back.

It was quiet for a short while after they went. Everything seeming a bit flat. Then Nora came across to Theda, exhibiting a look of horrified disgust.

'There's an airman in the netty vomiting his head off,' she said. 'You're the nurse – you see to him.'

Theda groaned and got to her feet. 'I'll give you a hand,' said Gene, rather unexpectedly. 'Scam never could hold his liquor.'

'Aye, well,' Matt commented. 'I suppose goat's milk and coffee and rum and blackberry cordial don't mix over well.'

The smell was overpowering in the ash closet at the end of the yard. Theda and Gene got Scam, the young rear gunner, out of there and into the fresh air. Too many people were using the outhouse, that was the trouble, thought Theda as they leaned him up against the wall and waited while his face took on a more normal hue. The ashes weren't enough to quell the smell.

Joss came out and leaned against the wall, offering cigarettes to the other two men and lighting a match, cupping it in his hands against the wind while they lit up. Superstitiously, he threw the match down and lit another for himself. Theda excused herself and went in to help her mother wash up the coffee cups and glasses.

'It went well, I think, pet,' Bea said complacently, and Theda agreed. It had gone well from her point of view too, she thought. There had been no time to mope.

'I suppose we should be on our way – leave you good people to yourselves.' Scam popped his head round the door. He looked a different man now: tall and gangly and healthy and clean-cut, though incredibly young. Surely he should be playing with a toy gun in his parents' back yard rather than flying over Germany in the tail end of a plane, firing at enemy aircraft which tried to stop them dropping their bombs?

Matt was behind him. 'Nay, lad. The club will be open in half an hour – we'll all go there. It's a free and easy night tonight. We can take the women an' all.'

Bea demurred only as a matter of form and shortly they were all on their way back to Winton Village, going past the chapel to the Working Mens' Club where there was no trouble signing in the Canadians at all. There were plenty of members prepared to swear they were their guests.

'Friendly folks in your little town, ma'am,' said Gene, taking Theda's arm and leading her to a set after the secretary insisted on buying their drinks.

'They've all heard about what Pilot Officer McMullen did,' said Theda.

'Oh, yes.' Gene's grin slipped for a moment and he looked thoughtful. Theda knew he was thinking about his dead colleague. Pilot Officer McMullen had brought his damaged plane home from a mission over Germany on 13 January, then found he was not going to make it to the airfield. They were over Darlington and in imminent danger of coming down on the crowded terraced housing. And so he got his crew to bale out, lightening the load so that he could take the plane away from the town before it fell from the sky. And then he had been killed as it crashed in the open country beyond.

'Something like you did when you came down on the Grammar School cricket field,' said Theda.

'No, nothing like it at all. We weren't going to crash on the houses. I just didn't know where we were.'

'Well,' said Theda, and smiled at him, 'come on, let's have a good time for a change. Forget the war for once.'

The evening flew, the concert room getting hotter and hotter and the crowd getting noisier. 'A bit of order, please!' called the steward, as one after another got up to entertain the company. Joss sang 'Just A-Wearyin' for You', reducing half the women to tears, and Matt sang 'The New Jerusalem', and everyone joined in songs from the present war and then songs from the Great War. No doubt some of them could go back to the Boer War but then it was time for Theda to go back to the hospital.

'I'll take you,' said Gene, who had his own car with him.

'You be careful, our Theda,' said Joss. 'You can't trust these Yanks. You know what they say: overpaid, overfed, oversexed—'

'An' you watch your language, our Joss,' said Bea, trying to look severe.

'—and over here,' he finished, unperturbed, and grinned amiably at Gene to show he meant no offence really.

'I can catch a bus just outside,' said Theda.

'No, I insist, I'll take you,' said Gene. 'I'm not drunk, honest.' And neither he was, Theda knew. He had only had a couple of beers all day.

They said their goodbyes and went outside to a chorus of catcalls and knowing looks from the company. 'Go to it, Gene!' the airmen called, and were still whistling as the door banged closed after them.

There had been a snowfall while they were inside the club and the street was deserted and dark. Gene's car was still parked outside the chapel and they walked up the street to it, the snow becoming thicker and faster even as they went. He held his greatcoat over her, shielding her from the worst of the storm, his arm around her holding her close against him.

A man passed holding an umbrella coated with snow. 'Good evening,' he said. 'Nasty night, isn't it?' Then he stopped and stared at her. 'Miss Wearmouth, isn't it?' he asked, and she saw it was the mine manager, Tucker Cornish.

'Good evening, Mr Cornish,' she murmured, keeping her head down, her heart dropping. The events of the day had kept her brooding thoughts of Ken away but seeing his uncle brought them back and it was like a blow. She was aware that he was standing watching as Gene opened the door for her and she got in.

Gene had to clean the snow from the windscreen before they could go and when the engine started it shattered the deep, muffling silence. But the snow soon stopped and by the time they got to the hospital what was on the ground had turned to slush and the roads were becoming bare.

'At least you'll be able to get back to base,' said Theda as she turned to thank Gene for the lift. All she wanted to do was get back to her own room, and to be by herself.

'Yes,' he replied, not very interested because he was leaning towards her and, taking her by surprise, kissing her on the lips.

'Please don't,' she said, her hand on the door handle.

'Too soon? OK, I can wait. I'll see you again?'

'I . . . I don't know.' Theda was miserably conscious that all day she had allowed him to think his attentions were welcome. 'I have to go now, or I'll be in trouble.'

He got out and opened the car door for her. 'I'll call you.'

'Yes,' she said. 'Goodnight. Thank you for the ride.' And she hurried away, not looking back until she got to the main door. Gene was still standing there, by the open car door. When he saw she was looking he waved and swung the door to and climbed back in at his own side. She watched as he did a three-point turn and headed back up the road.

Chapter Twenty-Three

'I don't know what's the matter with our Theda,' Bea confided to Matt. 'She's living in a world of her own these days.'

He looked up from his perusal of the *Daily Herald*. 'Aye, she looks a bit pale. I thought she'd got over Alan when she started going out with that doctor. But it's hard for the young ones nowadays, the men going off an' all. It's my belief she's working too hard. Same as most of us till this war's finished and done with.' Matt yawned and scratched his head and stretched his bare feet along the fender towards the blazing fire. 'I'm tired to death meself. By, that extra half hour on the end of a shift feels like half a day'

'Best get up to bed then,' said Bea. 'Let me get on with the baking. I don't get much help these days. When Theda does come home she spends half her time in the bedroom. I've seen the day she would come home and pitch in with the work almost before she's got her coat off.'

Matt stood up and curled his toes into the proddy mat.

He knocked the glowing end of his cigarette into the fire and carefully put the stub behind his ear. 'I'm off then. Don't forget, I want to be up early, I'm going to the match. The Bishops are playing Crook today.' He glanced out of the window at the empty yard before taking hold of her and nuzzling his face into her neck. 'I don't suppose you want to come up wi' me for a minute or two?'

'Oh, hadaway with you! It's all you men think about, it is an' all.'

'All what men? Who else has been in here making suggestions, eh? Best come clean, woman!'

'Who else would have me?' she asked, and watched as he went to the bottom of the stairs and turned and winked at her. She snorted and turned to the earthenware bowl by the side of the hearth. She picked up the tea towel covering it and prodded the dough with a fork. It could wait a while, it wasn't proved yet.

It was quiet with all the family out of the house. Chuck would be in off the back shift but soon he would be married and away an' all. Bea moved to the door and turned the key in the lock, then padded upstairs after Matt.

But still, she told herself as she took off her clothes and climbed into bed beside her husband, she would have a talk with Theda the very next time she came home. She would do her level best to get to the bottom of what was troubling the lass.

In the bathroom of the nurses' home, Theda leaned over the lavatory basin, retching. This was the third time this week, she thought. Standing up straight, she wiped her mouth with toilet paper and went over to the wash basin. She filled it with cold water and splashed her face and forearms, though she was already shivering in the glacial bathroom.

What was she going to do? There was no word from Ken, none at all. Perhaps she could go and see Mr Cornish? He would know where Ken was, wouldn't he? She shrank from going, though, the very thought humiliating. There was a knock at the door.

'You going to be in there all morning? Some of us are due on the ward, you know.'

'Sorry, I'm coming now.' Theda picked up her wash-bag and unlocked the bathroom door. She darted past the couple of nurses waiting with her head down and went into her room, closing the door behind her. She leaned against it for a moment. How could she even have thought of making a critical judgement on Clara? At least her sister had been going out with her Canadian for a few weeks, her child conceived in love.

My child is a love child, thought Theda. Trouble was, the love was all on my side. She smiled grimly and pushed herself away from the door, weariness in her every movement, and began to dress for her day on the ward. What she really wanted to do was go home and hide in her own bed, the bed that was hers alone now that Clara had got married. But she daren't do that. Bea would know straight away what was the matter in that bathroomless house.

Major Koestler was on the ramp just outside the prisoner-of-war section. Whether he had just come out of a ward or was waiting around for her, which was what

Theda suspected, she didn't want to see him. She couldn't deal with him at the moment.

'*Morgen*, Staff Nurse,' he said, clicking his heels and tipping his head forward in that foreign way he had. 'May I walk with you to Hut K?'

Theda was in no mood to be diplomatic. 'No, I think not, Major Koestler,' she said, walking straight past him, but he fell into step with her anyway.

'Your name is Theda, I think? A pretty name, though I haven't heard it before,' he said, and she stopped abruptly and turned to face him.

'Please, Major Koestler, stop following me about. If you don't, I will have to report you to the authorities.'

She was sorry she had been so sharp as soon as she saw his shocked expression but it was too late to take it back.

'I simply wished to ask you if you had heard from Major Collins.' He turned on his heel and walked rapidly away, disappearing into the next hut. His pride was hurt, she realised, but the realisation was overlaid by the pain his mention of Ken had brought to her. She carried on down the ramp, feeling more miserable than ever.

In her break, Theda made her usual fruitless journey over to Block One to check her pigeon hole for any post, most especially a letter from Ken. Still in the back of her mind was the thought that there must have been a mistake. Surely he would write to her. Was it possible for him to be in a situation where he couldn't get in touch? But the war was going well, it would be over soon, please God, and Ken was a doctor, for goodness' sake. He wouldn't be in the front line, now would he?

There was a letter in the cubby hole, a long brown envelope, and her heart flipped and began racing until she could hardly see the typed name and address. Typed. Why would Ken type a letter to her? She stared at it but the envelope gave nothing away and as her eyesight returned to normal she turned it over and tore it open.

It was from Sunderland Royal Infirmary. The disappointment was like a physical pain. It offered her a place on a course, Part One in Midwifery, beginning in March. Theda stared at it. It was useless, she couldn't go now. She stuffed the letter and envelope into the pocket of her uniform dress and walked out of the building and across the open space to the hutted section.

Somehow she had to get through the day. It stretched ahead of her, never ending, and would be followed by another and another just the same. And now there was not even any hope of getting away for how could she take her midwifery now?

Theda went back to Winton Colliery that afternoon. She was working a split shift and expected back on the ward by half-past four but she had foregone her lunch and it was only fifteen minutes past one. She had plenty of time. Not that she intended going home, not unless she was seen by someone who would tell her mother she was there. No, she was going to the gaffer's house to see Tucker Cornish. She had to find out if he had Ken's address.

It was a quarter to two when she descended from the bus, still the dinner hour. If she hurried she might find Mr Cornish at home. She paused at the gate, almost changing her mind, then walked up to the door and knocked, her heart thumping. Mrs Parkin answered the door.

'You're lucky to catch him – he's finished his dinner and will be going back in a minute. He hasn't got much time, mind. Is it important?'

'I won't keep him long,' Theda assured the housekeeper. She said no more though Mrs Parkin looked enquiringly.

'Well, then, I'll just tell him you're here,' she said finally.

Tucker was in his sitting-room, smoking his pipe before the fire. He rose to his feet as Theda went in, smiling coldly enough to make her rush into her explanation of why she was here, almost before they had exchanged polite greetings.

'Do sit down, Miss Wearmouth,' he said, cutting into her explanation, and she sat awkwardly on the edge of a chair. 'Now, what is it you want?'

'I wondered, Mr Cornish, if you could let me have Major Collins's address?'

Tucker looked at her consideringly. He took some time before answering by relighting his pipe. 'My nephew? Has he not written to you?'

Theda flushed. 'No.'

'Well then, Miss Wearmouth, I think perhaps you should wait until he does, don't you? In any case, I don't have his address. He could be anywhere in Europe.'

Theda got to her feet. Her flush had receded and she held her head high as she replied.

'It doesn't matter, it wasn't important. Look, I have to

go, I have to be back at the hospital . . .' She turned for the door and Tucker moved to open it for her but was too late.

'Goodbye then, Miss Wearmouth,' he said. He watched her going down the drive, unsure now that he had done the right thing. She wasn't the sort to chase after a man who didn't want her. Was she in trouble? There had certainly been an air of desperation about her.

He remembered the day he had come back from Marsden early in January.

'Major Collins must have brought a friend here over the holidays,' Mrs Parkin had said. 'A lady friend.' She was cleaning the sitting room and held up a green chiffon scarf she had found behind the sofa.

'Major Collins knows he is welcome to bring any of his friends here,' Tucker had said. And then there was the time Ken had taken Theda Wearmouth over to Marsden. Tucker's mother had been delighted that her grandson was showing an interest in girls again after Julie's tragic death. Perhaps he would write to Ken via Jane and ask him if he wanted Theda to know where he was? That was the best idea.

Still, he remembered the night he had seen the girl come out of the Working Mens' Club with a Canadian airman. The man had had his arm around her, and they were laughing together. And though he never took notice of the tittle-tattle in the village, he knew tales were going around about her sister's marriage to another Canadian – a flighty sort of girl, that one, according to village opinion.

Tucker had a horror of flighty women. The very thought was enough to make him shy away. There was the woman his father had run off with, or rather had gone to live with in Winton Village, leaving his mother with two small boys. The shame of it had ruined his childhood, leaving deep indelible scars. Wesley Cornish and his fancy woman had been the talk of the place. Ken wanted nothing to do with anything like that. The dirt would only rub off on the lad. Pulling on his overcoat, Tucker called goodbye to Mrs Parkin and went back to the pit.

Later in the afternoon, he sat in the manager's office at Winton Colliery. He was alone in the building though the activity in the engine house continued, the winding wheel buzzing and clanking as the steel ropes sent the cage back down to Busty number two seam to bring up the last of the back shift men.

Idly he thought about finishing up and going home. Mrs Parkin would have left him a meal in the oven. It was warm in the office, though. A coal fire had burned in the grate all day and the heat had built up even though the fire was beginning to die now. It was only a short walk to the house but rain spattered on the windows of the office and the wind swept up the pit yard, howling round the corners and even lifting the coal dust. The prospect of going outside was not very inviting.

It would have been different if Betty were there, waiting for him, the kettle humming on the hob ready so that she could mash a pot of tea for him as soon as she heard him open the front door. Or if he had been expecting Ken to come and eat a meal with him; he had enjoyed those times. But Ken was in Europe, probably over the Rhine by now, working in some field hospital. He would write to him tonight, get his address from Jane.

Maybe he had been too harsh with that girl, Theda Wearmouth. A good-looking girl she was, with her dark hair and eyes and that proud lift to her chin. Yet there was the night he had seen her outside the club with that Canadian and only a few weeks after Ken had gone . . . she couldn't have been serious about his nephew.

Perhaps he would drop Ken a line, telling him Theda had been to see him. And maybe he would mention too he had seen her on the day of her sister's wedding, and what a good time she seemed to be having.

Theda walked back to the hospital along the path through the fields, glad when she reached the cover of the wood. She walked blindly. Knowing the path she could find her way almost automatically, and it was just as well. She felt humiliated, dirty – used almost. No, that was silly. She had been a willing partner, an eager partner. What had happened to her was her own fault. It wasn't even unique: it happened to hundreds, thousands of girls. It was humdrum, banal.

The path was wet and muddy but she stumbled on, the mud coming over her shoes in one place and seeping through her stockings, clinging and icy cold. Her fingers were dead white with the cold, she had come out without her gloves. Gradually the cold seeped into her mind and she paused, realising with a last vestige of common sense that she had to get inside, somewhere warm.

She climbed the stile at the end of the wood and entered the cemetery, threading her way between the graves to cut off a corner and ending up in South Church Road, on the outskirts of the town. She paused. It was only three-fifteen, too early to go back to the hospital. In any case, she couldn't bear to see anyone she knew, not yet. Making up her mind, she turned down the road and headed for Rossi's coffee shop. It was warm in there, and what's more she could hide in one of the booths at the back.

The coffee shop was empty at this time of day. She bought a cup of Bovril and took it into a booth. She crumbled the free cracker into the drink and sipped the hot liquid, burning her tongue. But she could feel the warmth in the shop, and held her fingers round the hot cup, and slowly she began to thaw.

What right had Tucker Cornish to speak to her like that? she thought suddenly, her self-esteem rising with her body temperature. If Da had heard him he would have had something to say all right, even if he lost his job over it. Why the hell should she let what he said humiliate her? He didn't know her, and anyroad, who the hell was he? A Cornish, that's who he was, one of the family that had been the scandal of the place. Why, wasn't it his own father who had murdered the agent years ago?

Theda sat up straight and rooted in her bag for her compact, staring at her reflection in the mirror. Her hair was a mess, but otherwise she didn't look too bad. The cold had put colour into her cheeks and her eyes were beginning to sparkle with indignation. Taking out her comb, she pulled it through her tangled hair, taking it back from her face and pinning it with a clip over one ear. She found her lipstick and touched up her lips. Lipstick was frowned on at the hospital but just now she couldn't care less about that.

Finishing off her Bovril, Theda fastened her scarf under her chin and, picking up her handbag, slung it on her shoulder and marched out of the coffee shop and up Newgate Street to the hospital. Running a hot bath, she stripped off her clothes and lay in the hot water and made her plans. She would get through this on her own. Oh, yes she would. She didn't need a man. And it wasn't just bravado – she was capable of looking after herself.

Chapter Twenty-Four

So much for fine talk and resolutions! Theda told herself as she made her way wearily down to the dining-room a few days later. She still had no idea how she was going to manage on her own, none at all. Laura Jenkins was at her usual table and waved as Theda came through the door.

'Where have you been lately?' she asked when Theda had hung up her cloak on one of the pegs that ran along the wall and gone up to the hatch to fetch her tray of food. 'I was beginning to think you'd given up eating altogether. Either that or you were off sick, but Sister Smith said you were working all right. If you hadn't turned up today, I was going to come looking for you.'

'I just haven't felt like eating much lately,' said Theda. 'Stomach trouble. I've been living on Magnesium Trisilicate.'

'You look as though you have an' all,' said Laura, frowning in disapproval. 'You've certainly lost a lot of weight. I don't know, why didn't you go off sick?

267

Anyone else would have done. No sense in killing yourself, you know. Mag Tri is all right for a while but you can overdo it.'

'Well, I'm all right now.' Theda looked down at the grey minced beef on her plate, the plain boiled potatoes and watery cabbage. Picking up her knife and fork she attacked the food, unappetising as it was. Laura was right, of course, she had to eat. Her uniform dress was hanging from her as if on a coat hanger.

Laura put down her own knife and fork and gazed at her with concern. 'You don't look too clever even yet, it must have taken it out of you,' she observed. 'What time do you finish?'

'Six. I'll probably go straight to bed and try to sleep it off.'

'It'll do you more good to get out, forget about it for a while. Look, I'm going to the pictures in Darlington tonight, the Regal. We could go through on the train and get the last one back. At least we'll be getting out of the place for a while. What do you say?'

'What's on?'

'*Random Harvest*. Oh, I know it's been on before – but, ooh, I love Ronald Colman, don't you? And Greer Garson's all right, when she isn't being all noble and self-sacrificing and keeping the home front together against all odds. What do you say?'

Theda made her mind up all at once. She and Laura had gone from one cinema to another once upon a time just to see Ronald Colman. Her friend would definitely think there was something seriously wrong if she refused to go when she had the night off and nothing else arranged.

'It's a date,' she said.

Getting ready to catch the train she almost cried off. She felt so tired and slightly dizzy and her breasts ached. But in the end she brushed her hair and put on the brightest lipstick she had and she and Laura ran down to the station just in time to catch the train.

'We must be mad, going all the way to Darlington when there are three perfectly good picture houses in Auckland,' she said as they stood in a crowded compartment, swaying as it click-clacked over the tracks. Shildon tunnel loomed and abruptly they were swathed in darkness and someone must have left a window open for sooty smoke swirled down the corridor.

'Yes. But Ronald Colman's on at Darlington,' Laura pointed out as they came out of the Shildon end of the tunnel and the gloom lightened.

There was quite a walk from North Road station to Bondgate and by the time they got to the cinema, the lights were already down and Gaumont British News well under-way. They were shushed as they followed the torch of the usherette and groped their way to their seats. The audience's attention was on the screen where grubby-faced tommies were marching up a road in Germany, their guns at the ready and ruins all around them.

Theda closed her eyes. It was warm and muggy in the stalls, the only place where there had been empty seats, and to watch the screen she had to tilt back her head. But when *Random Harvest* came on she was feeling better and lost herself in the improbable story of the man who lost his memory and forgot he was an aristocrat, and the wife who pretended to be his nurse.

'By, it was grand, wasn't it?' sighed Laura as they stood for the National Anthem and then joined the crush for the exit.

'Theda? Theda Wearmouth?'

Both girls turned at the sound of the American voice. They were just entering the foyer and its brighter lights and Theda saw it was Gene Ridley and a friend.

'Gene, how nice to see you!' she cried. 'What on earth are you doing here? I would have thought the cowboy film down North Road would be more in your line.'

'Not me. I'm a sucker for films about the British stiff upper lip. Besides, I'm trying to learn a thing or two from Ronald Colman. There must be some tips on making women fall for you I can pick up from him.'

Theda laughed and introduced Laura to him and he introduced his friend. 'Scam – you'll probably remember him from Dean's wedding?'

'Oh, yes, of course I do,' said Theda, and smiled as she saw the look of embarrassment crossing the gangly young man's pleasant features.

'Don't remind me, ma'am,' he said. 'I truly thought I was going to die.' He turned his attention to Laura and fell into step beside her as Gene and Theda led the way out into the dark street. Gene hesitated, loath to let them go.

'Look, why don't we have a drink together? There's a pub just along here. It's pretty good too,' he suggested. 'Now we've just met up again, we can catch up on all the gossip.' He stopped walking and they formed a small group on the edge of the pavement. The crowds following them out of the cinema swirled round them as they stood close together though it was so dark they were simply black looming shapes to one another.

Gene was smiling eagerly at her and Theda couldn't help responding to his obvious interest after these last few weeks of feeling so rejected and unloved. She was tempted but Laura put in the voice of reason.

'We can't, we have to be back at the hospital. We're catching the last train as it happens and if we don't get a move on we'll miss it and then the fat will be in the fire.'

'AWOL, eh?' Scam said. 'We can't let that happen, can we, Gene? How about we give you a lift?'

'Oh, no, there's no need—' Theda began, but she was overruled and outnumbered and the four of them walked down the road to where Gene's old car was parked.

The car, a Humber, ate up the eleven miles from Darlington to Bishop Auckland and they laughed and sang the songs from *Rose Marie* with Scam doing the Mountie's song in a surprisingly melodious baritone in imitation of Nelson Eddy and the girls joining in with the 'Indian Love Call', which ended in a fit of the giggles as Gene joined in too in a squeaky falsetto.

'Don't go right up to the gates. We can walk from here,' said Laura as they drove along Cockton Hill.

'You ashamed of us, ma'am? We not respectable enough for you?' asked Scam, but he was joking really and Gene pulled up at the kerbside and they handed the girls out in the courteous way of the New World.

'Will I see you again?' Gene asked Theda. 'I've thought of you a lot. I was going to come looking for you. We can have some good times together, can't we?'

'Oh, no, I don't think so,' she said. Scam and Laura had walked a little way down the road and were out of earshot.

'Why not? You like me, don't you? I know you do, I feel it, and I like you a lot, you know I do. What's the harm? You don't have a boyfriend away at the front, do you?'

Theda was silent for a moment. He had made her think of Ken. With a brief stab of pain, she shook her head. 'No, I don't have a boyfriend,' she said. Not a boyfriend, no, she thought, just a man who didn't want her any more. But she couldn't say that to Gene.

'Well, then, why not?'

Theda hesitated. Why not indeed? Gene's attentions were like balm to her battered self-esteem.

'Theda? Are you coming?' Laura called softly from up the road, and in the muted beam of a car headlight, newly liberated from its blue masking paper, she saw that Scam was walking back to the car.

'All right,' she said rapidly. 'When are you free? I won't be until next Sunday afternoon.'

'It's a date,' said Gene, satisfied. 'I'll pick you up at the gate.' Scam was getting into the car now, studiously avoiding looking at them.

'No, here, in that cafe,' she said rapidly, starting to move away and at the same time indicating a small tea-shop on the other side of the road. She had almost said Rossi's but changed her mind at the last minute; Rossi's held too many painful memories for her just now.

Getting ready for bed later, she wondered why she had agreed to meet Gene. She could say there was no harm in it – after all, she and Gene could just be friends, and goodness knows she needed a friend just now. But in her heart she knew that he wanted to be more than a friend. She put out the light and jumped into bed and lay quietly in the dark, trying to sort out her feelings.

Gene was a nice man, of course he was, and there was a great temptation to lean on him, the knowledge that he was there and interested in her was comforting. What a drip she was, she thought, so determined one minute to rely on herself alone and yet now she was hoping for a manly shoulder to cry on. Poor man! He would run a mile if he knew the truth about her, she was sure. Theda turned over on to her side and closed her eyes, trying to sleep. There was no point in thinking about it.

'You were very friendly with that Yank, weren't you? Or should I say he was very friendly towards you?'

Theda glanced up from her mid-morning coffee to see Laura approaching her table, cup in hand. She shrugged. 'Not really. Well, I know him, I told you. He's a friend of Clara's husband. And, besides, you must remember – it was he who crashed his plane on the Grammar School field.'

'I never actually saw him at the time, though I heard all about it. It was nice of him to bring us home. He has an eye for you, I could see, though. You want to get yourself out with him, have a good time. It'll do you good.'

'I'm meeting him at the weekend,' Theda admitted.

'There you are then. It's time you went out with a man again. Go and enjoy yourself.'

'You don't follow your own advice.'

'No. I'm too old for men, I've given them up. Too set in my ways now.'

Laura finished her coffee and stood up. 'Must get on, there's a lot to do this morning.'

Theda watched her go, feeling depressed. If only things were as simple as Laura thought.

Gene was waiting for her in the teashop on Sunday afternoon and they went for a drive up the dale, Theda feeling guilty about wasting the petrol on such a frivolous outing.

'Nonsense,' he said firmly. 'You should learn to relax and enjoy yourselves, you British.'

The sun shone on an empty road as they drove on. Wolsingham in Weardale was closed and shuttered, the only signs of life in the chapel and church where children were coming out of Sunday School, looking unnaturally clean and tidy. As they climbed higher up the dale to Frosterley and then Stanhope, the tensions in Theda eased and for once she didn't feel the slightest bit queasy. They crossed over the ford at Stanhope and went up on to Bolihope Common where Gene parked the Humber by the side of the road, right on the summit.

'This place reminds me of home,' he said, staring out over the expanse of the moor, the miles of heather just coming into leaf, the white patches where snow still lay from the winter. His eyes had a faraway look as he sat back in his seat and opened the window so that the sharp moorland air came into the car. 'I can breathe here.'

The hardy black-faced sheep came right up to the car, searching for new blades of grass peeping through the gravel. There were a few tiny lambs beside them, bleating in terror when their mothers got too far away and running and jumping after them. Theda watched them, their coats so white and new compared with the bedraggled winter coats of the ewes.

'A sign of spring,' she said softly. They made her think of the baby she was carrying herself and she stirred uncomfortably. She didn't want to think of it, not now. Now as the time for make-believe, the time to pretend that she was just a girl out with a bloke on a first date – and perhaps more would come of it, who knew?

'Come on, let's take a walk,' she said, and opened the car door and jumped out. She pulled up the collar of her coat as the keen wind hit her, cutting through her clothes. She had forgotten how cold it could be on the moors.

Gene took her hand and they set off at a good enough pace to make the sheep, and especially the lambs, skip out of the way, up the track along by the snow poles. After a while they stopped by a low wall which was really part of a bridge over a burn. Out of breath, they leaned on the wall and looked down on the clear water tinkling away beneath.

'Cold?' asked Gene.

'I forgot my gloves.'

He drew her hands to him, wrapping them in his, and blew on them gently. 'The wind has blown colour into your cheeks. You look lovely, Theda,' he said.

She lowered her eyes and stared at their hands. His were so warm and capable; his shoulders broad in the Air Force blue uniform. He would make a good father, she thought. A grand man.

He put an arm round her shoulders and they walked on up the close-cropped verge and along a sheep track, which meandered round clumps of old bracken and heather. A curlew, disturbed in its nest-building, took to the air and skimmed low over the ground, calling its shrill, plaintive cry, which sounded almost human. Storm clouds gathered on the rim of the moor, threatening a spring shower. Theda shivered.

'Come on, we'd better get back to the car,' Gene said, and they rushed down the road and climbed in, just beating the first drops of rain.

'English weather,' he commented when he got his breath back, then leaned across to her and tilted her face up to his and kissed her on the lips. Theda sat there and just let him. She felt as though it was all unreal, nothing to do with her.

They drove down into Middleton in Teesdale and on up the road through Forest. The rain was lashing down now but it was warm and cosy in the car. At High Force they parked by the hotel and went in to the empty bar, and by some miracle Gene had a word with the barman and brought two brandies back to the table close to the fire where Theda sat.

They sat together and sipped the spirit and let the heat from the fire seep into their chilled bones. Gene held her hand. It didn't matter, she told herself, he just wanted the comfort of female company and he was far from home and anyway he would be going back to America soon, the war over bar the shouting. Why shouldn't they console each other?

Later they drove back down Teesdale, stopping in Barnard Castle to look for somewhere to eat and in the end having to make do with sandwiches and tea at a small cafe where they were the only customers. The owner watched them all the time, waiting so that he could close up and go home to spend Sunday evening with his family.

'Thank you, Gene,' she said when he dropped her back in Bishop Auckland. 'It has been the nicest time I've had in ages.' Her face darkened for a moment as she remembered the last time she had had such a lovely afternoon, the day she had gone to Marsden with Ken.

'Don't look so sad,' he said, mistaking her expression. 'You looked so lost there for a minute, I wanted to gather you up and run away with you.'

Theda smiled, forcing herself to speak lightly. 'I might just let you,' she said, and could have bitten her tongue as she saw his face brighten.

'I'll call for you tomorrow evening,' he said.

'Oh, no, I won't be free.'

'When then?'

'Er . . . Friday evening?'

If she was going to Sunderland – no, she *was* going to Sunderland, no ifs about it. She was going to start her midwifery course. She would be going at the end of the month, there was plenty of time to tell Gene. Why not go out with him meanwhile. They got on well together, didn't they?

Chapter Twenty-Five

'Well, thank goodness that's over for a while.' The speaker, a long-serving officer in the Queen Alexandra's Royal Army Nursing Corps, QAs for short, pushed the trolley of dirty instruments into the sluice for the orderlies to clean and sterilise and went with Major Collins into the make-shift office to write her report.

'If I were you, I'd have an early night,' she advised, casting a motherly eye over him. 'You look about ready to keel over. And God only knows what will come in tomorrow.'

Ken smiled briefly and went back to finishing his notes. 'No doubt you're right, Nanny,' he replied, giving her the nickname which she seemed to appreciate rather than resent. 'I'll just finish these and then I'm off.'

Later, the notes finished, he sat back in his chair and stretched his legs before him, easing the one that had been wounded, for it tended to stiffen after a day at the operating table. There had been a great number of casualties today requiring his services; at one point they'd seemed never-ending. And he still had to make his final rounds in the make-shift wards of the old German manor house, which by some miracle had escaped the attentions of the allied air forces and remained intact.

His mind drifted back to the letter he had received that morning from Uncle Tucker and he took it from his inside pocket and opened it out. Tucker didn't write that often, not unless he had something definite to say, and this time had wrapped his message up in chit-chat about the mine and the village and how the family had been the last time he had been over to Marsden. But his message was still clear.

'I saw that girl you sometimes gave a lift back to Winton and the hospital – Theda Wearmouth. I've seen her about a few times as it happens. She enquired after you a few weeks back, I think I told you. Now she seems to have a new boyfriend, an American, though he's in the RCAF. Her sister Clara married one of their pilots – you could hear the jollifications all over the village. Matt Wearmouth is a good worker and the younger son, Charles, shows great promise. He has ambitions to take over from me, as a matter of fact. But I'm afraid the girls seem a bit flighty, though now the younger one is married she might settle down.'

Even though the news that Theda had a new boyfriend depressed him, Ken couldn't help smiling at the old-fashioned term. Poor old Tucker. He always had been a stickler for moral rectitude. Not surprising really. He had been very young when his father, Wesley, Ken's gran's first husband, had left his family to move in with the notorious Sally Hawkins. And then all that trouble in the twenties. No wonder he had a horror of 'flighty women', as he was wont to call them.

Ken folded the letter and put it back in its envelope. Theda wasn't one of those women, he knew it in his heart. And anyway the war did funny things to women, and men too. It had been so good that New Year's Eve and she had been a virgin, he was sure. But what the hell did it matter anyway?

These last few weeks in Germany he had been thinking more and more of Theda Wearmouth, his memories of Julie fading naturally. He had been on the verge of writing to Theda more than once, the first time soon after he had left. He liked her, perhaps loved her or thought he did. But when you asked a girl to spend the rest of her life with you it was best to ask her face to face and he hadn't expected to be in Germany so long this time. Besides, he had sworn not to marry until after the war, not to get involved even. He couldn't go through all that pain, not again. Then he had almost forgotten his vows when he met Theda.

He had expected this appointment to be temporary. Relief surgeon, he had been told, six weeks at the most, just until the regular man got back from sick leave. Six weeks was not very long for a girl to wait. But the regular man was not returning, it seemed, he had been invalided out. So here Ken was for the duration. Like most other folk he had nothing to complain about really, except that it seemed the girl he loved had not waited.

An American. A Yank. Overpaid, oversexed and over here, as they said. Couldn't blame them, really – so far from home.

Ken's rambling thoughts went back to Theda as they often did these days. He thought about that day at Marsden – how he had meant to ask her to marry him after the war. Why had he let that stupid remark of Walt's about Julie disturb him? What a fool he had been. Now he had lost her, most probably. Still, nothing ventured . . . he might write to her tomorrow. So what if she was having dates with a Yank? There was probably nothing in it.

He got to his feet, feeling the familiar intensification of the ache in his thigh as it took his weight. Nanny was right. He'd better get some rest. There would be more work to do tomorrow, even if the war ended tonight.

'Are you not going to invite me to your parents' home?' asked Gene. He and Theda were sitting in the Bishop's Park, their backs against the ancient stone wall of the deer house. The sun was filtering through the branches of the trees, lighting up the green buds just coming into leaf. Though the summer was not yet in and there was a cool wind blowing down the dale, here in the shelter of the deer house it was pleasantly warm.

Theda looked at him. Oh, he was a nice man. Going out with him on the times they were both free together had been the only bright spots in the last few fraught weeks. He deserved the truth from her.

'You know my parents,' she said lightly.

'Not very well. Theda, you must know how I feel about you? I'm serious. I don't want this to be some hole in the corner affair. I want it to be out in the open. I want to meet your parents, come to supper maybe . . . try to convince them that I am just the man for their daughter. I want to court you properly.'

She felt dismayed and guilt-ridden at the same time. 'Oh, Gene, I don't know—' she said helplessly.

'I love you,' he said, and put his arm around her, drawing her to him. 'I want you to love me. I think you could if only you'd let yourself. Theda, you would love it at home – the space, and the folks are so friendly. My grandparents are from Newcastle, did I tell you? They still have the accent, a little anyway. You remind me of them.'

'No, I didn't know. But, of course – Ridley. It's a local name.'

'Tell me you love me?' he commanded.

She shook her head. 'I—' she began, but Gene stopped her mouth with his and his brilliant blue eyes hazed over as he kissed her, forcing her lips apart, slipping the tip of his tongue into her mouth. Theda closed her eyes and tried to concentrate on the feel of him. Where was the surge of feeling she should experience, the rapid pulse, the feel of her body responding to his lovemaking?

'Theda,' he murmured thickly, and put his hand on her breast. For a second there was a flicker of something but then all she could feel was a shrinking sensation for her breast was so tender she had to bite her lip to stop herself crying out.

'Don't do that,' she said, pushing his hand away and sitting forward. She only just stopped herself from jumping up and running down the grassy bank to the path which led out of the deserted park to the market place, where there were people and she wouldn't have to be alone with him. But she stopped herself, forced herself to sit back.

'Why not?' Gene bent over her again. He obviously thought she was just being conventional, protesting because she thought she ought to. He ran his hand down the length of her. 'What's the harm, Theda? I love you, I told you so. Don't act so cold to me.'

'No!' Her cry was involuntary.

This time he dropped his hand and lay back against the stone wall. 'What's the matter?' he asked. 'Is it because I'm scarred?' In a gesture that was becoming characteristic of him, he pulled his silk scarf up over the scar on his neck – a scar which in truth she no longer even saw.

'No, don't ever think that,' she said. 'I'm sorry. Oh, I'm so sorry, Gene. I have to talk to you, I haven't been fair to you at all. I shouldn't have done it . . .'

'Done what? Oh, come on, Theda. You can't have done anything which will make any difference to the way I feel about you.'

'I'm pregnant.'

In the silence that followed the chattering of a family of sparrows nesting in the battlements of the deer house sounded loud in her ears. Gene's arm remained around her shoulder. He sat very still. Along the path below them a man walked by followed by a labrador. It dawdled to sniff at something and the man whistled. The dog ran to him. Theda watched it as though in a daze.

Abruptly, Gene got to his feet and pulled her roughly after him.

'You're what?'

'I'm expecting a baby.'

He still had hold of her arms. They were standing very close, almost touching. She lifted her head and looked properly at him. His blue eyes were very angry and a pulse was visible in his temple.

'I'm sorry. I should have said from the beginning.' It sounded lame, inadequate.

'Yes, you damn well should!'

Gene dropped his arms and walked a few steps away, turned and came back. 'Whose is it? I suppose he's away in the war and you've been here, playing around to amuse yourself.' He began walking up and down, striding out, his fists clenched. 'Or is he dead?' He turned to her. Tell me is he dead?'

'No, he's in Germany. At least, I think he's all right, or alive at least. I haven't heard from him since he went away. He doesn't want me, Gene.'

'So you thought you'd palm the kid off on me, did you? Is that why you agreed to go out with me?'

'No!'

Had she thought she could do that? Bleakly, she wondered. He caught the guilt lurking in her eyes and came back to her, taking her by the shoulders and forcing her to him, lifting her so that her eyes were only inches from his.

'You couldn't do it in the end, could you? I suppose that's something to be said for you.' His eyes blazed with anger and she became alarmed.

'Let me go, Gene,' she said, trying to still the tremor in her voice.

'Let you go? Why should I? Don't you think I deserve something from you?'

His mouth came down on hers, hard and demanding. It was not at all like the kisses they had shared a moment or two ago. He wrapped his arms around her and held her in such a grip that the breath was driven out of her body, her lips were bruised, the pain in her back excruciating where his fingers were digging into the flesh.

Theda tried to fight. She kicked and struggled but it was no use. Her arms were pinioned to her sides and she felt herself losing consciousness so that she sagged against him. Somewhere close a dog barked. She heard it faintly.

'Hey, are you all right, miss?'

The grip on her slackened. She gulped in air and her vision cleared. The man with the labrador was there, halfway up the bank. The dog was barking furiously and he shushed it in an aside.

'We're all right, mind your own business,' growled Gene, and the man frowned.

'I was asking the lass,' he said. 'You bloody foreigners—'

'I'm all right, really I am. We . . . we were just having a bit of an argument. I'm OK really, thanks for asking,' said Theda. She pulled back from Gene and took her handkerchief out of her pocket and blew her nose.

'Sure?'

'Yes, I'm sure.'

'Aye, well, you young lasses want to be careful who you get friendly with, that's all. I mean, what do you know about these chaps? Where they come from?'

'Mind your own business, I said.' Gene stepped

forward and the dog set himself and began to growl. Theda put herself between them, hurriedly.

'No, really, thanks for bothering but I'm all right, I told you.'

'Aye, you did. Well, I'll be on my way.' Whistling the dog to heel, he went back down to the path and walked on. He turned and looked back once, but must have decided that Theda was all right after all. Beside her, she could hear Gene breathing heavily, felt the anger emanating from him.

'I'll go now,' she said, not looking at him. 'I'm sorry, Gene, very sorry. Oh, I am. You'd best go back to Middleton and forget all about me.' She set off, almost at a run.

She followed the man with the dog down to the path and out by the stile on to the broad gravelled drive which ran alongside the Bishop's Palace. The day had turned overcast and a shower of icy rain began to fall, sending people scurrying for shop doorways. Theda carried on walking regardless, making for the hospital and her room in the nurses' home. Her mind was a blank almost. She stared ahead unseeing, barging into people once or twice and murmuring an apology automatically.

Once back in the sanctuary of the home, she stripped and ran a hot bath and lay in it, soaking, until the water cooled. Then she climbed out and dried herself and went back to her room and bed without bothering about supper. She couldn't have eaten it anyway.

She lay awake for most of the night, not thinking of anything in particular, just lying there. About five o'clock, just as grey light was beginning to lighten the room, she got out of bed and sluiced her hands and face in cold water and dressed. She only had another two days at the hospital and then had a couple of days off before she had to report to Sunderland. She finished most of her packing and then went for a walk down Newgate Street, where the only people about were the milkmen and the paper boys from Armstrong's the newsagent.

She walked the streets for an hour, then returned to the hospital and went down to breakfast. Laura was there, eating a bowl of porridge with a dollop of golden syrup.

'When's the wedding, then?' she asked, grinning.

'What?'

'Well, I saw Gene the other day and I could see he's really fallen for you. I'm so pleased, Theda. Does this mean you've changed your mind about Sunderland?'

'It's all off, Gene and me,' said Theda. She collected her bowl of porridge and added sugar and milk and began eating stolidly.

Laura put down her spoon and stared at her. 'Come on, tell me all about it?'

'Nothing to tell, really. He doesn't want to marry me anyway. So I'm going to Sunderland. A girl has to think of her career.'

Laura was disbelieving. 'There has to be more to it than that,' she declared, and Theda sighed.

'Well, yes, there is,' she admitted, and paused for a moment. She needed to confide in someone. If she kept it to herself much longer she would go mad. 'If I tell you, will you promise not to breathe a word to anyone?'

Five minutes later, they were the only two still sitting

in the dining-room and perilously near to being late on duty. Laura was concerned, and for once she had forgotten all about the Children's Ward.

'But how are you going to manage?' she asked. 'How can you work and see to a baby? Don't be so soft, Theda. You're talking like a fool.'

'No, I'm not. I'll finish my first six months before the baby. Then, later, I can carry on. I've thought it all out. There's loads of mother and baby homes about these days, I'll have no trouble getting in one until I can find another place.' The baby will be better off if it's adopted by a couple, she thought. A couple who could give it a secure, loving home. But she did not say this to Laura. She would tell her, but not yet.

'I still think you should tell your parents,' her friend said firmly. 'Anyroad, who is the father, or am I forbidden to ask?'

'You can ask, but I'm not saying,' said Theda. 'Come on, now, back to the wards or you'll be in trouble.'

'There's trouble and trouble,' said Laura, rising to her feet. 'Eeh, Theda, I don't know what to say. But I can tell you this: if you need any help, you just have to let me know. If you're determined to go ahead, that is.'

'I am.'

Because they had sat so long in the dining-room, she didn't have the time to call to see if there was any post in her pigeon hole that morning. So she didn't know that there was a letter there from Germany. It was Major Koestler who found it. There was no one about so he had taken the opportunity to check over the post for anything interesting.

And letters from Germany were always interesting. Sometimes they showed small insights into the progress of the war and how they were faring on the home front – news which was sought eagerly by the other prisoners.

The following Sunday, Theda travelled up to Sunderland. She went on the Northern bus from Bishop Auckland, jolting along slowly from small town to small town for the hour and a half it took to get there. The last two days had been fraught for her at home in West Row, pretending to be bright and happy and looking forward to her new career. And Bea had been so proud of her, telling everyone she met that Theda was going to be a midwife and maybe one day would be back as a district nurse 'delivering all the babies in Winton'.

She had even told Tucker Cornish when he happened to meet them down by the pit gates, and he had looked puzzled.

'Oh, but—' he began, then stopped.

'Was there something?' asked Bea.

'No . . . I wish you all the best, Miss Wearmouth,' he replied, and Theda mumbled something, feeling hot as she remembered her humiliation the last time they had met.

There was a knock at the door on the Friday evening and as it happened Theda was in the kitchen on her own. The men were both on night shift and Bea was lying down with a headache. Standing there, when she opened the door, was Gene.

'Are you going to let me in?' he asked.

'Of course,' said Theda, and led the way, indicating that

he should sit in Da's chair. She herself sat opposite him in Bea's. She said nothing, simply waited for him to say what he had to say.

'How are you?' he asked, looking uncomfortable.

'Fine, thank you,' she answered, and waited while he cleared his throat.

'I can't stop thinking about you,' he said at last. 'I still want to marry you, no matter what you have done. Marry me, Theda, and I'll be a good father to your child.'

'No matter what I've done?' she asked, and he flushed and she was sorry. He meant well, she knew. 'I can't, Gene, I'm sorry,' she went on.

'Think about it, Theda, please. We'll have a good life, the three of us, you'll see. I do love you.'

But it was no good, she knew that now. The baby was hers and hers alone; she would look after it herself somehow. She tried to let Gene down gently but in the end he went off in a bitter mood.

'You're nothing but a tease, Theda Wearmouth,' he said. 'No wonder he went off and left you. No doubt he found out what you were like in time. Well, this was your last chance. I wouldn't have you now if you came begging on your knees.'

Sitting in the bus as it pulled out of Durham and set off on the Sunderland road, she sighed, remembering. But she had done the right thing, she knew she had. To marry Gene would have been to compound one mistake with another. She would get over this bad time, she would rise above it. And she would work hard, become better qualified, be a success. She didn't need a man.

Part Two
1950

Chapter Twenty-Six

'Richard! What on earth have you been up to?' Theda propped her bicycle against the school railings and went forward to meet her son. He was trailing out of the gates on his own, his cap awry, his shirt – pale grey and spanking new when she sent him out to school that morning – spattered with mud and half out of his shorts. Blood trickled down from grazed knees to his grey socks and she could see where tears had trickled through the dirt on his face and dried on his cheeks.

'I'm sorry, Nurse Wearmouth,' said Miss Robinson grimly, 'but we just can't seem to stop Richard from fighting.' She looked pointedly at her watch. 'I wanted to have a word with you about your so often being late to pick him up as well. I don't want to carp and I know you are a busy woman, but so am I and it's well past the time I should be on my way home.'

'Sorry, Miss Robinson, truly I am. I just couldn't get away. It won't happen again, I assure you.'

'Hmm.' Miss Robinson looked sceptical, which Theda

realised she had a perfect right to. This was the third time she had been a few minutes late this week.

''Bye, Miss Robinson,' said Richard as Theda collected her bike and they set off up the street. He smiled a bright sunny smile and Theda's heart swelled with love as his grey eyes – only a little darker than his father's – sparkled and lit up his face.

'Hold my hand, Richard,' she said.

'You can't wheel your bike properly with one hand,' he pointed out, and then, as she opened her mouth to say more, he sighed. 'All right, then. But I'm not going to run into the road, Mam. I'm not daft.'

'Daft enough to fight with the other boys and get your clothes in a mess. What was it about this time?'

'Nothing.'

She didn't press him. They walked to the crossing and waited until the light changed to green then crossed the road and went up the hill behind the prison. Theda had a house there, a pleasant house with a garden. The fact that it came with the job had been one of the main reasons she had come to Durham City. That and the fact that they were close to a good primary school at New Elvet.

'Go on up and take off those clothes. I'll be up in a minute to clean you up,' she told her son.

'You won't put iodine on my knees, will you, Mam?'

'Go on, don't be a baby,' she replied, and he stuck out his bottom lip and climbed slowly up the stairs, holding on to the banister, head down.

'I won't use iodine,' she said, relenting. 'I've got some Cetavlon. It doesn't sting one bit.'

Before she followed him upstairs she opened a tin of baked beans and slid a slice of bread under the grill of the gas stove. She didn't need to ask him what he wanted. At the moment it was baked beans every day.

In the bathroom, Richard had taken off his school clothes and was standing by the hand basin in his underpants and vest. He had run a tiny amount of water into the bowl and was busy making a lather with the soap, standing on tiptoe to reach so that the water ran down his arms and dripped over the black and white squared lino. He was very quiet, she thought, something on his mind no doubt. Well, she wouldn't press him, he would tell her in his own good time.

She cleaned his cuts and bruises, put on the antiseptic and covered them with sticking plaster. He struggled into a pair of old shorts and a jersey for he considered himself too old now to accept help with dressing. She took him down to the kitchen and sat him before the plate of beans on toast and glass of milk. And, sure enough, what was troubling him came out.

'You know Billy, Mam – Billy Carter?'

Theda, who was sitting at the other end of the kitchen table, drinking tea while she consulted her notebook on next day's visits, put down her cup and gave him her full attention.

'Yes.'

She remembered Billy all right, a boy a few months older than Richard, and taller, sturdy with blond hair like his mother's and a boisterous way with him. He always had a gang of small boys round him and Richard would hang about on the edges, obviously hoping to join them. Billy's mother was married to a college professor and lived over the footbridge in one of the detached houses that overlooked the Wear.

'Billy says I'm a Bassett. I'm not, am I, Mam? A Bassett's a dog. Mrs Smith had one where we lived before.'

Theda felt it like a blow to the heart. By, if she could get hold of that snobby Mrs Carter she'd knock her into the middle of next week! Who the hell did she think she was, talking about a little lad like Richard in those terms.

'Are you sure he said a Bassett, Richard? Maybe you were mistaken.' Theda forced herself to keep her voice calm.

'He did say that, Mam.' Richard nodded his head vigorously.

'He was just being silly, pet. Why would he say that anyway? Had you been fighting with him?'

'No, not then I hadn't. But then he said I had no daddy and it was because I was a Bassett. So I hit him.'

'Richard! You know you shouldn't have hit him. Not unless he hit you first.' Theda frowned at him. 'So that's how you got in such a mess. Did Billy do it?'

Richard sat up proudly. 'Billy couldn't hurt me, I knocked him down. But then his gang set on me and that wasn't fair, was it, Mam? I'd have won him if he'd been on his own. Next time I'll wait—'

'Richard! There's not going to be a next time. Promise me now?'

He stuck out his lower lip and bent his head over his plate. He mashed his beans with a fork and stirred them round and round. Theda could practically see his mind working. It was logical to him that if the other boy was bigger or there was more than one he had to use strategy. Despairingly, she picked up her cup and sipped her cooling tea, feeling inadequate. Was she bringing him up the wrong way altogether? Should she tell him what Mrs Carter had really said and what it meant?

There were lots of children Richard's age without fathers, a lot of men had been killed in the war. She had hoped that in a town like Durham where she was unknown, people would take it for granted that that was what had happened, his father had been a war casualty. How had that woman stumbled on the truth?

Theda's head throbbed. She leaned her elbow on the table and rested her forehead on her hand, closing her eyes. Questions buzzed around her tired brain. That was it, she was weary from lack of sleep. She had been called out in the middle of the night to a home delivery and the woman's labour had been protracted, the baby had not arrived until shortly before she had to pick up Richard from school, hence the reason she had been late.

That was the one fault with her job, though she loved it really. But every time she was called out of school hours she had to get Sheila from next door to look after Richard.

'Are you sad, Mam?' Richard had got down from his chair and was standing beside her; he slipped his hand into hers and leaned against her shoulder. 'I won't fight any more, Mam,' he promised. 'I don't care if Billy never lets me join his gang. I wouldn't join it anyway, they're just silly babies.'

Theda picked him up and sat him on her lap and hugged him. 'I'm all right, pet, just tired, that's all.' She dropped a kiss on his fine brown hair, so different from the strong black hair of the Wearmouths.

'Billy can't even tie his own shoelaces,' he confided, grinning. 'He doesn't know how to put the wireless on to the Home Service for *Children's Hour*.'

Theda smiled and set him down on his feet. 'Well, if you want to listen to *Children's Hour* you'd better go and put it on now. Go on, and not too loud, I want to be able to hear myself think.'

'You can't hear yourself think,' he shouted incredulously. 'Nobody can hear themselves think!' But he went through to the sitting-room obediently and in a minute she heard the introductory music through the open doors. Thank goodness for Uncle Mac, honorary uncle to most of Britain's children.

It would be better when she had qualified as a Health Visitor. At least then she wouldn't be called out during the night. She got to her feet and began to wash the dishes. There was the kitchen floor to wash too. By the time *Children's Hour* was over, she had finished the kitchen and put Richard's discarded clothes in to soak and laid out a clean set for tomorrow. As soon as he was asleep she intended to spend the rest of the evening studying. At least there were no births due for a couple of days.

Later, with Richard in bed and the curtains drawn to keep out the late-summer sun, she sat on the couch in the sitting-room with her books spread around her. But she was finding it difficult to concentrate; she kept thinking of

Richard and what Mrs Carter had obviously said. Smug, self-righteous cow!

Theda's mind flashed back to the one occasion she had taken Richard to Seaburn to meet the Sunday School trip from Winton Colliery. Her mother was travelling with them and she had thought it was a good chance to combine giving the child a day at the seaside and meeting up with Bea.

They had taken deck chairs onto the sands and it was a beautiful day with the sea sparkling in the sun and the children running backwards and forwards to the water's edge for tiny buckets of water to put in the moats round the sand castles they had made. A never-ending job really as the water soaked into the sand and the children had to go back for more. And Richard, who must have been three at the time, came back slopping his bucket so that there was only a table-spoonful in there and the women had laughed and he had flung down the bucket and howled his frustration.

'Hush now,' Bea had said to him, and handed him a lollipop. And as he stopped crying they could plainly hear the group of women behind them, talking.

'You'd think she wouldn't have the face to bring him here among decent folk,' one was saying. Theda turned her head, disbelieving.

'Aye, well, some folks has face for anything,' replied a fat, middle-aged woman with her legs spread out in front of the deck chair so that half-lying back as she was, a great expanse of pink knickers was exposed to view.

Bea jumped to her feet, fairly frothing at the mouth in

temper. 'Is that a fact, missus?' she demanded. 'An' some folks dare show more than their faces—'

'Mam, Mam, come away! They're not worth talking to,' said Theda, taking her mother's arm.

'Aye, you're right. Howay, pet. We won't stay where we're not wanted.' They had picked up the deck chairs and taken them further up the beach to howls of protest from Richard who, in picking up his bucket and spade, dropped his lollipop in the sand. Behind them, the two women flushed red and spluttered with indignation and muttered something about the Wearmouth lasses, both of them being no better than they should be. What about all those Canadians coming to the house during the war?

The sun had gone down now and it was too dark to read in any case. Theda sighed and closed the book on her lap and went into the kitchen to make a pot of tea. She remembered she had had no evening meal so rummaged in the cupboard and found a packet of mushroom soup. She mixed it with water and stood by the stove stirring the pan until the water boiled. It wasn't very palatable but she ate it steadily, together with a slice of bread. She was just depressed because she was hungry, she told herself.

Her thoughts wandered back to the time she had first left home and gone to Sunderland. What a nerve she had had, starting that course knowing she was already pregnant! But somehow she had finished the six months of the first part of midwifery and that had given her heart to go on later.

Her thoughts sheared away from the memory of the mother and baby home she had entered in the autumn of

1945. Such a dismal place it had been, yet full of young girls and even some older women. Not all abandoned by their men; some were just unlucky to have them killed right at the tail end of the war.

Most of them didn't know what they were going to do afterwards but Theda had laid her plans. She would have her baby and have it adopted and get on with her life. Further training was her goal. She would reach the highest point in her chosen profession, oh, yes she would, she was determined. Anyway, a baby would have a better life with a married couple who could give it a stable family life.

So there was no reason to distress Mam by telling her about the baby. It was best that she should never know about it. But that meant not going home at all after she had begun to show. The last time had been VE night, and Theda had gone home for the celebrations.

There had been a street tea party with trestle tables laid end to end and every house had a Union Jack fluttering from a bedroom window, or if not red, white and blue bunting. Pianos had been dragged outside on to the pavement and everyone sang until they were hoarse. They danced the hoky-cokey and every other daft dance they could think of and in the evening there was an enormous bonfire up by the old claypit just outside Winton Colliery and everyone in the rows was there. They roasted potatoes and even some sausages they had cadged from the butcher.

'Are you staying for the Victory dance on Saturday?' Norma had asked her, and Theda had shaken her head.

'Sorry, I have to be back on duty,' she had replied.

Privately, she thought she would never go to a dance in the church hall ever again, perhaps would never dance again. Look what it had got her into, she told herself grimly.

'You're putting a bit of weight on, Theda, maybe you could do with the exercise,' Norma said, and laughed. But Theda couldn't laugh. She knew she couldn't come back, not until the baby was born at least.

'I won't be back for a while, Mam,' she told Bea as she hugged her mother goodbye. 'I'm going to have to do a lot of studying on my days off for the next six months.' She had to steel herself not to tighten her arms around Bea, not to burst out crying and tell her everything. But how could she put her mother through that? Already Bea had found out the real reason Clara had got married in such a hurry.

She had gone to Darlington to see her younger daughter and found her hugely pregnant. 'By, daughters can break your heart,' Theda had heard her saying to Matt.

'What's the matter with you, woman? Our Clara's respectably married,' he had replied impatiently, but Bea had shaken her head and pressed her lips tightly together to stop herself from crying.

He had muttered something incoherent and gone upstairs to bed, out of the way of foolish women.

Theda wasn't going to shame her mother a second time, that was something else she had determined, though it was hard in a strange town with no one to talk to except occasionally Nurse Jenkins, her one confidante. Laura Jenkins had come through to see her twice on her days off but then she had gone away to train for her SRN in Cardiff, where her husband had come from.

Richard had been born on the first day of October when the leaves on the sycamore tree outside the delivery room had turned to copper and already some had fallen to the ground, presaging a long winter, the midwife had said cheerfully.

'We'll bind up your breasts to discourage the flow of milk,' she had added. 'In a few minutes, I'll be back. I'll taken baby along to the nursery first.'

'I haven't seen him yet,' protested Theda. All she had seen was the piece of cotton sheeting in which he was wrapped, covered by a threadbare blanket.

'Best you don't,' said the midwife calmly laying the baby in a cot and wheeling him to the door.

'Bring him back here!' shouted Theda, sitting up in bed, the after-birth tiredness dropping from her. She was ready to leap out of bed and seize the baby and keep him safe from all comers.

'It's for the best, Theda, really it is.' The midwife sounded as though she had been through this argument thousands of times before, which she probably had.

'Bring him here,' she said stubbornly. 'I haven't signed any papers yet, remember. And I probably won't. How do I know what sort of life he'll have with strangers?'

The midwife brought Matron and the doctor but Theda had made up her mind yet again and they brought her the tiny human being and she held him to her breast, and after that nothing they could say could make her give him up.

Of course, it wasn't the first time that had happened, so

they were used to it. And in the mother and baby home they were allowed to stay for three months while the authorities tried to teach the girls how to look after the babies on their own and helped them get work afterwards. With Theda that wasn't necessary. She told them plainly she could manage.

It was Joss who found out where she was and what had happened to her. One day Theda had an interview for a job at a small cottage hospital for a Staff Nurse's post. It was only until she got herself organised, she told herself. As soon as she had a little more money saved and could afford to pay for live-in help, she would take her second-part midwifery and be once more on her way up.

'Are you sure you can do it, Miss Wearmouth?' asked Matron, sounding very dubious. The woman peered at her over the application form and the references she had from Bishop Auckland and the Infirmary. Anyone would think that having a baby had made her half-witted, thought Theda. She felt like saying she could do the job standing on her head, having a baby had not made her lose her wits altogether.

'Of course, Matron.'

'Hmm. I can't have a member of my staff taking time off from work because her child is teething or has a rash. I need someone reliable. Are you sure you can get adequate help?'

'I am, Matron.'

In the end Theda got the job, though she knew it was because she was the only applicant. The salary was far from generous, but if she was careful she could manage to pay Ruby, one of the girls she had met in the home, to look after Richard while she was at the hospital. Ruby was unique among the residents in that she had a small house of her own; her parents had been killed in the war and the house had been theirs. So she planned to run a child-minding service.

Theda walked back to the home feeling happier than she had done for a long time. And there, in the entrance, was a tall soldier, standing with his back to the door and his hands on his hips. The home's Matron was flustered, Theda could see. Her face was red and she tossed her head at the soldier.

'I tell you, you can't come in. I don't care who you are. No male visitors allowed, can't you read the notice?' Matron had pointed to a large placard on the wall.

'And I'm telling you, I'm coming in. So stand aside, woman, and let me past!'

'Joss!'

Theda forgot all about keeping her secret from the family; the rush of feeling that flooded through her was so elating that there was only a great thankfulness that he was here, home from Germany or wherever he had been. She flung her arms around him and hugged him, laughing and crying together. For the first time she realised how alone she had been without her family. Not just lonely, but *alone,* which was so much worse.

'Well!' said Matron from somewhere over his shoulder. 'What do you think you are doing, Miss Wearmouth?' But nothing she said mattered any more.

'Right then, are you going to show me my nephew?'

asked Joss. 'I've come all the way from Dover since yesterday morning, and I don't mind telling you, you took some finding. So tell this woman who I am and let's have no more aggravation, our Theda.'

'Oh, Joss, Joss,' she said helplessly. 'By, I'm that glad to see you, you have no idea.'

'Aye, well, it seems I've come home none too early neither, what with Mam and Dad in a lather worrying about you, and our Clara going off to Canada.'

'You should have told me you were her brother,' said Matron huffily. 'Go on then, you can go up to the nursery for five minutes. But it's strictly against the rules, mind.'

Upstairs, a crowd of curious girls suddenly found it necessary to attend to their own babies in the nursery. They covertly eyed the handsome soldier as he stood for a minute over Richard in his cot.

'Aye, well, our Theda,' he said, ignoring the others, 'you'd best get your things together an' the bairn's an' all. You're coming along o' me. We're going home.'

Chapter Twenty-Seven

She had known it wouldn't work as soon as she walked into the house carrying the baby, with Joss following behind with her case. Not that Mam or Da condemned her; she had steeled herself for what they would have to say but they had said nothing, at least nothing in criticism of her.

'Our Theda!' Bea cried, rising up from her chair by the range where she was knitting a Fair Isle sweater. Needles and wool went flying perilously near the fire as she stepped forward and hugged her daughter. She looked down at the baby, protesting loudly now he had been woken up, and smiled.

'Aye, I wondered,' she said.

'This noisy little brat is Richard, Mam,' Joss announced. 'Two months old and with a voice enough to raise the dead.'

'Stand out of the way, woman, let me have a look at him,' ordered Matt. He lifted the baby from Theda's arms and undid the shawl wrapped around him, holding him on one muscled arm and regarding him solemnly. Richard opened his eyes and his mouth ready to yell his protest even harder, and stopped, staring up at his grandfather. Matt put up a blue-scarred finger and the baby grasped it tightly.

'A good, strong little babby,' he observed. He looked up at Theda, his gaze keen. 'Are you all right, lass?'

'I am, Da,' she answered.

'Howay in then, let's have the door shut. I don't know what that draught's going to do to my oven and I have some pies in.'

Bea bustled about, taking the oven cloth from the brass line above the range and opening the oven door to inspect the pies.

'I'll take these up then,' said Joss, and picked up the cases again and headed for the stairs. Chuck had not yet risen from the table where he was sitting in his black, only his hands showing strangely white where he had washed them for his meal.

'Hello, Chuck,' said Theda.

'Now then, our Theda,' he said grimly, his gaze sliding over her. Rising to his feet, he walked past her, ignoring the baby. 'I'll have me bath in the room, Mam,' he said to Bea. 'Seeing as you're so busy here.'

Maybe he was just tired and impatient to get his bath and go to bed, Theda told herself. But he could at least have looked at his new nephew. She laid the baby on the sofa and put the kettle on the fire and made up a bottle of National Dried Milk for Richard's feed.

'You're not feeding him yourself, then?' asked Bea,

watching her. 'Eeh, I don't think it's natural to give a babby cows' milk. Did you not have enough milk yourself, Theda?'

'It's 'specially prepared, Mam. It's perfectly all right, good nutritionally.' Theda tested the temperature of the milk on her wrist and picked up the baby. He took the teat into his mouth and sucked noisily. 'It was no good me starting him on the breast, Mam,' she continued. 'I'm going to have to go out to work.'

'No, you're not,' her father said sharply. 'I don't hold with a mother leaving a young baby. You can stay at home and help your mam, until the bairn's a good bit older anyroad. When he starts school then you can think about it.'

Theda bent her head over the baby, fighting to stop the sharp retort that rose to her lips. Already the happiness she had felt at coming home, the gratitude at not being condemned for what had happened to her, was dissipating. Instead depression was rising in her. She had been independent too long to give it up easily now. But it was no use arguing with her father.

Her silence was hardly noticed by the rest of the family for Joss was telling them about Germany – Cologne in particular.

'You can't imagine it, the whole place is in ruins. It's just like a giant builder's tip,' he said as they sat round the table eating the corned beef pies hot from the oven and chips made from potatoes from Matt's garden. Richard, replete after his feed, slept soundly on the sofa.

'Aye, well,' growled Chuck, 'they bombed British towns first. What about Coventry, eh?'

'Sunderland has some big holes in it, too,' Theda said. She thought about the streets with uneven gaps in them and rosebay, willow-herb and nettles growing amongst the rubbish.

'You can't help feeling a bit sorry for them, though,' said Joss. 'They have nothing left – nothing.'

'Only right—' Chuck began, but was interrupted by his mother.

'Eeh, Chuck, think about the bairns, man,' she exclaimed.

The argument went on but Theda hardly listened; she was going over and over her troubles in her own mind. How could she live here for five years without working? Oh, of course she could claim National Assistance and would probably get it and that would give her some independence from her family, but it wouldn't be enough. In any case, she needed to get on with her career. She couldn't afford to waste five years, not if she was to reach her goal.

'I'll borrow Renee's old pram and we'll take the baby for a walk after we've washed up,' suggested Bea. 'Fresh air's good for him.'

'Aye, you do that,' said Matt approvingly. 'On Saturday you mebbe can go into Bishop and get him a pram of his own. It'll be our Christmas present – what do you think of that?'

'Oh, Da, you can't afford to lay out such sums,' Theda protested.

'Aye, I can an' all, I'm earning good money now. Things is different around here, you know. And when the pits are nationalised and there are no owners taking fat profits out, we won't know we're born. The good times are coming at last, an' not afore time neither.'

'There never were such times,' murmured Bea, looking sceptical.

'You'll see, lass, you'll see,' he asserted.

'Well, good times or not, I'm not going back down the pit when I'm demobbed,' said Joss, and shook his head emphatically. 'No, there's plenty of jobs going elsewhere. Why go down the pit and flog your guts out for a pittance?'

'But I'm telling you, it's going to be—'

'Eeh, Joss, do you mean you won't be coming home to live?'

His parents gaped at him. Both of them seemed shaken by the thought that Joss was thinking of working away from home.

'You've been away all these years, I was looking forward to having you back,' wailed his mother.

'Well, I might be back, depends what work is on offer,' said Joss. 'Don't fret yourself, Mam. I'll still be coming home to plague you. You'll be sick of the sight of me, I'm telling you.'

Bea said no more but her agitation showed in her jerky, nervous movements as she got to her feet and began siding the table ready to wash up.

Later, as she and Theda walked the baby in the battered old pram they had borrowed from Renee, she seemed to recover some of her good humour, but not for long. It was a dark, overcast afternoon threatening rain and there were few people about, but those that were stopped to admire the baby and ask Theda where she was living now and was she well and all the usual small talk.

'She's coming back home to live,' Bea told them. 'In fact, she's back for good now.' Theda looked sideways at her mother but didn't contradict her.

'Oh, dear, I am sorry. Was your man killed in the war, then?' asked one woman, tilting her head to one side and folding her arms across her chest. 'Eeh, so many families being brought up without fathers these days, it's dreadful, Mrs Wearmouth, it is an' all.' She sounded sympathetic but her eyes were thoughtful.

Bea moved on suddenly, walking rapidly on to Winton Village.

'Come on, Theda, we want to get to the Co-op while they still have something left,' she called over her shoulder. The woman was left gazing after them.

'You might as well have told her the truth, Mam,' said Theda, almost running in her efforts to keep up with her mother. 'She'll find out anyway, it'll be all over the rows by tonight.'

'Aye. Well, let her find out, I'm not going to help her,' snapped Bea.

'I know it's hard for you, Mam,' said Theda. 'I'm sorry I've brought you this trouble home, I am. That's why I was going to stay away.'

'This isn't the worst trouble Winton has seen,' said Bea stubbornly. 'Just you remember Sally Cornish, and that murdering man of hers, and the lad, Ralph. It all passes, lass. If Tucker Cornish has the face to stay in the place, so have we.'

How could her mother class her with that old scandal? Theda was shaken to the core. She took hold of the pram handle, practically wrenching it from her mother.

'Hey, our Theda!' Bea protested.

'I'm sorry, Mam, but I think I'll just be getting back to West Row. It's a bit cold for Richard to be out. After all, he's barely two months old and I think there's going to be a bad frost tonight.'

'Well, I just want a few bits of messages at the Co-op—' Bea began, but was talking to Theda's rapidly receding back.

It was difficult telling her family that she was going back to Sunderland. 'I have to find a place of my own, you see, but I'll stay until tomorrow. Then I will have to pack, I have a new job to think about.'

'You're not going, our Theda!' Matt, who had been called early from his bed to add his argument to Bea's, tried laying down the law.

'I am, Da, I'm sorry.'

'But what will you do? You haven't even got a place in that home now you've walked out.' Bea was red in the face, her eyes bright with unshed tears. 'Don't be so daft, Theda, you never used to care what folk thought about you anyroad.'

'It's not that.' Though partly it was, of course, thought Theda. Not what they thought about her but how it affected her family. They would be upset at first, but it was better for them in the long run. And Chuck and Norma would probably be pleased if she went.

'I have a job to go to, Da, and I'll get a room. I might

even get a little house. I'm all right, I've got my nursing. I want to go on with my career.'

'An' never mind Richard!' shouted Bea. 'The poor little babby comes a bad second to what you want to do. You're selfish, Theda!'

'Aw, come on, that's a bit strong. Leave her alone to do what she wants to do – she's a grown woman. Mam? Da?' Joss appealed to them, but it was as if they couldn't even hear him.

Matt jumped to his feet. 'I'm telling you, our Theda, if you're going to leave this house you needn't wait until tomorrow – you can get yourself away now. But mind, if you do, don't come crying to me for help! Now, what are you going to do?'

'Eeh, Matt—' Bea began, eyes widening in shock.

'No, I mean it, Bea. If your daughter wants to go, then let her go. She's no daughter of mine. All this time we've been worrying about her, and what was she doing? Having a bairn out of wedlock! An' we forgive her and take her back, an' is she grateful? There's not an ounce of feeling in her, she's grateful for nowt!'

Theda listened to him ranting on, her head bowed. Never had she heard in him such a rage, never in her life. How could this be her da? It was a different man altogether. She trembled with shock, her mind numb, unbelieving.

'Well, Theda Wearmouth, what's it to be?'

From a distance she heard his voice and had to pull herself together. She looked at the baby sleeping through all the uproar in the borrowed pram. In the sudden silence there came a knocking at the back of the fire grate: Mrs Coulson alarmed at the raised voices. The wall between the houses was only one brick thick. She must have heard most of the argument, and probably Renee too. Still enraged, Matt took hold of the poker and knocked sharply back, bringing down a small shower of soot. Theda looked at it. It spattered out on to the clean tidy betty and enamel hearth plate and even reached the steel fender. It would have to be cleaned up, she thought dimly.

'Well?' he barked, making her jump.

'Da, if she goes, I'll go with her,' said Joss, and Matt looked at him as though he was a deserter from the front line. 'Have some sense, man,' Joss went on. 'She can't travel back to Sunderland on a winter's night with now-here to go when she gets there. Where's your common charity?'

'You must do what you must do,' said Matt. He turned to the fire and, putting a hand up to the rail, leaned forward until his head rested against the mantelpiece and stared into the fire. Bea sank down into her chair, looking stunned.

'Don't you worry, Joss. The home will take me in until I find somewhere. If you will just ring for a taxi . . . but you'll have to go up to Winton Village to the telephone box.' The baby whimpered and Theda went over to the pram and rocked it gently until he settled down again.

'I'll do that,' said Joss, and without another glance at his father, put on his greatcoat.

'Have you twopence for the call?' asked Bea, her voice small. Shocked as she was, she was still practical.

'I have, Mother.' He went out into the yard and on down the row. As he went he was making his own plans. He only had a few weeks left in the army; owing to his long service he was going to be one of the first to be demobbed. He had planned to leave the north-east but now he had to adjust his ideas. He could drive. He had driven in the army before he volunteered for the parachute regiment. He could drive a bus. He would apply to Sunderland Corporation for a job driving a double-decker. Then he could keep an eye on his stubborn little sister.

A taxi to Sunderland was going to be expensive as the distance was all of thirty miles. If he could only borrow a car, he thought. The idea was put into his head as he saw the Austin Ruby parked outside the manager's house. Joss looked longingly at it. It would have done the job nicely. But then, he didn't know Tucker Cornish well enough to ask them for a loan of a car. They were past commodities as no new ones had been made since before the war.

He walked around the vehicle. It was just the sort of runabout he would like to buy for himself when he got out of the army. Joss sighed and set off down the short cut and into the telephone box, which was at the entrance to old Winton Village.

Inside Tucker's study, Ken Collins stretched his feet out to the fire. 'I'm sorry I can't stay until tomorrow,' he said as his uncle handed him a glass of the brandy, which he had brought back from Germany only that morning. 'I have an interview at Sunderland tomorrow. But if you

want the Austin, I'll drop it off on my way back from the
farm on Sunday. What do you think?'

'Well, yes, of course I want it. A good car's harder to
get hold of than a hen's tooth. Thanks very much for
thinking of me, Ken.'

'Well, it belonged to a friend of mine from Darlington
who's lost a leg. It's been laid up for most of the war but
it's been well looked after. When I got the chance of it, I
jumped at it.'

'Yes, of course. I'll run you to Darlington for the train
on Sunday. It all works out very well.'

Ken sipped his brandy, a good one, he thought, smooth
as butter on the tongue. But somehow he was restless.
Maybe it was being back in Winton.

'Have you seen anything of that nurse? You know, her
father works at the colliery?' Ken hadn't meant to ask but
he did. But he was deliberately vague, though he remembered full well Theda's name, remembered a lot about her.
How strands of her hair hung black and curling at the nape
of her neck where it had escaped from her cap. Why
hadn't she answered his letter? He could only suppose she
didn't want to see him again. Maybe she was ashamed of
the way she had thrown him over when the Yank had
come on the scene. Ken sipped his brandy and looked out
of the window, disturbed by the bleak feeling rising in him.

Tucker moved uncomfortably, recrossing his legs. He
took his time lighting his pipe before he answered. 'Theda
Wearmouth, do you mean? No, she went away to work, I
believe. Newcastle or maybe it was York. You're not
interested in her, are you, Ken? I mean, you weren't really

keen on her?' He thought of the green scarf Mrs Parkin had found. It was still in the glove box of the hallstand. He could give it back to her family but it would be a little awkward. Best to leave it.

'No, not at all. I went out with her once or twice, that's all. Idle curiosity, I suppose.'

He'd taken her to Marsden. He remembered that day well. Her face had been alight with interest as he'd shown her round the farm and afterwards, on the edge of the cliff, watching the seabirds swoop around and the children let out of school, running and laughing around them. He remembered all right. But she must have forgotten all about him as soon as he left.

Ken shook his head to rid it of memories. Best be on his way. He said his goodbyes to his uncle and set out on the road to Sunderland.

Joss and Theda with baby Richard took a taxi to Spennymoor. It was well on their way and they could catch a bus there. They ran half-hourly. It was much cheaper that way. Joss studied the bus timetable, which was pinned up by the bus stop.

'Ten minutes to wait,' he said. 'It won't be long.'

'You could go back home from here, I can manage fine now,' said Theda. He looked down at her white face and strained expression. 'No, I said I was coming with you and I will. I can easily get a bed for the night, even if it's the Salvation Army.'

'I don't want you to fall out with Mam and Da, not over me,' said Theda. She looked down at the baby in her arms.

Sleeping, his lashes fanned out on his cheeks – such long lashes for a little baby boy. She tried to imagine how she would feel if she quarrelled with her son when he was grown but she couldn't.

The bus finally came and they were climbing on to it when a car pulled up behind, an Austin Ruby. Joss glanced curiously at the driver, a man in officer's uniform. He looked familiar and so did the car. But the lorry coming the other way, which had caused the car to stop, had gone by now and the Ruby was off, pulling round the bus and zooming down the road.

'That car looked like the one that was parked outside the gaffer's house,' he remarked to Theda, who had just sunk into a vacant seat with a sigh of relief. She looked up, alert suddenly.

'Where?'

'Oh, it's gone now,' said Joss.

Chapter Twenty-Eight

Thank God for Joss, thought Theda as she turned into the gate of 22 Laburnum Road – a grandoise name for a prefab in a sprawling estate of prefabricated houses, which they had shipped in from America at the end of the war. It was Joss who had insisted on their putting their names down on the waiting list, and his priority points as an essential worker, added to her own as a nurse, had secured them the two-bedroomed bungalow.

She remembered the small room in the home, which she had shared with Richard when Joss had only a bed in a scruffy boarding house down by the quay. It had been a few months – she preferred not to remember really. Inserting her key in the lock, she opened the door and held it open while she pushed the pram with the sleeping baby inside. And felt the familiar twinge of guilt that it was way past his bedtime and he ought to have been in his bed.

'Now then, our Theda,' said Joss, waving a large spoon at her as she put her head round the kitchen door. He was still in his bus driver's trousers worn with striped braces and shirt sleeves rolled up over his elbows. He had a tea towel fastened round his waist, already bespattered with fat and batter. 'I'm doing toad-in-the-hole with carrots and mash. I got a whole pound of sausages at the butcher's on my way home – I saw them being delivered on my way back to the depot. It'll be ready in half an hour or so if only you'll give me a hand with this batter. I don't seem to have got the hang of it . . . it looks a bit strange.'

'I have Richard to get to bed first,' she said.

'I'll see to the nipper. You're late anyroad – where've you been?'

'Oh, just painting the town red. Or at least washing down walls. Sister decided they needed doing and we all had to give a hand. And then when I went to pick up the little 'un, Ruby was in a flap. Little Jackie has the chicken pox.' Theda sighed. 'I suppose Richard will get it next.'

'Nay, man, don't cross your bridges afore you come to them. He might not. Here, give him here. I'll put him to bed while you take the lumps out of that disgusting mess.'

Theda beat away at the mixture until it was smooth then poured it over the sausages and put the lot in the oven. Thank God for the prefab, she thought again, with its light, bright kitchen such as she'd never seen before and its electric oven and that luxury of the rich, a refrigerator.

Richard had woken up and instead of whingeing as he was inclined to do, was laughing and splashing in the bath as Joss played with him. A satisfying smell was coming from the oven and the potatoes and carrots were bubbling on the stove. The kitchen was warm and bright and Theda began to relax.

Afterwards, with Richard in bed at the end of the hallway, they ate the meal at the kitchen table.

'I had a letter from the parents this morning,' Joss volunteered, putting his knife and fork on his empty plate and pushing it away. He poured himself a fresh cup of tea and lit a Woodbine cigarette with the lighter he had carried throughout the war. It was made from a brass .303 bullet case and the casing shone from the constant handling it received. Theda looked at his fingers playing with it, turning it round and round, flicking the light on and off.

'They all right, are they?' she asked.

'Fine. Mam says to give you her love and she'll be coming up to see you at the weekend.'

'And Da?'

'No, not Da.'

Well, she hadn't expected it. She hadn't seen him since the day she left Winton. But she missed him, missed them both. He's a stubborn old man, she thought, trying to channel her feelings into anger. At least that was better than the lost feeling inside her when she remembered how he had turned her out of his life.

'Well, I'm off out, got a big date tonight,' said Joss, breaking into her thoughts.

'With the lovely Beth, is it?'

'How did you know?'

'Just a lucky guess.'

Joss laughed easily. 'We're going to the pictures to see how John Wayne won the war. It's just as well to know in case we have to do it all again.' He stubbed his cigarette out on the ashtray and went off to the bathroom to get ready.

Please God, never again. The thought of Richard having to go through a war such as the last one or the one before that filled Theda with horror.

She took her cup into the sitting-room and put on the wireless. Soft music filled the room. She sat by the fire and sipped at her tea, wondering what she would do if Joss decided to get married and wanted to set up home on his own. Which he had a perfect right to do, she reminded herself. And if that was the way things were going, it would be just as well if she prepared herself for it.

First of all, she would have to go to a larger hospital and take her second-part midwifery. It would only be six months and then she would be well on her way to being qualified to go on the district. The thing was, would she be able to get a place in Sunderland or would she have to go elsewhere? If she had to, she didn't know how she would manage.

Finishing her tea, Theda took the cup out to the kitchen and began the washing up. Afterwards she would write a letter of application to the Infirmary.

The summer and autumn of 1946 passed in a whirl of work and study, rushing to pick up Richard from Ruby, and sometimes having to rely on Joss and Beth to look after him.

'Don't worry, I don't mind at all, I enjoy looking after him,' Beth reassured Theda when she apologised for the umpteenth time. And Richard enjoyed being with Beth.

Sometimes Theda couldn't help a pang of jealousy when she saw his face light up when Joss and Beth came in, how he laughed when Joss threw him up in the air, how it was her brother and his girl who were there to encourage him in his first attempt at crawling and when he pulled himself upright with the aid of a chair leg.

'You should have see it, Theda,' said Beth, laughing.

'I know.' Theda was not laughing.

'I meant – oh, I'm sorry, I know you would have loved to see it.' Beth was apologetic.

Theda leaned over Richard's cot one night as he lay sound asleep, his thumb firmly in his mouth, not stirring when she tucked the sheet round him more securely. Once again she had got in too late for his bedtime and Joss and Beth had seen to him.

'It's good practice for when we have our own,' said Joss. That was how Beth treated it too; she liked playing house in the cosy prefab.

But there were times when it was just impossible for any of them to be in two places at once. Beth was a clippie on the buses, usually on the same shift as Joss, and naturally they liked it that way. Often Theda thought she wouldn't be able to carry on for there was no one to look after the baby. Like the time he caught chicken pox right at the beginning of her course. But Theda was in quarantine too, she hadn't thought of that, and Richard was a healthy little boy and his a very light case of the disease.

One afternoon Theda walked with him in his push chair to the entrance of the hospital. Joss had been on early shift and had promised he would meet her at the gates and pick up the baby.

'I finish at twelve-thirty. I've loads of time to get there from the depot,' he assured Theda. But here it was, five to one, and there was no sign of the ancient Austin Ten which was Joss's pride and joy.

Richard was lying back uncomplaining, only his bright eyes darting about as he watched an ambulance negotiate the entrance and the people going backwards and forwards. Theda was gazing up the street where she expected the Austin to appear. If Joss didn't come soon, she thought, she would just have to go home again.

'Hello, it is you, isn't it?'

The well-remembered voice came from behind her. Theda turned round, disbelieving. Not now, not at this precise moment. Oh, no, she didn't want to meet him again now.

'Theda Wearmouth?'

She gazed at him. He was unchanged except that he wore a well-cut suit, not at all like the demob suits most of the returned soldiers she knew wore, ill-fitting and badly put together. His eyes were the same, though, cool and grey, and his hand as he held it out to her was the same surgeon's hand she remembered, so clean and firm and capable-looking.

'Doctor Collins,' she managed to say, and looked quickly away from him and fussed with Richard's blanket to hide the confusion she was feeling.

'I wondered where you had gone, Uncle Tucker didn't seem to know anything—'

'Theda! Eeh, lass, I'm sorry. I got held up at the depot but never mind, I'm here now. Let's have the little chap. Take him out of his chair and I'll put it in the boot.'

Joss had pulled up in his car and Richard was holding his arms out to him. 'Da, da, da,' he was gurgling, beaming at the sight of his beloved Uncle Joss. Theda lifted him out of his chair and it was all she could do to hold him for he was straining towards Joss, kicking and struggling and beginning to protest as she held on to him.

'Howay then, son,' said Joss, and put him in the seat beside him, bolstered on either side and in the front by cushions and tied round with a leather belt. Richard stopped complaining. He didn't mind at all being strapped in, so long as he could go with Joss.

'See you tonight, love,' he said to Theda and she nodded and watched as he pulled away from the kerb and out into the road. She turned back to Ken, hardly knowing what she was going to say to him, whether to shout at him for going away as he had or fall on him and weep. It was like a punch in the stomach to find he had gone.

She stared through the gates and up the drive to the main door. It was opening and shutting and a crowd of people were going in and out but she couldn't even tell if he was among them.

He didn't want to know her. Oh, he had been polite and friendly but obviously that was all there was to it. Slowly she walked up the drive and on to the ward.

'You're late,' snapped Sister. She was just coming out of a delivery room and hurried past Theda to go into another. 'Hurry up and get ready, Nurse,' she said over her shoulder. 'We have a busy afternoon ahead of us, I think.'

Fortunately from Theda's point of view it was very busy, which allowed her no time to brood or even to think about anything but her work. Later, as she took a break for tea, she put the question to one of her colleagues.

'Is there a Dr Collins working in the hospital?'

The other girl stared at her. 'Dr Collins? No, I don't – oh, do you mean, Mr Collins, the surgeon? Yes, of course there is. He's worked here for almost a year now. How come you don't know?'

'Oh, I suppose I don't notice much outside the department.'

'He's really quite a dish. I don't know how you could have missed him. Do you know him from somewhere?'

'I used to. A long time ago, during the war.'

'I suppose he's married? The best ones always are,' the other nurse sighed. 'Sod's law, isn't it?'

Theda felt a pang so strong she had to avert her face to stop it showing. 'I don't know, I suppose he probably is,' she mumbled.

On the other side of the hospital, Ken had just finished a theatre list and was sitting in the office, writing up the notes. He put the final stroke to the last report and closed the folder, putting it on top of the pile.

Sitting back in his chair, he picked up the cup of milky liquid which was served up as coffee, just the same as that served in most of the hospitals he had been in, and sipped the lukewarm stuff.

Dear God, he was tired, he thought, tired and depressed. And he had yet to go round the wards and check on his patients before he would be free to go home.

He was well aware of the reason for his depression. When he came face to face with Theda outside the hospital he had felt a surge of pleasure, delighted to see her again. So delighted that he even missed the fact that she had a child with her, a little boy by the look of things, he had noticed later. But at first all he could see was Theda and she seemed not to have changed at all; her dark hair still framed her face, pointing up the white of her skin, her dark eyes were as large and expressive as ever. He had greeted her without thinking, such a fool he was.

What a shock it had been when her husband drove up in that old banger of a car and the baby had smiled radiantly with her smile and held out his arms to his father. Judging by the baby's age, she must not have wasted much time after he himself had been sent back to the front line. Uncle Tucker must have been right about her. The thought brought a bitter taste to his mouth, which had nothing to do with the disgusting coffee.

Rising to his feet, Ken called goodbye to Theatre Sister and went out on his tour of the wards. At least he was free now to put her out of his mind altogether, as he should have done long ago.

Joss was married in March 1947 at a small Methodist chapel in one of the half-demolished streets of Sunderland. His parents travelled up with Chuck and Norma and all four stayed at a small hotel on the seafront at Roker. Da had declined to stay in the house in Laburnum Road.

'There isn't really room for us all, pet,' Bea had written in a letter. But Theda knew it was because of her that Da wouldn't stay with them. After all, on other family get-togethers they had all piled into the house in West Row.

Outside the church was the first time Theda had seen her father for fifteen months and he looked older some-how, greyer, but still as upright as he had always been.

'Are you coming home now that our Joss is getting married?' he asked her without any preliminaries. 'We can start again, I'm willing to let bygones be bygones.'

'No, Da. I'm staying here. I have a good friend to look after Richard when I'm working.'

'You know my views on that,' Matt Wearmouth said, and turned his back on her.

Theda refused to let it spoil the wedding for her. And if she felt an aching regret for what might have been, such as she'd felt when Clara got married, she put it firmly behind her. Ken Collins, *Mr* Collins now he had the letters FRCS after his name, had made it plain to her that he regarded her simply as an old acquaintance. Not that she would marry him now, not if he begged her. But she couldn't marry anyone else either, so no doubt she would stay single.

Listening to Joss and Beth making their vows before the minister, Theda looked down at Richard's bent head as he stood beside her on the pew seat, studying the hymn book with an air of concentration. Gently she turned it round in his hands so that it was the right way up and he looked up at her with wondering grey eyes, so like his father's.

The father who didn't want him, she thought, but that wasn't fair really. She should have let him know about Richard, he had a right perhaps. But no, he had not. He had gone off without a word, hadn't he?

The bridal party had gone into the vestry to sign the register and the congregation sat down. There was a buzz of whispered conversation.

'Go?' demanded Richard, losing interest in the hymn book.

'In a minute, darling.'

She picked him up and sat him on her knee and he leaned against her. After a moment the organ started up the 'Wedding March' and the company rose to their feet as the bridal couple led them out of the chapel into the pale sunshine. Bea, as she went past, smiled happily at Theda and Richard. Matt stared straight ahead of him at Joss's broad back.

Chapter Twenty-Nine

Theda was thinking about Joss and Beth and the fact that next weekend it would be their third wedding anniversary, as she walked up and down by the school gates. She would have to remember to send a card. She sighed. Durham City was a nice place to live and work, it was true, but she did miss having them near, being able to rely on them for help with Richard. And not only that, Beth was a good friend, and Joss – well, Joss was Joss; always the same ever since they were children.

Theda leaned against the school wall, staring at her feet as she waited for Richard's class to come out. A light drizzle had begun to fall and she turned up the collar of her uniform coat and pulled her hat more firmly on to her head. Today she had been so determined to get here on time that she had actually arrived ten minutes early.

A few more mothers were arriving now, some pushing prams or pushchairs. One or two spoke to her. She had become quite well-known in the few months she had been in Durham. Some of the babies in the prams she had delivered herself and these she had to admire and make favourable comments on.

'How well he's looking!' Or: 'Goodness, hasn't she grown?' she said when the mothers said hello and looked expectantly at her. It was when she lifted her head to reply to one such greeting that she noticed Mrs Carter by the gate, her shopping basket hooked over one arm.

Of course she should ignore the woman, Theda was well aware of that, but it had been a frustrating sort of day for her.

First of all, the letter she had been expecting concerning her application to become a Health Visitor had not turned up, then a mother had suffered unexpected complications so that Theda had had to call out the doctor to her in a hurry and her patient had been rushed into hospital for the delivery. Thankfully it had turned out all right in the end, but there had been a worrying hour or two first and not even the satisfactory lift of delivering the child herself. She looked at Mrs Carter and a surge of anger rose in her. On impulse Theda walked over to her, though she knew it was a mistake as she did it.

'Good afternoon, Mrs Carter,' she said, and even in her own ears she sounded aggressive.

The woman's eyebrows soared. Evidently she thought Theda did not know her well enough to greet her so familiarly. She murmured something non-committal in reply and stared into the middle distance.

'I understand you have been saying some rather unkind things about my son,' Theda went on, twin spots of colour brightening her cheeks.

'I have? You must have been misinformed. Why should I say anything about your son?'

'You called him a bastard.'

There was a murmur of shocked disapproval from the mothers near enough to hear.

'Really! I did nothing of the kind. You don't know what you're talking about.' Mrs Carter was disdainful. The other women were showing a great deal of interest now but Theda was at the stage where she didn't care.

'Do I not indeed? Richard tells me your Billy told him you did. In fact, they had a fight about it. Now I'm telling you: if you say anything else about me or my son, I'll have you up for slander!'

'Hoity-toity! Who do you think you are, threatening me? Coming out of nowhere with a bairn in tow . . . you're no better than you should be—'

'You mind what I said. Here are the children now. If you say anything before them, I'll have the law on you.'

Theda moved away. Battle honours to her, she thought. She had seen Miss Robinson come around the far corner of the building followed by the class walking decorously in twos. Right at the back came Richard, on his own. As he walked he was pulling off his coat and then he held it over his head to protect himself from the rain.

'Richard Wearmouth!' said Miss Robinson, stopping the column. 'Put your coat on at once. What do you think you are doing? Your shirt and trousers will get wet.'

'But my head is getting wet now, Miss Robinson,' he pointed out.

'Put your coat on,' she ordered. 'And don't answer me

333

back. How many times do I have to tell you? You should have remembered to bring your cap in any case.' She glared at him and then turned to Theda and glared at her, as though she had behaved very naughtily indeed in having such an awkward child, Theda thought, resisting the urge to giggle. Her brief spell of anger had evaporated.

The class moved on and stopped by the gate, waiting in silence to be dismissed. The mothers waited patiently in the rain.

'Class dismiss,' said Miss Robinson at last, and the children scampered out, Richard's face beaming as he saw his mother was there and he was not going to have to wait for her, all alone except for Miss Robinson.

Theda bent over him and helped him rebutton his coat. Out of the corner of her eyes she saw Billy Carter's mother grab him by the arm and march him off down the street, almost running him off his feet with the pace she was keeping. Theda's own mood was much lighter now, her outburst had done her good.

'Mam, can we go down by the river and have a picnic?'

'Richard, it's raining. We can't go for a picnic in the rain.'

'Why not, Mam? I like picnics in the rain.'

'A minute ago you didn't want to get your head wet,' she pointed out.

'But it's wet now, so it's too late. We can sit in that shelter anyway, the one by the cricket field, you know. It's got a roof,' he insisted.

Theda wavered. It wasn't too cold after all and she didn't often have the time to take him anywhere. So they bought pasties from the butcher on the parade of small shops halfway down New Elvet bank and two bottles of lemonade from the newsagents', and sat in the shelter and ate their pasties and drank the lemonade and watched the River Wear flowing past, swift and peaty.

A water vole slipped along the bank and plopped into the water and a family party of ducks sailed along serenely. Richard threw them bits of pastry and the mother duck led her ducklings over and they quacked excitedly as they gobbled them up, anxious not to miss any. The university rowing crew went past, practising despite the rain, the coach riding his bike along the towpath and calling the stroke. Richard was fascinated.

He watched them raptly, not speaking, forgetting his lemonade. But the light was already beginning to fall and a cool wind was blowing on the water, rippling the surface. I'm crazy, thought Theda, shivering. We'll have to go home. I'll put him in a hot bath straight away. Richard was tough, never seemed to suffer from coughs and colds – or not very often. But there was no sense in taking chances.

'Can we have a baby, Mam?'

The question took her by surprise. For a minute she could only stare at him as he turned away from the river. The rowing crew had disappeared round the bend. It was very quiet, even the birds seemed to have gone to roost early.

Theda took him on her lap and hugged him as she gathered her thoughts. 'Has one of your friends got a new baby brother or sister?' she temporised.

'Gary Nichols has. And he says his dad said you brought it.'

Theda remembered the Nicholses, of course, the baby boy was about two weeks old. She sighed. 'No, we can't have a baby, Richard.'

He clambered down and they began walking back up the lane to the main road. Waiting to cross it, he said, 'It's not fair.' But he didn't ask any more questions though she was dreading having to explain why a baby brother wasn't going to materialise and that once again it had something to do with his lack of a father.

Later, as she made toasted Marmite fingers for his supper and Richard was upstairs in the bath, the door bell rang. Her heart sank. She really didn't want to have to go out again tonight and it would mean getting Sheila in again to look after Richard and Theda hadn't even eaten yet. She went out into the hall and saw a dark shape through the ornamental glass of the front door, a man's shape. Best put on the chain, she thought, just in case.

It was a postman. Surprised, Theda took off the chain and opened the door wide and he handed her a telegram.

'Any reply?'

She hadn't even read it yet, just stared at the yellow envelope in her hand. 'Wait a minute,' she said. But before she could open it the telephone rang and she started, pulse racing.

What a fool she was, she told herself, and went to pick up the receiver. Maybe one of her patients was early. Everything always happened at once. That was one thing about midwifery: life was full of surprises.

'Theda?'

It took a second or two for the voice to register and she realised it was her mother. But why should she ring? Bea hated the telephone.

'Theda?'

'Hello, Mam? Is that you?' Something in her mother's voice alerted her, filled her with a nameless fear. 'What is it? Mother?'

'Where have you been, Theda? I've been trying to ring you for the last hour. I tried and tried, and managed to ring Joss and he tried to get you an' all. Eeh, Theda, where've you been? Did you get the telegram?'

Theda looked down at the telegram still unopened in her hand. 'I've got it, Mam, I haven't read it yet. Mam, *what's the matter*?' She was practically shouting down the phone now, the fear growing in her, choking her. Dear God, was it Da? Had he been hurt in the pit?

She could hear her mother begin to sob, great breaths being drawn in and whistling over the line. Tearing open the telegram, Theda had trouble focussing on the words and then she had trouble taking in the sense of them.

'Regret to tell you Charles had accident. Come home.' It was signed simply 'Mother'.

'Mam, what happened? Is Chuck all right?' But she knew he couldn't be, not when Bea called him by his given name.

'An accident. At the pit. My bonnie lad . . . oh, my bonnie lad.' Bea began to moan, a deep terrible sound. 'An' him just made under-manager an' all. Eeh, we were that proud, your da and me.'

337

'Mam?'

'He's gone, pet.'

'I'll come home, Mam. First thing in the morning.'

'Yes, that's right, pet. First thing in the morning.' Bea repeated the words but it was clear to Theda, even over the phone, that she hardly knew what it was she was saying.

'Mother, sit down, take it easy. I'll be there as soon as I can. You're not on your own, are you?'

'Nay, lass, of course I'm not. I'm at Norma's. We're both at Norma's. Of course we are, her family an' all. Poor lass is due next month. I'm coping fine, it was just with not being able to get in touch with you. No, I'm all right now, we're bearing up. We have to, for Norma's sake. She's having a lie down at the minute. I'll go now. See you in the morning, pet.'

The telephone went dead and Theda put it back on the rest.

'I'll have to go, missus. There's no reply, I take it?' She had forgotten all about the postman, still patiently standing at the door.

'No, no reply.'

Theda closed the door and went upstairs. Richard was already out of the bath and dripping water all over the bathroom linoleum but she hardly noticed, just wrapped him in a towel and carried him out to his bedroom and sat on the bed drying him. She put on his pyjamas and Mickey Mouse dressing gown and took him downstairs to sit him in front of a plate of Marmite toast.

He was quiet, drooping sleepily over it. She had to remind him twice to eat a little more. She warmed milk and made him a mug of cocoa and he only drank half of it before falling forward sound asleep. She only just caught him before he landed on the floor. Yet all the time she was doing it in a kind of shocked limbo, as though it was someone else dictating her actions.

Later, when he was tucked up in bed, she made her plans to get away, ringing up her supervisor and arranging to take compassionate leave, ringing Sheila to explain where she was going and that she wouldn't need her childminding services for a few days.

'By, I'm sorry,' said Sheila. 'What happened, do you know?' Theda had to admit that she didn't, she had just taken it for granted that Chuck had been killed in the pit. A fall of stone? A waggon gone amain, out of control? There were so many accidents that could happen in a mine.

'It doesn't matter how it happened in the end,' she said.

'No, of course not.' Sheila was silent for a moment.

'Well, look here, do you think it would be better if I kept Richard with me? I could you know, he's no trouble.'

'Good of you, Sheila. But no, I'll take him. I might be away for a few days.'

It was nine o'clock by the time Theda put down the phone. She went upstairs and packed a case for herself and Richard. She would go on the first bus, she decided. That would be the Newcastle to Bishop Auckland. It called in at Durham bus station at eight-thirty. She made a list and checked off everything she needed to take and tried to think of anything she needed to do before leaving, and all the time a part of her wondered at how she was keeping control when all she wanted to do was weep.

She had thought that she would not be able to sleep but somehow, round about midnight, she turned over on her side and next thing she knew it was already morning. She had missed the bus from Newcastle and caught the one from Sunderland at nine o'clock instead.

'But where are we going, Mam?' Richard asked, clambering on to the double-decker bus and making for the stairs. He loved sitting upstairs at the front and luckily the seats were vacant. 'Will Miss Robinson be annoyed at me for not going to school?'

'We're going to see Grandma and Grandda,' said Theda. 'And no, Miss Robinson will understand.'

'Where do they live, Grandma and Grandda?' asked Richard, and she realised with a sharp pang of shock that he had not been to Winton Colliery, at least not that he could remember. And with the shock came apprehension. Would she not be welcome in her father's house? Surely he would not turn her away, not now, not when Chuck . . . Suddenly she had to search in her bag for a handkerchief as the full force of losing her brother hit her.

Chapter Thirty

It was a quarter to four on the day before Theda and Richard travelled to Winton Colliery that Chuck joined the back shift men coming off shift as they walked to the shaft bottom. The men were tired and talk was desultory. It had been a hard day's work and they were hungry. Some of them moved over and made room for the young under-manager as a mark of respect, but after all it hadn't been so long ago that he had been working alongside them on the coal face.

'He always did have enough ambition for half a dozen,' observed Sam Hughes, the overman, as he watched Chuck stride through the crowd.

'Aye, he intends to be chairman of the Coal Board, that one,' someone else answered, and there was a general laugh.

Chuck heard it but it didn't matter to him; he got on well with most of the men and let them have their little digs. It was true, anyroad – he was going as far as he was able and had high hopes that under the Coal Board that would be right to the top.

Norma would have his meal ready, he thought. No need to go to the new canteen, which had been built beside the equally new pithead baths. There was his report to write but it wouldn't take long, the new coal cutter was working fine.

He rode up to bank in the cage with a group of young hewers, their spirits noticeably brightening the nearer they drew to the surface, and they all spilled out into the grey drizzle of the afternoon. Chuck shivered. It was cold after the heat of underground. What he needed was a hot shower. He marvelled that in such a short time the pithead baths had become so essential. He had almost forgotten the discomfort of going home black and caked with coal dust from the pit.

'Not before time an' all,' Da had said when the builders arrived to put up the baths, or showers as they were really. 'By, in my young day we would have thought we were in heaven, not having to travel home in our pit clothes. And to have a hot meal in the canteen. Molly-coddled these young 'uns are going to be.'

Chuck grinned to himself. He went into the dirty room of the baths and stripped off his pit clothes and put them in the drying locker. At the other end of the room a party of youngsters were larking about, laughing as they talked of the dance that was being held in the Miners' Welfare hall that evening, most especially the girls who would be there. Another cage load of men joined them as Chuck walked through to the main room with its open-ended shower cubicles. He could hear the laughing and joking getting more and more boisterous all the time, and smiled.

Just like bairns let out of school, he thought, but he himself was past all that. He was a married man with a baby on the way and hadn't time for messing about; he had better things to do. Picking up the soap, he turned on the water and stood for a minute or two, letting it sluice down his skin.

By, the hot water was grand. Thank God for the Coal Board. He threaded his fingers through his hair to loosen the dust and watched as the black water eddied round his feet and drained away into the plug hole. Soaping himself all over, he paid particular attention to his hair. He must remember to bring some of that shampoo Norma had bought him. Imperial Leather, that was it. He had felt slightly decadent, a bit cissy even, using special liquid soap to wash his hair but had to admit it made a better job than ordinary soap.

The suds ran down his face and stung his eyes. On the other side of the waist-high partition the young lads were larking about, flicking soap at each other, chasing round from one cubicle to another, laughing and shouting boisterously so that it sounded like a near riot in the echoing room. It was different for those who lived outside the village and needed to catch a bus home. He'd known that lot to come up in the cage at a quarter to the hour and be in the dirty end of the baths and out the clean side in time to catch the five to the hour Martin's bus.

'Bloody hell, man!' an older miner shouted as he was almost knocked off his feet as he stepped outside his cubicle. Chuck rubbed his eyes and looked across at him.

'Sorry, Grandda,' a lad said over his shoulder, his grin belying his words.

'An' I'm not your grandda!' shouted the older man. The others exploded into laughter as though he had made the joke of the century. It was time to intervene, thought Chuck.

'A little less hilarity, lads, if you don't mind,' he said, sounding only slightly pompous. They said nothing, though the laughter died in the air and they went back to their cubicles rather sheepishly.

Chuck felt a fool. Even to his own ears he had sounded fifty at least. There was a muffled burst of laughter from the other side and something landed at his feet. The lads weren't as respectful as all that. Not nowadays. Chuck rinsed himself off and stepped outside the cubicle, rubbing his eyes again as he did so, which were still stinging from the soap.

The fall was completely unexpected. One minute he was striding over for his towel on the other wall and the next he'd stepped on a sliver of soap and was flat on his back, staring up at the strip lights far above.

There was a splash of red on the white tiles of the cubicle. A drop was running down, ruby red turning to pink as it mixed with the water and he turned his head and saw the pink mingling with the coal-streaked soapy water, whirling round faster as it hit the drain. There were faces now bending over him, mouths working as though they were saying something, but there was no sound. And then everything faded from view.

*

It was just after ten o'clock when Theda, holding Richard by one hand and carrying her case with the other, walked up the yard to the back door of her parents' house. She hesitated before turning the brightly shining brass door handle that had replaced the sneck and went in.

It was dim in the kitchen, the curtains drawn against the light as was usual in a house of mourning. There wasn't even much light from the fire, which was almost out – just a few black cinders and a lot of grey ash. It wasn't like Mam to leave it like that, thought Theda as she dumped her case by the side of the press. Taking the coal rake, she pulled some small coal down on to the fire and then stirred the embers with the poker. It wasn't quite dead, smoke drifted lazily up the chimney.

'Does anybody live here?' asked Richard, looking round solemnly.

'Yes, Grandma and Grandda do.'

'I don't like it here. It's too dark.' He put his hands in his coat pockets and thrust out his bottom lip.

'Come on, we'll go and find them,' said Theda, taking his hand. Leaving the case where it was, they walked back up the yard and out on to the back lane. There was no one about. Whether the women were all out shopping or inside doing their housework Theda didn't know, in fact she didn't think about it.

It took only ten minutes to walk to the other end of the rows to where there was a small street of better-class accommodation, officials' houses. Chuck and Norma lived in the second house in Office Street. Theda knocked at the front door and after a moment it was opened by her father.

'Hello, Da,' she said. She gazed at him. He looked so old and bent and grey, his eyes puffy as though he had not slept for a week.

'Now then, lass.' Matt gazed back at her sombrely. Stepping forward she threw her arms around his neck and after only a slight hesitation his arms were around her too.

'Oh, Da. Oh, Daddy,' she said into his bristly neck.

'I know, lass, I know,' he muttered.

'Well, howay in, don't stand on the doorstep like that for all the world to gawp at,' snapped Bea's voice from behind him and his arms dropped to his sides.

'Mam? Is he my grandda?' asked Richard, and then turning to Matt, 'Are you my grandda?' he asked again, throwing his head back so that he could look up into Matt's face.

Some of the tension left Matt; he even managed a smile. 'I am that,' he declared. 'Mind, I never knew you were such a big lad. How old are you? Eight? Nine?'

Richard stood as tall as he could, proud that anyone could think him so much older. 'I'm only five,' he admitted. 'How old are you?'

'As old as my tongue and a little bit older than my teeth,' said Matt. He took hold of Richard's hand and Theda breathed a sigh of relief. At least there was going to be no bad feeling to complicate an occasion already so fraught with shock and sorrow.

Joss came, and solemn-faced he hugged his mother and Theda. Richard ran to him immediately and Joss sat him on his knee where Richard remained quietly watching the crowd of relations, all new to him except for Joss and Beth and his grandmother.

'I'll speak to Norma while you have Richard,' Theda said, and Joss nodded.

She was in the front room with her mother sitting protectively beside her. Norma wore a maternity smock printed with large sunflowers, which did nothing to disguise her late state of pregnancy, and her face was swollen with crying. Nevertheless, she accepted Theda's condolences with polite dignity.

'He was your brother,' she said. 'You'll miss him too.'

Theda had not seen Chuck since Joss's wedding yet she realised that didn't matter – Norma was right.

'Would you like some tea?' asked Norma's mother, but she looked frail and strained almost beyond endurance by what had happened and what was still happening to her daughter and the question was the automatic one asked of any visitor.

'No, thank you. I'm fine, Mrs Musgrave,' Theda replied. She sat with them for a few minutes more, noting the high colour in Norma's cheeks, the obvious weariness in her as she put a hand to her back and sighed. Norma probably had less than the supposed month to go, she judged, and hoped all this did not bring on premature labour.

'Perhaps you should lie down for a while, Norma?' she suggested, and looked at Mrs Musgrave who nodded her agreement.

'Oh, no, I must be here for him,' said Norma. Mrs Musgrave raised her eyebrows but said nothing.

Here for whom? asked Theda in her mind, though she did not put it into words. Here for Chuck, that was what Norma felt. It was an instinctive reaction.

'The minister is coming anyway,' she said. 'We have to arrange the funeral.'

'No, pet. There is to be a post-mortem and inquest first,' her mother reminded her.

'Oh, yes.' Norma turned to Theda. 'It was the tiles in the showers, you know. They're so hard, that's the trouble.' She looked puzzled. 'Though why Chuck should bang his head on them, I don't know.'

She ought to be in bed. Theda took hold of her wrist, feeling the pulse flutter. Norma was being entirely too reasonable and normal, she was liable to crack at any time. But what did she mean? Had Chuck not had his accident down the pit? But this was no time to enquire.

'Come on, love, we'll help you upstairs. You have to think of the baby, you know. Chuck wouldn't want you to get overtired, would he?'

Norma nodded. 'Maybe you're right,' she conceded. 'But there is so much to do. All the arrangements—'

'Me and your dad will see to everything, pet,' her mother assured her. 'Like Theda says, you have to think of the baby.'

With Norma upstairs lying down, the Wearmouth family made their excuses and walked back to West Row. On the way, Matt told them what had happened.

'All those years we campaigned for pithead baths,' he said bitterly. 'Who could have thought it?'

It was ironic, thought Theda. Oh God, how could this

happen? A stupid, stupid freak accident and Chuck was gone.

'I sent a cable to Clara,' said Bea. 'Not that she can come, of course, not with all those bairns.' For Clara had four children now. It was clear to Theda that Bea yearned for Clara to come, children or no, for she needed the comfort of her family with her.

'Never mind, Mam, at least you know she's all right.'

'Oh, aye, she is an' all. Happy as Larry, I shouldn't wonder.'

'She wouldn't get over in time for the funeral anyroad,' said Matt, and blew his nose loudly.

The funeral wasn't until a week later. Both Joss and Theda had had to return to work in the meantime. Joss had swapped days off with a mate to get down the day after Chuck was killed but got two days' compassionate leave for the funeral, as did Theda.

'I'll pick you up,' he offered when he rang her. 'What about Richard?'

'I'll have to take him,' she replied. She had no one to leave him with, not for any length of time. For the actual funeral, Renee had offered to mind him.

The sun shone through the windows of the Methodist chapel as the coffin was carried down the aisle behind the minister and the light glinted on the brass handles. It was carried by Joss, Norma's brother, and two of Chuck's marras. The family walked behind, Norma supported by her father, then the Wearmouths and the Musgraves. After the short service they drove off to the cemetery and stood round the grave with the sun still shining on the cross of lilies as it went down into the hole with the coffin and the brightly coloured wreaths as they were laid by the side. They all filed past and threw in the token handful of soil, and the men fingered their starched collars and took out their handkerchiefs to wipe their eyes and foreheads, ostensibly because of the heat though it was still early-spring.

Theda was aware that the chapel had been full and a lot of men off shift had followed Chuck's coffin to the grave but she didn't look at them and therefore didn't notice that Tucker Cornish was there with a younger man.

The funeral tea was in Norma's house and Theda and Beth helped pass the sausage rolls and plates of ham and beetroot salad while Richard followed them round, helping.

'He's as grey as a badger, isn't he?' Joss was saying to his father. They stood in the window that looked out over the rows of Winton Colliery as the shadow of the winding wheel lengthened over them.

'Who is?'

'The gaffer.' Matt turned to his daughter to answer her question and took a sausage roll. He looked at it and put it in the saucer of the cup of tea he was holding.

'I understand he worked his way up, just the same as our Chuck. You can tell an' all. He makes a good manager from the men's point of view as well as the bosses'. Maybe if it hadn't have been for his family he would have been area manager by now.'

'His family? But his mother and grandmother live over

by the coast. His brother is a farmer, his grandfather was too. How can they affect his work?'

Matt looked curiously at Theda. 'What do you know about it? Tucker Cornish's father and half-brother were the ones who were hanged for killing the mine agent. Did you never hear of that?'

Yes, she had, of course she had. It was a local murder and at school the children had sung rhymes about it. Just as they still sang rhymes about the West Auckland woman, Mary Anne Cotton, the woman who was hanged for poisoning her children. Absurdly that rhyme ran through her head, 'Mary Anne Cotton, she's dead and she's rotten'.

She shook her head. 'I'd forgotten that.' She almost said she knew Tucker Cornish's family and they were very respectable but to talk about anything connected with Ken was dangerous, well-nigh impossible.

'We can't be too late,' said Joss, putting down his plate. 'I have to get back with Beth and you have Richard, it'll be his bedtime soon enough.' He smiled down at the boy who was hanging on to his mother's skirt with one hand and had the thumb of the other firmly in his mouth. Theda followed his gaze.

'Don't do that,' she said automatically, and gently removed the thumb. Joss swung him up in the air and Richard broke into delighted giggles.

'Again, Uncle Joss, again!'

'Just once, then we have to go.' Joss swung the child in an arc and his legs stuck out in the air. Matt pretended he had to duck and the rest of the company looked on eagerly; the play with the boy broke the tension somehow.

They said their goodbyes and Theda promised to come again soon then they were away up the lane to Durham Road and the funeral was over.

'It went well, I think,' said Beth. 'Considering, I mean.'

'Yes.' Theda sat back in her seat and Richard dropped his head on her shoulder, eyes already closing with the motion of the car.

Chapter Thirty-One

'An unusually thin skull, eh?' said Ken. 'What a thing to happen.' The two men had just returned from the funeral and were having a drink together before Ken drove back to Sunderland.

'And who would have thought it? A man spends so many years in the pit where he could have all sorts of accidents – well, most miners have been hit on the head by the odd stone at some time or other. But he hits his head in the showers. Ironic, I call it.'

'Lost one son in the war, the Wearmouths, didn't they?'

'That's right – Dunkirk.'

Ken sipped at his whisky and water, a weak one because he had an hour's drive ahead of him. He pictured Theda as he had last seen her, standing by the grave, beautiful in a black suit with a pencil slim skirt and heart-shaped neckline. She had been so quiet, so sad. He had wanted to go over to her and comfort her, had had to stop himself from going. She aroused all his protective instincts.

He had looked around for her husband, feeling irritated. Where was he? Why wasn't he there, looking after her? He thought he recognised him but he was standing with a petite blonde so it couldn't have been him. Maybe her husband was looking after the child. The thought made him feel even more irritated, or maybe angry was the right word.

Which was silly; why should he feel like that about a girl he hadn't seen for years? A girl who made it plain all those years ago that he meant nothing to her by the fact that she hadn't even replied to his letter.

'Penny for them?' said Tucker.

Ken stirred and glanced across at his uncle. 'They aren't worth it,' he said. 'I was just thinking how little Theda Wearmouth has changed from when she was nursing the prisoners-of-war at Bishop. Even though she's married and with a family now.'

'Married? Is she? I didn't know that.' But Tucker's thoughts were still with his lost under-manager. 'You know, he was a good man, Charles Wearmouth. Reliable and that. He'll take some replacing.'

'Yes. I see his wife is expecting a baby soon too. Poor girl. Will she have to move from that house?'

'Not immediately, but eventually of course. Not while the enquiry is ongoing. But I should think she'll get some compensation, even though he had a thin skull.'

'Yes. Her husband drives on the buses, you know. I saw them together once as I was going into the hospital at Sunderland.'

'Who's husband?' Tucker was mystified, had no idea at all what Ken was talking about.

'Theda Wearmouth's. She must still be nursing. Though I haven't seen her lately. Maybe she has some more family.'

'What on earth are you on about? Theda Wearmouth has only the one boy, I don't think she's married. She never was, though there was talk for a while about that Canadian, or perhaps he was an American, she went out with during the war. But he'll be safely back in Texas or Michigan or some such place, I suppose. Now her sister, Clara I think her name is, she succeeded in marrying *her* Canadian. I understand she's living out there in the frozen north, a baby every year according to Chuck. He's always talking about his family.' Tucker paused. 'He *was* always talking about his family. Except for Theda, he didn't say much about her. She fell out with the family, you know, over the boy I should think. I was surprised to see her here, though I suppose at her brother's funeral . . . Ah, well.'

Ken shook his head. 'No, you're mistaken. I saw her with her husband. I told you, he's a bus driver.'

'Well, I hadn't heard about it. He must be a friend of her brother's. Now Joss, the one who was a paratrooper, *he's* a bus driver. He never came back to the pits. Left in the mid-thirties, I believe, joined the army then.'

Joss! Yes, of course, she had a brother called Joss. That was who must have been with the blonde woman today. He had had the looks of the Wearmouths, it was true. A lightness stirred in Ken. No doubt the whisky had given him a lift, he no longer felt down at all.

'Well, I have to go to the office,' said Tucker. 'There's

more paper work than ever now we're all working for the Coal Board. What are you smiling about?'

'Nothing. I was just thinking how we all assume things and half the time they aren't true. Anyway, I must get back too.'

Ken was whistling as he went out to his car. He had done his duty and supported Uncle Tucker through the day, as his grandmother had asked him to. Mind, his uncle did look old and tired, he thought as he drove up to Durham Road in his new Rover, only ten minutes before Joss in his old Austin Ten. Well, he only had a year or two to go before he retired. A pity Tucker had not married again after Betty died. He was the sort who needed a wife.

Sometimes Ken felt the same way himself, he mused as he drove past the inn near Spennymoor where he and Theda had once spent the night. How shy she had been, and inexperienced. He could have sworn he was the first lover she had had. He negotiated the roundabout at Croxdale and got on to the dual carriageway of the great North Road. Automatically he put his foot down, enjoying the way the Rover responded immediately with a surge of power. Now if Theda Wearmouth wasn't married as he had thought, well then . . . He felt a stir of excitement within him. So what if she had a child, even if the father had been an American? There had been a war on, hadn't there? A lot of girls had let their feelings run away with them. Theda would be older and wiser now and he had to respect her, bringing up a child on her own. Maybe if he himself hadn't had to go away when he did . . . Ken sighed. He didn't know now what he would have done, he had still been hurting from what had happened to Julie. Her dying like that. Oh, God, wars were so pointless. Though not the last one. They had had to defeat the Nazis, of course they had.

Ken smiled wryly. Theda had really got under his skin, and when he had sworn never to let another girl do that after Julie. It had taken him a long time to stop thinking of Theda. He had been determined to get over her and here he was, five, nearly six years later, still thinking of her. The only way was to find her, have it out with her. He would never be able to take an interest in anyone else, not properly, until he did.

Theda put Richard to bed, not bothering with his bath. He was already asleep and barely opened his eyes as she undressed him and put on his Rupert Bear pyjamas and tucked him up in bed. Though the day had been warm there was a frosty feel to the air and she opened the window just a crack and drew the curtains across. Then she went downstairs and made herself a bowl of spaghetti and cheese sauce and sat eating it at the kitchen table, a book on public hygiene propped up against the milk jug before her.

But she grew tired of reading and soon put down her fork too. The meal was uninteresting and the book held nothing she didn't already know. How could there be any sort of public hygiene around here until the mining villages were rid of their ash and earth closets, until they had proper plumbing and flush toilets, indoor toilets? No wonder disease still flourished.

But she couldn't even summon up indignation; she was

too full of sadness and not just because of Chuck and the funeral. She felt sorry for herself, she realised. She saw Joss and Beth together and was jealous of their happiness. What a stupid, mixed-up woman she was, growing into an embittered spinster even though she had Richard. She was filled with undefined longings, a restlessness.

Opening the kitchen cabinet she took out the half-full bottle of sherry left over from Christmas and poured herself a glass to take into the sitting room. She looked at her row of textbooks with distaste. Ambition wasn't everything. Chuck had had ambition but it availed to nothing in the end. It was family which was the important thing. And she had Richard, she reminded herself.

What she needed was a man in her life, she admitted. Maybe she should have settled for Gene, married him, gone to America. They could have had a better life, both her and Richard. Why had she let the memory of Ken Collins stop her? Many a girl had had to settle for second best, why not Theda Wearmouth?

Theda sighed. She sipped the sherry, Harvey's Bristol Cream, sweet and strong. Going into the kitchen, she poured another glass.

Next morning, she slept in and had to rush to get Richard to school. Her head ached and there was a sour taste at the back of her throat and she had to stop herself from snapping at Richard as he insisted on taking precious time tying his shoelaces himself and buttoning up his coat.

'You look a bit pale,' her first patient said. 'Out on the tiles, were you, last night?'

'It was my brother's funeral,' snapped Theda, and the woman was contrite.

'Eeh, I'm sorry, I didn't mean anything,' she said, lying down on the bed and allowing Theda to examine her distended stomach.

'That's all right, I didn't mean to snap either,' said Theda. 'Fact is, I do feel frail today.'

The day was got through, as was the one after that and the one after that, and gradually the pain of losing Chuck began to lessen and Theda began to feel better. She managed to buy a second-hand car, a Morris, and went to driving school in the city. After all, she reasoned, if she was going to be a Health Visitor it would be so much easier for her if she could drive herself around.

She passed her test at the first try and drove home on her own in triumph. And then it was Whitsuntide and the weather was warmer and she had the weekend off.

It was to be a surprise for Richard. She met him out of school on Friday teatime with weekend cases packed for them both.

'Where are we going, Mam?' he shouted excitedly as she opened the car door while he climbed in. 'Are we going to see Grandda or Uncle Joss and Aunty Beth?'

'No, it's a surprise. Just you wait and see.'

Theda drove out of the city and up the Sunderland road towards the coast. It took a while to get through the traffic in Sunderland, more and more people had cars now and it was a bank holiday weekend, but at last she was out on the coast road and past Roker seafront and on to Seaburn. For a minute or two she was tempted to go on to Whitburn and

Marsden, but common sense prevailed and she stopped the car outside a boarding house right on the seafront at Seaburn which had a card in the window saying 'Vacancies'.

'Are we staying here, Mam?' Richard was excited. He grasped his tiny attache case and stood on the pavement, waiting for her to lock the car. 'Can we go on the sands?'

'We are and you can,' said Theda. They booked into a modest room with a double bed and a single in the corner, which left no room at all for any other furniture except an old wardrobe in the opposite corner and, incredibly, a hand basin. Within fifteen minutes they had unpacked and were walking across the grass to the sands, Theda hanging on to Richard's hand as he pulled her along, jumping up and down with impatience.

The beach was still crowded with day-trippers. They took off their shoes and left them where the dry sand met the rest still damp from the tide and paddled along the water's edge. Richard squealed and jumped about as the cold water hit his bare feet and ran up the beach a way, but was soon back and wading happily.

'Are there any fish, Mam? Or crabs? We've been learning about crabs at school – they pinch your toes.'

'Well, you'll just have to watch out for them and not let one get you, won't you?'

They walked the length of the beach and after a while the water was no longer cold to their feet but delicious and refreshing, and their toes sank into the damp sand and that was delicious too. They bought sandwiches from a tea kiosk on the sands, spam sandwiches, which in normal circumstances Richard wouldn't eat but he ate every last crumb of these and an ice-cream after. And the late afternoon seemed endless, white clouds too small to obscure the sun for long chasing across the sky, and the North Sea was blue instead of the usual colour Theda remembered, gun-metal grey.

It was high tea in the boarding house at half-past six and in the end they had to run across the road in their bare feet for of course she had forgotten that the tide line was changing all the time and the sea had taken their shoes. They found them again, dripping wet, washed up by a wave and had to carry them. They were unwearable. So they bought sandshoes at another kiosk on the front, and a tin bucket with a picture of a boy with a ball on it, and a wooden spade.

There were fish and chips for tea and the cod was fresh and white and flaky, and rice pudding after. Well, what did she expect for nine and sixpence a day? Theda asked herself and ate it up with an appetite that matched Richard's.

'Can we go back on the beach now?' he asked. 'Aw, come on, Mam – just for half an hour.'

'Half an hour, then it's time for bed.' It was way past bedtime really, but what the heck?

But when they crossed the road this time the beach had disappeared. Or at least there was just a thin line of sand in places and waves were splashing up against the sea wall. Richard was disappointed and inclined to be tearful. Theda lifted him up in her arms but he struggled to escape and ran forward, not looking where he was going, straight into an enormous Old English sheepdog. Down he went, and the dog too, but the dog picked himself up and bent over the boy, barking furiously.

Theda ran forward. 'Go away! Go away, you brute,' she cried, waving her arms about. The dog backed off and she picked up the boy and sat down on one of the benches that lined the promenade and hugged him to her.

'Hush now, never mind, pet,' she said, and examined a graze, which had appeared on his knee.

'Let me look at that,' said a voice. It must be the owner of the dog, she thought, and cradled Richard protectively. Fury mounted in her at anyone who would let a great brute like that free in a place where bairns were playing.

'I'll see to it myself,' she shouted, not even looking at him. 'I'm a nurse. Why don't you keep your dog under control? He's vicious, that's what he is, great lumping thing!'

'In the first place, he's a she, and if you take a proper look at her you'll see she's not in the least vicious. It was the boy who ran into her. She wouldn't usually have barked at him, she was startled, that's all. Now come on, let me look at him. You may be a nurse but I'm a doctor.' He lifted Richard's leg up by the heel of his sandshoe and inspected the graze, and smiled at the boy.

Slowly, as Theda realized that Richard was not really hurt apart from the graze on his knee, for which the only treatment needed was a wash and a piece of plaster, she calmed down and began to realise she knew that voice. Oh, yes, she did. She couldn't believe it though. She looked up at him and saw he was gazing at her, open-mouthed.

'What on earth are you doing here?' she asked Ken.

'Theda? Theda Wearmouth?'

Chapter Thirty-Two

'She's called Flora, Mam, did you hear the man say? She's a lovely dog, isn't she, Mam? Can we have a dog? I'll look after it, I promise, take it for walks and that, find it stuff to eat. Please, Mam, can we have a dog, a big dog like Flora?'

'We'll see,' Theda temporised. Richard was standing by the wash basin while she dried him. She had sponged him down and for once he hadn't insisted on doing it himself, he was too busy talking.

'Yes, but can we, Mam?' Richard insisted. He looked anxiously at her with Ken's eyes and her heart turned over. Surely Ken had seen how alike they were? Trembling a little, she picked up the boy's pyjamas and put them on him.

'Into bed now, no more talking. I'll read you a story and then you must go to sleep. You want to go on the beach tomorrow, don't you?'

'I do, Mam, I do. Flora might be there, mightn't she? We can go in the water together. It won't matter if we get splashed, will it? I mean, I'll have my trunks on and Flora—'

'No more talking, I said. Now which story do you want?'

But Richard was already dropping off to sleep, his eyelids closing, lashes fanning out over his cheeks. 'Two more whole days,' he was saying, and turned over with his back to the light and was off.

Theda sat by the window in the near dark, looking out over the promenade. The window was open and she could hear the sea, like the wind soughing through trees, but rhythmically rather than wildly. Now Richard was taken care of, she could think about her own reactions to seeing Ken so unexpectedly.

'What on earth are you doing here?' she had asked, almost as though he had no right to be. And the scene repeated itself in her mind.

'I live here,' he said, and pointed to a pre-war villa just off the front. 'Do you see? The one with the lilac by the front door.'

'Oh, yes,' she said. 'For some reason I thought you lived in Marsden.'

'No, but my family does, if you remember.'

Oh, yes, she remembered. She felt hot all over at how much she remembered. Dear Lord, she wasn't prepared for this, she needed time.

'I have to go,' she said, setting the child down and getting rapidly to her feet. 'Come along, Richard.'

'Look at him, Mam, look at the dog! He's licking me, Mam, look!'

'She. Her name's Flora,' Ken said automatically, but he was still gazing at Theda. 'I'll walk with you.'

'No!' she said, and then realising she had been too vehement. 'No, there's no need. We're staying just across the road. The Britannia boarding house.'

'Oh, yes. Not far from me then,' he commented. 'I'll come along anyway. Heel, Flora.' Obediently the dog left Richard and went to her master, standing patiently while he attached a lead to her collar.

They stood in a row on the kerb, waiting for a gap in the traffic, and then crossed the road and were at the boarding house. Theda turned to Ken.

'We'll go in then. It's Richard's bedtime, he's tired,' she said.

'No, I'm not,' he declared. 'Are you going to be on the beach tomorrow, sir?' He was on his best behaviour, thought Theda, amused even in her confusion. He had to be to remember to call Ken 'sir' instead of 'mister'.

'My name's Ken, Ken Collins. Yes, I think we will. We're there most mornings I don't have to go to the hospital. What's your name, son?'

Theda caught her breath. 'Look, we really have to go—' she said, pulling Richard towards the front door of the boarding house.

'Richard, my name's Richard,' he called. 'Don't pull, Mam, I'm coming.'

'I'll see you tomorrow,' said Ken. 'Down by the ice-cream kiosk? Ten o'clock?'

'I . . . I don't know.'

'Aw, yes we will, Mam – say we will!'

Ken took a step towards her. 'Look, Theda, I was trying to find out where you were. In fact I'd just found out that you were living and working in Durham City. I was going to come and see you; isn't this a great coincidence?'

Theda's face closed up. 'Oh, yes, a great coincidence. Mind, there's likely to be a few great coincidences in five years, aren't there? Good night then. Richard, say goodnight to Mr Collins.'

'Goodnight, Mr Collins, I'll see you tomorrow. Will you buy me a cornet?'

'Richard!' Theda opened the door and closed it behind her, hearing Ken saying something behind her but not what it was. 'You don't ask strangers for treats, don't let me have to tell you again.'

'But he's not a stranger, Mam. You said you know him. You do know him, Mam,' wailed Richard, as they climbed the stairs to their room.

I do know him, thought Theda, going to the window and staring out to sea. There were lights out on the horizon, no doubt ships and small boats going into harbour at Shields or somewhere. Why on earth had she picked Seaburn? She could just as easily have gone to South Shields or Whitley Bay even.

Five years hadn't changed her much, thought Ken as he let himself into the house. Her hair was still as black and abundant and her eyes wide and brown with the brows arched over them. Funny that he should have been making enquiries about her these last few weeks without actually getting to the point of finding her, and here she was, on his own doorstep, so to speak.

He took Flora into the kitchen and put food in her bowl, made sure there was enough fresh water for her. 'Stay,' he said, and she looked up from the bowl and whined softly before accepting the fact that he was going out and returning to her food. Ken went upstairs and washed and shaved and put on fresh clothes then went out to his car. And all the time his mind was on Theda and the little boy who reminded him of someone, but he couldn't think who.

Half-heartedly he started the engine and drove out on to the road south. He was going to dinner at the farm; he had promised Gran he would go tonight.

'I'm getting on, you know,' she had said on the telephone, 'you should come more often.'

Ken smiled. So far as he could tell she was as fit as anyone who had reached the age of seventy-six could be, but she was not above a little emotional blackmail when she thought it was warranted.

It was only a short drive to Marsden and he had little time to think about his meeting with Theda and the boy. He ate dinner with the family and sat afterwards and discussed farm business with his brother and his Uncle Jack. But Walt soon went out, though when he was asked was cagey about where he was going, muttering that he might call in at the Whitworth Arms.

'I don't know why our lads have to be so secretive when they start courting,' Meg commented. I'm sure we'd be glad to get them off our hands, wouldn't we,

Jane?' She spoke to her daughter but she was looking at
Ken.

'Who do you mean, Gran?' he asked. 'I don't think
Uncle Jack is courting. You're not, are you, Jack?'

'Don't talk so soft,' growled his uncle.

'It's well time you sorted yourself out, our Ken,' said
Meg. 'If you're not careful you'll end up a grumpy old
bachelor. Time you were finding yourself a nice lass and
settling down.'

'I might just do that,' he agreed, completely taking the
wind out of her sails.

Driving back to Seaburn, he found himself looking
forward to the next morning. He had no clinic or theatre
list and wouldn't be going into the hospital at all unless
called. He could spend the whole day on the beach with
Flora.

He saw them cross the road and the esplanade and come
down the steps to the beach as Flora began barking in an
excitement that matched Richard's. They saw Ken and
Richard ran towards him and the dog ran to meet the boy
as though she had known him all her life.

Theda followed more slowly, feeling suddenly unsure
of herself.

'Good morning, Nurse Wearmouth,' Ken said, and
smiled down at her. 'I've been watching you.'

'Morning.' She gazed at him, this man who was a
stranger yet not a stranger, and thought, What the heck?
Why worry about being hurt again, sieze the moment.

'Can I take my shoes and socks off?' asked Richard,

and she took them and put them in her holdall, then she and Ken began walking down the beach just above the water line while Richard and Flora paddled at the water's edge. They walked in silence for a while, Theda searching for something to say though anything she thought of seemed unsuitable. In the end she took refuge in the banal subject of the weather.

'Nice morning, isn't it?'

'Yes. A cool breeze off the sea, though. I wouldn't be surprised if there's not a sea fret before the day's out. The North Sea doesn't warm up until the late summer and when the warmth of the sun hits it we get a fret. Or a haar, if you like.'

'Yes.' They walked on, watching Richard who had found a piece of driftwood and was throwing it into the sea for Flora to retrieve. Obligingly the dog brought it back and Richard threw it again.

'He'll tire before the dog,' said Ken.

'Yes.' He would be beginning to think that was all she could say. Theda cast a quick glance at him sideways and saw he was grinning, eyes dancing with merriment, and she grinned at him too and relaxed.

They found a place sheltered from the wind but close enough to the sea so that they could keep an eye on Richard and Flora. Ken got deck chairs and put them side by side. They chatted, carefully at first, talking about their time at the prisoner-of-war hospital and carefully skirting round anything at all about the time he went away.

'You remember Major Koestler?' asked Theda.

'Yes, of course I do.'

'Did you know they caught him sending messages back to Germany? He had a short-wave radio hidden in his room. The funny thing is, no one suspected him at all. It was a seven-day wonder when the radio was discovered. I never could understand how he could find anything of interest to send. Not in a little place like Bishop Auckland.'

'It's surprising. I did hear about it actually, I was questioned about him at the time. But the war was just about over anyway. I never suspected he was a Nazi, though. He was such a good doctor, a dedicated man.'

Theda remembered the disabled children in the small ward on Block Two, remembered the POW's attitude to them that Christmas of 1944. 'I did,' she said. Ken glanced at her and then away, over to the edge of the sea where Richard and Flora were still trotting in and out of the water.

'At one time I thought he was sweet on you,' he said. 'And you on him. I was jealous.'

Theda stared at him. Had she heard aright? 'What did you say?' she asked him, but Richard had come up and was tugging at Ken's sleeve.

'Will you help me build a sandcastle?' he asked Ken, then looked at his mother and added, 'Sir?'

'My name is Ken; you can call me that,' he said. And they built a castle, round and high with battlements the shape of Richard's little bucket, for they used that to shape the wet sand. Ken dug out a moat and build a drawbridge and marked out a portcullis and some windows. And Richard started the interminable journeys to the water's edge to bring back water for the moat. After a while another little boy joined him and the two of them trotted backwards and forwards to the sea, with Flora going along at first until she tired and flopped down beside Ken, her tongue hanging out.

The boys came back yet again and dropped their buckets. 'This is Brian,' Richard said to Ken and Theda. 'His mam's over there.' He pointed to a woman sitting knitting close by.

'Hello, Brian,' said Theda. 'Are you thirsty, you two? I'll get you some pop at the kiosk. Do you want dandelion and burdock or cream soda?'

'Dandelion and burdock, please,' the boys said together, and Ken hauled himself to his feet.

'I'll get it,' he said, and Theda enjoyed the unaccustomed luxury of sitting back and waiting while he did. He came back with four bottles.

'I knew you'd like one too,' he said to her. 'It's all those years of doing without such luxuries during the war that does it.'

'Your daddy's nice,' said Brian to Richard, and there was a sudden silence before Richard hooted with laughter.

'He's not my daddy!' he cried.

The sun went in, and as sometimes happens a fret rolled in from the North Sea, damp and clinging, and it started to rain.

'We'll have to go indoors,' said Theda, rising to her feet and pulling Richard's jacket out of her bag. 'Come on, Richard. Put this on, we're going.'

'I don't want to,' he wailed. 'I want to play with Brian.'

But Brian's mother was calling him and suddenly everyone was scurrying from the beach.

'Come back to my house?' said Ken.

'Oh, well, I don't think—' Theda began. Suddenly she thought of something which hadn't occurred to her before.

'Your wife . . . we don't want to be a trouble.'

'I'm not married,' said Ken. 'There's only Mrs Gascoigne who "does" for me. Every morning, nine till twelve.' Theda felt she had been too obvious for amusement was in his eyes once again but nevertheless she felt a lightening of the heart.

'We'll come. Richard loves to play with Flora.'

'And she likes to play with him.'

Richard brightened at the idea of going home with Flora and they hurried across the road and up the small drive and round the side of the house to the back porch where Flora had to stay until she dried out properly.

'I'll dry her,' said Richard eagerly, and Ken handed him the towel while he and Theda went into the kitchen. 'I'll make some lunch,' said Ken. 'Mrs Gascoigne has already gone, I didn't realise it was so late.'

'Oh, don't bother, we can eat at the Britannia,' said Theda.

But Ken wouldn't hear of it and in the end they made up a meal together, he washing salad stuffs at the sink while Theda sliced tomatoes and cheese to eke out the ham that Mrs Gascoigne had left in the fridge for Ken.

When it was ready they went to call Richard but there he was, beside Flora, boy and dog asleep on the rug, the boy's head on the dog's neck and one thin brown arm flung over her back.

'Leave them,' whispered Ken, and drew her inside, through the kitchen and the hall and into the sitting-room. She went obediently, drugged by his nearness and the feel of his hand on her wrist. He pulled her to him and kissed her on the lips, gently at first and then insistently, and it was as if the intervening years had never been. If a warning bell rang in her head Theda was quite deaf to it, all she could hear was the clamouring in her blood, the long denied desire for him, and could feel him harden against her through the thin cotton of her dirndl skirt.

She was drowning, smothered by the strength of the feelings she had denied for so long. His fingers moved on her back, sending electric shocks through her system until she thought she couldn't bear it. She was desperate, moaning, as she leaned into him. Ken was drawing her towards the couch, bending his head to her breast, pulling down her blouse impatiently, and there was no way she could have stopped him, though a flicker of sanity did run through her head and she knew she should. And then his arms were dropping from her and she swayed, eyes only half-open. For a minute she thought she would fall.

'Are you my daddy?' said Richard's voice and her eyes flew open. He was there, standing in the doorway, one hand on the door knob. Even in her febrile state she registered his expression of hope and eagerness. 'Daddies and mams do that, Billy Carter said.'

Chapter Thirty-Three

If the proverbial ground had opened and swallowed her, Theda felt she would have been happy. As it was, she sat in a corner of an out-of-the-way cafe with Richard and watched while he ate egg and chips. She drank a couple of mugs of tea and the rain trickled down the window pane, echoing her mood.

'I don't want to go now!' Richard had cried as she'd grabbed his coat and bundled him into it and out of the house, making an incoherent response when Ken tried to stop her, not looking at him, she couldn't.

'What about lunch?' Ken asked bewildered. 'Oh, come on, Theda, kids say these things. They don't mean anything. Why get in a state?'

'I'm hungry,' Richard protested, and she dragged him round the corner and another corner and away from the front of Seaburn to get as far away from Ken as possible.

'I'll have another cup of tea,' she said to the waitress, and watched as Richard puddled a chip round and round in his egg yolk, making her feel slightly nauseous. 'Stop making a mess and eat it up, Richard.'

His bottom lip jutted out. 'I wanted to stay and play with Flora,' he said, looking mutinous. 'Why couldn't I?'

'Because,' she said, sounding like a cross child herself.

What Theda wanted to do was go home now but she had promised the boy they were there for the weekend and it was only Saturday, Whit Saturday at that, and what was she going to do until Monday? How was she going to avoid Ken until then?

It wasn't the fact that Richard had embarrassed her by thinking Ken might be his father, although he had right enough. But Richard was looking for his father everywhere nowadays. No, it was the way her body had responded to Ken, her treacherous body. Why, she had been ready to make a fool of herself over him all over again. If Richard hadn't come to the door just then she would have done. And Ken . . . he seemed to think he just had to kiss her and put his hands on her and she was his for the taking. As she almost had been.

'Would you like to go and see Uncle Joss and Aunt Beth?' she asked Richard out of the blue, and he looked up at her reproachfully.

'You said we could stay here till Monday.'

'I know. But really, I have to go to see Uncle Joss. And it's not going to be any good on the beach, is it? It's raining too hard.'

Richard sighed. 'It might not rain tomorrow,' he pointed out. 'And if we stay in Ken's house we won't get wet, will we?'

'Look,' she snapped suddenly, 'I have to go to

375

Sunderland and you have to come with me. I'm your mother and you are just a little boy. So no more arguing, we're going. Or else we go straight home.'

'It's not fair!'

It wasn't fair, and she knew she wasn't being fair, but she had to go. She paid the waitress and hurried the boy out of the cafe. At the Britannia she settled her bill, not even protesting when the landlady insisted she pay for the extra two nights.

'You booked them, Mrs Wearmouth,' she said. 'This is a bank holiday weekend. I could have let the room over and over.'

'Well, don't let the room again for the two nights. I've paid for it and I might come back,' was her parting shot as she banged the front door behind her. It opened almost immediately.

'An' another thing,' said the landlady. 'This is a respectable place. I'm not having men hanging around the place after such as you!'

Theda stopped and turned round to face the woman who was standing, arms akimbo, in the doorway. She opened her mouth to demand what she meant but decided against it. She hadn't the heart for that sort of argument, not in front of Richard. So she took the boy and put the hastily packed cases in the boot and they got in the car and headed down the road for Sunderland and Laburnum Avenue, only ten minutes away.

Ken was walking up the promenade away from the beach when he saw the car heading south. He waved his arms, jumped in the air, but unluckily there was a Co-op van going past and it obscured his view for that vital moment and then she was gone. All he could see were her tail lights as she stopped for the crossing, too far down the road for him to run after though for one insane moment he started to.

He was stamping with frustration, and soaking wet with the rain for he hadn't even stopped to put on his mac. He had raced to the Britannia to catch her but the landlady had told him she wasn't there.

'May I wait for her?' he'd asked.

'Certainly not,' was the frigid reply. 'You're not her man, are you?' And when he admitted that, no, he wasn't her husband, 'This is a holiday boarding house. We can't have men hanging around waiting for young women.'

Theda's car was there, parked on the road. She must have taken the boy back on the beach, maybe to the fun fair, however unlikely in the rain. Ken hurried round the small resort looking everywhere, or so he thought. He had just decided to wait by her car since she must be coming back to it sometime; he would just sit on it until she did. But he was too late, though not too late to see her go.

Ken was in a lather, not a panic exactly but a lather. He dashed for his own car and raced after her, catching the lights on green so that in a very short time he was near enough to see her turn into the small estate of prefabricated houses and on to Laburnum Avenue. He saw her park the car and go up to one of the houses, and, from a short distance away, saw the petite blonde who had been with her brother at the funeral open the door.

He waited, considering what to do, but in the end drove up to the house and got out of the car and marched up to the front door and rang the bell.

If Beth was surprised to see them on her doorstep she was also welcoming and took Richard through to the kitchen to give him a bowl of homemade icecream.

'Joss is working this afternoon,' she said. 'I wasn't very happy about that, it being bank holiday weekend, but now the weather has turned out so bad I don't care. Come on into the sitting-room. We can sit round the fire and have a proper gossip. What's wrong? I can tell something's upset you, so come on, you can tell me all about it. I would have thought you were having man trouble except that you don't bother with men.'

'Well,' Theda began, sorely tempted to pour it all out to her sister-in-law, 'you won't say a word to Joss, will you? It's . . . it's about Richard's father.'

'What?'

Beth was shaken. In all the years she had known Theda she had never heard her say a word about who the father was or anything about him. But Theda was white-faced and obviously distressed.

'Are you sure you want to tell me? I mean don't, not if you're going to regret it tomorrow. What's brought this on, anyway? I thought you were over him, whoever he is. You haven't met him again have you?' Uncannily she'd hit on the truth.

'I have. I did. And he's just as big a bastard as he always was.' And Theda burst into tears.

'Howay now,' said Beth, putting an arm around her shoulders and leading her to the sofa where they both sat down. 'Don't upset yourself, pet – they're not worth it.'

Theda had just opened her mouth to start her story when there was a knocking at the door and Beth swore under her breath.

'Sit still, I'll go and see who that is. Probably the milkman, he hasn't been for his money yet. I'll soon get rid of him.'

But it didn't sound as though she had got rid of him, Beth saying, 'No, you can't go through,' and a man's footsteps in the hall. Theda jumped up in a panic as the door opened and there stood Ken. Beth was close behind him but he took one look at Theda and turned and took Beth's arm.

'You don't mind leaving us alone for a few minutes, do you?' he said, and led her out of her own sitting-room and closed the door firmly behind her.

'What . . . how did you get here? You have no right,' said Theda. Her chest felt tight, breathless.

'I followed you. I wasn't going to let it happen all over again. I want to know what I've done wrong. All right, I shouldn't have rushed you like that. I'm sorry. No, I'm not sorry, damnit! I wanted to make love to you. Why shouldn't I? Did you want me to ask your permission first?'

'Yes! You take too much for granted. You go off and leave me without a word all those years ago, don't even bother to keep in touch, and now, just because you're at a loose end or something this weekend, you think it amusing to take up with me again. I was just handy, that's all – handy!'

'It wasn't like that! I *was* looking for you, I told you. I was going to come down to Durham to try to find you.' Ken crossed the room to her and she backed away until the wall stopped her retreat.

'Of course you were,' she said. 'Why should I believe anything you say? You just want to get back to the way we were before, me here just for your convenience when you feel the itch!'

Ken looked so angry she quailed for a moment. He took hold of her by the upper arms and pulled her to him. 'So that's what you think, is it? That's your opinion of me?' He pulled her to him and held her so that the length of her body pressed against his. 'And what about you, eh? Tell me you don't care, tell me this doesn't affect you. And if you do, I won't believe you. I can feel you responding, see it in your eyes! I was fool enough to think you cared in 1945 but it didn't take you long to find someone else, did it? Once I'd gone.'

'Let me go, do you hear? Let me go.' She struggled ineffectively. 'What was I supposed to think anyway, when you went without a word? You weren't in love with me. Go on, tell me you were and I won't believe you. In lust, that was what you were, not love.'

Ken still held her against him, his face set. Then, gradually, his grip lessened, he let her go and stepped back. When he spoke it was quietly, almost unemotionally.

'Did you say "without a word"? What about that note I left you at the hospital?'

'I didn't get any note. Nothing. Do you think I didn't look for something? I couldn't believe you'd gone without at least trying to get in touch. You knew where I would be, where my parents lived even—'

'But I left a note. I was short of time and asked someone to put it in your pigeon hole.' Incredibly, he couldn't remember who he had asked. Another doctor, was it?

Theda sighed and sat down heavily on the sofa. She felt tired, really weary, to the extent that her bones ached. She put a hand up to her forehead, rubbing the spot where a headache was forming, just beginning to throb.

'Well, it doesn't matter now, does it? It's too late,' she said.

'I know who it was,' he said as though she hadn't spoken. 'Koestler . . . that's who it was. Major Koestler!' He sat down beside her and they looked at each other.

'Bloody Koestler,' said Ken. 'There was another letter too . . . What sort of devious game was he playing?' And Theda remembered the interest the Major had shown in where Ken had gone, it had seemed strange at the time.

'Bloody war,' Ken went on. 'Messed up everyone's lives.' He took hold of her hand and sat, looking down at their two hands joined together.

Theda nodded, a great sadness coming over her. 'Wars are hell,' she agreed. They sat for a while saying nothing while the day darkened and another storm sent the rain thudding against the window.

'Shall we go back to Seaburn?' asked Ken. 'I'm on call tonight, I have to be near the phone.'

'I don't know. It's too quick,' she said.

'It needn't be. We can start all over again. It'll be all right.'

They went out to the kitchen where Beth was playing snakes and ladders with Richard. The boy jumped up and ran to Ken and was instantly chattering excitedly to him. Beth watched him before gazing at Theda anxiously.

'Are you OK?' she mouthed behind Ken's back, and Theda nodded.

'Yes. We're going back to Seaburn. Ken has a house there and we're booked into a small hotel. We'll get things sorted, one way or another.'

Beth wasn't so sure. 'But he left you before—' she began in her normal voice, and Ken turned swiftly to her. But before he could speak, Theda intervened.

'No, it's all right, Beth. Look, thanks for all you've done. Tell Joss I'm sorry I missed him, but we're going now. I'll be in touch.'

While Ken was getting into the Rover she had a few more words with Beth in the doorway of the prefab. 'Don't worry, I'm older now, and wiser. We'll sort things out, as I said. There are two days before I have to go back to Durham. There's time.'

'I do worry, though. I don't know what Joss will make of it either. By, he'll be that mad, Theda, you know he will.'

'Don't tell him, Beth. I'm asking you not to.'

Theda went down to the cars, the Rover parked behind her Morris. She got into the driver's seat of the Morris beside Richard and waited while Ken pulled round her. Then, waving to Beth, she followed him back to Seaburn.

Chapter Thirty-Four

She would have to tell Ken about Richard, she thought as she drove along. She glanced down at the boy, huddled in the seat beside her, his head drooping as he struggled to keep awake. She pulled into the side of the road and put him in the back seat, stretched out with a cushion under his head.

'I don't want a nap, I want to go on the beach with Flora,' he murmured, but before she had the back door closed he was off, sound asleep. She started the car but before she could pull away, Ken was back, doing a U-turn in the road and pulling his Rover up behind her.

'What's wrong?' he asked.

'Nothing, nothing's wrong. I just had to make Richard comfortable. He was asleep.'

'I thought the car had broken down, or even that you'd changed your mind,' he said, bending over to speak to her through the car window. 'Follow me now and try to keep up with me. It worries me when I can't see you in the mirror.'

'You follow me then,' she said, and pulled away, leaving him standing. But she had a warm feeling. He worried about her and she had gone too long without a man worrying about her, a man she cared about. Except for her brother Joss, of course, she reminded herself, but that was different.

The late-afternoon sun was shining through the coloured glass of the vestibule as Ken carried the boy in and took him through to the sitting-room and laid him on the couch.

'Quiet,' he growled as the dog hurled itself at the door between the back porch and the kitchen, whining and giving excited little yelps. 'Don't wake him.'

Theda sat at the kitchen table while Ken filled the electric kettle and made tea. She watched him spoon tea into the pot and pour over the water. He reached up to the cupboards for cups and saucers and she told herself she had to keep her head, had to be sensible, she couldn't let herself be overwhelmed by the attraction which threatened her. All right, he was attractive, sexy even. But she was older now; she would wait until she was sure. At the back of her mind was the nagging thought that not even now had he said he loved her.

Ken brought the tray to the table and poured tea. She saw that his hands were trembling slightly and looked up quickly. She caught his eye and saw the uncertainty there and somehow felt reassured.

'Sugar?' he asked, and she shook her head.

'No, thank you.'

He stirred his tea and put the spoon back in the saucer

then reached across the table and took her hand in his.

'It was my fault, you know,' he said. 'I mean, that we lost touch.'

'No. Anyway, it doesn't matter now.' Theda shook her head. She didn't want to think of that time, once she found she was pregnant.

'If I'd written to your home, not the hospital. If I had come home sooner from Germany. If I'd tried—'

'Such a lot of ifs,' she said. The tea lay cooling between then, unnoticed, undrunk.

'I mean, perhaps you would not have met your American – not have had the heartache of being deserted by him.'

'Do you mean you think I wouldn't have had the boy? You're wrong.' She almost told him then that Gene was not Richard's father. How could a doctor be so dense, she thought?

'No, I didn't really mean – I know you would not be without him.' He had misunderstood.

'As it happens, I wasn't deserted by Gene. He wanted to marry me. I couldn't marry him. I didn't love him.'

Ken rubbed his thumb up and down her palm. He looked perplexed for a minute and then said, 'I don't want to pry, I have no right. If you don't want to talk about it, fair enough.'

Theda thought back to the episode with Gene but it seemed so unreal she couldn't remember how she'd felt about him at the time. Then something struck her.

'How did you know about Gene?' she asked.

Ken looked uncomfortable. 'It was just that Uncle

Tucker said he thought you were going out with an American. And then, when I heard you had had a child . . . well, I suppose I jumped to conclusions. Sorry if I was wrong.' He looked at her, a question in his eyes which she ignored. She didn't feel ready to tell him the truth even if it meant he thought Gene must be Richard's father.

The moment was interrupted by the boy himself, wandering into the kitchen rubbing his eyes, still sleepy and fretful.

'Mam, you left me on my own,' he wailed. 'And I want to go to the bathroom and I don't know where it is.'

It was just the distraction she needed. She rose to her feet but Ken was there before her.

'I'll take you,' he said. 'It's just at the top of the stairs.'

'He doesn't like anyone else but me when he first wakes up,' Theda began, but Richard had taken Ken's hand and stopped whingeing and was heading for the door.

'I'm too big for you to go with me now,' Richard said. 'Boys go together.' She was left on her own for a minute or two and for something to do she took the cups of tea and tipped them down the sink and rinsed out the teapot. The dog watched her, thumping its tail on the linoleum whenever she glanced down.

They took Flora for a walk afterwards, Ken and Richard together in front with the dog and Theda following on behind. They crossed the road on to the promenade and the beach. The tide was on the turn, the sands washed clean in its wake. Richard threw sticks into the waves and Flora obligingly retrieved them, barking furiously, looking suddenly skinny as her thick coat got wet and stuck to her sides.

Theda was glad of the respite, of the fact that there was no need to think or try to work things out, no strong emotions to battle.

She could just wander along behind Richard and Ken and smile at the antics of the dog and the boy. Sometimes Ken turned and shared an amused glance with her; most of the time he gave all his attention to Richard.

Oh, he was an attractive man, he was, she mused. But he was a stranger almost, after five years and more. She must be careful, reason told her. She hadn't even known him well before, not even when he had been her lover. Her lover. Her body tingled. Dear God, she was vulnerable. So long she had lived like a nun, her natural feelings frozen. No wonder she had no resistance. She had to be sensible, had to.

Ken came back to her, took her hand quite naturally. 'We'd better go in now,' he said. 'It will soon be dark.'

'Yes.' She called Richard to her and Ken clipped on Flora's lead. They went over the road as a family would, all in a row on the kerb, waiting for the traffic to ease and going together at Ken's say so. But when they got to the other side of the road, Theda halted.

'I'll take Richard to bed now,' she said. 'We'll go back to the Britannia.'

'Oh. but I thought—' said Ken, and started again. 'Come back to the house. We can have a meal. We'll make the boy a bed up in the spare room.'

'No.' Theda was determined. She knew how it would

go if they went back with him, Richard asleep upstairs and nothing to disturb them. She couldn't take that chance, not yet. If at all.

'But we haven't talked, not really talked,' he said.

'There's tomorrow. We don't go back to Durham until Monday.'

'But I have to go in to work tomorrow. I'll be away all day.'

'Maybe it's just as well. We both need time, Ken, things are going too fast for me.'

He was disappointed and showed it. 'I was banking on having this evening, a quiet evening on our own.'

'Yes,' said Theda, 'I know. But I need to be alone for a while, to think about things.'

'Don't push me out of your life again, Theda, I won't let you.'

'No. I'll give you my phone number and address in Durham.'

Richard was sleepy once again with the sea air and chasing after Flora and made no demur as she got him ready for bed. The landlady had been a little cool but their room was there, waiting for them, and Theda soon had him washed and tucked up under the bedclothes.

She had thought she would sit beside the window again with a book but in the event was so tired herself that she soon joined Richard and knew no more until he was bouncing on her bed next morning.

Theda and Richard walked along the banks of the Wear looking for ducks to feed. It had become a ritual this summer; every afternoon after tea they would take scraps of bread and walk down by the side of the chapel and over the broad street of Old Elvet and down the path by the side of the swimming baths to the riverside. It was a beautiful afternoon, the sun slanting on the water and swallows diving about after insects to feed their young. Richard had found some ducks to feed and was throwing his pieces into the water, watching closely as they were picked up.

Theda sat down on the steps leading down to the river from a college boathouse. 'Be careful, Richard,' she called, but she wasn't worried. He was a careful child, sensible and well used to the river. Ken would ring up this evening, she thought, her heart warm in anticipation. He had rung every evening since Whitsuntide; sometimes only for a minute or two, sometimes they chatted longer.

'Come up this weekend,' he had suggested the day after she returned from Seaburn.

'I can't, I'm on call.'

Ken sighed. 'I can't come down, I'm on call too.'

'Perhaps it's for the best.'

'I want to see you.'

'There's plenty of time.'

Somehow, the weeks had slid by and it was already a month since that weekend at Seaburn. But at least, she thought, she knew him better now. They had talked without her judgement being clouded by his nearness, his compelling attraction. He had even brought up the subject of Julie during one of their long conversations on the telephone.

'I was going to ask you to wait for me until after the war, marry me. You know, that weekend at Marsden?'

She had known there was something, of course she had. But she thought he had changed his mind, his feelings had cooled towards her.

'You remember Walt mentioning Julie?'

Oh, yes, she did, she remembered it well.

'We were engaged, going to get married before I went to Italy. We discussed the fact that I might not come back but it was just a supposition – we never really thought I wouldn't survive. I don't know why; I wasn't so daft as to think I bore a charmed life.'

'But you did survive,' Theda had murmured. She felt an intense pang of jealousy towards this unknown girl. Walt obviously hadn't liked her, and was probably a good judge.

'It was Julie who died. Killed in a raid on the quayside in Newcastle.'

Theda remembered the silence which fell then. She had felt irrationally guilty for thinking ill of the dead.

'I'm sorry,' she had said at last.

'Don't be. It's so long ago. But I think it affected the way I thought about you. I'd sworn I wouldn't get involved again, at least until after the war.'

Theda had thought about Alan. It had been different for her after him. She had mourned him, oh, she had. She had also bitterly regretted that they had not made love, as Alan had wanted to. She had denied him, and how could she have done? And then, with Ken . . . The bloody war, she thought, for the first time in ages. It had been an expression she used to herself almost daily when it had been going on. It was all the fault of the war. She felt all mixed up emotionally, even now, when it had been over for years.

'I'll come down tomorrow evening, and we'll go to Marsden,' Ken had said. 'Don't tell me you're on call. I know you can't be, you've been on call for the last two weekends as I remember.'

'Come Saturday morning,' said Theda. 'I have things to do tomorrow evening. Besides,' she added, 'what would the neighbours say?'

Ken had paused and she knew he was well aware of the real reason she had put him off. 'OK then, Saturday morning. Bright and early,' he said.

Sitting on the steps by the river, Theda watched Richard throw the last of his scraps to the ducks.

'Goodbye, ducks,' he said. 'I'll come back tomorrow and bring you supper, I promise.' He turned and saw Theda watching him and ran up to her. 'Is it tomorrow Flora is coming?' he asked.

'Now, I don't know if Uncle Ken is bringing the dog,' warned Theda. 'We'll wait and see.'

'I could ring him up and ask him,' Richard suggested.

'Oh, well, all right. Now come on, it's time to go home.'

She would soon be talking to Ken on the phone. The feeling of anticipation was delicious. But when Richard rang, Ken was out on a call. When Richard was in bed she had a bath and washed her hair and brushed it down, letting it lie in heavy, waving coils on her shoulders as she ironed a beige linen suit, the price of which had made her blink when she bought it at Doggarts in Durham. She pressed Richard's shorts and a blue cotton shirt and polished up his summer sandals.

Sheila came in from next-door and opened her eyes wide at such preparations. 'I do believe you've fallen at last,' she said. 'Come on now, tell me about it.'

'Nothing to tell,' insisted Theda, and just then the telephone rang and she put down the iron in a hurry and rushed to the door. Turning, she said, 'You don't mind, Sheila? Only it will be private.'

'No, I don't mind. I'll go. A wink's as good as a nod,' laughed Sheila, and went out. 'Tell me all about it on Sunday,' she called.

'Are you sure I shouldn't come down this evening?' asked Ken over the telephone. 'I want to come. Why not? Don't you want to see me?'

'Too many questions there for a yes or no,' said Theda, trying to keep it light. 'I do want to see you, I do. It's not that.' It was becoming very hard to say no.

'Well then. If you're worried about what people will think—'

'No.' Then she seized on the excuse. 'Well, yes, this house goes with the job. You know what it can be like. If anyone sees you coming at night and going in the morning it could cost me my place here.'

'I can be very discreet.'

'Ken—'

'All right, all right. I'll see you in the morning, darling.'

Darling. It sounded so good, thought Theda as she

climbed the stairs to bed. She looked in on Richard as she did every single night. He was fast asleep, his teddy bear, which he always insisted he was too old for now, tucked under his outstretched arm. It was hot in the room. She went to the window and opened it a little wider. She stood there for a moment or two, enjoying the feel of the cool air against her skin.

She should have let Ken come, she thought. It was hours before she would see him and she felt she would never be able to sleep.

Ken drove down to Durham next morning, very early. Today, he thought, before they went to Marsden, today he would ask her to marry him. He marshalled his arguments in his head. Richard needed a father, he would be a good father. Theda would be a good surgeon's wife, she knew what it was all about, wouldn't moan if he was called out during the night. He could provide well for them, Theda and her son. He was established in his profession.

He gripped the wheel hard, feeling the nervous excitement flow through him. There was a strange feeling in his stomach. He should have eaten breakfast but it had been too early. In fact it was only six o'clock now, he saw as he glanced at the dashboard clock.

He forced himself to relax, slow down. He stopped the car at the top of a hill and gazed out over the rolling farmland to where he could see Durham in the distant haze, the colliery winding engine of Sherburn Hill looking like a monument above the roofs of the village from the distance. He could make out the square tower of the Norman cathedral, the grey blur of the castle beside it. Somewhere in the city below was Theda.

Ken smiled and relaxed properly. He didn't need to marshal any arguments. There was only one that mattered – he loved her and he wanted to marry her.

Theda was wakened by the pealing of the doorbell, insistent, continuous. She practically fell out of bed, feeling groggy, and pulled on her old kimono, pushing her hair out of her eyes. Some panic-stricken young father, she thought, searching under the bed for her slippers. The bell rang again. She abandoned the hunt for the slippers and ran down the stairs. Richard would wake up in a minute, she thought crossly, then he would be tired at school.

No, it was Saturday, no school today. No panic-stricken young husband either, it was her weekend off. Her mind was clearing, though her eyes felt puffy with sleep and she had to squint through her lashes as the bright sunlight fell on her as she finally managed to get the door open.

'Ken,' she said. And stood there, stupidly, feeling the harsh fibre of the doormat under her bare feet. What a sight she must look, she thought dimly, hair all over the place, her faded old kimono over her nightie.

'Can I come in?' he asked.

She stood back from the door, opening it wide, and he stepped inside and closed it behind him. He moved forward to take her in his arms.

'You look adorable,' he said.

'Uncle Ken! Have you brought Flora?' Richard was standing well down the stairs in his pyjamas, a wide beam of delight on his face.

'That is the way of things when you have a child,' said Theda. 'No privacy at all.'

Chapter Thirty-Five

They walked Flora along the riverbank before breakfast, Richard racing ahead with her and scolding her when she panicked the ducks and they swam off to the far side, quacking indignantly.

'Naughty dog, Flora,' he said. 'Now you'll have to go back on the lead. Can I hold the lead, Uncle Ken?'

'If you're careful,' he answered.

Richard walked along importantly, talking away to the dog, and Ken and Theda followed, side by side. There was hardly anyone else about, it was still so early. The County Council offices, which backed on to the riverbank, were still empty, the workers – overspill from Shire Hall on the opposite side of the road – would not be there for another hour at least.

'I love you,' said Ken. 'I want to marry you. I thought I would ask you when we were alone and private but I can't wait any longer. I've loved you since I met you, I know that now.'

'It took a long time for you to say so,' said Theda. But

her heart was singing. She couldn't be bitter about the past, not now. She looked ahead to the outskirts of the cricket field where Richard was walking up and down with Flora.

'I know, I'm sorry. But I'm saying it now. The thing is, how do you feel about me?'

'I think you know,' she said.

'No, I want you to say it. I want no more misunderstandings.'

'I love you then.' There, it was out, she thought.

Ken stopped and took her in his arms, kissing her. 'When can we get married?'

'Not too fast,' she murmured. She still hadn't told him that Richard was his son. The longer she put it off, the harder it got.

'I'll make a good father to the boy,' he said, almost as if he was following her thoughts. 'I'll adopt him, give him my name.'

'It will only confuse him – he's got a name.'

'Yes, but when he's older, it will be better if he has my name.'

This was the time to tell him, she thought. But no, she didn't want to spoil the moment with explanations.

'You haven't given me an answer,' said Ken. 'I want it settled, once and for all. Please, darling.'

She looked up into his clear grey eyes, so like Richard's. Why did he not guess? He smiled and pushed her hair back from her ear. He bent his head and nibbled at the lobe and she trembled.

'I'll marry you,' she said. 'Whenever you like. Well,

I'll have to put in a month's notice. I will probably be able to work in Sunderland, I intend to become a Health Visitor.'

'Do you?' he said, looking doubtful. 'If you must. Until we have a child, that is.'

'We have a child. We have Richard.' There now, she'd said it. She braced herself for the questions, the demands to know why she hadn't told him before, why she had waited five years. Her heart beat painfully.

'I know. I meant another. Richard is a child to be proud of too.' For a minute she thought he really did know and didn't mind. But then she realised that he had misunderstood once again. He kissed her lightly on the nose and walked up to where Richard and the dog were lying in the grass, panting after a run. Ken picked Richard up and to the boy's huge delight put him on his shoulders, with the child's legs straddling his neck.

'Come, Flora,' he said, grasping her lead, and she trotted beside him obediently. 'It's time for breakfast. And then we're going to a farm, Richard. You'll like that, won't you? I'm sure the farmer will let you help him feed the animals. He will because he's my brother.'

Walking up the path by the side of Old Elvet chapel, they saw Billy Carter and his mother.

'Hello, Billy,' Richard called, beaming with pride from his seat in the air. He waved his hand and arm so vigorously Ken had to grab the top of his leg to hold him on.

'Well, that'll give Mrs Carter something else to gossip about,' said Theda. Ken shrugged, as far as he was able with Richard on his shoulders.

'What does it matter?' he said indifferently. 'We're getting married, aren't we?'

'We are,' agreed Theda, and opened her front door and led the way inside for breakfast.

They drove up to Marsden in Ken's Rover, Richard sitting in the back seat with Flora. Theda was quiet. In spite of herself she wondered how she would be received by Ken's family, a woman with a child of almost five. After all, they didn't know who Richard's father was either.

'It will be fine, you'll see,' said Ken quietly as they drove up the lane to the farm. 'They liked you the last time you were here, didn't they? In any case, you're marrying me, not the family.'

She glanced up at him, surprised. He had practically read her mind once again. Yet on that most important thing . . . But they were entering the farmyard now so there was no more time to talk privately.

'Now then, Ken. How're you going on? Be careful with Flora, the bitch has puppies,' called Walt as they were getting out of the car. 'We don't want a dog fight on our hands.'

'Puppies!' breathed Richard, his eyes alight. He looked longingly at the kennel by the back door where the sheep-dog was lying, watching the newcomers suspiciously.

'I'll fasten her in the scullery,' said Ken. But there was no need. Flora was a sensitive, intelligent dog. Before Ken could take hold of her she approached to within six feet of the kennel and lay down, wagging her tail to show she meant no harm. The sheepdog gave a warning growl and turned to nose the puppies further inside but she obviously saw no real threat in Flora.

'Look at that, then,' Walt, who had been forking manure out of the stable, put down the gripe and wiped his hands on a piece of sacking. 'Hello, there.' He nodded to Theda. 'I won't shake hands – you can see why.' He grinned and she saw his face light up in the way of his brother's. He turned to Richard.

'Would you like to see the puppies? If you come with me and don't try to touch, I'll show you. They're only a few days old, you see, their eyes aren't open yet.'

Ken and Theda left the boy with Walt and went inside. Meg was in the kitchen with Jane. Surprisingly, to Theda at any rate, the two women looked exactly the same as they had when she had last seen them. Ken's mother as pale and ethereal and Meg, his grandmother, as sturdy and bright-eyed. Perhaps she had a few more lines on her face.

Solid as she was, Ken stepped forward and lifted her up and gave her a smacking kiss on the cheeks, swinging her round as she did so. 'How's my best girl?' he said, laughing.

'Go on, you daft beggar!' Meg cried, slapping out at him. 'What will Theda think?'

'What should she think?'

He went over to his mother and bent over her chair. She lifted up her face for his kiss eagerly, cheeks flushing pink with pleasure.

'How are you feeling, Mother?'

'Not bad, Ken, not bad. All the better for seeing you.'

'Come and sit down, Theda lass, I'll have the tea made

in a trice, the kettle's boiling.' There was a new electric cooker to the side of the fireplace but an old iron kettle was singing on the hob of the coal range. 'Call Walt, will you, Ken? Jack's in the byre an' all.'

Walt came in, Richard at his side. A little shy at first, he went straight to Theda and leaned against her knee.

'This is Richard,' said Ken.

'Now then, Richard,' said Meg. 'Howay, sit down. I bet you're hungry, aren't you? I've got some nice new scones and strawberry jam, would you like one?'

'Yes, please,' said the boy, and he scrambled on to the chair by his mother. 'The puppies have no hair and they can't open their eyes,' he told her. 'Uncle Walt says I can come back and see them when their eyes open. He says their eyes will be blue at first.'

Meg sat down suddenly. 'How old are you, Richard?' she asked.

'I'm five. But I've started school, you know, I can read.' Honesty got the better of him and he added, 'Little words, I can read.'

Theda stared down at her scone. She could feel the heat in her face, even the tips of her ears. There was a silence in the room. Ken, who had taken a bite of his scone, put it down on his plate and swallowed.

Meg gazed hard from him to the boy. 'So you're getting married, are you, at last?' she asked Ken. 'An' not afore time, I'd reckon. By, lad, what've you been thinking of all these years?'

Ken jumped up from the table and rushed out of the room without looking at Theda, and Walt mumbled something about having things to see to and drank his tea in one swallow. Taking his scone in his hand, he went out to the scullery and could be heard putting on his farm boots.

'Eeh, lass, do you mean to say Ken didn't know?' asked Meg. Jane had risen from her customary seat by the fire and came to sit beside her mother. When Theda raised her eyes, both women were looking at her.

'Richard, why don't you go and see if Uncle Walt needs some help?' suggested Meg, and they waited while he picked up the last drop of jam from his plate with his forefinger and sucked it.

'All right, Mam?' he asked, and she nodded.

The women were left on their own and Theda met their eyes. 'I meant to tell him, it just never seemed to be the right time,' she said. 'How did you know?'

'There's eyesight in it,' declared Meg. 'Anyone can see the bairn's a Grizedale; he has the family face. Even if he has his Grandfather Collins's eyes. Not to mention Ken's.'

'He's my grandson too,' said Jane. 'You shouldn't have kept him from us, Theda. I'm sure if Ken had known he would have done the right thing by you. He's an honourable man.'

'Yes.'

'Best go out there and find him, lass,' advised Meg. 'Go on now. So you made a mistake. You'll just have to put it right, won't you? Walt will watch the bairn or we will.'

Theda went out through the scullery, passing Jack in the doorway and acknowledging his greeting. As she went into the farmyard she could see Walt and Richard just closing a field gate after a herd of cows.

'Get along there, Daisy,' Walt encouraged a straggler. And, 'Go on, Daisy,' echoed Richard. Walt saw Theda and nodded down the lane. 'Ken went off down there, I think,' he said. 'That's where he always went when he was out of sorts. The lad'll be all right with me if you want to go.'

She walked down the lane, feeling sick with a misery that was all the stronger after the happiness of this morning. She should have told him; he had had a right to know. She was in the wrong, oh, yes, she was well aware of that. She walked over the road and along the top of the cliffs to where the Souter lighthouse stood. And there, near the edge of the cliff, she found him sitting with his back against a wall, staring out at the seabirds swooping and diving around Marsden Rock. She sat down beside him.

'I don't think I told you,' he said, 'Gran left school at nine-years-old and her first job was scrubbing down the steps of the lighthouse. Did I tell you?'

'No. No you didn't tell me that.' She swallowed and looked out to sea. 'Ken, I'm sorry, I am. I can understand how you must hate me for it.'

'Hate you? No. I just feel such a fool. It's you has had all the worry, all the trouble of bringing the boy up on your own.'

'Yes, but . . . oh, I should have made more effort to get in touch with you. I went to see Tucker Cornish, you know. He said he hadn't the authority to give me your address. But he didn't know about the baby, mind.'

Tucker, thought Ken. Well, he couldn't blame him. It was his own fault, no one else's. When he first walked out of the farmhouse he had been furiously angry – angry that he hadn't recognised his own child, angry with Theda that she hadn't told him, angry at the war, the flaming, bloody war, which had separated them in the first place. He had missed the first few years of the boy's life. But hadn't that happened to thousands during the war? He wasn't alone in it. And why let that poison the rest of their lives? They had had their time for war, now it was a time to heal. Beside him, he could feel how miserable she was. Scrambling to his feet, he held out a hand to Theda and after a moment she put hers in it and allowed him to pull her up.

'Never mind, sweetheart, never mind,' he said. A cold wind blew over the North Sea, though the sun shone bravely enough. He opened his coat and held her to him, holding the coat round them both as she laid her head against his.

'I thought it was over, finished. I thought you wouldn't want to marry me now,' she said.

'Well, like Gran said, it's about time too.'

'But it's not just because of Richard, is it?'

'Theda, I know I've been stupid, but really, you sound as dense as two short planks. I love you, you daft lass. I love *you*. How many times do you want me to say it?'

She buried her head in his chest. They stood for a few minutes then turned together and walked back to the farm, arms entwined.